Heart Magic

Heart Magic

Magic, Love, and Mischief Book 3

Kait Disney-Leugers

4 Horsemen Publications, Inc.
1497 Main St. Suite 169
Dunedin, FL 34698
4horsemenpublications.com
info@4horsemenpublications.com

Cover by J. Kotick
Typesetting by Autumn Skye
Edited by Kristine Cotter

Library of Congress Control Number: 2023946027

Paperback ISBN-13: 979-8-8232-0324-1
Hardcover ISBN-13: 979-8-8232-0326-5
Audiobook ISBN-13: 979-8-8232-0323-4
Ebook ISBN-13: 979-8-8232-0325-8

For my mom, Teresa Leugers. You told Dad I write smut, so here's some smut! Share with your friends.

Acknowledgements

To all the people who wanted Wes's story, this is for you. As always, I must thank the usual suspects. To my editor Kris, who puts up with my illiterate ass and makes my work shine. To Linda Stewart, always Linda, my best friend, and a master storyteller. Thank you for always being my hype person. To Storm, my sister, who will insist she doesn't read romance, and yet... A big thanks to Leslie Sommers, my fellow Horsemen and friend for listening to me whine about why nothing was working, and for sharing spoilers for her books. To Greg and my goblin babes, y'all wouldn't let me get anything done, but I somehow managed despite your best efforts! Also to Jordan, not for any reason other than you are my friend and I'm stuck with you.

Mom and D

Table of Contents

Chapter 1

The house was quiet. No sounds of drunken college student neighbors stumbling around the halls or into the door. A gentle hum came from the refrigerator, not a single death rattle to break up its properly functioning state. The air conditioner kicked on by itself, adding another soft noise to the quiet space. Air circulated the living room, fresh and cool. No stale air or must, and absolutely no fish smells or the reek of someone else's dinner. It was perfect and clean, with plenty of space to live, and a quiet street outside. The house was a proper adult home, exactly what a professor should live in.

Wesley St. James hated it.

The lack of noise was jarring after living so long in student housing, and, before that, in an array of foster homes that were always too packed and too loud. Even the house he'd spent his happiest years in with Maddy had always been filled with the smell of spices from his foster mom's Cajun cooking and loud music from the iPod and speaker set she always kept in the kitchen.

His house was also mostly empty. He had moved his stuff in, but after years and years of trying to shove too much into too small a space, now that he had the space to spread out, it looked like he owned almost nothing. It didn't help that all the plants that had always filled his apartment were gone. Not that Wes had any sort of green thumb, he definitely didn't, but green things had been a constant in his life until that point.

But plants and green things were his sister Bridget's domain, and for the first time since they were teenagers, they didn't live together. Sure, she had spent the last few years living with her boyfriend, now husband, but she still kept her room at their apartment. They had dedicated hang-out nights where they would order in, drink too much, and watch bad tv with their friend Lily. Brie and her new husband Ezra were off on their honeymoon for a few weeks and Wes was alone in his new faculty housing–with no plants, no roommate, and more books and rocks than clothing.

Wes never planned to stay in New Britain. Not that there had ever been a plan for his life. He had liked rocks and minerals before Maddy taught him all about their magical properties and importance in Pagan rituals. Rocks made sense; rocks endured for millennia. In thirty years, few things in his life had endured. His parents were killed when he was young, too young to really remember them. Foster home after foster home was taken from him, mostly because they simply started running out of space or he was too much trouble. Then Maddy died. She had been his guiding light, a stalwart rock in a sea of shit. That small woman with a big heart saw something in the surly teenager she took into her home and made him fall in love with her. Maddy had been his mother. It just took them some time to finally meet.

And now Brie was gone.

A honeymoon isn't gone, gone, asshole. She'll be back soon and ready to annoy you with all her stories about sex in exotic locations.

He flopped down on the couch, the same one from their old apartment. It was more than a little worse for wear, but Wes couldn't bring himself to throw it out. There was history in those cushions, told in every stain and bad patch job.

Wes was moody, and being a generally depressing mess for no reason. It wasn't like his sister had left him for good. And a new place was nothing to mope over, especially since it wasn't a shitty apartment. This was an adult home, an actual house that was all his. Next week, he would start teaching classes as a real college professor. Well, adjunct professor, but still a professor. And he wouldn't have to deal with just gen-ed classes and bored undergrads. He would get graduate students too. People who actually cared and wanted to learn about geology. Then there was also the geology lab, which he had full access to, to do whatever he wanted. Within reason, mostly.

He also had Apollo.

Well, mostly had Apollo.

Wes had been seeing the incubus since they met when Brie started working at Spirit Antiques, the place her husband owned, three years previous. It had been super casual for the first year or so. They would plan to go out and end up just having sex before they had a chance to go anywhere. By the second year, they did start going on actual dates, but then, again, they would end up back at Apollo's penthouse and stay there the rest of the night. The past year had been a little different, more relationship-like in a way. But that was all still unclear. They did things as a couple and presented to others as a couple.

But Wes didn't feel like part of a couple.

Instead, he felt like he was still a booty call. Or like a boyfriend for hire. There when Apollo wanted attention or sex, or he needed somebody on his arm for an event. Wes knew they were not exclusive. He and Apollo had discussed it before, and neither were willing to commit to monogamy.

Well, that wasn't true, exactly. Apollo made it clear he wasn't willing to commit to monogamy. He was an incubus after all, and therefore relied on sex to sustain himself. Wes was perfectly fine with monogamy. Preferred it, actually. But he was willing to compromise for Apollo if that was what he needed and made him happy. While he wasn't thrilled with the arrangement, he dealt with it.

Wes placed the palms of his hands over his eyes and tried to empty his head. He didn't want to think about Apollo, or being alone, or how much he couldn't stand his new place. What he needed was a serious distraction. Not that there was much to help in that case. Without Brie around, he didn't have much of a social life. There was Lily—the two of them had become tight over the years, especially after they were part of the rescue squad to save his sister from a totally crazy warlock together.

It was still daytime, so Lily would probably be in her garden, rather than hanging out with her own partner, a vampire named Albert. He was a total dick most of the time, but Wes didn't have any issues with the vamp.

Maybe they'll let me crash in one of their guest bedrooms for a night.

What was he thinking? He was an adult man who could definitely sleep alone in his own house, in his own room without his little sister, or a partner, or a friend, staying with him.

I am a badass dude. I can be alone, no problem.

"Fuck, I hate this," he said loudly to the empty room.

Wes had to get out of the house. The quiet was simply overwhelming, and he didn't want to deal with it any longer. Now that he was getting a higher-than-minimum-wage paycheck, he could actually afford to go grocery shopping properly. His fridge was empty anyway and it would get him out of the house for a while. Then he would make himself a nice meal and go over the syllabus he had written one more time.

Not that he didn't know it thoroughly. Besides having obviously written it, he had read over it at least a dozen times and arranged the required reading into a stack in several different configurations. He was nervous. There was no way to deny that.

Wes had never given much thought about what his life would look like at thirty. Maybe, he might admit to himself, he never thought he would make it that far in life. He suffered from depression as a teen and was diagnosed with bipolar once he was in college. So many nights he lay in bed in a crowded room, wishing he wasn't around anymore.

For as long as he had them, his parents had trained him to be a guardian. He could call up a meager amount of magic to that end. Fight training had started when he was young, but then his parents died when he was seven and the training stopped. Instead, Wes bounced around the system with no direction, no one to tell him how to handle the small magic that lived inside him. Even when he went to live with Maddy, she didn't know how exactly to train him. But she encouraged him to seek out resources and had tried to help him with whatever she could find.

Maddy had been on the fringes of the magical community, though she had no magic herself. She was a human guardian, a connection between the magical world and the human one. Her job was to help bridge between the two. She knew all about what Wes was born into. And she knew when she took Brie in that she was the reincarnation of the goddess that Wes's family served. If only they had more time with her, Wes and Brie would have had more of a connection to the world that they were a part of. But cancer was a real bitch, and not even the indomitable Maddy St. James could fight it for long.

Yeah, he definitely needed to get out of the house. He was too much in his own head. Wes grabbed his bike from the hook at the front of the house and carried it outside. The grocery store wasn't far, and the day was warm and bright. The summer sun had darkened his already tan skin, but he couldn't wait for the heat of summer to end and the chill of autumn to start. Wes hated the summer.

He mounted his bike, pushed a stray lock of black hair from his face, and rubbed a hand against the shaved side of his skull. He had rocked the same hairstyle, one side shaved, one side long and brushing his ears, since he was in high school. It was his signature look, much like the band t-shirts he always wore. Sure, they were faded and ratty after probably hundreds of washes, but since he grew up with very little to call his own, he didn't get rid of anything.

It took only a few minutes for Wes to reach the grocery store. He hated shopping, but he couldn't bring himself to have his groceries delivered. It was an extravagant expense. Once the essentials filled his cart, and an indulgence or two, he headed for the self-checkout, the better to avoid interacting with anybody. Just as he finished paying, his phone vibrated in his pocket.

[Apollo: I'm bored. Come keep me company?]

That was Apollo-speak for, "Come over and have sex because I'm between people at the moment." Wes hated these types of texts. They made him feel like he was only a warm body and not a real person. But it didn't matter how many times he brought it up, Apollo just brushed him off. Wes told himself time after time that he was done with it, that he would set a boundary and tell him no, but then he would always run to Apollo the minute he texted.

Every single time.

[Wes: Finishing shopping. Be there soon]

A sick feeling settled in his stomach as he sent the text, but it didn't matter. He would still go, still enjoy himself, and then go back to feeling sick after he returned home. Because he never spent the night with Apollo. Even after three years of whatever they were, he always left Apollo's place after. And Apollo never came to him. Not once had he set foot in Wes's apartment.

I know why I keep going back to him. It's the sex. Fuck, is he good at that.

But, then again, he was an incubus, a sex demon by nature. It wouldn't do to be a sex demon who was bad at sex. Apollo knew how to please. He wasn't a selfish lover, unlike most of the men and even some of the women Wes had slept with before. Apollo had the largest collection of sex toys Wes had ever seen, most of which had some kind of magical property to enhance pleasure. And, as Apollo loved to tell Wes, he got them all from Ezra and it delighted him to no end to tease Ezra about it. Which only served to weird Wes out, since he was talking about his brother-in-law.

It wasn't a healthy relationship and Wes knew that he deserved better. Knowing and actually doing something about it, though, were two different things.

I'm sure a therapist would say something about my desire to be loved because I didn't get enough of it in my childhood. They would be right, obviously, but who really got enough love in their childhood?

The ride back to his new house was short, and he took his time putting the groceries away, dragging out the chore longer than it needed to be. Yet another sign he really should break things off with Apollo. He couldn't even bring himself to be excited to see his pseudo-boyfriend. Sure, the sex would be great in the moment. After, though, he would be left feeling used and ashamed, especially since Apollo would likely kick him out immediately after to go off and do whoever else he wanted.

Goddess, he wished his sister was around to tell him how much of an idiot he was being. Not that she hadn't been trying. When he and Apollo had first started hooking up, Brie was, while not super thrilled, accepting. Mostly. She knew very well what Apollo was. But after Wes wanted to get more serious, Brie hadn't taken it so well. But just like she hadn't listened to him when she started to catch feelings for Ezra, he wasn't listening now. The only difference was that Ezra had committed to Brie. Loved her. Fuck, he'd even married her. He didn't string her along for three years.

But Apollo? He couldn't even commit to keeping his dick out of other people for a night. He didn't even call Wes his boyfriend. They had dates, lots of them even. But whenever Apollo had to introduce him to new people, it was always, "...my friend, Wes." And every time it was a knife to Wes's heart.

I like having fun with him. But I don't want to love him. And he will never love anyone but himself. Wes's thoughts were bleak as he knocked on Apollo's penthouse apartment door.

It only took one knock for Apollo to open the door, and all Wes's thoughts went out the window and all the blood in his brain rushed straight to his dick. Because the sex demon was standing on the threshold wearing nothing but a sock, and it was not on his foot.

Apollo was golden all over, like he was made from a bit of sun. Tall and fit, with sun-kissed skin and shining bronze hair in gentle waves above his ears, and blue eyes that popped, he could only be described as beautiful. "I was listening to some old Red Hot Chili Peppers. I love them, and I felt like I needed to get into the vibe. What do you think?" Apollo thrust out his pelvis to bring all attention to the sock barely hanging on for dear life, as if Wes's attention wasn't already on that part of Apollo's anatomy.

Wes tried to remember how to form words, but he was failing miserably. Not that Apollo cared. He didn't need Wes to say anything as he grabbed one of Wes's limp hands and dragged him inside the penthouse. He followed the incubus into the living room, which was an open-concept space that flowed into a chef's kitchen. All of Apollo's furniture was leather, and not all of it was for company to sit on. It was like he had his own private sex dungeon sitting out in his living room.

Music blasted through the sound system as Wes was led through the room to a stack of pillow pads near the window. Wes was already taking one of the pads and setting it on the floor before Apollo spoke. He knew how this game went. "I'm going to keep dancing, but why don't you show me a good time," Apollo purred, his voice just loud enough to make it over the music.

Wes eagerly complied, falling to his knees in front of Apollo and adjusting the pad beneath them to keep his knees from getting sore. Apollo kept moving his hips to the music while Wes stayed on the floor at eye level with the sock and all that it contained within. He looked up at Apollo once and noticed that the incubus's eyes were closed as he enjoyed the music.

Is he even going to pay attention to me while I do this?

Old insecurities bubbled up within Wes, but he pushed them aside. Apollo would either watch or he wouldn't, but Wes was still going to suck him off.

With eager fingers, he reached out to remove the sock when Apollo batted his hand away. "No hands, bunny, I only want that pretty mouth of yours today," Apollo drawled, then closed his eyes again. Instantly, Wes's face felt warm with shame, like he should have already known what Apollo wanted.

And once again, Wes questioned why he put himself through this. He wasn't happy with their arrangement, wasn't happy with the way Apollo treated him like a toy to be used instead of a boyfriend. Because that's all he would ever be. Even though Apollo said the words, said they were more than casual, that they were a real couple, he didn't mean it. Wes was just another notch on Apollo's already impressively whittled bedpost. One that he liked to come back to because it was convenient.

Knowing this, feeling everything he felt, Wes still found himself leaning into the task of removing the tube sock from Apollo's length. Careful to avoid biting down on any part of Apollo's generous anatomy, he slowly pulled the soft fabric down Apollo's dick and spat the sock out of his mouth once it had cleared the head.

Wes shifted on his knees and tilted his head to get a better angle, all the while staring at the dick waiting erect in front of his face. Then he took just the tip into his mouth and began his work, hating himself with every bob of his head and yet enjoying the act itself.

Sometime later, when they both had satisfied their lust, Wes clung to the hope that Apollo would ask him to stay, to do something that was coupley. But it was a Saturday afternoon, and his hopes were quickly dashed.

"That was wonderful, bunny. You really do have a gifted mouth. Now, I hate to cut this short because I love having you around, but I have a party to get ready for, and perfection doesn't just happen, so I need to get ready." Apollo was already heading toward his bedroom, still completely naked, but clearly unbothered by that fact.

"Were you even going to invite me to come along? I thought we could spend more time together before classes start," Wes said, sounding whiny even to his own ears. And Goddess, he hated himself even more. Today was not getting any better the more it went on.

Apollo stopped at the threshold of his room and turned back to Wes. His customary smirk slipped from his face only a little, but his lips remained turned up at the edges. "No, I wasn't. I'm tired of going over this with you, lamb. This is who I am. This is what I do. Please stop trying to change my nature. We have a lot of fun together. I don't want that to change." The full fledged smirk returned, and Apollo was his usual self again. They had this conversation at least once a week, and every time Apollo brushed him off, this was the first time he'd confronted Wes about it directly.

Wes hung his head, unable to look at the incubus any longer as disappointment flooded him. Apollo took a few steps closer to Wes and cupped his jaw, but Wes didn't raise his head. "Don't be upset, bunny. We really do have a lot of fun together. I enjoy being with you. But I can't change what I am, and as much as I like you, I'm never going to love you. So let's enjoy this for as long as we can."

It felt like a dagger plunged into his heart at Apollo's words. *I'm never going to love you.*

Not that it was the first time Wes had heard them. Apollo made sure to remind him occasionally. Maybe a part of Wes hoped that Apollo would change his mind, that he would find he really did love Wes. But it was never going to happen. Maybe it had been fun for the first year, but now Wes wanted more. Apollo wasn't going to be the one to give it to him. And Wes could either be okay with that or move on because he would never ask Apollo to change for him. He could never ask that of anyone.

Wes finally looked up and nodded, forcing a weak smile on his face. "Yeah, let's just enjoy it. Well, I'll get out of here. I have like a ton of stuff to do anyway and a big night." He started to turn away so that Apollo wouldn't see the hurt in his eyes.

"Bye, sweetling. You were wonderful today," Apollo said, his voice bright, his smile wide as he turned away again toward his room. Wes couldn't stay a second longer in his shame. He left the penthouse quickly and made his way home.

The house was still too quiet. And now he didn't feel any better than he did before he'd left the house the first time. Instead, he felt worse, if that was possible. Once again, he found himself wishing he could call Brie. He needed his little sister to comfort him and then kick his ass to knock some sense into him. But as much as he needed that, there was no way he was disturbing her on her honeymoon.

Despite it being early afternoon, Wes headed for his room and flopped onto his bed. He would just suffer alone. Again. As usual.

CHAPTER 2

If Wes had any whims that being an adjunct professor would be in any way better than a teaching assistant, that hope would have been dashed at exactly 9:01 Monday morning on the first day of classes. His first class ever as an actual professor of geology was to a bunch of freshmen taking Geology 101, and he only needed to do a quick scan of the large lecture hall to know who was going to show up beyond today and who would disappear within the next two weeks.

Sure, he wouldn't be the one doing the grading for the most part, that's what teaching assistants were for, but there was the soul-crushing knowledge that basically everyone else in the room was only there to get easy credit. And Geology 101 was easy credit, for the most part.

If you show up, he thought, his inner voice grumpier than his outside one. It was best to appear somewhat happy to be there on the first day. Try to inspire the students to come back to class, even if he wasn't feeling all that inspired.

Shouldn't I be more excited about this? Isn't this what I wanted for my life?

Wes knew being a professor was exactly what he wanted. He enjoyed teaching. He enjoyed sharing his passion for all things rocks. Maddy had given that gift to him, and even though she wasn't here to see how that influence paid off, he would always honor her memory by doing what he loved.

The problem was his personal life, not his professional one. Being in love with someone who would never love you back really took a hit on his mental state. The whole thing was sending him into a bit of a depressive episode. It was an effort to get out of bed that morning. Like it was going to be the hardest thing he did all day.

He decided the best thing to do was call his psychiatrist after class to see about upping his dosage. Wes had been on the same dose of Lamictal since his early twenties. When he was still in the foster system, nobody cared about his depression or manic episodes. Most homes didn't have the means to focus on one kid's mental health problems since most of the kids there had their own, so they, including his social worker, chalked it up to run-of-the-mill teenage angst and left him to languish in his own head.

Life was overwhelming—too many changes, not enough coping mechanisms.

The first class ended with appreciative laughter. Wes liked to end his class with some bad rock joke. Dad jokes were his specialty. Students seemed to like him for his corny humor and the fact that despite all attempts from Apollo to take him shopping for better clothes, Wes was a t-shirt and jeans kind of guy. He just didn't feel comfortable in anything else. And not just in a personal choice kind of way, but in that, collared shirts and turtlenecks sent him into sensory overload and he spent the entire time he wore them clawing at his own neck kind of way. He could rock a sport coat with a v-neck shirt and be totally fine, but add a button-down in place of the shirt and he wanted to rip his clothes off.

Lucky for him, geology wasn't one of those sciences that rested on formality in the workplace. Dumb, rock-pun shirts were actually encouraged, at least in his department. Today, Wes went with a simple black shirt that said, "Of Quartz I Love You," with line-art of a piece of quartz in place of the word. Brie had gotten it for him when he first started college and though it wasn't quite so black anymore, it was still one of his favorites.

"Geez, who shit in your coffee?" A voice cut through his thoughts. Wes focused in on his surroundings. He had been sitting alone in his office in the geology department, where he finally had a window. At the door stood Candy Thermpoli, his brand-new graduate student.

Candy was the complete opposite of her name—whereas someone would think she would be bubbly and colorful, Candy was a goth queen, who never wore a shade outside of black, and rimmed her dark blue eyes in heavy liner. Though Wes considered himself fairly tall at six foot one, Candy easily had about two inches on him, and that was without her thick boots adding a few more inches. She came from a long line of geologists. Her family were rock hounds in their spare time, traveling all over the country to hunt for minerals and fossils to add to their collection.

While Wes's area was mineralogy, Candy specialized in geochemistry and was probably, no definitely, the smartest person he had ever met.

"The only shit coffee around here is what they serve in the staff area. Fuck, it's like they haven't cleaned the damn thing in thirty years," Wes responded, staring at the half-empty coffee mug on his desk. It was cold now, and he didn't mind wasting the brown sludge.

"Oh, they haven't. Definitely not since my mom started teaching at least," Candy said, as she entered the office and plopped down into one of the two worn chairs across from Wes's desk.

Wes leaned back in his own chair, feeling at ease for the first time in days. Candy had that effect on people once you knew her. Sure, she might scream *don't talk to me* when you first looked at her, but she was an empathetic and all-around nice person once you got past the exterior.

"Well, nepo baby, maybe you could work your connections to get us a coffee maker from this century." He laughed.

"Yeah, laugh it up, asshole. I earned my spot here, just like everyone else. Mom wasn't allowed to give me a recommendation," she said, though there was no bite to her words. It was a running joke with them anyway. Wes knew very well that Candy worked her ass off to get into the geology graduate program. She had been accepted to CalTech's program, and Columbia's, but had chosen to stay in New Britain to attend CCSU and be close to her mom after she was diagnosed with early onset Alzheimer's. With her dad already gone and her siblings living scattered across the country with families of their own, she had elected to stay home and attend the university her mom had taught at for thirty years while also taking care of her.

"So, what's got you glum, chum?" she asked in a cheery voice.

Wes ran a hand through his hair on the long side, letting his fingers tangle a little in the curled strands. "Just some personal stuff has got me off my game," he said with a shrug. His problems weren't Candy's problems, and he didn't like to dump on people.

She nodded her head with a knowing look. "Boy problems again?" Even if he didn't like to dump his problems on others, Candy knew all about his troubles with Apollo. Well, most of them. She didn't know Apollo was an incubus, only that he liked to sleep around. Candy wasn't part of the magical community, and had no idea it existed, as far as Wes knew.

The hand that ran through his hair again acted of its own accord; Wes couldn't help himself. "Another weekend of booty calls and then see you later. It's like I'm just a piece of ass to him. It's been three years of this, Candy. Three fucking years!" He sighed deeply and flopped his head onto his desk with a loud thunk. It hurt a little, but the pain was welcome.

"Listen, I'm going to give you some tough love because I care," Candy started. Wes looked up and gave her a small nod before putting his head back down. "It doesn't matter that this guy has a golden dick and is a veritable sex god. He treats you like shit and you deserve better. You deserve love, Wes.

You deserve someone who will dick you down and then cuddle you the rest of the night. Stop thinking with your downstairs head and start thinking with your upstairs head and get out of that relationship."

It was harsh, but Wes knew she didn't mean for it to be. He needed to hear this because even if he said it a million times to himself, he didn't believe it. "You sound like my sister," he said, lifting his head again and leaving it up this time.

Candy gave him a half smile. "Smart woman. How's Brie, anyway? Back from her honeymoon?" Wes and Candy had started hanging out a few years back when they were both TAs and Brie was added into the fold when they all started playing Dungeons & Dragons with Periwinkle Montgomery, the pixie who owned Tower Books and the Goodberry Café. Though Candy didn't know Perri was a pixie because there were charms to keep her looking human when she was working around humans.

"They got back last night. I still haven't seen her yet, but they are coming over tonight for dinner. You're welcome to join us." In truth, Wes was just being polite. As much as he liked Candy, he really wanted some time with his sister. Well, and now his brother-in-law. But he wanted to hear all about their travels, and knowing them, there were plenty of magic-related stops that they wouldn't be able to discuss in front of Candy.

Luckily, Candy gave him an out. "Can't. Mom has a doctor's appointment this afternoon, and she's usually pretty agitated the rest of the night. I need to stay with her." It took until that moment for Wes to fully see the dark circles under Candy's eyes. It was more than just her eyeliner. She looked like she hadn't slept well in ages. How she was able to juggle school, helping her mom, and even a modicum of a social life was amazing to Wes. But it was clearly starting to take its toll on Candy.

Wes sat up straighter in his chair. "Hey, Candy, if you need anything, just let me know, okay? I might be a whole-ass disaster, but I'm here for you."

Candy's smile was thin, but her eyes were warm. "I know, Wes. I know. Goes both ways, you know." Wes nodded his head in return, because he did know. Candy was a good friend and Wes had had so few of those in his life that he appreciated her all the more.

Candy slapped her hands on her knees and stood from the chair. "Well, I gotta jet. I have class soon, and I want to snag some food before all hell breaks loose." Candy didn't waste time making an exit. She was gone in seconds, the door pulled closed behind her with a quiet snick.

Wes slouched down in his chair and stared at the coffee mug still on his desk like it would hold the secrets to fixing all his life's problems. But in the end, it was just a half-filled mug of terrible, cold coffee and no secrets of the universe were to be had.

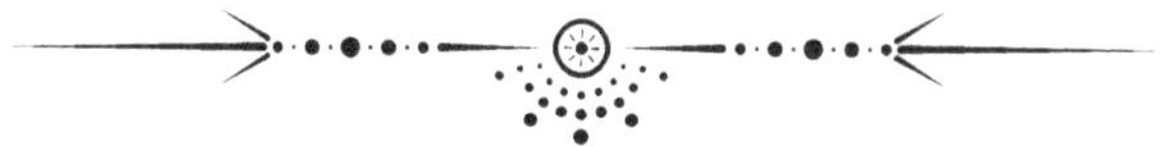

It felt like the couch was pulling him into its cushions as Wes stretched out his legs, resting them on the coffee table in front of him. He wasn't sure if that was just because it was a comfortable couch or if his body just felt so heavy. Either way, he let himself sink into the plush fabric. A nap sounded nice after a long day.

Just as Wes's eyes closed, his door burst open, the frame of it glowing an orangish-yellow. Half a second later, his sister Brie walked through the doorway, followed closely by her new husband, Ezra, the angel turned magic antique shop owner. Wes nearly fell off the couch completely, but instead he slammed his ankle against the coffee table hard. *That's going to leave a bruise.*

"Don't you knock, woman?!" he grumbled as he rubbed his sore ankle.

Brie bounded over to the couch and threw herself into Wes's arms. "Nice to see you too, dick. Didn't miss me too hard, did you?" Wes hugged his sister back and let his heart rate settle down. She could bust through any door any time if it meant he got to be around her. She was all he had left of family in the world, and being apart for weeks had been a lot for him to handle. He sounded like a needy child rather than the grown-ass man he was, but with his sister embracing him, he couldn't care less.

"Sorry about barging in. My wife insisted we set up a direct route from the Storage Room, and the magic doesn't lend itself well to knocking first. I hope that's alright. We can always remove it if you're uncomfortable with it," Ezra said, shutting the door behind him. Wes really liked Ezra; he was a good guy who treated his sister well. Hell, he had brought her back from the dead years ago and for that, Wes would forever be thankful.

"Nah, it's cool. Easy for all of us. Means I can get out of this house and to people I like that much easier." He wasn't going to pretend things had been great living on his own, because it hadn't. "Turns out I hate the quiet. I've never lived alone like this and it's the worst. The wooooorst," Wes whined, while Brie laughed into his shoulder. "Keep the portal, so I can come bother you two when the kitchen appliances start talking to me."

"And let you miss your 'Be Our Guest' moment? No way, shut it down, babe, the portal has to go. Wes needs to be a Disney princess," Brie said, laughing over her shoulder to address Ezra.

"I'm going to take a hard pass on the singalong, since I definitely do not have the hair or the grace to be a Disney Princess. What I will take is some food," Wes replied as he playfully shoved his sister off him. Brie fell back on the couch with a wide smile on her face.

"Darling husband, will you go get the pizzas? Please? You big strong angel man." She batted her eyes at her husband. Ezra responded with a roll of his eyes, something he had learned from Brie, and walked back through the portal door. In a moment, he stepped back again with the food in his arms and shut the door. A little pop sounded, and a small four-numbered panel appeared next to Wes's front door. There used to be one at their old apartment too.

"Number one will take you to the shop, and two will take you to our place. If you would like, I can connect one of them to your office or anywhere you like. Let me know, and I will take care of it," Ezra said, setting the stack of pizzas with a small plastic bag balanced on top on the coffee table.

"What's in the bag? Doesn't look big enough to be breadsticks." Wes reached for the bag first, while Ezra walked off to the kitchen for plates and napkins.

It was Brie's turn to roll her eyes. "Salad, of course. We let him into our lives, Wes, for years, and he is still trying to stuff us with healthy foods." The siblings groaned loudly in unison. They would still eat the salad, obviously. They both had a complex about wasting food, another gift from the foster system. And really, neither of them minded the healthy eating, it was more about being dramatic and keeping the joke going at that point. It had taken several years, and a lot of Ezra's home-cooked meals, but the St. James siblings were no longer the trash pandas they once were, and instead, opted for a few green foods now and then.

It took no time for all of the food to be consumed, including the salad, which Wes had to admit there was some merit in eating greens. They talked a little through the meal, mostly Brie, as she told Wes all about her honeymoon, making sure to keep it rated for older-brother consumption. Occasionally, she thrust her phone under his nose to show pictures of some magical shop in Morocco or the Midsummer celebrations in Belarus.

"I can't believe you got Ezra to do the fire jump with you," Wes said with a laugh, handing the phone back to Brie.

"It's cheating when the wings come out." She turned and shot her husband a glare. Ezra lounged on the other end of the couch, a soft grin on his face. His angelic wings were not visible now, he rarely showed them off except on special occasions, but the picture Brie showed didn't do their beauty justice.

"My wings were nearly singed. I would hardly count that as cheating," Ezra responded, as he leaned forward and started to grab the empty plates. Wes jumped up and made a move toward the dishes.

"Hey, I got it. You're my guest. Sit back." He tried to take the plates from Ezra's hands, but his brother-in-law pulled them back.

Ezra waved him off with a free hand. "Don't worry about it. I know where the sink is. You two need to catch up." Wes didn't put up much of a fight, and instead returned to sit next to his sister on the couch. He saw her staring at her husband as he walked off into the kitchen, nothing but pure love in her eyes. Wes wished he had that. Wished he had someone who would look at him like he was the moon and stars. As unorthodox as Brie and Ezra's relationship had started out, they really were stupid in love and complimented each other well.

I'm going to end up alone and jaded as fuck.

Wes had spent his twenties in various friends-with-benefits situations. None ended up being anything serious. For the most part, he'd never wanted anything serious while he was still in school. As for his partners, he always ran into the same problems. The men he dated thought he was gay and lying to himself, and the women he dated constantly thought he was going to leave them for another guy. It was exhausting.

It was better to just have a series of flings and one-night stands than a real relationship back then. But

Wes was older now and wanted someone to do the mundane things with him. Sex was great and all, and that was absolutely a necessity in any relationship, but he wanted more.

Later, as he waved to Brie and Ezra as they stepped through the magicked door, he thought about how he wished he had what they had. They got to wake up every morning and just be together, through good and bad. And in the years they had been together, there had been a lot of both.

Meanwhile, Wes's life had felt like a string of mediocre and bad. The teaching job was the good. Wes loved his work. The small group of friends he had acquired over the last few years was great. The sex with Apollo, outstanding. But that was all it was with Apollo. Sex. There was no completion in his life. Just a series of endless goals with no end in sight.

"You're letting yourself spiral again, Wesley," he said aloud, though there was no one but himself to hear. Staying conscious sounded like too much effort now that his sister and his brother-in-law were gone, so Wes slunk off to his room and flopped down on the bed face down. He didn't care that he was still in his clothes. The thought of getting up now was too much to deal with. Sleep came quickly, deep and consuming.

Like the rest of his life, even his dreams were empty.

The first month in his new role as a professor passed uneventfully. After the initial rush of full attendance, the class size began to dwindle. That wasn't unusual. People stopped showing up for class until it was test time. He was sure he would hear from them around mid-terms when suddenly they would have a million questions. All of the material was on the class portal anyway, including recordings of his lectures, so it wasn't like they didn't have access to literally everything. He could always unload those questions on Candy, but he wouldn't do that to her. She had enough on her plate to worry about without a bunch of dumb questions from undergrads who couldn't even be bothered to put in the effort until the last minute. Not that she wouldn't get her own share of them.

After class, he stopped by the Chinese takeout place he and Brie used to live over, more for a taste of the familiar than that the food was particularly good. He ordered enough to feed at least four since he was headed to the antique shop and Lily was joining them. It had been a while since he had seen the green witch. He had spent the summer solstice at her family farm, but ever since then, she had been working on some potions for a new line of products for the aging witch. "Magical Botox," Wes had called it, and Lily had laughed at that.

Her mate, Albert, would be out on his weekly feed. As a vampire, he drank from a human source once a week–always a willing donor. Most were dying and wanted some peace and dignity in their death, so they volunteered to be drained. Albert was an asshole most of the time, but he was their asshole and had actually grown a little on Wes as the years progressed.

The antique shop, Spirit Antiques, that Ezra and Brie owned was empty. Not surprising since it was a Wednesday afternoon, barely time for dinner. Most of the customers who frequented the place came out after dark, and the random humans who would sometimes stumble in during the day never stayed long. Mostly because Brie or Ezra shooed them out pretty quickly.

Wes made his way across the shop and since the door was already set on the Storage Room, he went through the one and only door into the cavernous room that housed all the shop's stock. They always ate in the Storage Room for some reason, even though the door also led to a staff room and Brie and Ezra's apartment. There was something nice about eating in the large magical space. Not just because the sort-of sentient room liked to be helpful by providing just about everything, but because there was this feeling, a tingling sensation of magic arcing all around them. The whole Storage Room was packed full of magical things: enchanted items, potion ingredients, and powerful magical talismans. It was a wonderful space, if a little intrusive at times.

Right on cue, Brie and Lily rounded a corner, talking excitedly as they stepped up to the platform that led to the door. "Wesley!" Lily shouted, running up to Wes and throwing her tattooed arms around him. Not too long ago, only her right arm had been covered in plant tattoos, but she'd recently started adding to the other arm. As usually is the case with Lily, Wes got a face full of her dark curls and the scent of herbs and strawberries washed over him. Were she not with

Albert, he knew he would marry her in a second just so he could have her hug him every day.

"Nice to see you too, Lils. I thought you had forgotten about me," he said with a grin. *Everybody else does, it seems, so why wouldn't she?*

No, he wouldn't think like that. His sister hadn't forgotten him. She had just been on her honeymoon. He couldn't be upset about that. Lily had her own life and partner, which again, he couldn't be mad about.

The only person I can be mad at is myself. I let myself be alone. I let Apollo jerk me around and play with my heart.

Wes pushed all those thoughts aside; he didn't want them to see him hurting. His feelings were not Lily's or Brie's problems. And they both would try to help him if they knew. That's just who they both were. So he kept it to himself and plastered on his best smile.

"Never! Actually, I was just thinking about you earlier today. So I've told you about my friend, Cameron. You know, the baker? And he and his girlfriend broke up last year. Not that I've been talking to him about you, but I totally have. Do you want his number?" Lily gave him a huge grin.

For the past two years, Lily and Brie had been not so subtly trying to set him up with people they knew. And while he appreciated the effort, Wes still hadn't taken them up on any of them. He hadn't received the same loyalty from Apollo in those two years, but it just wasn't Wes's style. There was also the certainty, though they never talked about it, that while Apollo could continue to sleep with whomever he wanted, the same allowance was not afforded to Wes. And anyway, he didn't want to be with multiple partners. He wanted one person who was going to love him.

Maybe I should take Lily up on her offer and move on from Apollo.

That was the logical choice. If Wes wanted more from a relationship than Apollo was willing to give, then it was time to end it. Wes had met Cameron many times over the years since Lily had started bringing him around, and he was a total snack. Wes had been caught staring at the man on more than a few occasions.

"I'm not sure... you know how things are with Apollo," he started, but Brie cut him off.

"Things are shitty with Apollo. He doesn't respect you, Wes. He won't commit to just you. Fuck, he still flirts with me constantly at the shop, and I don't mean the fun, innocent type of flirting." Her voice was hard. She had never liked Apollo all that much. During their first meeting, she slapped him after the incubus had tried to hypnotize her into sleeping with him. Wes couldn't blame her. When he'd met Apollo, Wes was overworked, underfed, and a little sex-crazed. He liked the attention he got from Apollo, loved the open flirting, and how handsy he was no matter where they were. He wasn't overly fond of him constantly hitting on his sister though. A complaint that clearly kept falling on deaf ears.

"Why don't I just give you his number and you two could hang out as friends? It's always nice to make a new friend. He's from an old witch family, so you know, you don't have to hide anything about yourself," Lily said, a hopeful look in her eye.

Wes thought it over. He really could use another friend that wasn't his sister or her group. Not that he didn't have any of his own friends, just not many. He had Candy, and he was friendly with some of the other associate professors around campus. But he didn't have much of a social life outside of this little found-family he had been brought into. And since Candy spent most of her time either in school or taking care of her mom, she really wasn't a great avenue for hangouts.

Cameron was a good guy from what Wes knew, and it would be nice to hang out with someone else for a change, another guy who wasn't a package deal with either his sister or Lily. Especially now that he was living alone full time. "Sure, give me his number. Would be good to have someone around who wasn't you two. You guys are just okay." Wes kept his face neutral. He really loved both of them, but he loved messing with them more. Laughing everything off made him feel a little like he was normal. Like he wasn't a total emotional and mental mess.

"Hey, we are both fucking delights, and you should feel privileged we let you hang out with us," Brie shot back. "Now, I'm starving, and you are just standing there holding food. Can we get a table up in here, please?" She addressed the second part toward the room. It was strange to talk to the Storage Room though. It wasn't like talking to a person, there wasn't anything in front of you to speak toward. It was more like putting your request or comment out into the world with no direct target.

But the Storage Room delivered when a gilded antique table walked itself up to the platform where they stood. Four chairs followed behind the table. Bowls and chopsticks popped into existence on the table, along with a napkin at each setting. Except at one spot, which had a whole stack of napkins. "Once again, this place insults me for being a messy eater," Wes said, taking his spot next to the large stack of napkins. The Storage Room always provided extra for him, and even if he wouldn't admit it aloud, it was an endearing gesture. It made it feel like he had his own place in the world.

Ezra joined them after they all started eating. He was still working on the inventory project he had started when he'd brought Brie on at the shop. It was a real testament to just how large the place was, since he wasn't even halfway done.

The four of them sat together, talking and eating, and it felt like a real family dinner. Which it pretty much was, since this was the family Wes had chosen. They all took turns talking about their day. "Samhain prep starts next weekend and I'm already exhausted just thinking about it. Dad and Bertie have been testing recipes for days already. I can't even look at an apple anymore."

"Well, you have us if you need anything," Brie said, volunteering the rest of the group.

"Hey, you don't speak for me. Maybe I have a busy schedule, and you know, a life," Wes said back with faux indignance.

Brie leveled a look at her brother, skepticism written all over her face. "You don't, and no, you don't." It was true, but she didn't need to say it like that. But then again, little had changed since they were teenagers. Wes may enjoy the more amorous company of individual people, groups he couldn't stand. They overwhelmed him, and he went into sensory shutdown if there were too many people, or he got too uncomfortable. He mostly enjoyed the comfort of a small group of people and his rocks.

Wes crossed his arms and leaned back in his chair. "Just because you're right, doesn't mean I'm yours to command. You're not the vessel of the Morrigan anymore, Little Witch. But fine, yeah, should you need us, Lils, just say the word." His sister flipped him off, but she was smiling, so it evened out.

They all stood to collect their dishes and trash, hauling it over to a normal trash can Brie had put in when they started having family dinners in the Storage Room. The magical room felt like part of the family too, in its own way, so it just felt right to take their meals in there. Once everything was cleared up, the dirty plates and chopsticks blinked out of existence and the table and chairs walked themselves back to wherever they came from. Another bonus of being in a magical room.

"I have to get back to work, sweetheart. See you at home later?" Ezra kissed his wife's cheek, and she nodded. He hadn't said much during dinner, but Ezra wasn't a chatty person by nature anyway.

"I have to be off too. Bertie will be home soon, and we're doing some moonlight harvesting," Lily said, shouldering her customary tote bag. "Anyone want to do a movie slash wine night this weekend? I need some chill time before the chaos starts."

It was exactly the thing Wes needed to get himself feeling normal, at least for a bit. Just some chill time with his favorite people, sans significant others, to complain about life and drink too much. Though, maybe he would cool it on the drinking too much. Being over thirty, the hangover was a real bitch to deal with.

They made plans for Saturday night, and then Lily was off, while Ezra slunk back into the recesses of the Storage Room. "Guess that just leaves us," Brie said, throwing her arm around Wes's shoulders. He snaked an arm around her waist and the two of them walked back into the front of Spirit Antiques.

Just as they stepped through the door, Wes's phone vibrated in his back pocket.

[Apollo: Picked up something fun at the shop the other day. Come over and we can try it out.]

Wes really didn't feel up to it. He wanted to spend time with his sister and not have any expectations of him for the night. On top of that, Apollo always came into the shop on Thursdays, so whatever he got was purchased last week and had undoubtedly already been used several times by that point.

Next to him, Brie let out a heavy sigh. "You can go if you want. At least one of us should get dicked down tonight." Was that a note of disappointment in her voice? But for which part?

"Ezra not giving up the goods lately?" Wes asked, avoiding answering her just yet.

She laughed. "Are you kidding? That man is insatiable, and I love it. No, my period has decided to make an appearance. Turns out being immortal does not get rid of the crimson tide."

Wes scrunched up his face. "Ew, TMI."

Brie punched him on the shoulder. "Don't act like periods gross you out. If I recall, since we were kids, you would always prepare me a care package whenever it was really bad. You were the one who got me on Diva Cups because you gave a whole presentation on why they were more sustainable." It was true. There was a PowerPoint and everything. There were two women in his life that were the most important people, and Brie was one of them. He focused all his love and attention on taking care of his little sister, especially after their adoptive mom, Maddy, died.

Wes looked down at his phone again. He shouldn't go to Apollo's. What he should do was stay with his sister and enjoy some time with his sibling without her husband around. Or he could go home and call it an early night since he had to teach classes the next day.

But Apollo was like an addiction. Wes knew the relationship wasn't good for him, knew it was destroying his self-worth. And yet, he still couldn't stop himself from heading straight to Apollo the second he snapped his well-manicured fingers. A pang of self-loathing hit him suddenly, and he knew he was going to leave Brie and head over without putting much thought into it.

"You sure you're okay with it?" he asked tentatively.

Brie snorted. "No, I'm not okay with it. Apollo treats you like shit. He uses you when it's convenient, and then leaves you hanging until he wants to screw you again. How long are you going to put up with this, Wes? I don't like seeing you hurting like this." She didn't reach for him, which was something Wes was thankful for. He didn't want to be touched right now. Just the idea overwhelmed him. Yet, he was still going to make himself go to Apollo and let him touch and use him as he saw fit. Even if it made Wes's skin crawl.

"I know you're right, but I've already spent three years with him, at least in some capacity. It's not easy to walk away from all that. Maybe, if I just stick it out a little longer, he will love me like I love him." It sounded pathetic even to his ears, and clearly, it sounded pathetic to his sister.

"Are you serious? That's not how love works, and you know it. If he won't commit to you exclusively after three years, he never will. But you need to figure that out on your own, so go if you want. I won't stop you." With that, Brie turned, punched the number three on the keypad next to the door, and opened the Storage Room door. "I really hope you get your head out of your ass soon, Wesley," she said over her shoulder. The door slammed behind her and Wes was left standing alone in the shop feeling like absolute garbage.

CHAPTER 3

Wes stared at the text box, the cursor blinking at him, trying to prompt him to actually type something. He had pulled up Cameron's contact information after he returned home from Apollo's and thought about texting him that night. But he convinced himself it was too late and instead went straight to bed, despite it being only nine.

Now it was Thursday afternoon and he once again attempted to send a text to Cameron. *It shouldn't be this hard. Just a "hey, Lily gave me your number. Wanna hang sometime?" Easy enough.* Wes had sent dozens of those types of messages.

And yet, he kept typing and deleting, typing and deleting every sentence he tried out. Nothing sounded right. Everything sounded like he was a desperate dork.

Why did it feel like he was cheating on Apollo by just asking if Cameron wanted to hang out? Apollo clearly didn't have a problem screwing everyone in town. It wasn't even like he wanted to pursue anything with Cameron, he just wanted to hang out and broaden his friendship circle. Maybe get some free baked goods out of it. There should be benefits to being friends with a baker, right?

He just needed to stop overthinking everything. Wes was going to text Cameron to hang out, and it was just going to be that, two people looking for new friendships. Wes would tell Apollo, and Apollo could think whatever he wanted. There was nothing to feel guilty over.

Except he did feel guilty, because even if Apollo didn't see it as cheating, Wes certainly did. By Wes's definition, he was in a relationship and while he couldn't control Apollo's actions, he could control his own. And his mind decided it would be going down the road to cheating to hang out with another guy he found incredibly attractive.

Wes set his phone down next to him on the couch and stared at the powered-off tv in front of him. How did he get to this point? Too afraid to break things off with Apollo and too afraid to move forward with his life. Logically, Wes knew he should either be alone or with someone who wanted the same things he did. But Wes wasn't being logical, he was thinking with his libido instead, because as awful as Apollo was at the romantic part of being a boyfriend, he was an exceptional lover, and for the last three years, that had been enough to keep Wes coming back.

What he needed was someone to talk to about all this. Someone that wasn't his sister. Brie had made it abundantly clear how she felt about his relationship with Apollo, and she was already biased since Apollo constantly flirted with her.

Tomorrow he would talk to Candy. She was a good third party, who didn't know Apollo. Not that he felt great about dumping his relationship problems on her, since she had enough to worry about in her own life. But she knew he had problems in his relationship, and she would pry it out of him anyway. Given enough time.

Wes had nothing to do for the rest of the day, so he decided to take himself out to an early dinner and head home. As he sat alone at his table in a diner far enough away from campus that it was mostly student-free, he looked at the empty seat across from him. It should be filled by someone who loved him. Someone who wanted to spend their life with him. But that person didn't exist. So instead, he sat alone.

"Do you actually sleep, or do you naturally look like shit all the time?" Candy said, as she walked into his office and sat down on one of the chairs.

"Good morning to you too," Wes grumbled into his coffee. If he thought talking to Candy was going to make him feel better, he really needed to examine his life choices.

"It's morning, but the good part is questionable. You look like you slept about as much as I did last night." She had bags under her eyes that not even her heavy eyeliner could hide.

Wes studied her face. Worry and guilt filtered through him. Here he was fretting over his romantic troubles, and Candy was dealing with real issues. Her mom had been getting progressively worse, and between college and being her caretaker, Candy was visibly cracking under the strain.

"So who talks first? You talk first? I talk first?" Wes said with a weak smile. Levity was his default. It didn't matter that inside his head, he was a mess. The only way to get through the day was to keep it light.

"You talk first. I've got nothing to say." Candy waved her hand dismissively, but it was all bravado. She threw her arms around the back of her chair and leaned back, her body language demonstrating she was ready to listen to his whining.

Wes slouched in his chair. He felt like a total asshole for wanting to unload on his friend. But it would just annoy Candy more for him to say nothing. "So, Lily gave me the number of one of her friends, this cute guy who is a total sweetheart. And I chickened out on texting him."

Candy raised a perfectly shaped eyebrow. "So you feel guilty because you are in a pseudo-relationship and you think Apollo will accuse you of seeing other people if you text this guy?" It wasn't a question, even though she posed it as one, Candy just read him that well. There was no judgment in her features, or in her tone. It was a simple statement, her reaction flat.

"Listen, boss, you are a grown-ass man. You need to make your own decisions. However, as a third-party observer with absolutely no stake in the matter, I can tell you that Apollo is never going to commit to you. If you're okay with that, then just keep doing what you're doing. If you're not, maybe it's time to stop pretending that you are in a real relationship and go find someone who is on the same page as you. Or better yet, forget people for a while and just date yourself."

"You really are the smartest person I know. You are the whole package, Candy, brains, beauty, and wit. I'd say marry me now, but you're out of my league." Wes laughed. He had to laugh, because if he didn't, he would have to let her words fully sink in. She was right, of course, he knew that he would never get what he wanted out of a relationship with Apollo. The sex was great, but that could only carry him so far. Wes wanted more from life. He wanted a partner who was invested in him and wanted to spend time with him, even if it was just sitting at home watching Netflix.

Candy chuckled. "Damn right I am. But you're not my type, boss. Now, maybe if you picked some clothing that wasn't so tragically mid-twenty-tens pop punk, I might be interested."

Wes's smile this time was genuine. "Do you even like men?" Not that it was any of his business. Sure, he had poured out all his problems to her, but there were still things he wasn't privy to when it came to her personal life.

Candy gave him a thoughtful look, but stayed silent for a moment. "I don't like anybody. Well, that's not totally true. I'm open to the idea of people. I'm just not interested in being with anybody like that. I'm ace."

Oh, well, that's surprising, Wes thought. Though it didn't change anything about how he thought about her. He always assumed she didn't date anyone because she was too busy looking after her mom. That's what he got for making assumptions.

Wes shrugged. "People suck anyway. Relationships are a headache." Again, the levity took control when he couldn't think of anything else to say. He was grateful that Candy trusted him enough to tell him. Even with people being more accepting now, it wasn't easy to disclose your sexuality to others. When he came out as bisexual to Maddy and Brie, his heart had hammered in his chest. He thought he was going to pass out. Both of them had simply hugged him and told them they loved him. Then they had a family pizza party where every pizza was half cheese, half pepperoni, because, as Maddy said, "Well you like both".

"Thank you for trusting me. I know it's not always easy." The smile was gone. He wanted her to know how much it meant to him.

Candy rolled her eyes. "Don't make it weird. We're friends, and that's the kind of shit friends share with each other. Besides, it's not like you can judge me. You're a full-blown bisexual disaster."

Truer words were never spoken.

"Valid point. So, you think I should call it off with Apollo?" Again, she rolled her eyes. Maybe Wes was being too tedious about this. Enough people in his life had told him that Apollo wasn't good for him. Maybe he should actually listen.

"Wes, I will reiterate that you are an adult who can make his own decisions. I'm just saying that maybe you should have a little more self-worth." She sat up straight in her chair and grabbed the bag she had set beside her on the floor. "I should get going. I have shit to do before I can head home."

Goddess, he was being a bad friend again. "Do you want to talk about it? You look like you haven't slept in days." He had spent all this time whining about his love life, knowing full well what kind of stress Candy was under.

I'm a selfish bastard, he chided.

But Candy stood anyway and hefted the bag onto her shoulder. "No, I don't." That was all she said before slipping out the door. Wes tried not to take it to heart. If Candy didn't want to open up about her problems, that was okay, and he would respect that. Candy was the type of person to keep it close to her chest, and it wasn't Wes's place to pry.

No, he needed to worry about himself and be a supportive presence for Candy without knowing the details. Instead, he should focus on getting his own shit together and figuring out what he was going to do about Apollo.

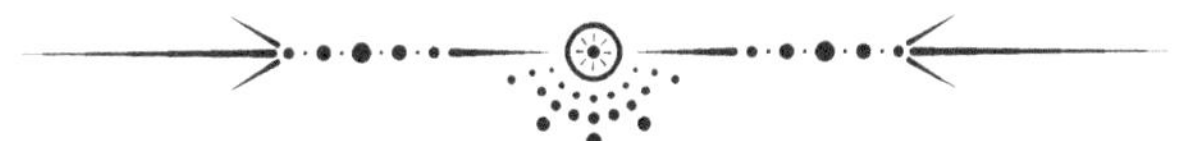

Wes was standing in front of the class finishing up his lecture when he saw the door open in the back of the large hall. His eyes followed Apollo as he slid into one of the back seats next to a pretty blonde freshman. She turned her head toward him and gave Apollo a big smile, which he returned.

Wes watched as Apollo threw his arm around the back of her seat, leaned over, and whispered into the girl's ear, and she pulled back, giggling softly and blushing. It was with no small amount of difficulty that he finished his lecture without staring at the two of them at the back of the room.

As he dismissed the class for the day, his gaze found them again, and he caught Apollo handing the girl back her phone, giving her one of his most seductive smiles, which she returned with more giggling.

Once the class cleared out, Apollo made his way down the stairs to the table Wes stood at, packing up his things. "She's barely legal," Wes said by way of greeting, keeping his focus on his bag. He didn't want to even look at Apollo. The man was shameless. Flirting with college girls right in front of him, in the class he was teaching.

Apollo just laughed. "Barely legal is still legal, my dove." And that was the end of the conversation. Apollo rounded the table and pulled Wes to him and kissed him passionately. Despite himself, Wes moaned against Apollo's lips and let the kiss wash away his irritation. Like he always did.

It was already halfway through October, and still Apollo hadn't brought up their going to the Everett Samhain celebration. Maybe Apollo just assumed they would go together, like he did years previous. But Wes was always the one doing the asking. He wanted Apollo to show a bit of initiative and make plans and ask him. The chances of that happening were looking less and less.

This year, Wes wasn't going to cave and ask Apollo. Either Apollo asked to go with him, or Wes would just catch a ride with Ezra and Brie and hang with his family all night. Not that he minded. Samhain was about remembering ancestors, and it was meaningful for him and Brie to take Maddy's photo to the altar and spend some time talking about her.

This year Celeste, their late mother's partner, would be attending. It had been years since he had seen her. After Maddy's death, she had taken to traveling, giving up her position as coven leader. It was her own way of letting her broken heart heal. Wes was excited to see her again.

"Let's get lunch, I'm starving," Apollo said, drawing Wes out of his internal fuming.

"Didn't get enough to eat this morning?" Wes couldn't stop himself from biting out. There was no chance that Apollo woke up alone today and Wes was feeling surly.

But Apollo didn't acknowledge his tone. Instead, he shot Wes a mischievous grin that was all bright teeth. "Oh, I ate well this morning, but I find myself absolutely famished now. I want something a little different from breakfast." Apollo's eyes shone with lust and it wasn't hard for Wes to figure out what Apollo expected of their time together.

Minutes later, Wes thought he really should have insisted on getting lunch without the innuendo, as he pulled tightly on Apollo's golden hair while the incubus sucked him off in the empty lecture hall. As he climbed closer to his climax, his thoughts dissipated, and he leaned into the pleasure Apollo's mouth brought.

CHAPTER 4

Brie chattered loudly in the front seat of Ezra's SUV. Wes sat in the back, barely listening as he stared out the window into the darkness. He had been brooding all day because Apollo never even mentioned Samhain to him. For once, Wes's resolve stayed firm, and he didn't ask Apollo about it. So here he was, hitching a ride with his sister and his brother-in-law because his boyfriend couldn't be bothered to do anything with him.

Hyacinth Everett was the first to greet them when they entered the circle of celebration. She hugged both St. James siblings tightly and kissed Ezra's cheek when he bent down to her level. "Why don't you go set your stuff down on the altar and then get some food. You know how fast things go around here," Hyacinth said, looping her arm through Brie's and leading the trio over to where a table was already piled full of pictures, paintings, trinkets, and food–all as mementos of those who had passed beyond the veil and who they all remembered tonight.

"Hey gang, glad you could make it!" Lily bounded over to them as they turned away from the altar a few minutes later. "Grab some food. We have a space over near the fire." They piled plates full of the amazing food that Lily's dad, Damien, and Albert had worked on for days. It was all amazing, of course, but that was to be expected from a kitchen witch and a vampire who had spent the better part of a century perfecting recipes.

They followed Lily over to where several blankets were set up on the ground and a few people sat chatting over half-empty plates. Albert Hsu, Lily's vampire mate, sat on the edge of the blanket with a cup of what was likely blood next to him. In the center of the blanket was Periwinkle Montgomery, the pixie owner of the bookstore and Goodberry Café. She was a slender woman with toned arms, silvery blue hair, and iridescent wings on her back.

Finally, sitting cross-legged on the other blanket, was Cameron Griswold. Tall, even sitting down, and broad, he looked like he was trying to compact his body to leave space for others. His chocolate brown hair hung just over the tips of his ears, and a bit of dark blond scruff covered his chin and around his upper lip. Even in the firelight, his eyes were a captivating, shimmering light green. He smiled while he waved, and it was blindingly brilliant and transformed his face into something exceedingly beautiful.

Wes had met Cameron on several occasions over the years, and he could count on one hand how many of those times he had seen the man without flour somewhere on his body. He had a trusting vibe around him, like he wasn't anything more than what he appeared. Not to mention, he was ridiculously handsome. Not the unrealistic and unattainable hotness of Apollo, but instead a rugged handsome that was only enhanced by a wide smile and sparkling eyes.

Wes's stomach filled with butterflies at the sight of Cameron, just like it always did. He had been so tempted to text him the other day, and now he cursed himself for chickening out. Who wouldn't want to spend time with a man like that?

"You can sit here," Cameron said, patting the empty space next to him on the blanket. Jolted from his appreciation of Cameron's form, Wes realized that he was the only one still standing. He flushed and quickly took a seat next to Cameron and focused on the food sitting on his lap.

"Lily told me you started teaching full time at the university. I'm sorry, but I forget what your field is." Cameron gave Wes a sheepish grin, like he felt embarrassed that he didn't remember. Not that Wes would expect him to. He couldn't recall ever talking about his work to Cameron in the times they had spoken.

"Geology. My specialty is mineralogy," Wes said between bites. Cameron may be good to look at, but the food was fantastic and Wes couldn't keep himself from it.

Cameron nodded. "That's really cool. I don't know much about rocks, other than what they teach in grade school about igneous and whatever the others are. Science wasn't my forte." When he smiled at his self-deprecating comment, a dimple appeared on the right side of his mouth. Wes had the overwhelming urge to kiss it.

"Dude, you are a baker. That's all chemistry," Wes said, and he couldn't stop himself from putting a hand on Cameron's shoulder. It was a little cooler out, being the middle of autumn, but Cameron felt like an inferno. Wes could practically feel the heat radiating off him through the man's sweater. He didn't even wear a coat, just a burnt orange knit turtleneck.

If Wes wasn't mistaken, a small blush formed on Cameron's cheeks. Wes wanted to make the big man blush more. It was entirely too cute. "It's more magic than chemistry. Perks of being a kitchen witch. But all the Griswolds have been bakers, probably since we settled in Connecticut a million years ago." His laugh was infectious and Wes found himself chuckling along with him.

"Well, I think there's some science in magic. It's not just wand waving, there's intent, and visualizing how all the components of the magic work. Essentially science in its own way." Wes had always been passionate about magic. He found that he sometimes felt a deep sadness that his family didn't live long enough to teach him more of what it meant to be a guardian, all the magic that was lost to him because of their deaths. The magic Maddy had taught him was the human kind, no real power behind it. At least not one that was recognized by the magical community. Their Pagan ways had a magic of their own, though.

The smile never left Cameron's face. It was like his default was a beautiful grin and bright eyes. Wes wanted to just stare at him all day. Conversation was so easy with him, even when Wes found it hard to talk to others. "You're a very passionate person. I bet everyone loves your class," Cameron said, and Wes felt himself swell with pride and a warmth spread through his body. Was this how it was supposed to be with another person? They complimented you and took an interest in what you were interested in even if they didn't understand it?

They continued to talk as they ate and even after their plates were long empty, Wes and Cameron kept their attention on each other. It was like the rest of the world didn't exist to Wes. "Wouldn't you agree, Wes?" Brie's voice cut through the contented haze he was in around Cameron.

Wes reluctantly turned his attention to his sister. "Huh?" was his brilliant response.

Brie, Lily, and Periwinkle giggled amongst themselves.

"Totally called it," Brie said, smirking. The other two women nodded their heads, wearing matching grins. Ezra's face was neutral. He had no stake in the conversation, clearly, and Albert looked bored, his hand creating circles on Lily's arm. Next to Wes, Cameron looked on with an adorably confused face.

"Called what?" Wes asked, suspicion coloring his tone, though he suspected he knew exactly what his sister called. Just because she was right, didn't mean she needed to call him out in front of Cameron.

But Brie didn't answer, because two dark shadows fell over the group. Wes looked up, and though his face was clouded in darkness since the fire was to his back, he could tell it was Apollo. The second shadow looked to be Esmerelda, a pretty nymph who Wes knew was a frequent partner of Apollo's. "Hello, darling," he said, staring directly at Wes, his blue eyes the only thing shining through the shadows of his face.

Guilt washed over Wes in waves. Here he was having a great time talking to Cameron, maybe even flirting a little, and his boyfriend had caught him.

No, I'm not doing anything wrong by talking to another person. Especially since he's here with one of his fuck buddies. Wes had to focus on those facts or he would tear himself apart with guilt.

"Hi," he responded sheepishly, but he looked past Apollo's shoulder. He couldn't meet the other man's eye.

Apollo flopped down on the blanket next to Wes, tugging Esmerelda down with him, though she huffed in protest. He threw his arm around Wes's waist and pulled until Wes felt obligated to scoot closer to him. Apollo's other hand rested high on Esmerelda's thigh. He was staking a claim on both of them. "I thought you would invite me as your date tonight. I was disappointed when you didn't say anything." His pout was faked, of course, and Wes could now clearly see the mischief in his eyes.

Wes turned his gaze to his lap, wishing he could push away from Apollo. "I always ask. I thought maybe this year you would take the initiative to invite me. Looks like you found someone to replace me."

"Someone is moody tonight. Come now, lamb, you know my nature. You do the begging and I give you whatever you want. And I know a way to get rid of that bad mood." Apollo stood and pulled Wes up with him. Esmerelda started to get up too, but Apollo stopped her with a hand. "Why don't you stay here, Ezzy. I'll be right back." He threaded his fingers through Wes's and led them away from the blanket.

Wes didn't want to go with Apollo, but he was helpless against Apollo. He turned and looked back, his eyes locking with Cameron's. He thought he would see hurt or disgust, especially since they had been having a great time together until Apollo arrived. But the look he saw on Cameron's face was sympathetic. The man looked poised to spring up and follow them, but Esmerelda put a hand on his forearm and slipped it up to his shoulder. Their gazes broke and Wes turned back, letting Apollo drag him away from the circle surrounding the fire.

Wes thought Apollo would lead him off into the woods surrounding the clearing, but instead he took them to an area that was far enough from everyone else, but still near enough to see the fire. It quickly became clear that Apollo had not led Wes away for a tryst in the great outdoors.

"Are you having a good time, Wes?" Apollo stopped and turned to look at Wes. He dropped their hands and crossed his arms. Wes was instantly on edge. Apollo rarely called him by his name, instead opting to use a myriad of ridiculous pet names that Wes couldn't stand.

Wes decided to go for the truth. "Yeah, it's been nice so far. Until you showed up with your date, that is." He wasn't trying to be combative, but he was angry. No, that wasn't right. He was trying to be combative. Wes wanted to show Apollo that he wasn't going to wait around for him, that he would still have a good time without his supposed boyfriend around.

Apollo chuckled and dropped his arms. He closed the distance between them and cupped Wes's cheeks. "Sweet lamb, are you jealous?" The tone he used was sickly sweet and a little condescending.

It only served to make Wes angrier. "Fuck yes, I'm jealous! We're supposed to be in a relationship. And rather than ask me to be your date to one of our biggest celebrations of the year, you blow me off and bring Esmerelda of all people with you instead." He stepped back out of Apollo's reach. If he let the incubus touch him too long, Wes would let himself melt into Apollo's arms and forget and forgive everything again. He wanted to be angry and stay angry for a little longer.

But Apollo gave him no room. He stepped back into Wes's space and took his hands. Wes wanted to rip his hands away, but stopped himself. Apollo's face was surprisingly sober. "Wes, darling, it's my nature to seek out companionship from anyone and everyone. You know this about me. I know you don't see it as fair to you, but you know what I am. I'm an incubus. I am driven by lust. I can't change my stars, Wesley. This is my curse, and it doesn't care who else it hurts in the process."

Wes had never, in the three years he had been seeing Apollo, heard him speak so somberly, so directly, and without affectation. It was jarring, and Wes found he couldn't hang onto his anger. He may not know everything about incubi, but he did know they survived by feeding on lust. It didn't matter that Wes wanted them to be exclusive, Apollo's very nature kept him from doing that. And Wes knew, though it hurt his heart to acknowledge it, that he would never be enough to fulfill Apollo. Not because of a lack of trying, but because there just wasn't enough of him to give. He was disgusted with himself for wanting more from Apollo.

"I know I'm being selfish. I can't change who you are, and I would never expect you to change. I just... I don't know. If you could at least not parade your hookups around me, I might feel better about it." Wes averted his gaze, because he didn't want to look at Apollo, didn't want him to see how much he hated even having to say any of this.

Apollo pressed his lips to Wes's, and it was one of his rarer kisses. It wasn't devouring or fast, or even passionate. It was soft, gentle, adoring. He so rarely gave those types of kisses, that Wes was stunned for a moment before he started to kiss Apollo back.

"I'm sorry for making you feel uncomfortable. I think I was just a little hurt that you didn't invite me. I didn't want to come alone," Apollo said, resting his forehead against Wes's. His words made Wes feel even worse, like a knife to the heart. He felt callous for not asking, when that had always been their way. How was Apollo supposed to know he wanted to change it up this year?

Apollo wrapped his arms around Wes's middle, and after several beats, Wes returned the embrace. They held each other for a while, and silence fell between them. Wes found himself wishing things could always be like this with Apollo, where they talked about their issues and just held each other. He wanted that easy intimacy with Apollo, because even if it was a twisted and one-sided kind of love, he still loved Apollo.

Or maybe I'm just trying to force myself to love him. Because this doesn't feel like love.

He squashed the thought down instantly. Later, he would examine it further, but he wanted to stay in the moment for as long as he could, where everything felt like it should be between him and his boyfriend.

Too soon, though, Apollo pulled away. He kept only one arm around Wes's waist as he pulled them back into the celebrations around the fire. For the rest of the night, Apollo kept close to Wes's side, always touching him in some way like he was staking his claim and letting everyone else know. Esmerelda lurked not far away wherever they went, visibly pissed off that Apollo had all but ditched her. Wes knew very well that Apollo would make it up to her later and she, like Wes, would come crawling back and forgive him for all slights against her.

Wes saw Cameron a few times throughout the rest of the night and each time tried to give Cameron a sheepish smile, but it never reached his eyes, even if Cameron flashed him a large toothy grin in return. They didn't get another chance to talk one on one for the rest of the celebration. Apollo barely let Wes near the group again. At the end of the night, Wes only got a few seconds to say goodbye to his sister before Apollo whisked him off to his car. Wes could practically feel Brie's disapproving glower prickling on the back of his neck.

The drive back to Apollo's penthouse was quiet, though Apollo kept his hand on Wes's thigh. Claiming him, reminding him who he belonged to. "No talking tonight, sweet boy, this is just about feeling everything together," Apollo instructed, as he pulled Wes back to the bedroom.

Apollo's bedroom was the ultimate seduction space. The lights were dim. The bed had cotton sheets in deep burgundy with the highest thread count Wes had ever felt. The duvet was downy soft, and the bed held enough spring for a good rhythm when thrusting, but was pillowy enough for ultimate comfort. Not that Wes had slept in the bed, only laid for a few dazed minutes before Apollo kicked him out. Everything in the room was tastefully decorated with antiques that Wes was sure Apollo had collected over the centuries, but managed to compile into a modern look.

Apollo was in Wes's space in seconds, hands resting on Wes's hips as he tugged him close and gently kissed him. Tonight had been full of soft kisses, and Wes felt unbalanced at the gentle way Apollo had been treating him. Apollo began to trail kisses down Wes's jaw, then his neck, sucking lightly on his pulse points. A quiet moan escaped Wes, and he closed his eyes and let himself get lost in the feeling of Apollo's warm lips on his flushed skin.

Slowly, Apollo pulled off each piece of clothing Wes wore, letting them drop to the ground before taking off his own clothes. He laid Wes down on the bed, returning to Wes's lips, keeping them locked together. Wes relished the feel of Apollo's skin on his. Warm and soft skin pushed against each other.

All the while, Wes kept silent, his only sound the noises of pleasure that came out as breathy moans and sharp intakes of breath. Apollo settled him on his back, throwing Wes's legs over his shoulder when he finally pushed into him. They stared deeply into each other's eyes while Apollo set a slow rhythm with the rocking of his hips.

Wes searched Apollo's eyes, searching for something, a spark, or a hint that what Apollo felt was deeper. Even through the fog of lust and satisfaction, he could see it wasn't there. Apollo was being gentle, making love rather than quickly fucking, but there was no sign of actual love in his eyes, simply pure lust and restraint.

They came seconds apart, and Wes let his disappointment abate as his climax relaxed the tension in his body. Apollo made quick work of cleaning them both up before doing the most out-of-character thing that night. He laid back down on the bed and wrapped his body around Wes, letting his hands settle on Wes's chest, and nuzzling his chin at the crock of Wes's shoulder. They cuddled in Apollo's bed, the quiet becoming more comfortable, the only sound breaking the silence was that of their slowing breaths.

It was late, and Wes felt his eyelids dropping. His mind started to drift off. Part of him expected Apollo to kick him out, maybe offer to pay for his ride-share home. But he didn't. Instead, he pulled Wes close and kissed the spot behind his ear that made him weak in the knees.

"Goodnight, sweetness," Apollo said sleepily, and in seconds his breathing evened out and he was asleep.

Wes lay in the circle of Apollo's arm, unsure of what he should do. Not once in the three years they had been seeing each other had Apollo let him sleep over. Conflict swirled in his head about whether he should see himself out or stay in the bed and enjoy the opportunity to just cuddle.

His body made the choice for him. Wes was too tired to get out of the bed, let alone try to make his way home this late at night. So he allowed himself to snuggle closer to Apollo and fall asleep.

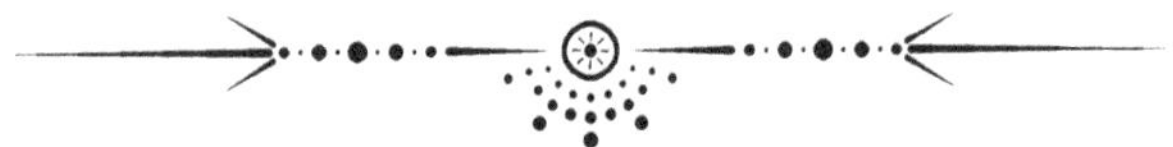

Even though Wes and Apollo had slept late into the morning, by the afternoon Wes was exhausted. And despite having ended the night wonderfully, he still felt like he could barely move from how low he felt.

Brie had texted him several times, but even the thought of picking up his phone to text her back seemed like a monumental effort. So he lounged on his couch instead, staring at some show on HGTV that he didn't remember turning on. He didn't know how long he sat there, just melting into his couch, when his front door burst open and his sister stomped inside.

"What the fuck, Wesley?!" She slammed the door behind her and crossed the room to the couch, where she stood looming over his prone form. Wes tipped his head up to look at her, seeing the conflicted look on her face. She couldn't seem to settle on anger or worry. Wes said nothing, and the look he gave her must not have been a good enough answer. "You just dipped out last night with barely a word. You didn't show up for breakfast at Lily's like we'd planned, and then you didn't answer your phone all day. So again, what the fuck?!" She was shouting by the end, and her eyes were hard, her mind finally set on anger.

He felt guilty. He had completely forgotten about breakfast at Lily's. They had planned it last week as a post-Samhain hangover cure. But Wes barely had enough energy to get home that morning, and since he didn't check his phone other than to see that Brie had texted and called, he didn't remember the breakfast at all. "I forgot. I stayed at Apollo's and we slept late," Wes said, his excuse falling flat even to himself. Normally, Wes was meticulous about his schedule, putting every single event into his phone calendar so he wouldn't forget. But he didn't even bother to look at that notification either.

Brie's face melted into sympathy and she sat down heavily next to her brother. "Well, that explains it. I'm guessing you didn't take your meds with you and forgot to take them when you got home."

Clarity flooded through him. His meds. His mood-stabilizing bipolar medication that was sitting on his dresser in his room, where it always was so he could take it first thing in the morning. But because he got home so late that morning, he had forgotten to take them. Forgotten all about them, actually.

Well, that really did explain everything. It had just been so long since he had missed a dose that he forgot what it felt like to go without. No wonder he couldn't bring himself to get off his couch. "Stay here, I'll go get it for you," Brie said, like she could tell he wasn't capable of moving his body. She got up and walked into his room before returning with an orange pill bottle. She grabbed a soda from the fridge and brought both the pills and the drink to Wes. He took the offered items, and quickly swallowed the white pill before setting the bottle and soda can down on the coffee table.

"Goddess, I'm a fucking idiot. I can't believe I forgot my meds." He flung his head back against the couch and closed his eyes. For fuck's sake, he was in his thirties and had been taking the medication since he was a teenager.

He felt Brie rest her head against his shoulder as she snuggled in next to him. "Don't worry about it, Wes. These things happen. I was just worried about you. I just wanted to make sure you were okay. It's not like you to miss out on our plans."

Wes lifted his head from the couch and moved instead to rest his cheek against Brie's head as he threw an arm around her shoulders and pulled her into his side. "I'm sorry for making you freak. Honestly, I wasn't anticipating staying at Apollo's. He never lets me stay. He was just so different last night. It was nice, but kind of weird too."

Brie scoffed and sat up straight to turn her body toward Wes. "Yeah, he was different because he saw you enjoying yourself with someone else and got jealous. Which is insane because that asshole showed up with a whole other person as his date." Wes had tried to forget that part and just wanted to focus on how nice things had been between him and Apollo last night.

Still, what she said was true. Apollo never acted that way, but Wes had never given him a reason to think he wasn't completely committed. Just because he was an incubus, didn't mean Apollo didn't experience jealousy, it just never was an issue before. Wes was an introvert who mostly stuck to his sister and limited friend-group at events.

And Wes didn't want to think about Apollo trying to sabotage his good time simply because he was enjoying someone else's company. Not after last night and this morning. Instead, Wes was going to let himself bask in a rosy idea that their relationship was at a turning point and Apollo was going to try more. The little voice in the back of his mind kept trying to push through, to remind him that what Apollo was doing was love-bombing, making him feel special and showering him with the affection he always craved. It wouldn't last.

Eventually, Apollo would feel secure enough that Wes wasn't looking for more elsewhere and go back to the way things were. The thought was depressing. "You're right, and I know that. But I want to enjoy a little bit of it before he's back to being an ass." Wes scrubbed a hand over his face, knowing full well things were going to suck with Apollo again eventually.

"Why don't you just break up with him and explore how things go with Cameron? The two of you were vibing last night. We all saw that. And he's a great guy." She wasn't wrong. Cameron was a great guy, and they totally had a connection last night. But that didn't matter, because he was still with Apollo and it didn't seem right to break off things with his long-term boyfriend because he had half of a great night hanging with another guy, and especially not when he saw Apollo trying to make up for how things had been.

"Cameron is great, and if I wasn't with Apollo, I would totally go for it. But I'm not going to jump from one guy to the next." He held up a hand to stop Brie from responding. He knew what she was going to say. In his twenties, Wes had definitely hopped from boyfriend to girlfriend. As soon as one relationship ended, he was hooking up with someone else. "I'm not looking for that anymore. I want what you and Ezra have, someone to spend forever with, who wants to settle down into a loving relationship."

Brie sighed. "So, why are you wasting time with Apollo? You know he's not going to be that person for you." He did know. If Wes was being honest with himself, it was because he was scared that he would end up alone. Even if Apollo never gave him the type of relationship he wanted, at least he wasn't on his own. Wes knew what it was like to be alone, but he also knew what it was like to finally have a semblance of a family. He couldn't handle being alone again. He wasn't strong enough for that.

So he shrugged at his sister's question, and even though he could tell Brie wanted to keep arguing, she didn't say anything further about Apollo. Wes felt when the medication finally started to work because his energy began to return and he felt incredibly hungry.

"Let's get lunch or dinner or whatever it's time for," he said, effectively ending further conversation about his love life.

Chapter 5

"I rolled a one again. These dice are cursed." Brie stared at the sparkly purple 20-sided die like she could make it roll higher just by shaming it with a glare. The table in the back of Goodberry Café was full that night. Wes came with Brie and Albert, while Periwinkle, the owner, sat at the head of the table. They were playing Dungeons & Dragons, something Wes had pulled his sister and his brother-in-law into a few months after all the shit went down with the creepy warlock, Moloc. But eventually, Brie let Ezra off the hook and he stopped coming. She brought Lily and Albert one time and Albert got hooked on the game, much to Lily's amusement and Brie's annoyance. Though it had helped to make them sort of friends.

Periwinkle hosted and ran the game, offering up her café, which was already open late. There were three others in the group: Tobias, an accountant who was also a gnome, Chel, a siren who had a strict ban on playing bards in the game, and Samson, a vampire who couldn't play on Friday nights because he was Shomer Shabbos. So they played Sunday night once a month, and all drank too much coffee while they played. In the summer months, when the days were long, they had to start later, and it was always a super late night. But on a chilly November evening like that night, they got to start much earlier, so maybe Wes would get home before midnight.

In the center of the table was a large grid-shaped map where miniature characters were placed. Hovering over the map, a hazy cloud showed in animated detail the scene that was happening in the game. Periwinkle used her magic to create images of the combat, creating full visualizations of their characters that would act out whatever each player commanded. It was more than just traditional D&D and more like a video game mixed with tabletop gaming. In Wes's opinion, it was the only way to play Dungeons & Dragons.

In the hazy cloud, the dwarven paladin character Brie played fumbled her axe and missed the goblin in front of her completely. Everyone at the table laughed. It was always entertaining to watch a character fail, but even better when they epically succeeded. Periwinkle was talented with her magic and it made the game even more exciting.

"Alright, Wes, why don't you finish him off. If you can." Periwinkle smirked and with a wave of her hands, the image focused on Wes's halfling bard. Wes rolled his die and whooped when it came up with a twenty. He rarely had good rolls, but this was perfect. The whole table cheered when he announced his roll.

Periwinkle waved her hands again and the image in the haze was of Wes's bard strumming a chord on his mandolin and the goblin disintegrating from the blast of magical music. "Don't bother rolling damage.

The dude had one hit point left. He's basically a smear now. And I think that's where we'll end it tonight. I have a meeting with my suppliers in the morning and need to sleep."

They packed up their stuff and began to head out of the café. "Will you remind Ezra that I won't be in Thursday, but Wednesday instead? Twig's baby dance recital is Thursday, and I am obligated to attend," Albert said, referring to Lily's sister Ivy's two-year-old daughter. Her name was actually Tiger Lily, but Albert started calling her Twig because he said she was tiny, like a twig, and the nickname stuck.

"Baby dance! I bet that'll be hella adorable!" Brie said with a delighted shriek. Wes hoped she wasn't feeling the baby craze yet. Not that he didn't want her to have kids. He would love to be the fun uncle, but it would be weird to think of her as a mom. He wasn't sure where his sister stood on the whole "kids" front. That was something for her and Ezra to discuss. They never talked about it as teenagers, probably thinking the same thing. If they could get other kids out of the system, they would.

Albert rolled his eyes. "Ah yes, a bunch of toddlers completely forgetting a dance they've been learning for weeks, or worse, having a meltdown on stage. Sounds like a riveting good time, and definitely a good reason to waste good magic so I can be out in the daylight." They headed out of the café and continued talking on the sidewalk.

"Take lots of pictures for me," Brie said, rummaging through her messenger bag for her keys.

Albert let out a long-suffering sigh that Wes knew was just for show. He adored Twig and doted on her constantly. "I was already planning on it. Twig loves the camera." Wes and Brie gave each other a knowing look. It was more like Albert's camera loved Twig. He couldn't get enough of her toddler antics, and they had seen enough pictures of the two of them together to know that.

They all waved goodbye to each other, and Periwinkle headed back into the café to take over from one of her employees. She worked pretty much whenever she felt like it. The whole place was a well-oiled machine.

"I don't know about you, but I'm exhausted." Brie stretched her arms over her head and yawned. Wes could relate. He felt absolutely beat. He had to teach an early class the next day, and all he wanted to do was crawl into his bed and pass out.

"If I could lay down right here on the sidewalk, I would. I could sleep anywhere at this point," he responded. They got into the black Audi that was technically Ezra's but was basically now Brie's car since she used it more. Nobody liked Ezra's driving much.

"Gross, don't. I can take you home, or you can stay with me and Ezra. We're closer if you're that tired," she said, pulling away from the café. Wes considered it for a moment. There was something comforting about the idea of staying with his sister. Last year they even created a second room so people, mainly Wes, could stay over.

"And run the risk of hearing you two have sex? No thanks. I'm going to keep pretending my little sister doesn't have sex," he joked. The rooms at their place were pretty soundproof, so it wasn't like he would actually hear anything, but that wasn't the point.

Brie flashed him a grin. "Hate to break it to you, big brother, but I'm a married woman and we most definitely have sex. Lots of it, and it's not always in our bed."

Wes put his hands over his ears. "I don't want to know how you've defiled the whole house and shop. My poor virgin ears." His whine was loud and exaggerated, and quickly they both started to giggle.

"Just you wait. Maybe, one day, Ezra and I will have kids and then we're going to have to talk about where babies come from." Brie laughed, keeping her eyes on the road. Silence filled the car for the rest of the drive, but it was a comfortable silence. The St. James siblings never minded the quiet when they were together. Both relished some peace, so long as it was with someone else around. Not everyone could understand their desire not to fill every moment with noise.

Brie pulled up to Wes's house, and they hugged across the console before saying goodbye. Wes had just made it through his door when his phone vibrated with a text.

[Apollo: My bed feels lonely without you. Come snuggle with me.]

Wes knew very well there would be a lot more than just snuggling. But it sounded also like Apollo wanted him to stay, to spend the night. He had already done so twice since Samhain, and it was nice to not be kicked out immediately after sex and to wake up in Apollo's arms.

Still, Wes was tired, and he had an early start to look forward to. Apollo would understand. Wes wasn't at his beck and call and if he wanted to stay home for a night, that was okay.

[Wes: I just got home and I need to get to bed.]

[Apollo: Boo! I don't like that answer. Please come over. I will make sure you get plenty of sleep. I know just the thing that will help with that.]

Yeah, Wes knew exactly what Apollo's sleep aid was. And he just didn't have it in him to go over. He would either have to bike over or take a ride share and it really was getting late. Wes wanted his own bed, without the expectation to perform before sleeping.

[Wes: Maybe tomorrow. I really want to sleep.]

Apollo wouldn't offer to come over. He never did. Even if he had been on his best behavior since Samhain, giving Wes more attention than he ever had before, it didn't matter. It was time to set a boundary on Apollo's love-bombing, starting here.

[Apollo: Don't make me beg, lamb. I need you.]

That was almost enough to make Wes's resolve crumble. Almost. Instead, he made his way to his bedroom and got undressed. Another excuse not to go over to Apollo's. He would have to get dressed again, and that was simply too much effort.

[Wes: Goodnight, Apollo. I'll talk to you tomorrow.]

And with that, he put his phone on "do not disturb" and then set his alarm. That was the only thing that was going to wake him for the rest of the night. He finished his nightly routine before climbing into bed. The urge to check his phone before sleep was strong, but he resisted and left his phone where it was. He would only be dragged back into a conversation with Apollo if he looked now.

Instead, he turned off the light and rolled over. Sleep claimed him quickly, and for the first time in a while, his sleep was deep and pleasant.

"Who's up for harvesting some nightshade with me?" Lily asked the group over dinner the following Thursday.

"It's the middle of November. How do you still have nightshade growing?" Wes asked though the answer was pretty obvious. Magic. When you were a green witch of Lily's caliber, established growing seasons meant nothing.

Lily gave him a bright smile, never judging. "I have to keep a steady harvest of the stuff. A lot of my customers use it. So I keep that field climate controlled.

It's a simple spell. I just have to update it once a month. I could show you if you like."

Wes hadn't given much thought to his magic lately. He could call his sword, but no one had ever really worked with him beyond that, not since his parents. He took Lily's offer into consideration for a second. "You've got the wrong St. James sibling. That's all Brie. I'm not much of a plant person in general."

Lily hummed her acknowledgment. Brie didn't have a magical bone in her body, not anymore, since the spirit of the Morrigan had left her. Though she was immortal now, so she had that going for her. A thought neither St. James liked to dwell on. Wes didn't know if he had a prolonged life span like the rest of his friends and family, but he knew that one day he would die and his sister would live on. A sobering thought that he couldn't stomach, so he tried not to think about it ever.

"When do you want to harvest? I have literally nothing going on the rest of the week." Brie's voice cut through Wes's thoughts.

"I was thinking Saturday around nine, if that works for you?" Lily replied, looking between the siblings and Ezra, who so far had sat quietly eating his salad.

Brie and Wes glanced at each other and then each nodded toward Lily. "Works for us," Brie said, digging back into her own salad. After years, Ezra had finally gotten her eating greens, something Wes had also been roped into. There was something to the healthy eating, but that didn't mean Wes had completely converted to clean foods. He was still a lazy cook and all problems could be solved with pizza.

Ezra made a noise in the back of his throat. "I suppose that means I have been volunteered?" He sounded put out, but Wes knew he would do anything Brie told him to. Ezra was completely crazy for his sister, and that was what she deserved, someone who loved her without question. And he would absolutely do whatever Lily asked since nobody was capable of saying no to her.

"You bet your ass," Brie responded, batting her lashes at her husband. He made another noise and went back to eating, unfazed by the fact that once again he had been volunteered for something. It would mean closing the shop a little early, which neither of them ever seemed to mind. Things had gotten a little lax at the shop since Brie had mellowed Ezra out.

"Great, that'll make things go a lot quicker. Ever since Bertie bought the land next door to our house, my garden has basically become its own little farm. Bertie will make dinner, of course, and we can break into his good alcohol." Lily's laughter filled the room, and Wes felt his mood lighten even more. Lily had a way of making everyone around her feel better. It wasn't magic, it was simply her personality. Lily was sunshine in human form.

When Saturday rolled around, Wes was in a bad mood. Apollo had been icing him out since he had told him he wasn't coming over the previous Sunday. There was no way he wasn't hooking up with other people, since Apollo would literally die if he went a day without sex. Wes wasn't sure if he was being hyperbolic or if an incubus could die from lack of daily sex.

Either way, Apollo had not spoken to him, in person or via text since that night. Seemed the love bombing had ended, and things were right back to where they were, only worse. Wes thought about texting him first to apologize. But it wasn't like he had done anything wrong. All Wes had said was that he was tired. He wasn't going to haul himself across town in the middle of the night for a booty call, when all he wanted to do was sleep and be prepared for a day of teaching. His boundary should have been okay. Except it wasn't for Apollo, apparently.

Wes arrived at Lily and Albert's minutes after Brie and Ezra, hoping like hell that Lily hadn't invited Apollo to join them, though he doubted she did. Lily generally liked everyone, but she tolerated Apollo at best. Still, she had known him a lot longer, but like everyone else he had ever met, Apollo hit on Lily regularly too. He had at least waited until she turned eighteen to start making advances on her from what Lily said.

Lily and Albert, well Lily, had an open-door policy at their large home, so Wes let himself in. The place was warded to hell, so only those who were friends and family could pass through them anyway, which meant they kept the door unlocked when company was coming over.

Wes tried not to stomp his way to the kitchen, where he knew everyone would be gathering before heading out to the garden, but his bad mood made his footsteps heavier. Lily, Brie, and Ezra stood around the kitchen island, while Albert stood at the stove stirring something that smelled amazing, though Wes couldn't place the scent exactly.

"Wow, grumpy gills, what's wrong with you?" Brie asked as Wes walked up to the island and set down the bags of chips he brought with him. He always brought something but knew better than to encroach on Albert's meal territory, and Wes was terrible at baking.

Wes sighed heavily. "You know, the usual. My boyfriend is ignoring me because I dared to say I was tired and didn't want to come over."

"You should dump him already," Albert said from the stove, not bothering to look back at Wes. Albert especially didn't like Apollo. While everyone else tolerated his antics, Albert automatically hated him simply because he flirted with Lily. Albert handled Apollo's advances toward him, because of course Apollo even propositioned surly vampires, but Lily was another matter.

"Yeah, what Albert said," Brie chimed in. It was still weird to hear her be agreeable with Albert, but they had both grown on each other over the years. Still very weird, though.

"Relationship drama aside, should we head out?" Ezra asked, clearly wanting to avoid any talk about romantic entanglements. It wasn't like he hadn't heard it all before, and he was by no means an expert on relationships after how he'd initially handled things with Brie.

Lily checked her phone. "Hang on, I'm expecting one more person to help out." She smiled at Wes, and he knew with absolute certainty who she invited, and his heart flipped in his chest.

Not five minutes later, Cameron walked into the kitchen, filling the space with his large stature and brilliant smile. He carried a basket overflowing with bread and baked goods. “Hey everyone! I brought treats.” He lifted the basket to indicate the goodies, like every eye, save Albert’s wasn’t on the food already.

Albert left the stove and took the offered basket and set it on the counter. “Bread is exactly what we needed for this dish.” If there was one thing Albert appreciated, it was food. As a vampire, it didn’t do anything for him nutritionally, but he was a damn good cook in Wes’s opinion, maybe even rivaling Damian Everett, Lily’s dad, and the family kitchen witch.

Just seeing Cameron though, standing taller than everyone except Ezra, his perfectly sculpted body in a white t-shirt and jeans and a jean jacket thrown over the whole thing made Wes feel warm all over. His light green eyes glinted with mirth and complimented his huge smile so well, Wes felt weak in the knees. Wes felt flushed, and he was sure his cheeks were turning pink. And were those butterflies in his stomach?

Cameron sidled up to the island, leaned over, and settled his elbows on the countertop next to Wes. It was like heat rolled off him in waves, and Wes had to stop himself from inching closer, just for a bit of that extra warmth. “I didn’t know you were going to be here,” Wes said, turning just slightly to address Cameron. He was afraid to look at him directly, fearful he would do something stupid like throw himself directly into the larger man’s arms. The thought was incredibly tempting.

Cameron scratched the back of his head, and it was too adorable for words. "Lily asked me last week; thought I would help out. She's been such a good friend and there was a promise of food. I'm a bit of a homebody anyway. This is the first time I've done anything besides work since Samhain." His chuckle was a little self-deprecating, which only served to endear him more to Wes.

"I know what you mean. It's pretty much work and D&D for me, and then home all the time. Since my sister abandoned me to live with her husband, it's been a quiet life." Wes wished his laugh didn't sound so unhinged, but he couldn't help himself. He was nervous. Cameron made him nervous and not because he was intimidating. Wes just couldn't seem to think around him. It was like he was a teenager all over again around the man.

"Ah yes, I've had first-hand experience with the whole moving in with someone you married." Cameron's smile was wide. He wasn't laughing at Wes, but with him.

Wes gave Cameron a puzzled look. "You're married?"

Why is Lily trying to set us up if he's married? I'm not into the group thing.

He tried not to let his thoughts get away from him. With things being what they were with Apollo, he was firmly sure of his desire not to share.

Cameron suddenly looked a little shy, an adorable look that Wes had to turn his gaze from. "Was married. We were middle school sweethearts and got married way too young. We divorced while I was still in college.

Clean break though, you know. She realized she was a lesbian, and I was still grappling with my own sexuality. We're still good friends, and I actually introduced her to her wife. I'm their daughter's godfather."

He said it with such a cheerful tone it was like he wasn't talking about his ex-wife. And Wes supposed there were different types of families. Wes had never kept in contact with any of his exes, preferring a clean break and to never speak again. It had worked out well enough for him. He couldn't imagine not only being friends with an ex, but being an active part of their life as well.

"You are like probably the nicest person I've ever met," Wes blurted out before his brain could filter his words. When it finally did catch up to him, he blushed furiously. Wes was the one who always thought through what he said. It wasn't like him to just word vomit without thinking. His logic seemed to short-circuit around Cameron.

"Are you guys coming, or are you just going to make out here in the kitchen? I don't think Albert wants to watch," Brie called from the doorway that led out to the gardens.

Albert sniffed indignantly. "I really don't." He turned his attention back to the food, ignoring them completely.

Leave it to Brie to totally embarrass Wes. He wanted to smack his sister as he flushed all over, and he couldn't look at Cameron at all. From the corner of his eye, though, he saw that the taller man was blushing a gorgeous shade of pink; the color accentuating the freckles on his nose and cheeks. "Yup, uh...

I'm coming... we're coming. Together. Not like... fuck it." Wes couldn't seem to get his words right, so he opted to just stomp past his sister and out to the garden without looking anyone in the eye. From behind, he heard Brie laugh, and it only annoyed him further.

As he passed Lily, she smiled knowingly at him. While Wes knew Lily's smile didn't exactly mean anything other than Lily that smiled at everyone, he snatched the wicker basket she offered from her hands. "Don't say anything, Lily. I know what you're doing." He narrowed his eyes at her, but it only served to make her smile brighter.

"I don't know what you mean, Wesley. I just needed the extra help with the harvest. I planted a lot of nightshade." She flounced off to her garden, a spring in her step and an aura of mischief around her.

It would have been best to spend the rest of the evening avoiding Cameron, and Wes had all intentions of doing so. But somehow, Cameron kept finding his way close to Wes's side. Judging from the giggles and smirks shared between Brie and Lily, he knew that it was orchestrated. It wasn't like Cameron intentionally wandered over to hang near Wes. Lily directed them all where to go and which areas were ready for harvest.

"I'm sorry I totally word vomited back there. My head is all over the place lately," Wes finally said, breaking some of the quiet tension between them.

Cameron cut a plant free and placed it in his half-full basket. The pinkish color on his cheeks was visible in the bright moonlight. "No worries. I forget how to word all the time. Just talking to people in general makes me pretty nervous. But then I don't say anything, and, well, people tend to think I'm stupid. Better to let them think that than confirm their suspicions, right?" He laughed like it was funny, but it didn't meet his eyes.

"Well, I don't think you're stupid. You are a fantastic baker, and you're easy to talk to when I'm not putting my foot in my mouth. You have golden retriever energy." Wes kept his focus on the plants as he talked. It was easy to talk to Cameron when he wasn't looking at him. At least he could keep his head clear and not let his mouth run off completely.

"Not sure if that's a compliment or not, but I'll take it," Cameron said, a small chuckle in his words.

Wes looked at him from the corner of his eye. "Definitely a compliment. One of the highest I can give." Wes was good with words usually, despite the signs tonight that said otherwise. He liked to compliment people, not just because it made them feel good, but because it gave him a lightness too. And Cameron was easy to compliment. The man had so many good qualities, he was genuinely a good person.

If only I could spend more time with him. Just enjoy his company.

Wistfulness flowed through him. This was something he would never have with Apollo. They didn't converse so easily, if they talked at all. Apollo didn't like to waste time talking when they could do something else that didn't involve so many words.

"You're an interesting person, Wesley St. James. I wish we had met under different circumstances." Wes tried not to read too much into that, but his mind immediately went to what could have been. But what if that wasn't what Cameron meant? He tried to recall their first meeting. The memory came back to him with staggering clarity.

They had been at the Everett's farm for Ivy's baby shower, eating too much and playing silly baby games that Wes was definitely losing terribly. It had been fun and Wes had stared at Cameron even then.

But then Ivy started having contractions. Her water broke, and everyone was rushed out so Ivy could get to the hospital. Her husband Jamie had kept everyone calm, his hands a flurry of motion as he signed what everyone should do. The man didn't crack under pressure, even when it affected Ivy. Twig was born in the early hours of the morning, apparently super eager to be out in the world.

The only thing Cameron had said that night to Wes was, "What a crazy night. I'm Cameron, by the way." They had shaken hands and then went their separate ways. It was certainly a memorable meeting.

"Okay gang, I think we have what we need. Let's head in and get something to eat," Lily called across the garden. Cameron and Wes hefted their baskets and headed toward the house, walking without speaking. Wes found it comforting.

Wes was feeling better as he walked back into the kitchen. The work of harvesting had melted away his anger and frustration, and talking to Cameron had certainly helped his mood even more.

That all changed the minute he entered the kitchen. Leaning against the island, looking for all the world like he owned the place, was Apollo. He sipped on a glass of red wine, while Albert glared across the island at him from where he stood at the stove. "Hello, darling," Apollo said to Wes with a cheeky grin, his eyes solely on Wes.

"He just showed up. I didn't invite him. He's been annoying me for half an hour," Albert grumbled, accepting Lily into his arms.

Wes's good mood instantly dissolved at seeing Apollo. He couldn't have this time away from him. He knew Apollo would try to pull him away quickly and insist Wes come home with him. But all Wes wanted was to stay with his friends and family and enjoy Albert's cooking.

Next to Wes, he felt Cameron move just a half step closer to his side, like he was prepared to protect Wes. "What are you doing here, Apollo?" Wes tried to keep his tone neutral and not accusing, but he wasn't sure he was successful as he watched Apollo's eyes narrow.

"You didn't answer my texts, so I decided to come find you." Apollo recovered quickly, letting his customary lazy grin spread over his lips.

Wes hadn't checked his phone the entire time he was in the garden, hadn't even felt it vibrate. "We were helping Lily, so I didn't look at my texts." He wanted to cross his arms in defiance, but thought better of it. But then he didn't know what to do with his arms, so they hung loosely by his side.

The tension between them filled the room. Luckily, Lily knew how to handle any situation, and broke it with her words. "Well, you're here now, so why don't you stay for dinner? Though, you've been here half an hour and didn't bother to help, so you owe me a turn in the garden soon."

Apollo's plush lips turned pouty, but there was a gleam in his eye. "Can't I instead get a free meal? I'm so hungry. Starving really." Lily wasn't taken in by that look. She had a way of assessing true emotions that had nothing to do with her sight. Her look told him she was holding him to a future task.

The thought hit Wes, and he wondered if Lily saw this happening. Her sight got stronger every year, but she couldn't always pinpoint events, especially if she wasn't looking for them. Why would she use her magic to see if Apollo would party crash? He couldn't blame Lily for this. But he could blame Apollo. After Samhain, Wes had appreciated all the attention Apollo gave him. Now he just felt smothered, like he couldn't have anything for himself without Apollo being there, or demanding his attention.

They took their seats around the table that Albert had already set, a hearty beef stew the centerpiece. Apollo inched his chair closer to Wes's, crowding his space like he couldn't let Wes have even an inch of his own. Across the table, Brie glared daggers at Apollo as the incubus swung his arm around the back of Wes's chair, much to Wes's annoyance.

Sitting on Wes's other side, Cameron kept a respectful distance, but Wes noticed he looked a little uncomfortable. Not that he could blame him. The table had gotten very coupley quickly. He was the odd man out, and Wes found himself wishing his chair was closer to Cameron's than Apollo's.

"Why don't we get out of here and head back to my place? Maybe Albert will let us take some with us and we can eat it after taking a bite out of each other,"

Apollo whispered in Wes's ear. His hot breath tickled Wes's ear, and he almost flinched from the feeling of it. But Wes held himself in check, knowing full well that Apollo would read into his body language, and probably ice him out for another few days again.

The chatter around the table kept them from being overheard. "I want to stay and finish dinner with my family," Wes whispered back, keeping his focus on the hot food in front of him. Albert really was an amazing cook, and the food warmed his insides immediately. A basket holding one of the loaves of bread Cameron brought was passed around the table and Wes tore off a hearty chunk and took a large bite.

The bread was magnificent, crusty on the outside, while inside it was chewy and yeasty. It was warm, either because Albert had heated it up before they came in or from the magic that Wes knew was infused within it. There was a hint of rosemary and it paired so well with the stew, it wouldn't be a surprise if Albert and Cameron had collaborated beforehand.

Wes ignored Apollo for the rest of the meal. If he didn't respond or look at him, Wes reasoned, then Apollo couldn't talk him into leaving. Instead, Wes focused on the food and the rest of the conversation around the table. "Albert, if you weren't with Lily, I would ask you to marry me right now. We could get an enormous farm table and adopt a whole brood of children that you could feed," Wes quipped. He and Albert had gradually started to joke with each other over time. It was still awkward at times, but never as weird as Brie and Albert's slightly antagonistic friendship.

Wes heard Apollo huff beside him, and if possible, he crowded Wes's space even more, to the point where he couldn't move his right arm much to eat. Albert gave Wes one of his customary scowls. He only ever smiled for Lily, but his eyes glimmered with amusement. "If you had such a beautiful future planned for us, you should have been quicker to the punch and got to me before Lily."

The table burst into laughter, including Wes. Though Apollo laughed along, Wes could hear the tension in the sound. It wasn't the carefree chuckle that was Apollo's norm. The rest of the meal was spent with Wes trying to ignore Apollo, despite the other man's constant attempts to get Wes to leave. The conversation flowed easily despite Apollo's best efforts and Wes made it a point of trying to include Cameron in conversation as much as possible.

"We should be heading home. I have a special order coming in and the delivery window is literally like sometime after eight in the morning," Ezra said, rising from his chair and helping Brie out of hers.

"Which means we'll sit around all day and Gunther, the delivery guy, will show up at like eight at night instead." Brie pulled on her coat, picked up her plate, and took it to the sink while Ezra followed behind her, doing the same.

Wes thought about asking for a ride with them, but decided to ride his bike home rather than leave it behind at Lily and Albert's. Then again, he was prepared for Apollo to insist they go back to his place and he would still probably have to collect his bike in the morning.

Cameron, Wes, and Apollo started to head out at the same time. Lily instructed them to leave their dishes at the sink, where with a flick of her wrist, the dishes began to wash themselves. She followed them down the hall and to the door. Cameron left them first, giving Lily a big hug before heading down to his car with a quick wave and a giant smile.

Wes said his goodbyes with a one-armed hug, and Apollo tried to kiss Lily before she gave him a rough shove away, with a smile on her face. As the door shut behind them, Wes grabbed his bike from beside the door and started to head toward the street. "You can just leave that here, darling. I drove, and I'll bring you back tomorrow to pick it up. We have more pressing matters to attend to, and none of it involves clothing." Apollo's smirk was inviting, despite Wes not really being in the mood.

But against his better judgment, Wes nodded and followed Apollo to his ostentatious sports car that was so low to the ground, it was a wonder either of them could contort themselves enough to get in. Apollo drove it entirely too fast for the city streets and cornered like a manic. There was a sort of thrill riding with him though, like at any moment the vehicle was going to flip and they were riding that edge of danger all the way to their destination.

Careening around the streets of New Britain was enough to get Wes's blood pumping and ready for a few rounds with Apollo before sleep. It took no time to make it to Apollo's building, where he pulled into his parking space with practiced ease, though he parked sideways like an asshole, taking up as much space as possible for his outrageous car.

Apollo practically pulled Wes into the building and into the elevator up to his penthouse. He didn't even wait for the doors to finish closing before he pulled Wes close and started kissing him passionately. It was a wonder they weren't naked by the time they reached the top. The moment the door shut behind them, Wes's coat was on the floor and Apollo tugged his shirt over his head. Wes's jeans and boxers were off before they even reached the living room, while Apollo remained entirely clothed, even his expensive wool coat remained on.

Wes ran his hands down the soft material of Apollo's coat while the incubus dragged him to the center of the room with one hand on the back of Wes's head, the other gripping his shaft. Apollo captured Wes's moan with his lips and started to stroke him with agonizingly slow, languid motions.

It was pure torture and it was delicious. Wes closed his eyes and threw his head back, loving the way his calloused hands caught on the fabric of Apollo's clothing. There was something incredibly erotic about being completely naked while his partner remained fully clothed.

With each moan of pleasure pulled out of Wes, Apollo speed up his rhythm until his strokes were just on the right side of painful.

"I'm ... going ... fuck ... I'm gonna–" Wes's words were choked off by Apollo dropping to his knees and sheathing Wes in his mouth. It took the barest of sucks before Wes was spilling into Apollo's eager mouth, the groan that came with his release echoing around the room.

This. This is why I keep coming back to him, why I won't break things off.

Wes managed to form the thought through the haze of his orgasm. And in that haze, he let Apollo lead him back to the bedroom and followed his instructions to undress him, before climbing on the bed to rest on his hands and knees.

"You've had your fun, lamb. Now it's my turn," Apollo said, his voice low and seductive. Wes flinched as Apollo poured a cool liquid down his backside, but the sensation lasted only a moment before Apollo pushed into him, and Wes could no longer form thoughts while Apollo began to fuck him hard and fast.

When they finally collapsed on the bed together, they were both panting heavily and shining with sweat. Neither said a word for a long time. Wes hoped they would stay like that, basking in the afterglow of mind-blowing sex, comforted by the closeness of each other's bodies.

Naturally, Apollo had to ruin the moment. "You seemed really cozy with that witch tonight. Should I be jealous?" Apollo's tone was light, but Wes could hear underneath it was a bit of hardness.

Wes laid on his back, staring up at the ceiling, while Apollo turned on his side, propping his head up on his hand, and looked at Wes. "Hanging out with someone while in the garden makes the work go faster. I'm allowed to talk to people without it being something more," Wes said, the lightness in his body growing steadily heavier by the second.

Apollo dragged a warm finger down Wes's chest, cloying and deceptively intimate. "You can talk to anyone, Wes. I merely observed the two of you being pretty friendly. Are you going to see him again?"

The gentle touch on his chest started to grow irritating. Wes wasn't sure he wanted Apollo's hands on him now. "He's Lily's friend. I'm sure I'll see him around," he said, trying to keep his voice neutral so Apollo wouldn't think he was having an effect on him.

Apollo seemed to be done with Wes evading his questions. He rolled on top of Wes, straddling his hips, and splaying a hand across his chest. His eyes were intense, like they were trying to see into Wes's mind and pick through his thoughts. "What if I didn't want you to see him again?" And for once, Apollo looked serious, his lips pinched in a tight line.

Wes could only stare back up at him, unsure of what to do, of how to respond. He took a moment to collect himself, deciding whether he should placate Apollo's strange mood or take a stand against him.

"I would say you're being a huge hypocrite, then. Considering all the seeing you do with other people. Nothing I say stops you from fucking everyone else in this town, so don't expect me to stop having friends because you suddenly feel jealous." They glared at each other; the tension thick between them. Wes rarely spoke up against Apollo and had stopped telling Apollo how much it hurt him that his supposed boyfriend slept around. Maybe Wes was just hitting his breaking point.

Apollo placed his other hand on Wes's chest and stared even deeper into his eyes, focused. And then his eyes began to glow. It was hypnotic and beautiful and Wes could feel himself getting lost in those eyes. They promised pleasure and bliss and everything Wes could ever want to be happy. He could fall into that feeling, open himself to Apollo and let him take whatever he wanted because Apollo would take care of him in the end. Everything would be all right, and all Wes would ever know was pleasure.

A jolt of panic cleared his head, cutting through the dreamy glow of his mind. With a strength he rarely, if ever, used, Wes pushed Apollo off of him. "What the fuck? So now you're trying to use your magic to get your way. What the fuck is wrong with you?" Wes couldn't stop himself from screaming. He flew off the bed and out of the room. His clothes were scattered everywhere at the front of the penthouse, and he made quick work of retrieving every piece and putting it on.

Behind him, Apollo walked out of the bedroom with lazy strides. The levity returned to his countenance, and he smirked at Wes from across the room, his arms loosely crossed over his still-naked chest. "Don't be mad, sweetling, I can't help myself sometimes," he said, though he didn't make a move toward Wes, which was a small blessing.

"I am mad and I'm allowed to be. I'm not just one of your random hookups who you can hypnotize into doing whatever. I'm supposed to be your boyfriend, and right now, I can't even look at you, and not just because I think you'll take advantage of me and try your magic on me again." Wes pulled his coat on, and without a backward glance, walked to the elevator, wishing there was a door to slam.

The elevator came quickly enough, and Wes leaned against the far back as it took him down to the ground floor. There was no chance of Apollo following him, so he let his shoulders relax. He would have to get a ride share home since Apollo insisted he leave his bike at Lily and Albert's. Wes pulled out his phone and requested the ride.

For ten minutes, he waited inside the lobby of the building before the car showed up. It was late enough that he didn't have a chatty driver and Wes tipped well once he was dropped off in front of his house.

Before he fell into bed, Wes checked his phone to see if Apollo had texted, but there were no messages, not even from Brie telling him he was being an idiot.

CHAPTER 6

"How's your mom doing?" Wes asked as Candy took a seat across from his desk. She looked so tired. The bags under her eyes were massive and she hadn't bothered to even put on her heavy makeup today. Candy always looked so put together in her gothic style, but today she looked completely rung out.

Candy sighed and rubbed her palms against her eyes. "It's been a bad few days. She's been waking up in the middle of the night confused about where she is and she thinks I'm a burglar and started hitting me last night." She never shared much about her mom's condition, so the fact that she opened up so quickly made Wes extremely concerned.

When Candy removed her hands from her eyes, Wes could really see how bloodshot they were, and there was a sheen of what could only be tears, though he had never seen Candy cry before. "I'm so sorry. I can't imagine what you're going through. Have you thought about ... alternative care?" He didn't want to ask if she considered putting her mom in a home. He couldn't imagine having to do that. Not even when Maddy could barely stand did he ever consider putting her in a nursing home. Celeste stayed with her most of the time, while Brie and Wes had taken turns staying with her because Maddy insisted they not miss class.

Candy's sigh was deep and belied the heaviness she was clearly feeling. "I've thought about a nursing home, or at least an in-home nurse. It just feels wrong to make someone else take care of her, you know. She's my mom. She was the one who took care of me all my life. Don't I owe it to her to do the same when she needs me most?"

Wes reached across the desk, and Candy brought her hand up so he could hold hers. She wasn't normally a touchy-feely person, so things had to be incredibly bad if she was letting Wes comfort her like this.

"Sometimes the best way to take care of someone you love is realizing you can't do it alone anymore. You can't run yourself down. It's not fair to you or your mom. I hate seeing you like this, Candy. You look like shit, and I say that with love. You know if your mom was still in charge of her mind, she wouldn't want this for you." Wes hoped he wasn't overstepping. Candy had put up with enough of his bullshit that he felt like he owed it to her to give it to her straight, to let her know it was okay that she was struggling. And that she could ask for help.

Candy squeezed his hand and then withdrew it and slumped in her chair. "I know. Fuck, I know what I have to do. I just feel like I'm letting my mom down. But like, my siblings have been saying the same thing for months, and I told myself it was just because they didn't want to deal with her. Ugh, I don't want to admit they were right. They give me enough shit for being the youngest as is."

Wes hated to see his friend like this. Her vibrancy was gone. Even if Candy was a gloom-and-doom type on the outside, she was still full of life. But this person before him was diminished, her spark now smoldering, fading. "Don't worry about what your siblings are going to say. If they love you, they will know that you have limitations and need the help. They aren't around every day to see how much you struggle. Do what's best for you and your mom."

Even if he couldn't get his own life in order, Wes wanted to be a rock for Candy. She was a great person, someone he deeply admired, and he would be a bad friend if he didn't do what he could to help her. He just wished he could do more.

"Why don't you come over to my sister's place tonight? My brother-in-law is a great cook, and I can promise it'll be better than anything I could make for you." Wes didn't stop to think about what Candy might see at Ezra and Brie's place, but that really wasn't important right now. She needed a support network and Wes was determined to be part of that.

Candy looked unsure. "I don't know. I'm not sure how Mom is going to be tonight. I don't want to leave her if she's having a really bad time. But I can always have my neighbor come over. She watches Mom sometimes when I can't be home and the part-time nurse is unavailable. Honestly, I really need a night away, and I feel like a shitty person for even thinking it."

"You're not a shitty person for needing time away. It makes you human. So, six o'clock at Spirit Antiques.

My sister and brother-in-law live at their shop, and you can take that time to relax and let someone feed you." Candy gave him a grateful look with a tired smile. They said their goodbyes, and Candy left for class, still looking worse for wear, but at least her shoulders had relaxed a little.

Wes sent off a quick text to Brie to let her know there would be one more at dinner and then settled back at his desk to work on writing the final that was coming up in a few weeks. December was just around the corner and Wes was ready for the end of the year already. He was tired in his own way.

It had been radio silence from Apollo. After Wes's outburst at the penthouse, Apollo must have not felt it necessary to even send a text to Wes about their fight. Apollo icing him out had started to become a more frequent thing. It had happened on a few occasions over the last three years, but never as much as it had the last few months. Before, it used to hurt Wes deeply when Apollo stopped talking to him for a few days. He would send message after message to the incubus, apologizing for things he didn't do, or for perceived slights.

But this time, Wes found he didn't care all that much. If Apollo didn't want to speak to him, then he didn't want to speak to Apollo. He wasn't going to cave and apologize first. If Apollo wanted to talk to him, he would. Maybe Wes would actually get a little peace at night, and not be coerced into leaving the house late at night. If Apollo wasn't going to care, then neither was Wes.

Instead, Wes focused on his work, and let himself be consumed with something that actually mattered and that he enjoyed.

"So how do you propose we explain the magic door to her?" Brie asked, though her focus was still on the ledger book and computer sitting on the counter. Both Brie and her husband had a bad habit of working while in conversation, and Wes couldn't help but marvel at how well she multitasked.

Wes shrugged. "It wasn't like Ezra did anything to explain the door to you when you started. So I'm not sure what you expected."

"That's because she worked here and it's already strange enough not counting the door. She was going to find out sooner or later. But your friend is a one-time, or at least infrequent, guest who won't be subjected to my customers," Ezra said, slipping out from behind the Storage Room door.

Brie looked up from her work to accept the kiss she knew Ezra would give her. It was a quick peck, but it still spoke of a deeper love. Wes felt a pang of longing at the sight. He wanted to have that easy love, where you could just expect a token of affection when your partner entered the room, nothing extravagant, just a quick reminder of their love. But he didn't have that. Maybe he never would.

Brie looked away from her husband and leveled a gaze at her brother. "Telling a human about magic is a big deal. You sure you want to open that can of worms? Not that I don't want to see Candy. I love her. She's great with all her doom and gloom. Just, think about how you're going to explain a few things to her."

Wes nodded, though he really didn't have an idea of what he would say. *Oh hey, here's a magic door that leads to a few places. One of which is a magical Storage Room that shouldn't exist in this space, but does house a ton of enchanted historical things. Totally run-of-the-mill stuff.*

Yeah, that wasn't going to fly. Maybe he should have thought this over first, before inviting Candy. It would have been simpler to invite her over to his house and just have Ezra cook there. Why didn't he think of that before? There was still time to text Candy and tell her there was a change in venue, but Wes knew Ezra had already started cooking and even if Wes's house was literally a step through the Storage Room door, he doubted Ezra wanted to haul everything out of his apartment and over to Wes's house.

The next thirty minutes were spent in the break room, trying to come up with something to tell Candy. But in the end, Wes's best explanation was to say it was magic in a dorky voice and hope she didn't question further. It was a long shot, but what else could he do?

Wes stepped out of the break room minutes before the bell above the shop door tinkled Candy's arrival. While she still wasn't back to her normal gothic princess self, she at least had changed out of the sweats she had on earlier, and had donned a pair of black jeans and a plain black long-sleeved shirt.

"Hey, Candy. You look better," Wes said, giving her a thumbs up as she crossed the room. She returned his gesture with a raised middle finger and a deadpan stare.

Brie popped out of the Storage Room door, probably alerted to Candy's entrance by the spyglass of Charles Vane above the Storage Room door. It creeped Wes, and just about everybody else out, but it was a necessary security feature.

"Candy! It's been a while," Brie said as she walked up to the other woman and opened her arms. She waited to let Candy decide if she wanted to be hugged or not. But Candy stepped into her embrace, and Wes saw that she sagged into Brie's arms just a little more than usual. The two women parted after a few seconds. "Dinner is almost ready if you guys want to head to our place." Brie turned back to the Storage Room door, hit the number two button on the panel beside the door, and opened it after it made a small *snick* sound.

The hallway beyond was painted in dark colors and dimly lit. Wes realized immediately another oversight he had made in inviting Candy over to Ezra and Brie's. Their living room was enchanted to resemble a living forest. The leaves moved and there was sometimes a breeze. Even sunlight occasionally broke through the canopy during the daytime. He really didn't think this through at all.

Brie walked through first, not waiting to see if Wes or Candy followed. Wes gestured for Candy to walk ahead of him and then he followed behind, closing the door behind him. "I thought this was like a storage area," Candy said in front of him as she took stock of the hallway. The lights brightened as they stepped inside, and the dark green walls of the hallway showed off dozens of framed photographs.

Most were newer pictures from the last few years. There was a picture of Brie and Wes after he graduated. Another of Brie, Ezra, and Wes after Brie received her Ph.D. There were other photos of them all with Lily, Albert, and Apollo throughout the seasons, including one where they were all completely sopping wet from a snowball fight after a huge blizzard. Everyone was smiling except Albert, though it was a false grimace. If anything, Albert had been the most ruthless and enthusiastic about the snowball fight.

Toward the end of the hall hung the two most important pictures in the little gallery. On one side was an intimate photo of Brie and Ezra on their wedding day. They weren't looking at the camera, instead, their gazes were fixed on each other. Brie wore a blue dress in memory of their adoptive mother. And hanging across from the wedding picture, on the opposite wall, was a picture of a teenaged Wes and Brie, flanking their mother Maddy, with their arms wrapped around her. Maddy was just under average height, with dark black hair curled around her light brown skin. She had been a Cajun woman who somehow found herself in New England, where she ended up changing the lives of two misfit kids. The picture was taken just a year or so after Brie came to live with them. Before Wes had left for college, and years before cancer tore their little family apart. Wes had the same photo hanging up at his house.

Candy studied the pictures as she went, not seeming to be in a hurry to get to dinner. Wes wasn't surprised when she stopped in front of the photo with Maddy. "Is this your mom?" She pointed directly at the picture but didn't touch it.

Wes stared at the picture for a second, letting his mind drift to the day they took that picture. It was at the Mabon festivities their coven held. The day had been sunny and still slightly warm. Celeste, Maddy's partner, though she wasn't at the time, had taken the picture of the three of them. It was at that moment Wes realized he had family, and he had pulled the two women close to him and wanted nothing more than to hug them close all day.

"Yeah, that's Maddy. It's been just over a decade since she died. And I miss her every single day," Wes said, not taking his eyes off the picture. He and Candy weren't so dissimilar. Even though her mom was still alive, she wasn't really there anymore. The difference was that Maddy went quickly; the cancer took her in just a few months. Candy was actively watching her mom slip away slowly, knowing she could live a long time still, never knowing her own daughter.

"Come on, I'm starving. My sister will eat everything if we don't go in," Wes said, turning from the wall. Sometimes, it just hurt too much to think back to that time, to think about how much he had lost in his life.

Wes braced himself for Candy's reaction as they entered the living room. The apartment was an open concept, with the living room flowing into the kitchen. A breakfast nook was off to one side, which was a newer addition, since Ezra and Brie had added more people to their circle. Down another hall were three doors; one to the master bedroom, one to a guest room, and then the bathroom. But the first thing anyone saw was the living room, with its forest walls and furniture that looked to be made of living trees. There were shelves of books, which made it look like they stood on their own in the middle of the woods. It was the most soothing room Wes had ever been in.

Still, to an outsider, it might freak them out. Candy entered the room and stopped. Her eyes darted around the room, taking it all in. “What the actual fuck?” she said, though her voice was barely more than a whisper. She spun around slowly, looking over every inch.

From the kitchen, Brie watched Candy’s reaction silently. Ezra continued to move about the kitchen, finishing dinner. He didn’t appear to take much notice of Candy’s reaction. After several minutes of slacked-jawed awe, Candy turned her attention to Wes. “What the fuck?” She gestured wildly at her surroundings.

Wes fidgeted with his hands, unsure still of how to approach this. “Magic?” he said, his voice raising higher at the answer, and he shrugged his shoulders. It was probably too much to hope that Candy would just take that answer and move on, but it was all he had.

“Magic? Are you kidding me? Seriously?” She crossed her arms tightly across her chest and jutted out her hip, disbelief coloring her face.

Wes was at a loss for what else to say. He turned toward Brie for help, but she rolled her eyes in return. She was no help at all. His gaze turned to Ezra next as he finished chopping vegetables for the salad. Wes gave him his best pleading face.

Ezra responded with a deep sigh and an eye roll of his own, a trait he had absolutely picked up from his wife. "It's all magic. I'm an angel, my wife is an immortal, your spineless friend here is a magic user, and my home and business are magical spaces. No, we're not crazy. Yes, it's all true, and yes, there are a lot more things out there than us. Now, dinner is ready." He sounded bored and long-suffering and didn't stop his movements around the kitchen while he talked.

Candy didn't look mollified, though. "Yeah, I'm a scientist, so I'm going to need to see some proof of all that." Wes had expected that of Candy. She was never one to just accept an answer without something to back it up.

Ezra barely acknowledged her words, but without any indication he was doing it, a pair of magnificent white wings suddenly sprang from his back. He paused his bustling around the kitchen for half a second to let Candy take in his appearance before he moved on to set the food on the table. Brie came up behind him to place down the plates and silverware, both acting as if nothing out of the ordinary was going on. Which, for them, it was normal.

"Huh" was the only response from Candy. She crossed the room to join Ezra and Brie at the table. Wes was left standing in the middle of the living room, confused.

"That's it?" he asked, finally heading to join the rest of them at the table.

Ezra's wings disappeared the instant he started to sit. He never kept them out long, probably because he was more used to keeping them hidden. "What else can I say? I'm not going to demand a demonstration when there's food ready. Though you can talk during dinner."

The four of them spent the next few minutes filling their plates and taking the first couple of bites. They each, in turn, complimented Ezra on the quality of the food. Wes loved coming over to his sister's place for dinner. Ezra was an exceptional cook, even if he did make them eat green things.

They chatted about their days, Brie casually discussing the various customers who came in, clarifying to Candy the nature of each person she talked about. Candy seemed to take that all in stride, nodding her head to accept that a minotaur or a fairy frequented the shop. Beneath the surface, though, Wes knew she was bubbling with questions. He would answer them, each one to the best of his ability, and rely on his brother-in-law and sister to supply info in the gaps of his knowledge.

When her plate was half finished, Candy began her interrogation. "I'm open to the idea that magic exists and that there's a whole magical community in town. But how has nobody ever noticed? I mean, like non-magical people. Does the city government know? Is it like this unspoken agreement, or something, where they know but keep it from the general public?"

Right off the bat, Wes had to defer to Ezra. "The thing about humans is that they try to make sense of everything. Their minds are incapable of accepting something they believe can't be true. They could see magic performed right in front of them, see an enchanted item react under their hands, and they would still try to find a reason based in science or faith for why it happened." Ezra took a bite of his food and then a sip of wine, unhurried in his response.

"As for the government knowing about us, they do not. We have our own form of government in the Council. They oversee the magical community in New Britain. I'm sure other cities and towns have something similar. We keep to ourselves and have our own laws, while still adhering to those of the human society. Our kind coexists with humans and they don't need to know anything else about our true nature. Indeed, most in our community navigate through the human world like any other person." Candy nodded her head along with Ezra's words, absorbing all he had to say. She cleared her plate and sat back in her chair, holding her glass of wine between her hands.

"That makes sense. So, you're an angel, she's immortal, and Wes, you are what kind of magic user?" She pointed to each of them in turn, and then kept her attention on Wes.

Wes thought a moment about how to phrase what exactly he was, not that he really knew. Not anymore. "I'm a guardian. Was a guardian. My family served the Morrigan. She was a goddess for thousands of years. But she's gone now. That's a whole other story. I didn't get to finish my training, but I can conjure a pretty cool light sword. It's like a lightsaber."

"People have offered to train you more, but you keep turning them down," Brie added, pointing her fork at her brother. Wes waved her off. Lily had offered, but she was busy most of the time and he didn't want to be a bother to her. Sure, she was a patient person and was very encouraging, but there was something about taking magic lessons from a friend that made Wes self-conscious. Like she would see all his failures and judge him, not that it was Lily's nature.

"It's not that I don't want to learn. I just don't want to waste anyone's time. Maybe I'll get a magic tutor outside of the group someday," he said, though, by the look Brie shot him, she knew he was just saying that to appease her. Wes wanted to be in touch with his guardian magic. It was one of the many things he wished his family had been alive for. Even though he did end up with a loving, if small, family. But Maddy couldn't teach him about magic. She knew about the magical world beyond her Pagan beliefs, but she wasn't part of it other than to be a bridge between the two worlds.

If only there was another guardian out there he could train under. But as far as he knew, there were no guardians, either of the Morrigan or who served another god, anywhere near New Britain. And it wasn't like he had any idea how to find them if they were out there, not that he had even tried to look.

"So, what are the limitations of magic? Can it heal anything? Or change the outcome of certain scenarios? Can you see the future?" Candy kept her questions in a steady barrage, preferring to ask in clusters rather than one at a time.

"Why don't we move this to the living room and get comfortable? Something tells me we're going to be at this a while. As you said, you are a scientist, and from my experience, you lot are a relentlessly curious bunch," Ezra said as he stood and began to clear plates.

They all gathered their dirty dishes and placed them in the kitchen before adjourning to the living room.

Candy sat in one of the chairs, Wes sat opposite her in another, while the married couple took the couch. Brie tucked herself against her husband, seemingly content to stay at his side.

"Now, to answer your questions. There are many limitations to magic, but most depend on the individual. There are many species and types of magical creatures in the world, some with very powerful magic, and some their only magic lies in existing." Candy nodded along; her attention focused completely on Ezra.

"Some can certainly heal. There are doctors in your world who are part of ours. They use their magic on patients in subtle ways. Then again, there are hospitals devoted exclusively to treating the magical community. But magic cannot heal everything. Some wounds are beyond healing, not just of the body, but the mind as well. Especially the mind, since it is such a complex thing."

"You literally brought my sister back from the dead," Wes deadpanned. It used to be a sore subject around Brie and Wes. Seeing her lying dead in Ezra's arms had been the worst sight in the world. Wes's heart had shattered. Before he could fully process the loss, though, Ezra used his divine magic and brought her back to life. Brie had nightmares about it for months, and even though she joked about it now, it still gave her anxiety occasionally.

Candy's gaze narrowed at Ezra. "You brought your wife back from the dead? Can you do that with anyone or just her?" Questions upon questions, Wes should have expected this from Candy. She wouldn't be content to ask only a few questions. She needed to have a full picture of what magic was.

Ezra shrugged. "I honestly don't know. I don't make a habit of bringing people back from the dead. Though I'm sure that beyond a few minutes, it would become extremely difficult. By then, the soul would have left the body, and calling a soul back is far more difficult than repairing a body."

"Yeah, I was dead for like less than five minutes, so it wasn't a big deal," Brie added, though Wes knew it was an extremely big deal to her. Years of therapy had told him that much.

"What about someone who is not all there? Mentally, I mean?" Candy asked, her tone casual. It came to Wes with clarity now. She wanted to see if magic could heal her mom's Alzheimer's.

"Candy," Wes began, and waited until her attention turned to him. "Magic doesn't work like that. I may not know much about healing magic, but I do know that healing the mind is one of the hardest things to fix. Nearly impossible. Magic has limitations and there has to be a balance." He watched as her face dropped, then harden into resolve.

She threw her shoulders back, her spine ridged. "You said nearly impossible, not entirely. So that means there's a chance one of your magic healers could help my mom, right?"

But Ezra was already shaking his head. "That's not how it works. I don't know the details of your mother's illness, but magic can't fix the mind. It's too delicate, and more often than not, can make the issue worse, or even kill someone in the pursuit of healing."

Candy shot to her feet, surprising Wes, though Ezra and Brie looked nonplussed. "Then what good is magic if it can't help her? I can accept that magic is real, that creatures exist that seem impossible. But I can't accept that it can't help my mom." She stormed away from them toward the hallway, but stopped and turned. "Thanks for dinner," she said, and then walked out of the apartment, the door slamming shut behind her.

Wes stood from his chair and shot an apologetic look at Brie and Ezra. "I should go after her. I didn't expect things to go this way."

They both nodded. "Some people are open to the idea of our world, but fairy tales and stories make it hard for them to believe that magic can't simply fix everything," Ezra said sagely. Wes thought about that as he walked out of the room and into the shop proper. Candy hadn't gone far. She stood at the counter, staring out at the wares around her.

"Figured you would follow me," she said, keeping her face turned away from Wes. Her voice lacked any inflection, she just sounded tired. Wes walked up behind her and put a hand on her shoulder. She turned, and surprising Wes even more, wrapped her arms around his middle and buried her face against his neck.

His arms went around her shoulders and when she started to quietly cry into his shirt, he didn't say anything. Candy needed this, and Wes would be there to listen and let her fall apart. She was such a rock for her family all the time, stoic around everyone else. Candy never let herself feel anything, and now Wes knew why. Because if she let herself feel something, let down her guard a little, she would fall apart like she was now.

They said nothing for several minutes until her tears started to slow. "I'm so tired, Wes. I thought I could do it all, but I can't. I just want my mom back." She choked on her words and kept her face buried against his skin. Wes rubbed her back in slow, comforting circles.

"Yeah, I know how you feel. I would give anything to have both of my moms back," he said, thinking of the woman he never really got a chance to know, and the woman who showed him what unconditional love looked like.

Candy stepped back finally and wiped at her eyes. "Okay, now I feel like an asshole. I'm blubbering over my mom who is still alive, and you've lost two moms."

Wes brought his hands up and wiped her remaining tears away with his thumbs. "We can't quantify grief. Just because both my moms are dead, doesn't make what you're going through any less hard." He pulled Candy close again and hugged her tightly to his chest. He wanted to let her know she wasn't alone, that he would help her through whatever she was going through. He planted a soft kiss on the top of her head, which he could only do because she was bent over slightly, and they held each other in the quiet of the darkened antique shop.

CHAPTER 7

Apollo finally texted Wes after two weeks of silence. Wes wasn't sure if he even wanted to talk to him. Two weeks was a long time to give your partner the silent treatment for setting some simple boundaries.

The text came in the evening, of course, just as Wes was settling in for the night. Winter break was coming up, and he was exhausted from all the exam prep he was running with his classes. He was ready for the break, probably more than his students were.

[Apollo: I miss you. Please come over.]

Wes nearly leaped from his seat that instant to run over to Apollo's place, so used to doing exactly what Apollo wanted. Apollo rarely, if ever, said please. Maybe he would even apologize to Wes for the way he'd behaved, though that was certainly a stretch.

But Wes decided to set his phone aside and think it over for a few minutes. It wasn't okay for Apollo to just ignore him like that for weeks. Wes would not be the kind of person who sat on the side waiting for their partner to decide they had been punished enough and then go running the instant they were ready to show affection again.

Well… I'm not going to be like that anymore.

The decision was made quickly. He would leave Apollo on "read" until the morning. After that, he would message him back and let the incubus know they could meet up for coffee. Under no circumstance was he going to go to Apollo's penthouse, because then nothing would change and Wes would just fall right back into bed with Apollo and it would be like nothing had happened.

Once he had laid comfortably on his couch, Wes put his phone on "do not disturb" and settled in to watch a movie. Things were going to have to change with Apollo. Wes was tired of all the bullshit and of making up excuses about why it was okay. When things had been casual, sure, that was fine. But Wes had made it clear things weren't casual anymore and Apollo didn't care. He did whatever he wanted, even when he had agreed to be in the relationship.

The next day, Wes would lay it all out on the table for Apollo, and whatever happened, he would accept the outcome.

In the morning, when he checked his phone, there were dozens of messages from Apollo, all more or less saying the same thing.

[Apollo: I miss you.]

[Apollo: Come over.]

[Apollo: I'm lonely.]

That last one Wes highly doubted. Apollo never spent a night alone, and Wes knew he wouldn't have waited around for Wes to suddenly show up to find a willing partner.

The final text arrived around three in the morning and simply said, "Don't sulk, darling." Like Wes was sulking over Apollo. No, he had been peacefully sleeping in his own bed, not having to worry about finding a way home in the middle of the night.

After showering, getting dressed, and taking his Lamictal, which he had been extra diligent about taking since the incident, he finally deigned to text Apollo back.

[Wes: Fell asleep early last night. Want to meet up for coffee today?]

[Apollo: Counter offer, you come here and we can have coffee after I make you cum.]

Frustration welled up inside Wes at Apollo's message. Why couldn't the man just hang out with him in public like a normal couple? Why was everything always behind closed doors unless it was a special occasion?

[Wes: I'm on campus all day. I'd rather just hang out between classes.]

[Apollo: Fine, I guess we can do that. But you owe me sexy time tonight. I have something new to pick up from Ezra that will blow your mind.]

[Wes: 11 at Goodberry. See you then.]

He chose not to acknowledge Apollo's comments about potential sex or new toys. Things like that used to thrill him, but not anymore. Was it too much to want something simple every now and then in the bedroom? More cuddling, maybe? Apollo didn't do vanilla, didn't really do sweet.

Picking up his bag, Wes grabbed his bike and headed out the door. It was cold as hell outside now that it was early December and the ride to campus was miserable, but refreshing in its own way. The chilly air helped clear Wes's mind. For months, he had been living on autopilot, observing his life rather than living it. He had been relying on his relationship status and job to give him meaning and identity. But he wasn't a student anymore. He was an associate professor of geology. And as for his relationship, it barely existed and what did exist was toxic and unfulfilling.

A gust of icy wind nearly blew his helmet off his head, and with it came absolute clarity. Wes was riding to meet Apollo and end things. It was time. Their expiration date had already come and gone and Wes was ready to move on. Whether that was onto another relationship or some time alone, it didn't matter. It was time to end whatever he and Apollo had for good. Wes just hoped it would be an easy break since he would still have to see Apollo around. Knowing Apollo, he would hardly care and by the end of their talk, he would likely have someone else lined up to sleep with and carry out his plans with his newest toy.

It hurt worse to think about how little Wes meant to someone he loved, or thought he loved, than the idea of breaking up with Apollo. Wes wasn't even sure if he would be heartbroken, maybe just relieved.

Goodberry was bustling when he walked in after locking up his bike. Most of the seats were taken, people crowding around tables and stuffed next to each other on couches, all hiding out from the weather. Inside was toasty warm and the smell of coffee was soothing and inviting.

The line wasn't terribly long. Wes enjoyed taking the time to warm up, then he ordered a sugary latte for himself and wandered around the space looking for a place to sit. A small table in the back was the only open space that could accommodate two, so Wes set his bag down on the table and took a seat, waiting for his order to be called. He had considered ordering something for Apollo, but he knew very well that the incubus wouldn't show up on time and he wasn't going to waste his money on cold coffee that Apollo would only complain about.

There was nothing to do but wait and people-watch. Goodberry attracted CCSU students, professors, and a myriad of magical people who used glamours to fit in during the day. Many of them bought glamour charms at Spirit even, so Wes was familiar with many of the patrons of Goodberry from hanging around the shop.

From his vantage point, he saw a group of encatados, shapeshifting river dolphins. All three women were absolutely gorgeous, the better to entice any would-be lovers, and they each wore knit hats to hide the blowholes that remained on the top of their heads even in their shifted form. They looked trendy and stylish as they chatted amongst themselves. A quartet of human college guys shot glances at them periodically, giving them goofy smiles each time they were caught looking.

He recognized one of the encantados from a party he had attended with Apollo a few months ago, though he couldn't remember her name. Encantados were creatures of sex and pleasure, much like Apollo. He had probably slept with at least one of them, if not all three.

Wes quickly turned his attention away from them. The last thing he wanted to think about was who else Apollo fucked. It only hardened his resolve to end things today. Human watching was the safer option. They just weren't as interesting, since most were students studying for finals in large groups.

By the time Apollo finally showed up, Wes had already finished his coffee and had nearly given up on the incubus showing up at all. Apollo gracefully took the other chair at the table, a piping hot cup in his hands, which was undoubtedly a chai latte.

"What a morning! I about froze my dick off out there. Can you imagine if I lost that? I would literally die," Apollo said dramatically.

Wes scoffed internally. *Might not be such a bad thing.* He felt guilty immediately after thinking it, but he couldn't help how he felt.

"It's cold, but not that cold. Besides, I'm sure you can find someone to stick your dick in to warm it up." Wes rolled his eyes and tried to keep the anger that was bubbling under the surface at bay.

Apollo leveled a look at him and then lounged back in his chair with a grin. "Someone is feisty today. I like that, means we can have a lot a fun once we get out of here." He sipped his latte, running his tongue over his bottom lip to savor every last drop.

Used to be that one gesture would send Wes spiraling into lust, but now it only annoyed him further. Everything had to be so sexual with Apollo all the time. It was only Apollo's nature, though. He was an incubus, after all. Dating a person who was literally designed to always be sexual, to always seek pleasure without regard for monogamy, wasn't for Wes. He needed exclusivity. He needed someone who wanted to be with only him forever. And that would never be Apollo, because he couldn't change his nature.

"Doesn't it get tiring always being like that?" Wes tried to make his tone even. He didn't want to make it seem like it was a judgment. In three years, he had never asked Apollo how he felt about being an incubus. He wasn't born one, but he never talked about his time before becoming an incubus. He didn't say much at all about his life.

At some point in Apollo's long existence, he had been an angel, like Ezra. But then he had fallen and was cursed to be an incubus. Did he miss being what he was? Having wings and magic that didn't involve sex and hypnotizing?

The long sigh that came out of Apollo was unexpected. For a moment, his blue eyes looked distant, like he was seeing beyond the café. "When I was first cursed, I hated every minute of it. I missed being myself. Then I grew to love it, because what else could I do? And now... well, I've accepted what I am, and what I will never be again."

It was more than Apollo had ever shared with Wes in all the years they had been together. Wes's heart ached at the confession. Apollo really did sound tired at that moment. His shoulders slumped. He may have accepted what he was, but Wes could see the longing in his eyes for what he once was. How had he never seen that before?

But the moment ended quickly, and Apollo's smirk returned. "Enough of that. Why don't we get out of here and warm each other?" He waggled his eyebrows at Wes, and the ache in Wes's chest dissipated instantly. Instead, he steeled his nerves. This was way overdue.

"I want to break up," Wes blurted. It was clunkier than he had intended. The speech he had practiced while waiting for Apollo completely flew from his head. But it was out there, and Wes couldn't take the words back now.

Across the table, Apollo's smirk slowly faded away, until his plump lips were set in a hard line. There was confusion in his eyes as he kept his focus on Wes's face. "What do you mean by 'break up?'" His words were slow, like he was thinking them over as he went.

Wes forced himself to keep eye contact, though he didn't know what to do with his hands, so he put them in his lap and tried to keep them still. "I mean that I think this relationship has run its course. We want different things. You are happy with casual, and I'm ... not. I want commitment and that's not something you can give me." Wes's heart pounded so loudly in his chest that he thought Apollo could probably hear it. He bit his bottom lip and waited for Apollo to reply.

"Wes, lamb, I thought we were past this, that you were okay with where we stood. What's changed? Is it that guy you were talking to at Lily's? Because if you wanted to add a third to our little party, I am open to that." Apollo let a little of his usual flirty tone come through, though his face was still screwed up in a blank mask.

Wes shook his head. "No, we weren't past that. It's my own fault. I kept telling myself that I could handle what we have, but I can't. It has nothing to do with Cameron, and the last thing I want is to add another person to whatever this mess is. I can't even handle just the two of us. So, this is it. I'm done."

With nothing left to say, Wes stood, grabbed his empty coffee cup, and began to turn away. "I'm sorry, Apollo. I really did love you," he said, his tone dripping with sorrow.

Wes only took one step before he felt Apollo's fingers wrap around his wrist. He stopped moving, but he couldn't turn and look at Apollo. "We can still make things work, Wes. I know I can't give you everything you want, but I can still make things good for you." If Wes wasn't sure that Apollo never begged for anything, he would believe there was a note of pleading in his voice.

"It can't be good for me when the love is only one-sided. Goodbye, Apollo," he said sadly, and then Wes tugged his wrist out of Apollo's grasp and walked out of the café without a backward glance.

When he planned the breakup, Wes thought he would feel sadness or regret once he told Apollo. But as he unlocked his bike from the freezing bike rack, he only felt relief. It was as if a great weight had been pushing down on his shoulders and was suddenly lifted. Wes could finally breathe again.

There was no doubt in his mind that Apollo wouldn't take the break up right away. There were still going to be booty calls and texts for him to come over. Wes was done with it all. Before he got on his bike, he took out his phone and blocked Apollo's number; leaving no room for him to be tempted. With that done, he slipped his phone back in his pocket and took off toward his office, the only regret in his mind was that he had wasted so much time with the wrong person.

CHAPTER 8

Yule was coming up and Wes had spent the last week doling out final exams. Lily had sent a message to everyone about a pre-Yule party she and Albert were hosting. It was the only thing getting Wes through Friday, knowing that the next day he would be with family and friends, having good food, good drinks, and exchanging homemade gifts.

He sat at the lectern reading a sci-fi novel that had been on his to-read list forever, while a room full of first-year students took their final exam. It was so quiet, with only the scratching of pencils and pens and the occasional cough filling the lecture hall. Occasionally, Wes lifted his eyes from the book to scan the room. Candy walked the aisles, observing for any signs of cheating. They would have to be total idiots to try to cheat under Candy's watchful eye. She had a way of striking fear into the hearts of freshmen.

Since the dinner, she had been constantly asking questions about magic and the creatures that lived in New Britain. Candy was a scientist through and through. She didn't bring up the idea of magic healing her mom again, and Wes didn't ask, though he was sure she hadn't let the idea go yet. Talking to Candy about everything made him realize how much knowledge he actually lacked. Now that things were calming down in his life, without the stress of Apollo keeping him on edge, maybe he would take the time to learn more magic.

Students filtered out slowly over the hour, placing tests and Scantrons on the table at the front of the room. Wes noticed the difference in the students who passed by. Many looked completely exhausted, like they spent all their time studying late into the night and were now wiped after a week of exams. But then there were those who looked completely unfazed, and those tended to be the same people who he didn't recognize because they hadn't shown up to class since the first week. First years were idiots most of the time, with no study habits at all. No doubt he would see a few of them again next year to repeat the course.

"I swear I saw a guy mark igneous for literally every answer. Pretty sure it's the same one who's slept through every single class since the first day," Candy said, as she grabbed the tests and Scantrons from the table. It was her job to grade them all. One of the perks of being the professor, Wes had an underling to do his work for him. He was going to help her, obviously, Candy still had a lot to deal with. Her siblings were coming in for the holidays and they were making plans to put their mom in a nursing facility. But until then, she was still under enough pressure with her own classes still taking up the rest of her time.

"If these kids spent less time partying and more time actually, you know, going to college, they wouldn't need to sleep in my class. But at least they show up. Were we that out of control as freshmen?" Wes had been a little wild in his first year or two of college, but he still showed up to class, got good grades, and mostly had a good balance.

"I know it's hard to believe, but I don't like people all that much, so partying wasn't much of my thing," Candy deadpanned.

"I'm shocked," Wes responded in a monotone, with a roll of his eyes. They walked out of the lecture hall together before parting ways. "You'll be at the Yule party tomorrow, right?" he asked, knowing full well that she would be since he'd practically begged her to come.

She paused to think for a moment, like she might not actually attend. "Well, I can't pass up free food and a chance to hang out with your super special friends. So yeah, I'll be there." With a backward wave, she left him standing in the hallway, and Wes headed in the opposite direction. A little time in his office to unwind was a welcome thought. A cup of coffee from the old drip coffee maker, while not exactly the height of luxury, was also something he was looking forward to, so long as it was still hot.

Once firmly ensconced behind his desk, Wes leaned back in his chair, wonky though it was, and closed his eyes. A break from classes and time with his friends was exactly what he needed. Tense weeks of dealing with Apollo's bullshit had run him ragged. But days of getting to bed at a reasonable hour and no late-night texts had been glorious. For once, Wes felt well-rested and relaxed.

Which, of course, meant that it wouldn't last. His phone vibrated with an incoming text on his desk. Reluctantly, he opened his eyes and sat up, cursing himself for being a punctual texter. It was from Lily.

[Lily: I just remembered that I invited Apollo to the party. I did it before you guys broke up. I'm so sorry!]

[Lily: I can uninvite him if you want.]

Wes let his head fall against the desk. Why didn't he think of that before? Naturally, Lily would invite Apollo. He was part of their group, despite the fact that he got on everyone's nerves at some point. And they had been together for years, so of course she would invite the pair of them.

[Wes: No, it's fine. I'm going to have to see him at some point. Just seat him as far away from me as possible.]

It wasn't an ideal solution, but he wasn't going to make Lily uninvite Apollo just because Wes didn't want to see him. Whether he liked it or not, Apollo would be around. Wes couldn't avoid him forever.

[Lily: I'll keep your glass full the whole night. And if he makes a scene, I'll kick his ass.]

[Wes: Lol, appreciate it, Lils.]

He set his phone back down on the desk and resumed his lounging position. And here he had been really looking forward to the party, but now a sense of dread filled his stomach. Apollo was definitely going to make a scene. That was his nature. Besides sex, Apollo thrived on drama. Though he knew Lily would do everything in her power to keep Apollo from messing up the night, including using magic against him.

The bike ride home seemed to take longer than normal. All the excitement he felt about the party had quickly evaporated. At least he would have his sister, Ezra, and Candy as a shield around him. Maybe Cameron would be there too. That thought cheered him a little. Cameron was likable, easy to talk to, great to look at, and always brought something tasty to eat. Even though the party would be a small affair, Wes was confident he wouldn't have to deal with Apollo much during the night. He hoped anyway.

There wasn't a strict dress code for a Lily Everett party, but everyone dressed up a little, anyway. Wes put on a nice pair of dark slacks and a forest green button-down, one of only two he owned. Immediately, he rolled the sleeves up to his elbows. He couldn't stand the feel of the cuffs on his wrists. He cleaned up the shaved side of his head quickly with his razor before styling the rest of his dark waves so the strands flopped just so.

At the door, he debated between his comfy, yet scuffed-to-hell Converse, or his one pair of loafers. Comfort over style was usually always the case.

But he chose the loafers in the end to complete his grown-up look.

His Uber showed up minutes later. If Lily followed through with her promise to keep the alcohol flowing, and she would, Wes didn't want to bother with his bike. He grabbed his overnight bag from where he had placed it on the couch, knowing full well Lily would insist on everyone staying over if they wanted. He offered to ride over with Candy, but she insisted she would meet him there after procuring the address. "I don't know if Mom will need me right before I leave, so I don't want to make you wait for me if she starts having a bad time," she had said. Wes worried that Candy wouldn't show at all, but she had assured him that a night nurse was coming over so she could have some time outside of the house.

The ride over to Lily and Albert's took several minutes since they lived in one of the more residential areas of the city, where all the old money houses were. He stared out the window, watching as the world turned pink and red with the setting sun.

I'm going to have a good night. I'm not going to let Apollo ruin it.

He just had to make himself believe the words.

Lily greeted him at the door with a glass of red wine and a hug. "You're starting me off right away. Have I told you lately how much I love you? Because I think I love you even more than I did yesterday." Wes accepted the glass and returned her hug with one arm, squeezing tightly to show his appreciation.

"You can tell me you love me anytime. I enjoy hearing it. Just don't let Albert hear you. He'll think you're trying to steal me away," she responded with a laugh. She led Wes into the house, where there was a flurry of activity.

"Hey Wes," Lily's older sister Ivy said as she finished hanging a strand of garland above the threshold into the sitting room. Her husband, Jaime, waved a greeting before placing his hands on Ivy's waist to help her down from the step stool. Wes waved back before he continued to follow Lily through the house to the kitchen. The space served as the central hub of the house and where they spent most of their time whenever Wes or anybody was over. It allowed Albert to feed everyone quickly and had easy access to Lily's gardens.

Brie and Ezra were already sipping drinks around the island, chatting with Albert while the vampire worked around the kitchen. Cameron stood next to Brie, assembling a tray of vegetables. Wes crossed the room to hug his sister and Ezra. "I see you made sure to be just late enough to avoid any help with setup. Slacker," Brie said and gave his arm a light punch.

"You think it's easy looking this good? No, no, Little Witch. This takes time." Wes twisted one way, then the other, to show the look that in truth only took him ten minutes to pull off. He hadn't meant to slack on helping. His mind had been so preoccupied that he forgot the time. Brie rolled her eyes in return while Wes hugged Ezra and shot a wave toward Cameron, who waved back with a large grin on his handsome face.

"You look like the Ghost of Christmas Present," Wes said, laughing as he gave his sister a once over.

Brie was dressed in an emerald dress that brushed the floor. The long sleeves were lace and the neckline scooped low. She wore a wreath of garland atop her ginger waves.

Brie scowled at him. "Joke's on you, asshole. He's my favorite ghost." She snagged a carrot on the tray in front of Cameron. He playfully swatted her hand away, but let her take the carrot, anyway.

Ezra was in a pair of black slacks and a black button-down; the man never wore color. Honestly, it would be weird to see him in anything other than black at that point, but he contrasted nicely with his wife. Wes's eyes moved back to Cameron. He was dressed a little more casually in a red Henley and dark jeans, no flour in sight. Wes had never seen the man not covered in flour and he admired how well Cameron cleaned up.

"How's it going, Wes? You look good," Cameron said, his smile all bright teeth, and an adorable crinkle formed at the bridge of his nose. Wes couldn't stop the color rising to his cheeks, or the warmth that filled his body.

"I'm good. You look good too. No flour tonight. Not that you don't look good with the flour. You look great with it. It's just a change, ya know?"

What the fuck is wrong with me?

He couldn't stop talking, he was word-vomiting all over the place. But Cameron didn't seem to mind as he chuckled and his eyes grew brighter.

"I know, right! My sister said the same thing before I left the house. Said it had been like three years since she had seen me completely clean. We live together, me and my twin sister Camilla. She's great. I think you would like her."

Wes wasn't sure if he was sharing this to be friendly or if Cameron was hinting at something between Wes and Cameron's sister. Not that he was ready for anything yet. It had barely been a week since his breakup. And he really enjoyed Cameron's company.

"She's probably better than my sister. I mean, look at what I'm stuck with," Wes said, pointing at Brie with a mischievous smile on his face. Brie scowled at him as she flipped him off.

"I'm a godsdamn delight, and you are lucky to have me," she retorted haughtily.

Wes shrugged. "Eh, you're okay." She flipped him off again, but the smile behind it diminished the gesture.

"I think you're more than okay, sweetheart," Ezra said, wrapping an arm around Brie's middle and pulling her close to his body. She actually giggled and turned her head up to kiss him. They were a cute couple, and Wes was glad that his sister had found her happiness, but sometimes they acted so in love it was nauseating.

Lily bustled back into the kitchen with Candy in tow a minute later. Candy looked sharp in a perfectly tailored suit jacket and slim-fitted trousers that ended just above her black, heeled shoes. Rather than a dress shirt under the jacket, she wore a stylish lacy crop top. She looked like she was either ready for the red carpet or a rock concert. Candy could probably pull off both in one night. In her hands, she carried a large covered tray.

"I made baklava. It's my yaya's recipe," she said, raising the tray a little higher.

Albert didn't turn toward her when he spoke. "Desserts over there." He pointed to a little sideboard where a Yule log cake and a basket of pastries already sat. Candy quickly deposited the tray where Albert indicated before taking a spot at the kitchen island like everyone else.

Lily placed a glass of clear liquid in front of her, a wedge of lime balanced on the rim. "How did you know I like gin and tonic?" Candy asked as Lily walked back over to the drink cart in the corner of the kitchen.

"She's a witch, and like psychic," Wes said. "She sometimes knows more about you than you know about yourself. Which is weird and a little unnerving." All save for Candy laughed. Each of them, probably Cameron too, had at some point been the subject of one of Lily's visions.

Candy's face was a mix of awe and skepticism. She was still coming to terms with magic, despite Wes's best efforts to tell her about what he knew. For some people, it was harder to accept that magic was real, that witches, vampires, and angels existed. And that was just the people in the kitchen. "Can you read my mind? Or see my future? Will there be a tall, dark, handsome stranger in my future?" There was a hint of sarcasm in Candy's words, but Lily was too good-natured to take offense.

Instead, the witch smiled brightly. "As I've told everyone else several times, it doesn't work like that. I can't read your mind, and my visions have a way of doing their own thing. They let me see what I need to see when I need to see it. Sometimes I can target something, but that takes a lot of time and energy. I kind of just roll with it."

"Often, it ruins surprises," Albert grumbled from where he stood at the stove. Last year, they had tried to throw Lily a surprise party for her birthday. Wes couldn't remember who came up with that stupid idea. Lily, at least, had the good grace to feign surprise, which nobody bought.

Ivy and Jaime entered the room, and Jaime made straight for the tray of veggies they all had already been picking at. There was an assortment of crudités across the counter, the usual veggies, cheeses, and fruits. Every few minutes, someone would ask Albert if he needed help finishing dinner, and they would receive a sharp "no" in return. Albert let nobody around his food while in the cooking process, not even Lily.

Wes found himself standing in a small circle with Cameron and Candy. It wasn't a surprise to himself that he was near Cameron again. He always seemed to gravitate toward the friendly giant of a man. And now, without his attachment to Apollo, he didn't feel guilty about talking to another person that he found attractive.

Candy seemed content to stick by his side, but not in a smothering way. She knew Brie, Ezra, and Lily a little, but Wes was her only real friend. Now that Candy knew about what they all were, she seemed somewhat wary about mingling with the rest of them. She would come around given time; Wes knew. She needed to examine all the facts and come to her own conclusions first.

"So you're a geologist like Wes?" Cameron asked Candy, his great big smile plastered on his face, green eyes shining. When Cameron spoke to you, he looked you right in the eye and gave you his full attention.

After taking a sip of her gin and tonic, Candy responded, "I'm still a student, but I'm his teaching assistant. He's a slave driver and a pain in the ass. But yeah, I come from a long line of geologists, so it's pretty much in my blood."

"That's really cool. My family has been bakers forever, so I know how it feels to be surrounded by the same thing all your life, including the pressure and expectations," Cameron said, his eyes taking on a faraway look for only a second before he snapped back to his cheerful self. Candy nodded enthusiastically.

Wes didn't miss the look. Had his parents lived, Wes was sure he would understand what that meant more. He came from a long line of guardians, those who had served the Morrigan for hundreds of years. But he didn't get to know that side of himself, not really. There was never anyone around to push him, to heap expectations on him. Maddy guided him the best she could, but she wasn't that kind of guardian, and she had no magic of her own. She couldn't give him that legacy.

"I'm not really a hard ass. I only flog you once a day. You have it easy compared to the other TAs," Wes said, hiding his laughter behind a serious tone. He broke easily when the other two laughed. His smile broadened at hearing Candy's light laugh. It had been a long time since he heard genuine levity in her voice, had seen the worry lines melt from her face. A night out was exactly what she needed.

Hell, they all needed a night out to just enjoy themselves, Wes included. There was nothing to worry about other than eating and drinking too much. He didn't have to think about who he was talking to or being pushed to leave before he was ready to go. There was no expectation that he would jump at the whim of another person and upend his night to suit someone else's needs.

Wes had started to realize how much he had let Apollo take over his life the past few years. And for what? Great sex. That was it. Wes had taken on all the emotional labor of that relationship and gotten little in return.

Now he didn't have to worry if he wanted to spend the rest of the night talking to Cameron, or if he hugged Candy tightly because she needed it. No one was going to pull him away from a good night.

That didn't mean his night couldn't be ruined, though. Just as they all sat down to dinner, Wes seated between Candy and Cameron like he had been all night, they heard the door open and two people walked into the dining room.

Wes had held out hope that Apollo would ditch the event and he wouldn't have to see him at all. But that was too good to hope for. And Apollo made it worse by walking into the room with not one date, but two. The first was a man, well, a satyr, with curly brown hair, and downy ears on either side of small horns on the top of his head. He had pouty lips set in a frown and was impeccably dressed in a gray suit with the jacket unbuttoned, and the pants tailored perfectly around his goat legs.

The other was Esmerelda. Wes guessed she was going to be Apollo's go-to event date now that they were no longer together. Her gaze was locked on Wes, and she gripped Apollo's arm a little tighter while she smirked, like she thought she won a prize.

The satyr, maybe his name was Graydon, Wes had a hard time remembering every person Apollo introduced him to over the years, looked annoyed as his eyes roved over the table. "I thought you said this was a party," he said, sounding bored already.

Apollo grinned at everyone, his eyes lingering on Wes the longest before he snapped his attention to the hosts. "Sorry we're late. We got a little carried away with our pre-party fun." Was his voice always so oily? Wes was used to Apollo sounding smarmy, but if anything, his voice was just annoying.

"Lily said you were bringing a guest, not multiple," Albert said sharply from the head of the table. Lily's style was the more the merrier, a sentiment her mate did not share. Especially when it involved Apollo.

Apollo didn't seem to care, like the rules of etiquette didn't apply to him. Albert's scornful look didn't even phase the incubus, who only smirked at the vampire as he took a seat at the table. Maybe-Graydon took the empty chair next to him, but because they weren't expecting Apollo to bring two people, there was no empty chair for Esmerelda. She didn't waste a beat as she plopped herself onto Apollo's lap, staring at Wes the whole time with a triumphant smile. Her arms wrapped around Apollo's neck and he nuzzled her hair, his nose grazing her cheek.

Wes thought he would feel something. Maybe not jealousy, but a tinge of regret at seeing Apollo with someone else. It was a surprise to him that he felt nothing at all. Not in a hollow way, but that he simply didn't care about what Apollo did. The situation wasn't unusual even when they were dating. It hurt then, but Wes had no claim over Apollo, and his constant flaunting of his other partners had stopped hurting Wes some time ago.

"Gonna introduce your friends, or do we have to watch random people hang all over you all night?" Brie glared so hard it was a wonder Apollo didn't burst into flames. If Brie still had the power of the Morrigan, Wes was pretty sure she would have set him on fire or done something equally destructive.

Apollo smiled brightly, thinking he could charm the people in the room. But they were all his friends, of a sort, and nobody was fooled or charmed by his look. "This lovely creature here is Esmerelda. I believe a few of you are already acquainted. And this fine-looking specimen," here he indicated the satyr, "is Graydon. Wes, I believe you've met Graydon before."

Wes made no acknowledgment that Apollo had even spoken and opted instead to take a gulp of his wine. He had met Graydon a few times, the first of which was walking into Apollo's penthouse to find Apollo on his knees with Graydon's massive dick in his mouth. Graydon had panted out a gruff hi, while Apollo didn't acknowledge Wes until he was finished. It was quite the introduction.

Under the table, Wes felt a large comforting hand squeeze his knee, while a smaller warm hand grabbed his on the other side. Cameron and Candy offered their support with the simple gestures, and Wes had never been more grateful to have two people in his life. He didn't look at either of them. He didn't want Apollo to think he had gotten to him. But he did squeeze Candy's hand back, and placed his other hand on top of Cameron's acknowledging them both.

Lily, ever the dedicated host, steered the dinner back on track to keep it from getting more awkward than it already was. "So Ezra, Brie, how are things at the shop? Is the inventory project going well?"

Nobody actually cared about how the inventory project was going. The two of them had been working on it since Brie started at the shop over three years ago. It was a long tedious process since Ezra had been hoarding magical items since Goddess only knew when. And he added to the collection every week. Luckily, they both had eternity to work on it.

And Brie seemed to think the project would take an eternity. "If I had known it would take this long when I applied for the job, I wouldn't have bothered. I'm pretty sure the Storage Room has been expanding and lost treasures have rematerialized." She swung her fork in the air for emphasis. Most of the table laughed, save Graydon, who didn't even crack a smile.

"It has, actually. The Storage Room has a ... complex about its girth sometimes," Ezra said matter-of-factly, like it was totally normal for a room to be size conscious.

"Poor baby, I love it no matter its size," Lily cooed. It was a truth universally accepted that while the Storage Room wasn't *alive* in the traditional sense, it certainly had a mind of its own and was treated like a member of the family.

Candy furrowed her brow. "You talk about it like it's actually a living thing. Which, by the way, is pretty weird."

Esmerelda sneered at her across the table. "There's nothing weird about magic. Gods, that sounds like some backward human mentality."

Wes leveled a glare at Esmerelda. "That's because she's human, Ezzy." He used the nickname he knew she hated, but it gave him some satisfaction to see her perfect face turn red.

"So you don't know anything about magic? Why are you even here?" Graydon drawled, his tone bored, his face hard. The conversation was quickly getting hostile, and it was Apollo's fault for bringing both of them to what should have been a nice party.

"What are you even doing here? You weren't invited," Albert sounded annoyed, though he kept his face blank. It was pretty standard for Albert. But he also hated everyone who wasn't in his very tight inner circle, which basically consisted of Lily, certain members of her family, Ezra, and, most recently, Brie. Wes didn't even make the cut; he was tolerated at most.

"Alright, why don't we move on and enjoy the company we do have? We have a lot of great things to eat. Bertie, the food is perfect! And Cameron, I swear you put a little extra magic in this bread. I'm addicted." Lily steered the evening back on track, tactfully keeping the attention off Apollo and his guests. Even when Apollo and Esmerelda started to get a little extra cuddly at the table, Lily shot a few magical zaps across the table to keep them from going full PDA while they ate. Apollo laughed while Esmerelda sulked. Graydon continued to frown and look mostly uninterested, though he seemed to eat with gusto.

Throughout the whole of dinner, Lily's sister Ivy and her husband Jaime remained quiet. Ivy observed the conversation, while Jaime focused solely on his food. Jaime had a tendency to turn off his hearing aids when he didn't want to engage in conversation, especially when there was conflict or tension.

After they finished eating, rather than sit around the table with drinks and dessert like normal, Lily led them to the living room, where the layout was more spread out and there was more comfortable seating. Despite the abundance of couches and chairs, though, Esmerelda remained firmly perched on Apollo's thigh, with Graydon snuggled close to them, though the satyr didn't look particularly thrilled to still be there.

Wes sat next to Candy while they munched on the dessert she brought and a few of the pastries Cameron had baked. The large man himself was ensconced in a plush chair close to Wes's other side. It was like he and Candy had separately decided they were Wes's bodyguards for the night. There was a warm feeling in Wes's chest at their consideration. He felt cared for by a good friend and someone who was slowly becoming one.

Nearby, his sister kept darting glances his way, like she was checking on how he was feeling. Even though she was the younger of the two, she was protective of her older brother. Wes felt so much love at that moment that any thought of Apollo was pushed from his mind. Even as the incubus sat across the room from him, in full view, Wes didn't bother to spare a glance his way. Not because he was avoiding him, Wes just didn't care. Apollo hadn't really cared throughout their relationship, and now that it had ended, Wes was enjoying being around the people he actually did care about.

At least he thought so until he saw Esmerelda's lips latch onto Apollo's throat. She slowly kissed up his neck and Wes knew the soft moans that came out of Apollo were exaggerated. They were baiting Wes. Esmerelda certainly was. That much was clear. Apollo was probably going along with it just because he enjoyed the exhibition.

Wes was on his feet before his brain could process anything further, and he stomped out of the room and made his way to the back porch. At some point in the night, it had started to snow. Big fluffy flakes that had barely begun to stick to the ground. Wes hadn't brought his coat, and he shivered in the cold air, his thin button-down doing little to stave off the chill. But he was protected from the snow by the porch roof and he sat on the frozen step just outside the door.

He pulled his knees up and rested his forearms on top. Logically, he knew the display in the living room was just to get at him. Apollo liked to tease, and Esmerelda thought there was some kind of competition between her and Wes. His emotions were a jumble. It wasn't like he was upset that Apollo had moved on; he had never really been devoted to Wes anyway. For years, Apollo had slept with everyone while being with Wes, so it really wasn't a shock.

Wes could honestly say he didn't care. At least he didn't care to get back together. It just hit him hard that Apollo would do that in front of him right after they broke up. He told himself it wasn't jealousy. Okay, maybe it was a little. But more than that, he was upset that Apollo didn't seem to care at all. That their three-year relationship had meant nothing.

Maybe it had meant nothing to Apollo. Maybe Wes had been just another person on his arm to flaunt, fuck, and then forget. Wes was there in an instant whenever Apollo needed someone, whether that was to fulfill a need or because he needed someone on his arm for a party. Even though Apollo had said the words, said they were a couple. But clearly, those had been empty words. Empty words that Wes had fallen for time and again, and had accepted for years, even when the evidence suggested otherwise.

Goddess, he had been an idiot. An idiot who wanted someone to love him like he gave love. Apollo had never and would never love him like that. Wes just never wanted to admit it to himself. And yeah, it was ridiculous to be upset that Apollo wasn't pining over him or that he didn't seem to care at all about their breakup, when Wes felt only relief now. Wes admitted to himself that he was a hypocrite, but Apollo's behavior confirmed what he already knew; Apollo never saw Wes as anything more than a fuck buddy.

Behind Wes, he heard the door open and close a second later. A large warm body plopped down next to Wes on the step. Cameron sat next to him, his posture mirroring Wes's, though he looked more cramped with his knees up.

"You okay? What am I saying? Of course you're not. What Apollo did was super messed up. He could have at least come alone if he was going to show up. I'm so sorry, Wes." His tone was comforting, if a little self-deprecating. Like he was afraid he was offending Wes by not understanding his emotions entirely.

Wes shrugged. "I'm okay. I'm honestly not surprised, probably should have expected it. I don't know why it's bothering me."

They were quiet for a moment, both of them watching the slow fall of the snow. "Do you miss him?" Cameron asked, so quietly Wes almost didn't hear.

But Wes shook his head quickly while he kept his face forward. "No. I feel like I should be more broken up about it, but honestly, I'm not. I spent so many years being disappointed by him never really committing to me that it doesn't really feel any different than when we were together. I think I'm angry more than anything. Like shouldn't he be upset at least a little? Rather than letting someone hang all over him right in front of me just a few weeks after I ended things. Goddess, I sound horrible." He let out a humorless laugh and hung his head.

Two fingers touched under his chin and lifted it. Wes's face turned toward Cameron, who looked at him intently. "You're not horrible for wanting someone you expected to love you to actually care that you are not together. You expected him to care a little, and he's showing that he didn't. I'm sorry you have to go through that. You deserve better. You deserve someone who actually gives a shit about you."

They stared into each other's eyes. Wes was absolutely mesmerized by Cameron's green eyes and how the light shining through the kitchen window reflected in them. His fingers still touched Wes's chin, and that simple touch reverberated through Wes's whole body.

Wes couldn't be sure who leaned in first, but an instant later, Cameron's lips were on his. There was no urgency or heat to the kiss. It was gentle, surprising from a man as big as Cameron. His lips were pillowy soft and tasted like sweet syrup and pistachio. Cameron's tongue swept across his lips, begging for entrance, and Wes quickly opened his mouth. Their tongues twined together in a slow dance, neither rushing, or pushing.

Cameron cupped the back of Wes's head, pulling him just closer, deepening the kiss a little more. All thoughts fled from Wes as he reached a hand out and placed it on Cameron's expansive chest. He could feel Cameron's heart beating quickly under his palm, and Wes knew his own heart must be beating just as quick.

It felt like a lifetime before they pulled away from each other, breathing heavily. Their foreheads pressed against each other, and Cameron still held the back of Wes's head. It was intimate, their breaths warming each other's faces.

"I've been wanting to do that for a while," Cameron whispered against his lips, and Wes felt a smile spread across his face.

"I would be lying if I said I hadn't wanted to do the same," he admitted. Wes had once felt so much guilt even thinking about Cameron, let alone thinking about kissing him. But he had. Many times. And it was better than anything he'd imagined.

They were too close for Wes to fully appreciate Cameron's grin, but it was enough to fill his whole body with a fuzzy feeling. "So what now?" Wes asked tentatively.

Cameron pulled back to take in Wes's whole face, but he kept his hand where it was, and Wes loved the heavy feel of Cameron's palm against his scalp. It was a possessive gesture, and Wes was more than willing to surrender to it. "Now, I want to take you on a date. Not like right now. That would be weird to ditch the party. Plus, it's like nearly midnight. But like soon. I would say tomorrow, but is that too soon?" Cameron seemed a little shy all of a sudden. He seemed worried that Wes would say no, that it was too soon for him.

But Wes was glad he suggested the next day, because he definitely didn't want to wait to spend more time with Cameron. Wes leaned forward and planted a quick, chaste kiss on Cameron's mouth. "Tomorrow sounds perfect," he said as he pulled away.

The door opened again, and Albert's bored drawl filled the night. "Can you please stop making out on my porch and get out of my house?" The door shut again immediately, and Wes felt his face burn. He looked at Cameron and his cheeks were flaming red.

"We should probably head out," Wes said as he stood, reaching his hand out to help Cameron up. When they were both standing, neither moved right away to head inside. Their hands remained clasped together, and they fit so perfectly together, Wes couldn't bring himself to let go.

But he dropped Cameron's hand after a moment and they headed inside with matching smiles on their faces. They tried to keep at least a foot of distance between them, lest anyone else know what they had been doing. Albert would be sure to tell Lily and Lily would tell his sister, and pretty soon everyone would know. For a moment, though, the kiss was just between them. Well, and Albert.

Wes said his goodbyes to Lily with a giant hug, ignored Apollo and his entourage completely, and waved at Albert sheepishly. He walked with Candy, his sister, and his brother-in-law out of the house. Cameron was just behind them.

He waved a shy goodbye to Cameron, his cheeks coloring at the smile Cameron returned. Wes followed Candy to her car, since she offered to drive him home. With a parting hug for Brie and Ezra, Wes climbed into Candy's car, his eyes watching Cameron as they pulled away.

CHAPTER 9

[Lily: It's going to go well, just so you know.]

[Wes: What???]

[Lily: Your date with Cameron. It's going to go really well.]

[Wes: Why do you even know that?]

[Lily: I have a special interest in the relationship working out.]

[Wes: Because your sister tried to set you up like forever ago?]

[Brie: Hella awkward]

[Lily: Quiet Bridget! No, because I saw this happening ages ago.]

[Wes: Define ages.]

[Lily: Like ... two years ago.]

[Brie: Why am I just now hearing about this?!]

[Wes: So full of secrets, Lils. But I'm with Brie, why are we just now hearing about this?]

[Brie: He could have been smooching Cameron's cute face instead of stuck with Apollo!]

[Lily: It wasn't the right time.]

[Lily: But now it is, and it's going to be great.]

[Wes: I'm holding a grudge.]

Wes tossed his phone onto the couch with a huff. He should have asked Lily how his life was going to go down. She probably knew for years things with Apollo would implode and Cameron was in his future.

Or maybe not. Well, the Cameron part anyway, but Lily wasn't one to push the future to happen. She knew there were several versions that could come to pass and she was only seeing one.

It was late, but Wes was still buzzing from the kiss with Cameron. The soft way Cameron's lips had touched his was now imprinted on his brain. Now that he had one kiss, he craved more. Apollo kissed like he wanted to devour Wes's very essence. But Cameron's kiss was like he wanted to cherish every part of Wes, like he wasn't taking. He was giving a piece of himself to Wes and only asked for a little in return. Wes had experienced a lot of kisses in his life with many different people, but none could match the simple beauty and joy of Cameron's plush lips.

Wes needed to get to bed. He had a date the next day.

His whole body vibrated with nerves, though Wes couldn't say why he was nervous. It wasn't like he hadn't spent enough time with Cameron, laughed with him, hell, even kissed him.

But this is different.

And it really was different, because this wasn't some hangout in a group setting. This was one on one with a guy he was really starting to like. Cameron seemed to be a monogamous relationship guy, which was definitely a point in his favor. Though now that Wes thought about it, did he really know what Cameron wanted out of whatever was going on between them? What if he turned out to be like Apollo? Just because they knew each other and had shared a moment didn't mean they knew each other well.

There was no way Wes's heart could take another one-sided relationship. He didn't want casual sex and lack of commitment. But that was what a first date was for, to suss out what they both wanted. So Wes decided that he would lay it all there on the table. If he was in, he was all in. No casual hook-ups, no booty calls in the middle of the night, and absolutely no other partners. If Cameron couldn't commit to that first thing, Wes would walk. He was over being played around.

Was that what people talked about on a first date, before they were even official? Yeah, probably. Wes had never gotten that far into a relationship before dating Apollo to have that conversation. But Wes was sick of having his heart broken day after day. And if Cameron wouldn't commit to that, to him, Wes was done with all magical beings. Humans may be boring, but there were fewer complications. Or more, really, depending on how you looked at it. He would have to introduce them slowly to his sister and his brother-in-law and what they did and then his friend-group. There wasn't a good way to hide all the magic in his life, and Wes had no intention of pulling away from that world. He was still technically a part of it himself, and he wouldn't push the magic inside him away.

So maybe he would just be done with men in general. That seemed easier. You didn't have to deal with an alpha male ego when you were dating a woman.

Wes spent all morning fretting over what could be with Cameron, and the clock ticked slowly toward their one o'clock coffee date. He rode to Goodberry Café. It was a safe space for Wes. It wasn't busy; most of the students had already left for winter break. The place was only half filled with the local creatures of New Britain, most looking a little hungover still from their own Yule celebrations.

He arrived early to scope out a table and wait for Cameron, but when Wes walked in the door, Cameron was right there, sitting at a table next to the window. Two cups of coffee sat on the tabletop in front of him.

When he spotted Wes, he pushed to his feet and gave Wes a sheepish smile.

"Hi," Wes said, and heat rose to his cheeks. He felt jittery all over and he hadn't even had the coffee yet.

"Hi." Came Cameron's shy response and he blushed such a pretty pink color. If Wes wasn't careful, he would fall in love with Cameron on the spot. Two awkward nerds in love. It sounded like a cliché. But they weren't there yet. They still had to get through the first date.

"I got you a coffee. Caramel latte with almond milk, extra whipped cream, right?" Cameron bit his lip, like he was worried he got the coffee order wrong. Wes wouldn't have cared if he had gotten him a decaf drip, he'd drink it, anyway.

Wes sat first to push past the awkward tension. "No, yeah, that's my order. How did you know? Wait, let me guess. Lily?"

Cameron nodded sheepishly. "Lily," he said with a small grin. "She called me at like six Friday morning to tell me. Said it would make a good impression, but gave me no other context. Guess a vision hit her early that morning." He chuckled, and it was so full, so joyful, that it made Wes's heart melt. He wanted to bottle that laugh, save it for a bad day.

Wes let his smile stretch wide even as he shrugged. "She was probably just getting up for the day. Lily happens to know my coffee order off-hand, anyway. And my dinner order, and my favorite snacks. It's basically like having a wife, but Albert takes care of her."

"More like she takes care of Albert and he feeds her in return," Cameron said, his own grin reflected all the way up to his green eyes. "And it's not the first time Lily has called or messaged me early in the morning for something that seems random until the moment occurs."

"Yeah, I'm pretty sure we've all had many of those calls. Her visions do not care about anyone's sleep schedule," Wes added with a smirk before taking a sip of his latte. He was delighted to find that it was exactly how he liked it. Lily could call Cameron up all she liked to tell him all of his favorites and he wouldn't mind. Was it cheating the dating system? Maybe. But it made it so much more convenient for them.

They sat across from each other, shy smiles on their lips. Wes had no idea what he should say next. Last night at the party they spoke so easily. Actually, every time they had been around each other, they spoke with such ease, like they had known each other for years. But now Wes knew what Cameron's lips tasted like and he couldn't get his brain to completely function and form the words to flirt, or say anything at all.

"So," Cameron began, but then he stopped, a blush creeping across his cheeks again, but he kept his eyes locked on Wes.

Wes rubbed the back of his head, unsure of what to say at first. "So ... this was a lot less awkward before we kissed. Not that kissing you was awkward. It wasn't. Just now what?"

Now what, indeed?

Wes thought as he forced himself to keep eye contact with the gorgeous brown-haired man across the table.

"It wasn't awkward. I really enjoyed it. Like really enjoyed it. I'm ... well ... listen, I know you just got out of a bad relationship with Apollo, so I want to be upfront with you. I'm not like that. I'm a one-person relationship guy. I'm not looking to mess around. And when I say relationship, I mean like I will be the best boyfriend you've ever had. Or, I mean, I'll try to be." Cameron averted his gaze, his face completely tomato red, embarrassed that he had said too much too soon.

But it was exactly what Wes wanted, needed to hear. It was all laid out there, and they were on the same page. Wes audibly sighed in relief.

With his gaze still averted, Cameron's face fell. It was so sudden that Wes feared he had done something wrong by simply sighing. He scrambled quickly to answer. "That's good, because I was going to say the same thing. I'm all in if you are. I'm honestly really sick of being a doormat to someone who won't commit."

Cameron's green-eyed gaze quickly swept back to Wes's face, a relieved yet small smile there. "Oh, great! I thought for a minute that wasn't something you were into. I mean, you were with Apollo a long time, so I thought ... maybe ... that was your thing. But I'm glad it's not." If the man could blush even more, he would probably combust right there in the chair.

Time to open up a bit, I guess, Wes thought, putting his hands on the table. If he didn't give Cameron the details of what he wanted and what he didn't, they would be starting off whatever their relationship was going to be with half assumptions. "Listen, I spent three years with Apollo, thinking one day he would commit to me. It was stupid, I know that now, but when you think you love somebody, well, it makes you kind of stupid. I like you, Cameron, like a lot. Not just because you are literally the polar opposite of my ex, but because you are genuinely a good person. I'm not saying things will last forever and we'll ride off into the sunset. I don't want to get ahead of myself. But I know whatever we have together, it'll be just the two of us, nobody else."

Cameron nodded, his grin quickly widening. "I like that idea. So, awkward part of the date over?"

Wes took a large gulp of his cooling coffee. "Abso-fucking-lutely over. Let's talk about literally anything else. Tell me something I don't know about you. Like, I know you're a baker. A fantastic one, I might add. But like what else?"

Cameron beamed under the praise. He grasped his coffee cup, like he was trying to keep his hands contained while he talked. "Um, there's not a whole lot to me. Baking is my profession, hobby, and passion. I come from a very long line of bakers. I left my parents' bakery when I was nineteen and set up my own across town. I didn't want to compete with them, but I liked focusing more on bread and pastries, while my mom and dad are more into cakes and desserts. What else? My most treasured possession is my some-odd great gran's sourdough starter. That thing goes back generations, and it's been infused with so many different types of magic that it always makes the perfect loaf. I hope to one day pass it along to my kids with all the love and magic I've put into it."

The man flushed a little and rubbed the back of his neck. "So you're saying you want kids someday?" Wes wasn't sure how he felt about that. Losing his parents young and having no stable father figure in his life, he wasn't sure how he would handle fatherhood.

Cameron didn't look at him when he responded, instead keeping his gaze on the cup in front of him. "I come from a big family. Four sisters and I'm the only boy. Not that not wanting kids is a deal-breaker for me. But yeah, someday I would like that."

The color in his cheeks seemed more from embarrassment now. Wes leaned back in his chair, quiet while he contemplated his words. Several moments stretch out, and Wes worried he was making it more awkward by not saying anything. "It's probably a little early to have this talk, but I'm not against the idea of kids. It's just ... you know, I was orphaned really young. I honestly have no idea what it takes to raise kids. Hell, I don't even know how to be around them. Pretty sure I've never even held a baby before. Still, I'm, you know, open to the idea."

First date and they were already talking kids. Wes could see how easy it would be to plan their whole life together. He needed to slow down. Granted, these were things he never discussed with Apollo. There was no future planned for them. Never in three years did they even discuss moving in together. Apollo lived a day at a time and didn't make plans beyond the week, let alone a lifetime. Maybe Wes was rushing into things with Cameron.

"Anyway, this is date one. Assuming we have more of these, there's plenty of time to talk kids and family, and all that. You should at least take me to dinner first before we start planning the wedding." Humor was

Wes's fallback in this scenario, and it did the trick of eliciting a grin from Cameron, who could finally look him in the eye again.

The large man chewed on his bottom lip for a second. "Would you be open to that? Dinner, I mean? I would love to take you out." His fingers drummed on the coffee cup.

Wes smiled widely. "Let's get through the coffee date first, and then yes, I would love to get dinner with you."

I would love to do a lot of things with you, he thought.

But there would be plenty of time for that. He wasn't going to repeat the same mistakes he made in his last relationship. Wes didn't want things with Cameron to be all about sex. Not that sex wasn't great and important to him, but like he had told Apollo for years, he wanted more than just that. He wanted passion and compassion, love and laughter with his partner. That person needed to be someone he could rely on and would rely on him. Wes wanted a partner, not to be a sex toy for an emotionally unavailable person.

Wes contemplated laying out all his emotions now, getting it out of the way, so Cameron knew exactly what he was looking for in a relationship, but then thought better of it. That needed to be a gradual process, not necessarily a slow one, but things they could discuss over a series of dates, rather than dump his heart out on the table and hope Cameron didn't split. More time with the witch was what Wes wanted. He didn't want to drive him away on their first date.

Instead, they spent the next hour talking about their families and growing up. Cameron was patient and kind and didn't pry when Wes wasn't comfortable talking extensively about his childhood. Their upbringings were so completely different. Cameron was surrounded by a large family, with his sisters, including his twin, and more cousins than he could keep track of. His was an old magic family, some of the first in America. Their family grimoire was so stuffed full that they had to keep adding blank pages every decade or so.

"Do you want to learn more magic? I don't know much about what being a guardian means, but I'm sure there's still lots you can do," Cameron asked, his chin resting on his hands.

Wes leaned against the table, wanting to be closer to Cameron so much he didn't even realize how far he had moved. He was used to the question; Lily and Brie brought it up all the time. "I mean, yeah, I would love to know more. Right now I'm a one-trick pony kind of guy. It's just, I don't want to waste anyone's time if that's all I can do."

Cameron didn't hesitate in his response. He eagerly dropped his hands and leaned across the table, mimicking Wes's posture, their faces nearly touching. "My sisters could help. Well, my twin Camilla could. She actually teaches young kids the basics of magic, so she's used to working with newbies."

Wes screwed up his face, unsure if he was offended or relieved at Cameron's offer. "Are you calling me a child?" He kept his face neutral, not accusing, but also kept himself from smiling at the way Cameron's face turned to horror.

"Fuck, no, that's not what I meant. Goddess above, I am so sorry. I didn't mean that... you clearly aren't... no, you are definitely a man, not a child. It's just that ... I..." Cameron stumbled over his words, face red with embarrassment. Wes needed to put him out of his misery.

He reached across the table and placed a slender hand on Cameron's large one. "Relax. Breathe. I was just joking. I'm sorry, I didn't mean to make you panic. Honestly, I am basically a child when it comes to magic. If she's up to teaching a hopeless guardian like me, then I would love her help. I need to stop putting it off." Cameron's shoulders eased away from his ears, and the horrified look melted from his face. His smile returned, though it was more tentative, and his cheeks held the light blush.

"Sorry, I didn't mean to offend you. I let my mouth go faster than my brain sometimes. All the time, actually. Moral of the story, I don't think you are a child, obviously, otherwise I wouldn't be here. My sister is a great teacher and I may have already asked her if she would give you magic lessons. Did I screw that up too? I shouldn't have presumed you would want that. Just thought I should ask before, just in case." Cameron was spiraling into embarrassment again. Wes couldn't help the smile creeping across his face. The man was too cute and flustered so easily.

Wes didn't remove his hand from Cameron's, opting instead for a gentle reassuring squeeze of his fingers. "It was very thoughtful of you. Even if I said no, it was good to give her a heads-up. Don't worry, okay? I'm really grateful that you thought of me, that you remembered."

They stared into each other's eyes, and Wes was mesmerized by Cameron's striking gaze. Green eyes that he could get lost in drew him in, offering promises of sunlit mornings and endless joy. Wes wanted so badly to reach out and take that. Craved it. Still, there was hesitation lingering in the back of his mind. As much as he wanted that joy, he was afraid of being hurt all over again.

Cameron flipped his hand over and held onto Wes's hand, finally drawing Wes out of his own head. Cameron's hand was warm and rough, much larger than Wes's own slender fingers and narrow palm. A tingle ran up Wes's arm and filled his whole body with electricity from that point of contact.

Wes turned his attention to the table where their hands were joined, loving the image of his hand encased in Cameron's dominating grip as the larger man began to run his thumb along Wes's knuckles. "I really like you, Wes. And I'm trying not to mess this whole thing up by being weird and awkward. But that's who I am. I'm a very awkward guy. If you give me a chance, I can promise I get a little less awkward with time."

There was a pleading in his eyes mixed with a small bit of trepidation. Wes needed to erase that look. He didn't want Cameron to plead or be worried about rejection. While he wasn't sure how things would go relationship-wise, Wes knew with absolute certainty that falling in love with Cameron would be as easy as breathing. And maybe, he would be okay with that.

Maybe.

"Just so we're clear, I am the epitome of awkward, so I think we'll be good," Wes said, his tone light and playful.

Cameron smiled so big that the crinkle on the bridge of his nose appeared. It was the cutest thing Wes had ever seen, and he wanted to make it appear as often as he could.

CHAPTER 10

Wes didn't expect to start magic lessons so soon. He figured it would take a few weeks for Camilla to have a break in her schedule and then he would meet her and they could set up some time.

So Wes was pretty nervous as he sat in his living room the following Friday evening with Cameron and his twin sister, Camilla, parked on his couch for his first magic lesson. Cameron had offered to stay with him and give him tips if he wanted, and Wes had eagerly accepted. Not that he didn't feel comfortable at the idea of being alone with Camilla, though he didn't know her. It was just an added comfort having Cameron there.

He needn't have worried, though. Camilla was as warm and inviting as her twin. Her hair was the same shade of chocolate brown and fell in long waves down her back. The same green eyes as Cameron's twinkled with pure happiness. She was just as tall as Cameron, a towering Amazon of a woman even in flat, stylish shoes. In almost every way, she was identical to Cameron, save for a few softer places in her slightly pronounced curves and smooth face.

"So you two look scary similar. That must have been fun growing up," Was said lamely, for lack of a better opening. He had no idea how he was supposed to approach this.

Camilla's answering laugh was booming and filled the whole room. "Yeah, we get that a lot. We're actually identical twins, even though I'm definitely prettier. We did used to swap places when we were kids just to mess with the adults, which I'm sure every set of twins does at some point. But then I started estrogen and well, Cam here doesn't have boobs, so the game was up."

Cameron smiled at his sister. "She's definitely prettier than me. Even when we were young, she rocked a dress way better than I did. How that happens when you're identical, I don't even know. Probably has to do with confidence." The two of them laughed, sharing a knowing look between them.

"Sounds like you two had a fun childhood." Wes kept his tone neutral. Just because his childhood was shit, didn't mean others didn't grow up with loving full families. Maybe when he was younger, he was bitter and jealous about that. But after he was placed with Maddy and then Brie came along, he realized that while his family was unconventional, they still loved each other fiercely.

"It was pretty great. And our family was very supportive of us. I would say we came out well-adjusted. Mostly," Camilla said, winking at Wes. Heat filled his cheeks because it turned out that Camilla was just as charming as her brother.

"Excuse you, Cammy, but you have a very serious partner, in case you forgot. Stop flirting with my boyfriend." Cameron's eyes widened, realizing he let something slip. "I mean, we haven't made anything official. I... it was just something I said. We can talk about it, but like, we don't have to label anything yet. I'm sorry?" Wes enjoyed how flustered he became. But he loved it more that Cameron had called him his boyfriend. It felt right, even though they had only had one coffee date and a dinner date. And that was all in one day. They had talked every night on the phone over the week, something Wes never did, and texted all throughout the day. Wes could just picture Cameron's phone screen covered in flour while he texted from the bakery, that adorably shy smile on his face.

"Tim is the love of my life, and knows I'm with him until the day one of us dies," she laughed, and it was so loud and joyful that Wes couldn't help but smile. "Anyway, enough chit-chat boys. It's time to get to work. First, I want to see what kind of magic you can do, Wes, and then we can go from there."

Now it was Wes's turn to be flustered. It was one thing to use his magic in the heat of the moment; he didn't have to think about what he was doing or have someone actually study how he did it. This was different. Camilla was essentially expecting him to do a placement test of his magical abilities. Babies had better magical aptitude than he did. Probably.

"It's not much. I'm just letting you know now so you won't be disappointed," he said, with the hope that would lessen her expectations.

Camilla smiled reassuringly. "Just do your best, and don't be embarrassed." Easier said than done.

But then he felt Cameron's hand on his and a comforting squeeze there. While Wes didn't feel at all confident in himself, the gesture still settled his anxiety. Cameron was not the kind of person to judge someone for their shortcomings, and if Camilla was anything like her twin, she wouldn't either.

Wes took a deep breath and reached into his magic. It was like a warm light inside him, its own little sun that sat nestled within his ribcage, cozied up to his heart. The warm feeling moved outward from its contained space as he called upon it. Down his arm, he felt the light tingles start to form and in his mind's eye, he pictured the glowing blue light sword. One of the last bits of magic his parents taught him before their death was to create the symbol of the guardians, their sword.

It barely had any weight in his hand as he called it forth. Wes could vaguely remember when he was young and trying to adjust to using a sword that barely weighed anything. There had been a lot of bruised knees from over-extending. Wes wished he could remember more of that time. Not just his magical training, but the everyday life he had with his parents. The foods they had for dinner. What his parents talked about around him. He wished he could remember the flow of Spanish around him, but that was something lost to him once he was placed in foster care with non-Spanish-speaking people.

"Well, that's impressive. And it's functional?" Camilla asked, her eyes examined the glow of the sword.

Wes held the sword for a few seconds longer before letting the magic dissipate and the warmth retreat back into his chest. "Functional against dummies, sure. I've only used it in combat once against a werewolf, which would have worked out better had I known what I was doing." His laugh was self-deprecating, but it was the truth. He may have landed a solid blow against the werewolf while trying to save his sister, but if Ezra hadn't been there, Wes would absolutely be long dead.

"An offensive weapon is good to have, and we can definitely work with that. Show me what else you can do? Doesn't have to be anything as showy as a sword," Camilla urged. She sat back in her chair, and waited, one ankle crossed gracefully over the other.

Cameron shot Wes a wide smile and gave him a reassuring nod. Wes took a deep breath and closed his eyes. He wracked through his brain trying to think about what he knew. There was nothing. Besides the sword, what did he even know? Lily had taught him a few tricks over the years while she worked with Brie to see if any magic would materialize with her. It didn't, but Wes picked up a few things. Not that coaxing a flower to bloom would be helpful right now, which was the bulk of Lily's lessons.

Camilla seemed to sense his turmoil. "Let's try this a different way so you don't feel so put on the spot. Why don't you try conjuring a light? Nothing too big, just a small manifestation of the magic within you will do." Wes's eyes opened and snapped to hers. The woman smiled, her demeanor soft and encouraging. Though he knew she didn't intend for it, she made him feel like a child.

"Hey, you got this. Okay?" Cameron said with a soothing voice, and Wes let his shoulders relax a little at Cameron's comforting words. He hadn't even realized how tense his body had become.

Wes nodded, then closed his eyes again and held his hands out to focus on that magical warmth within. It filled his veins, spread through every inch of him. This was what Wes loved most about magic; not about what it could do for him, but how it made him feel when he called upon it. It made him feel closer to the family he couldn't remember, to generations of guardians that had faithfully served the Morrigan. Not that he cared much for that old bitch. It was her fault Brie had died. It didn't matter that Ezra had been able to bring her back to life; she was still dead for a few minutes. But that connection to his ancestors was what mattered the most, what made the magic so special to him.

His focus started to waver. The warmth that spread through his body started to heat up, and what was once a cozy feeling began to feel like an inferno. Wes opened his eyes to see a ball of light had formed between his palms. But it grew larger, more unstable, and before he could stop it, the light expanded into a miniature explosion.

The three of them were blown back into their seats and the windows in Wes's living room blew out. Glass rained down onto the floor and onto the grass outside.

"Is anyone hurt? Camilla? Wes?" Cameron's voice sounded far away to Wes's ears, muffled by a much louder ringing in his head.

"Wes! Wes! Wes!" But he could barely hear through the ringing and his own disorientation. Warm hands gripped his shoulders and gave him a light shake. Wes turned his attention upward to Cameron's concerned face, his big green eyes widened in fear, his plush lips moved to form Wes's name again.

Then sound, and a bit of his senses, came rushing back to him, and with it came the crushing weight of humiliation. "I'm fine. Fuck. Fuckity, fuck! What just happened?" Wes gripped his head, fingers tangling in the long curls on one side of his head while on the other his fingers scrambled through stubble.

"Well, it seems like you were, to put it bluntly, feeling some shit. And sometimes when we have big emotions, we have big explosions," Camilla said, then made a face. "Sorry, I work with kids, and explosions are pretty common. That wasn't even in the top ten biggest I've been through. Six-year-olds with ADHD can level a city block given the right conditions."

She turned in her seat to face the mess of windows. With a gentle wave of her hand toward the gaping hole where the windows should be, the glass on both sides rose into the air and fit itself back into place until the windows were whole again. It was as if they had never been broken to begin with. She faced Wes and Cameron again. "I'll teach you that one. I came up with that specifically because of the six-year-olds."

"I think you're going to have your work cut out for you," Wes grumbled. Magic lessons somehow seemed even more daunting now.

"Hey, don't think like that. That was a really impressive explosion. The last time I had a magical freakout, all the dough I had proofing baked instantaneously. Hours of work and none of the bread was worth eating. Perfectly baked bread isn't worth eating if it's still underproofed." Cameron laid a hand on Wes's knee, and that was more than enough to bring Wes out of his own head. He was heating up from something entirely different from magic.

There was a charged moment between them, with Cameron looking Wes in the eye and the two of them simply stared at each other. Wes felt his whole body concentrate on that one point of contact. Cameron's cheeks colored, a pretty pink flush to his cheeks.

"Okay, well, I'm going to go, because this is getting awkward for me." Camilla's voice broke through the spell. For a minute there, Wes had completely forgotten that he wasn't alone with Cameron. He felt his face warm from embarrassment this time, and he turned his face away from Cameron.

Cameron moved away from Wes and back toward his sister. Camilla stood, a towering figure over Wes's seated form. "Wes, it was good to meet you. Why don't we call it a day and we can meet up again this time next week to officially start some training? I have an idea of what we're dealing with so I can come up with some kind of lesson plan. Cam." She turned to her twin. "Try to keep it in your pants today. He just had an emotional moment, and doesn't need your tongue down his throat right away."

With that, Camilla sauntered out the door, hips swaying as she went. Wes didn't know who was more embarrassed, him or Cameron. But both of them were bright red at Camilla's parting words.

"Don't listen to her. I wasn't... not after... not that it was a bad thing. I ... uh ... don't want to take advantage of the situation. You know what, I'm just going to stop talking now before I dig myself any deeper." Cameron promptly shut his mouth and wouldn't look at Wes.

A laugh bubbled up in Wes's throat. It was so adorable the way Cameron got flustered so easily. It was so cute that he blushed so easily around Wes. Not that Wes was any better. The feeling of being desired was intoxicating. It had been so long since Wes had felt that way.

Wes scratched a frayed edge on the knee of his jeans. "I mean, we could do some kissing without tongue. I'm not that emotional. Maybe it'll even calm me down."

He felt Cameron's stare on him, heating his skin further. Tentatively, Wes turned his face toward Cameron. The look the bigger man gave him was serious and sultry. "Wes, let me be perfectly clear. When I kiss you, you will be anything but calm."

If he hadn't been sitting, Wes wasn't sure he would have been able to stand from how weak his knees went and how hard his dick got from that look alone. Cameron's words sent shivers down his spine, and more than anything, Wes wanted him to make good on that promise.

"I'm not opposed to that," Wes said, biting his bottom lip. He wasn't sure if he was flirting well or not. He was a little rusty because, with Apollo, flirting stopped happening a long time ago.

Cameron's eyes were dark, his pupils blown wide. Before Wes could process what was happening, Cameron pulled him up out of the chair, gripped the back of his neck, and kissed him.

There was nothing soft about the kiss. It was fire and claiming and despite the promise of no tongue, it took no time for Cameron's tongue to brush over Wes's lips anyway, demanding entrance. Wes didn't hesitate to open up and let Cameron claim his mouth. And it wasn't just his mouth Cameron claimed, it was Wes's whole body. Cameron pulled Wes close, his strong arms wrapped around Wes's waist and his large hand pressed against the small of Wes's back.

Wes didn't know what to do with his hands. What did anyone do with their hands when a gorgeous green-eyed giant kissed the life out of them? With nowhere else to consider, Wes snaked his arms around Cameron's neck, draping them behind his head. He wanted to fist his fingers in Cameron's hair, but thought better of it. The other man was in control and Wes was along for the ride.

Long minutes after they started kissing, Cameron pulled away. Their foreheads rested together, noses touching as they breathed heavily together. "That was ... wow. Um... well, hello to you too." He couldn't think of anything witty or charming, and certainly not cool to say. Wes's mind had been blown by that kiss. It was everything he had ever hoped for, not just with Cameron, but with anyone. No kiss had ever come close to that. He was ruined for all other kisses.

Cameron gently rubbed the tip of his nose against Wes's, his eyes closed. It was so intimate and so soft. It made Wes's soul cry out with joy. Nobody had ever held him like that, never made small gestures of affection. He didn't even know he had been missing it because it had never been there. Not in a romantic sense, anyway. With Maddy and Brie, there were always physical shows of affection and love, but this was different.

Cameron's laugh was breathy, and his smile was blinding as he pulled away. He opened his eyes, and they sparkled with mirth. Wes was completely mesmerized by that look. "Hi. Sorry, I didn't mean to just attack like that. But you just looked so cute and I couldn't help myself. Camilla said I should take things slowly after all that, but she's used to me not listening to her." He laughed again and his warm breath washed over Wes's face.

"I should probably get going. I have some prep to do for tomorrow's bakes." Cameron drew away, though reluctance showed on his face.

Wes felt a pang of disappointment and with it came the realization that he wanted to spend the whole day with Cameron. But that was asking too much too soon. The last thing he wanted was to be needy again. Apollo had made him believe that it was not becoming of a partner. Not that he thought they were partners yet, even if Cameron had called him his boyfriend.

His face must have betrayed his emotions, because Cameron stepped back into Wes's space and cupped his cheeks in his large, calloused hands. "I really don't want to leave. I like spending time with you, Wes. Do you think we could get dinner after I'm done at the bakery?" Cameron's eyes were large and earnest, and Wes melted at the sight. How was Cameron so in tune with his emotions so quickly? Wes wasn't even that aware of his own feelings most of the time.

"I would like that," Wes said, leaning into the comfort of Cameron's palms. The smile on Cameron's face stretched even wider, and he leaned in and pressed a soft kiss to Wes's lips. Minutes later, he was out the door with a promise to text Wes later once he left the bakery. Wes watched from the newly repaired window as Cameron made his way to his car, waving at Wes before he got in and sped off.

CHAPTER 11

"So you guys are like a thing? Officially?" Brie asked, a slice of pizza poised in front of her mouth. She took a large bite after her question was out there. She and Lily sat perched on the couch, hovering over the pizza boxes on his coffee table; pepperoni lovers for him and Brie, and a veggie pizza for Lily, which both St. James siblings scoffed at. Without Ezra around, there was no one to shame them into eating vegetables. Candy lounged in her own chair, a Hawaiian pizza on her lap that held her full attention for the moment.

Wes quickly swallowed the last bite of his first slice. "Yeah. I mean, we've had a few dates. A lot of kissing, which holy shit, he could go pro with those lips, and yeah, we're like a thing." He couldn't help the grin that spread over his face, so he kept his focus down on the plate of pizza balanced on his lap. If his sister caught his face, she would no doubt tease the hell out of him.

But it didn't matter, because Lily definitely saw. "Oh my Goddess, you are smitten! I knew you would be! You two are perfect for each other. I'm not saying

I made this happen, but I was a small influence." She sat back in her seat, a playfully smug smile on her face.

Brie gave her a light backhanded slap. "Small influence, my ass. You literally orchestrated things so they would always be around each other. Don't tell me you didn't start getting chummy with Cameron because of that vision. You've spent a solid year, at least, trying to get them together."

"A year? Lils, seriously?!" Wes glared at her. He didn't know exactly how he felt about that. Could he have spent the last year in a loving relationship with Cameron instead of the torture that came from being with Apollo? Or would things have worked out at all? Maybe Wes would have been too needy and scared him off. He wished he would have seen the signs that Lily was pushing them together. He just thought they naturally gravitated toward each other and he really liked Cameron as a person, anyway. But would they have done anything if Lily hadn't been pushing behind the scenes?

Wes couldn't decide if he should be angry at Lily's interference, or if he wanted to kiss her for helping him have a chance with Cameron. Lily being Lily made the decision for him, because he could never be angry at her. "You should have been more overt about it. Your subtlety cost me a year of wasted time with Apollo," he said, his tone snarky.

"*You* wasted your time with Apollo. We all tried to tell you the relationship was bad," Candy said, though she didn't lift her attention from her pizza. She looked at it like she was having a spiritual experience.

She was right, obviously. Every person in the room had told him on multiple occasions that he needed to end things with Apollo and he hadn't listened to any of them until he was too miserable to go on.

"Nobody asked you, Patrice!" Wes exclaimed loudly and then started to crack up with laughter. Lily and Brie laughed along with him, while Candy shoveled the rest of the slice in her mouth. "But yes, you're right. It's 'I told you sos' around the room. You ladies are so smart. Now shut up." Wes turned his attention to the TV screen that had been playing *Clueless* for the last hour, which Brie had deemed an underrated classic and the best interpretation of *Emma* ever created. An opinion with which Wes heartily agreed.

"So, is Paul Rudd like a vampire or something? Is that why he hasn't aged since this movie?" Candy asked the group, finally setting her pizza box on the coffee table. Ever since she found out about magic and the magical world, she would ask random questions to anyone nearby. Usually, they were about spells and the different creatures that lived in New Britain. But occasionally, she would ask about random celebrities or bizarre myths. Those questions usually were directed toward Lily.

"He's actually a lich. He's been around forever. From stories my granny has told, he's actually called something like Paltranko Rudnitsky and he was a powerful wizard before he liched himself. Now he just gets bored every few centuries and tries something new and big. He'll eventually have to disappear and go off to where he goes for another century or so," Lily explained as she sipped on her second glass of wine.

"How does somebody 'lich' themselves?" Candy leaned forward in her chair and kept her focus all on Lily.

But Lily only shrugged. "It's nasty business. You have to be insanely powerful, and probably just plain old insane, at least a little. I mean, it's basically like killing yourself and stuffing your soul into another object for all eternity. I've never seen it done, and I'm hoping to keep that track record." Lily's tone, while light and airy, as Lily always was, had just enough edge to end the conversation there.

Wes knew very little about liches, but he knew enough to understand why Lily didn't want to think about it. That kind of magic didn't just change you physically, but it left a permanent stain on your soul.

"Couldn't do it the old-fashioned way and get a vampire to bite him. He had to get immortality the hard way. Work smarter, not harder, Paul," Brie yelled at the screen. "Not that I'm one to talk. I work slow and dumb." His sister laughed to herself. He knew she was struggling with some of her research, and the never-ending digital records project at the shop was, well, never-ending. All of it frustrated Brie to no end.

"Anyway, enough about Paul Rudd, tell us more about your new boyfriend and when you're seeing each other again!" Lily clapped her hands, getting them all to focus back on Wes, who blushed under the scrutiny.

"There's not much to tell. It's not like we've fucked yet, but like I said, the kissing is nice. He's having me over for dinner at his place this weekend. I really hope the man can cook as well as he bakes because I am not eating all that day in preparation." One of Maddy's lessons stuck out in his mind at the thought. *People show you how much they appreciate you by how much of your food they eat.* Not that Maddy ever had to worry about Wes and Brie not eating her cooking. The pair of them as teenagers had been bottomless pits when it came to food, especially Maddy's cooking. She gave them their appreciation of spices with her Cajun cooking, something she tried and only moderately succeeded in teaching her adopted children. Wes and Brie could cook, they just didn't want to take the time.

"I bet he can cook really well. I mean, I've had his baked goods, and damn, they really are pure magic. Do you think maybe we could double date and he could cook for all of us?" Brie turned toward her brother with big pleading eyes.

Wes shoved her away with a hand on her face. "Your husband feeds you enough good food. You don't need to encroach on my dates, scavenger."

Brie pouted for a second. "But he's always trying to feed me greens and vegetables. It's like he just wants me to die." She threw herself back against the couch dramatically while the rest of them chuckled at her antics.

While he wouldn't mind a double date with his sister and his brother-in-law, right now, all he wanted was as much alone time with Cameron as he could get. No dick-blocking sister was going to get in his way of becoming more acquainted with Cameron in so many different ways.

"Because that's what anybody wants; their younger sibling tagging along for date night," Candy deadpanned, and Wes was starting to wonder if Candy wasn't the physic one in the bunch with how often she had been calling him out on his inner thoughts. She continued before Wes could think about it further. "My mom made my older brother take me on a date once with his girlfriend because she didn't know about the girlfriend. I was thirteen. It was the worst. For all of us. And then we had to lie to Mom about having a good time bowling." She closed her eyes and shuddered, repressing a memory.

The St. James siblings caught each other's eye and for a second, there was silence. Then they burst out laughing, falling onto each other's shoulders while they did. Laughing with his friends and sister was the perfect way to spend the evening.

For so long, Wes had felt like he had to force himself to laugh and enjoy himself, knowing that at a moment's notice, he would be expected to upend his night to snap to Apollo's whims. And the time he did spend with the people who were important to him, well, that was mostly filled with him feeling sorry for himself because of his relationship. Being happy and excited about a relationship was much better than the alternative.

Wes didn't find himself constantly checking his phone throughout the night like he used to and instead got to enjoy every bit of the time with his friends. Cameron texted him at the start of the evening to tell him to have fun and to confirm their dinner plans for the next day. Wes was already amazed as he discovered what a healthy relationship could be.

Hours later, after everyone had gone and Wes had just slid into his bed, he sent a message off to Cameron.

[Wes: Took your advice and had fun tonight.]

[Cameron: I'm glad. Now get some sleep, I don't you falling asleep during dinner]

[Wes: Night!]

He plugged his phone in and turned away from it. It was best that it was out of sight. Otherwise, Wes might have picked the phone back up and called Cameron. He wanted to hear his voice fill the quiet, dark room. But that would come off as too clingy and Wes didn't want to feel like he was demanding attention. Then again, he also didn't want to force attention onto Cameron. The whole complexity of what it meant to be a partner in a healthy relationship seemed more nuanced than being in a toxic one. Wes didn't know the rules yet, didn't know how much he could push or pull, what would elicit emotion, and what would leave him feeling empty when it came to Cameron.

No wonder he had stayed with Apollo for so long. Wes had learned all the rules about what their relationship was. And there had been a lot to learn and most of it the hard way, leading to a lot of personal embarrassment for Wes. But then it got easy because he knew what he could do. Even then, Wes slipped and tried to push what he and Apollo had into being something more. Something it was never going to be.

Now, with Cameron, everything was so new. Wes didn't know the rules, didn't have the playbook for this relationship, and that scared him more than he wanted to admit. Because with Cameron, it wasn't about sex. They hadn't even slept together yet. There was a deeper connection between them, one that wasn't purely physical. Cameron didn't see him as another conquest or an on-call fuck buddy. Cameron actually wanted to spend time with him and be around him, and just enjoy his company. The thought alone made Wes completely happy, and he fell asleep with a smile on his face at the thought of seeing Cameron the next day.

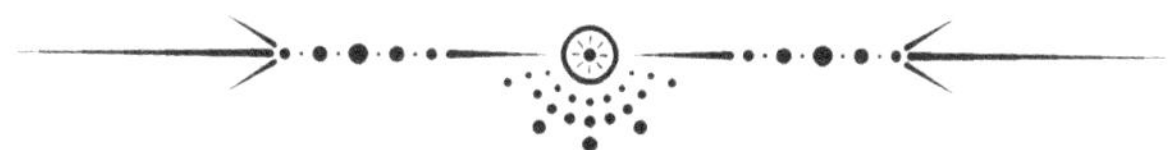

Wes didn't know what he expected Cameron's house to look like. He said he lived with Camilla, but Wes figured it would be something like his house, a cute bungalow-style only stuffed with more people.

Cameron's house was not a cute, small bungalow.

For one, it was not small. The house was at least three stories tall and seemed to expand in each direction. The whole thing was painted a light yellow that was either welcoming or needed to be washed. That there were not enough windows for the amount of wall space was the second thing Wes noticed. Which led him to his next observation. He could see several entrances into the house from where he stood on the sidewalk. At least three, and he was sure there was at least one behind the house if he had to guess. The pathway up to what Wes assumed was the main door was cleared of snow and ice.

Careful steps took him up to the nearest door. The front door opened just as he raised his fist to knock. Standing there, in a well-worn yellow apron, was Cameron, a flour smudge on his left cheek and a wide grin on his face. "You made it!" He sounded delighted and surprised, like he wasn't entirely sure Wes was going to show up.

"I made it. And I brought wine," Wes said, holding up the bottles of wine he'd brought, one red and one white, since he didn't know what Cameron was making. Wes prided himself on the fact that both wines cost more than ten dollars and, hopefully, wouldn't give him a headache.

Cameron's beautiful green eyes lit up with his smile. "Perfect. Come in. I'm just finishing up in the kitchen. Camilla is at Tim's tonight, so we have the place to ourselves." He stepped aside to let Wes in and then walked down a bright hallway toward the kitchen. The house smelled amazing, like bread and spices.

The kitchen was huge, a true chef's kitchen, and clearly indicated the house had seen a remodel or two since it contained a large island in the middle, as well as a full range stove. The most surprising thing, which took the place of honor in the kitchen, was a large wood-fired oven. It was set into the wall, a hulking brick thing, and was clearly well-loved.

"You built your house around a whole-ass pizza oven?" Wes asked, his tone incredulous, and his eyes firmly fixed on the thing in question.

Cameron rubbed the back of his neck sheepishly, and Wes found his attention turning toward how Cameron's large hands slipped through his shiny brown strands. "I wouldn't say built. This house is like two hundred years old. But we did a few modifications to incorporate it into the kitchen. One of the handy things about magic is saving on contractor bills and rearranging the structure of the house." Cameron let his hand fall to his side, his cheeks a little pink. "Besides, it's my favorite part of the house. I bake everything in it. All my breads and pizzas. Which, speaking of pizza, that's what we're having tonight. I know it seems basic, but trust me, you've never had my pizza. My nan perfected the sauce recipe and so far, I'm the only one she's given it to."

He beamed with pride at that fact, and Wes had to laugh. "Bet she tells all her grandkids that," Wes said with a chuckle.

Cameron's smile didn't waver, though. "Probably. She gives out her recipes to the family constantly. But only the family."

"For the record, pizza is literally my favorite food. There is no more perfect food out there. Fair warning, if it's as good as everything else you make, then I will probably move in and stay with you forever just so you can feed me." Wes let the lightness in his chest expand. Even with things being so new with Cameron, the idea of spending forever with the giant man actually sounded like the perfect thing. It would be the kind of life Wes always wanted.

In three quick strides, Cameron invaded Wes's space. His smile was no longer innocent, it was a true grin, with his eyes dark and lids heavy. Wes wasn't a short man, he was over six feet, but Cameron still had a few inches on him. With a firm grip on his chin, Cameron tilted Wes's face up to his and before Wes could fully prepare himself, Cameron's lips were on his. The thumb resting on Wes's chin pressed against his skin, urging him to open farther. With a soft moan between them, Wes opened to Cameron's tongue, and the larger man wasted no time in deepening the kiss.

Wes wanted to be closer. There was still too much space between their bodies. He wrapped his arms around Cameron's middle, pulling him close, erasing the space between their chests. With his hand still gripping Wes's face, Cameron snaked his hand around Wes's waist and pushed against the small of his back. His hand moved lower, palming and gripping tightly at Wes's ass. Wes moaned and his hips bucked involuntarily at the touch. His jeans felt too tight suddenly as his dick strained against the fabric of his already tight jeans. Against his stomach, he could feel Cameron was equally affected, an impressive girth rising between them, if not obscenely long.

Never in his life had Wes been so turned on. Nothing with Apollo had ever been like this, where he felt so claimed, so desired, and yet so cherished. Without meaning to, Wes's hands started to work on autopilot. He released his hold around Cameron's middle and brought his hands between their bodies. His fingers scrambled for Cameron's pants, but he forgot the apron was still tied around the other man, blocking his hands from latching onto Cameron's waistband.

Wes made quick work of pulling the offending garment aside and reached to unbutton the other man's pants. But Cameron pulled away half a step, putting space between them. He placed his large hands over Wes's, stilling them on the button of his jeans. "Wes," he breathed, resting his forehead against Wes's, breathing hard against his lips.

Mortification coursed through Wes, and he took a large step away from Cameron. "Fuck, I'm sorry. I ... I thought you wanted me to like, you know ... I fucked this up." He couldn't even look at Cameron. Being with Apollo had made him immediately go to sex, whether he was in the mood or not. He was used to it. Walk in, make out a little, and then get on his knees. It was the routine Wes knew best.

But Cameron wasn't Apollo. Maybe he didn't even want to sleep with Wes yet, or at all. And there was Wes, pushing things before Cameron was ready because he had been trained to keep his dick out of his pants.

"I should–"

"Don't go! You didn't do anything wrong. I want that, I do. I just don't want you to feel like you have to, you know? I," Cameron stepped forward, back into Wes's space, crowding him, "I just want us to enjoy being around each other. We don't have to rush into anything. You just got out of a bad relationship, and I'm guessing since it was with an incubus, everything revolved around sex. I want to do that with you, Wes. But let's take things slow. I want what we have to be more than just sex."

He pulled Wes into his arms, not tight, but gentle, and warm, and safe. Wes still felt overwhelmingly embarrassed, despite Cameron's words. "I'm fucked up. I know. I really like you and you're right. I'm so used to how things were with Apollo that I don't know what a functional relationship is anymore." Things had started off so well, and now Wes felt like he had ruined it.

Cameron cupped Wes's cheeks and tilted his face up so Wes couldn't avoid his green-eyed gaze. "I can be patient. You're not fucked up, you were just in a fucked up situation. You don't owe me anything and we don't have to do anything because you feel like you have to. So yeah, let's take things slow for now."

Wes searched his face, looking for any signs of an ulterior motive, something he would expect to see from Apollo. But all he saw with understanding, gentleness, and still a hint of lust. It was everything Wes wanted, and he wasn't sure he deserved it. No, fuck that, he did deserve it. Wes deserved to be happy and to get what he wanted for a change.

"Yeah, slow. I need to, like, reprogram my brain. And I can start doing that by eating pizza. You lured me here with the promise of food, you should deliver on that," Wes said lightly, trying to break the mood so he didn't have to continue with his introspection. Maybe it wasn't the smoothest segue, but it was the best he could come up with to salvage the night.

It was the right thing to say, apparently, because Cameron's face broke out into a huge grin, and the little crinkle between his eyes was visible. Wes had already decided that was his favorite part of Cameron's body, that little crinkle at the bridge of his nose. That, more than his laugh or smile, meant he was truly happy, that nothing about his smile was fake. And every time Wes saw it, which was often during their dates, he wanted to lean forward and kiss it.

"I did lure you with food, and I will deliver on that now. You have your pick of toppings. But I warn you, this is a test and you will be judged on your choice of toppings." Cameron led him farther over to the long island where a ball of dough sat waiting next to a pan of red sauce. Several bowls were lined up beside the dough, filled with various freshly chopped vegetables and meats.

Cameron took his spot in front of the ball of dough and began to work it on the already-floured surface. In no time, he had the dough rolled out into a perfect shape for a pizza.

"What, you don't flip the dough into the air? What kind of cut-rate pizza joint is this?" Wes tried not to laugh, but he cracked a smile, anyway.

"You don't want to see me toss dough. I'm actually forbidden from doing it again," Cameron said with a straight face.

Wes raised a brow. "Why?"

Cameron simply pointed up, directly above his head. Wes followed his finger and saw a large splatter of red on the ceiling, with crusted bits around it that looked a lot like dried dough. "I may have gotten drunk at a family dinner and decided to try a pizza toss ... after I had put the toppings on. Camilla won't let me magic it away because she says it's a reminder to, and I quote, 'not let drunk Cameron do stupid shit.' So far it's worked."

Wes stared at the stain a second longer. "How long has it been there?"

"A while," Cameron laughed. Then he reached out his flour-covered hands and pulled Wes close. "Here, want to add the sauce with me?" His arm came around Wes and up to a ladle in the saucepan. Wes was forced to move right up to Cameron, leaving their bodies squished together. "Take this," Cameron said, waiting for Wes to bring his arm up to take the ladle.

Cameron's hand fell over Wes's as soon as he took the handle. Wes could barely breathe. The smell of flour and sweet dough, and a hint of cinnamon, hit him so fully that he thought he felt a little dizzy from the smell. Of course, Cameron would smell like a bakery.

"Like this," Cameron said, his voice barely registering in Wes's fuzzy head. He manipulated their hands to pour out the sauce over the dough and spread it around in circles using the back of the ladle. It was a rhythmic motion that kept Wes's eyes locked onto the sight of Cameron's hand eclipsing his own.

Once the sauce was evenly spread, Cameron took the ladle from Wes's hands and placed it back in the saucepan. He still kept his front pressed against Wes's back, warm and solid. "What do you like on your pizza?" Cameron whispered into his ear. An innocent enough question, but Wes couldn't help but shiver as Cameron's warm breath tickled his skin.

It took longer than Wes wanted for him to collect his thoughts and speak. "Anything. Unless it's green.

Basil being the exception." Why were words so hard all of a sudden?

It's pizza toppings, for fuck's sake! Wes's inner thoughts chastised himself for being so turned on by something so simple.

Cameron's laugh reverberated in his chest, and Wes felt it against his body. The feeling was delicious, and he wanted more of it. He wanted to feel all of Cameron's laughs. Every chuckle. Every smile against his lips. It had only been a few weeks, and Wes already felt himself falling and it was like nothing he had ever felt before.

"So not a health nut, I guess," Cameron said, as he reached around Wes and started to add handfuls of cheese. Wes let his body relax against Cameron's, tilting his head back until the back of his head rested on the other man's shoulder.

"Not at all. I am a teenage boy when it comes to my eating habits. But only in my eating habits," Wes added with a smirk. The rumble of Cameron's chest sent another spark of desire through his body.

"You're so godsdamn cute," Cameron said, placing a tender kiss on Wes's ear before resuming his pizza-making. Color rose to Wes's cheeks at the compliment, but he said nothing while he watched Cameron's large hands dip into a container holding pepperoni.

Wes leaned against the counter; elbows pressed against the thick wood while he watched Cameron slide their finished pizza out of the oven. It only took a matter of minutes before it was ready, half covered in pepperoni and basil, while Cameron's half was loaded with meat and a full garden's worth of veggies.

They chatted over dinner, and Wes still marveled at the ease of their conversation. Talking to Cameron was so natural, like they had known each other for years and had long established a comfortable camaradery. Except Wes spent half the time staring at Cameron's lips, watching as he took every bite of pizza. He should feel like a creep, but everything about the man was perfect.

After dinner, they cuddled on Cameron's large couch and watched a movie, though Wes couldn't recall what it was since he was so focused on the feeling of Cameron's body against his, snuggled as he was under the man's arm.

There was a tinge of disappointment when hours later Cameron announced it was getting late. *We agreed to take it slow*, Wes reminded himself as Cameron walked him to the door. At the threshold, Cameron seized him by the hips, pulled him close, and kissed him so fiercely, Wes's head began to spin. Then they said good night, and the perfect date ended.

CHAPTER 12

It was late January when the sound of Wes's phone woke him in the middle of the night.

[Unknown: Come over. I miss you.]

Wes stared at his phone, his eyes still unfocused as he read the text over again. It could only be one person. He had blocked Apollo's number. Guess he found a way around that little problem.

He hadn't heard from the incubus since the Yule party, and Wes had been thankful for the silence. For a week after, he expected Apollo to randomly show up or to find him somewhere, but he never did.

Until now.

[Unknown: Lamb, I gave you space, now let's stop playing around. Come over, I need you.]

Wes felt a pang in his heart as he read over the second text. Of course Apollo would do this after things had been going so well with Cameron. Wes was finally happy. He was enjoying his time with the witch.

Sure, they hadn't done anything more than make out so far, but Wes liked that they weren't jumping right into everything, despite how much time they spent talking or getting together. And here was Apollo trying to derail that with his booty calls and love bombing.

[Unknown: Wes, baby, I need you.]

With a sigh, and against his better judgment, Wes typed back a response.

[Wes: We're done. Please leave me alone.]

[Unknown: I don't accept that. We're good together. Why don't you come over and I'll show you just how much I appreciate you.]

There was only one way to deal with this.

[Wes: No.]

Then he blocked the number, placed the phone on his side table, and rolled over. But sleep didn't come easy. Wes expected to feel sad or regret when he thought about his former relationship. Instead, he felt angry. How dare Apollo try to pull this shit? Did he think a late night text for sex would mean everything was okay? That Wes would just up and leave his new relationship because Apollo snapped his fingers and promised blowjobs?

Yeah, he did. That's exactly what Apollo thought, because he didn't consider anyone but himself and his wants. Wes laid awake for over an hour fuming over Apollo. Again.

He didn't want to think about Apollo anymore. He had to teach in the morning and wasn't going to let his incubus ex ruin another night of sleep. Wes reached for his phone and pulled up his meditation app, putting on a sleep story to help him drift off again. He glanced at the time, it was nearly four in the morning. Cameron would be getting up in an hour to start the day's baked goods.

Wes contemplated texting him, and before he could talk himself out of it, he shot off a quick message.

[Wes: I hope you have a good day at work.]

Then he set his phone down, smiling at the thought of Cameron in his bakery, covered in flour, with a large smile on his face. It was enough to calm his emotions and let the sleep story do its work.

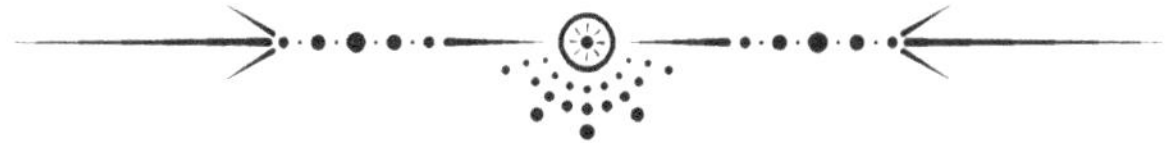

"Why don't you go visit him at the bakery?" Candy said, lounging in the chair across from Wes's desk. She had seemed lighter the last few weeks. Now that her mom was getting proper care in the Alzheimer's wing of a care facility, she was able to have a life again. Not that the guilt didn't show sometimes, but her older siblings had convinced her it was best for her and their mom, and they had been constantly checking in with

Candy to make sure she felt supported even if they couldn't be around.

"I don't want to bother him while he's working. Besides, he might be out on a delivery and then I'll probably miss him," Wes said, not looking up from the papers he was reading over.

It was like he could hear Candy's eye roll without even seeing her face. "They have these things called phones where you can just text someone and ask if they're around, Grandpa."

"Then it wouldn't be a surprise. Isn't that a romantic gesture?" Wes retorted, taking a sip from his mug, the coffee long since gone cold.

Candy scoffed. "Nobody likes to be surprised at work. It's bad form."

Wes looked up and smirked at her. "Who says 'bad form' like that anymore?"

Again, Candy rolled her eyes. "Shut up. I watched Hook last night and I've always loved Dustin Hoffman's performance. So shut up and text your boyfriend that you want to stop over."

Wes fought the urge to roll his own eyes. He wouldn't stoop to her level. "Fine," he said with some reluctance. Truth be told, he was nervous about asking to visit. What if Cameron thought he was smothering him? It was one thing to see each other at their homes or with friends, but at Cameron's place of business, that was something completely different. Wes couldn't even imagine what it would be like to have Cameron visit him at the university.

And yet he still found himself standing outside of Cameron's bakery, the Loaf Oaf, trying to tell himself that he wasn't being a total stalker. After a few minutes of standing outside the entrance, a chiming broke the quiet as the bakery door opened and Cameron popped his head out.

"Hey, Wes. Are you going to hang out here all day, or do you want to come in?" His eyes sparkled in the winter sun and his smile was just for Wes. He extended his hand out the door toward Wes, and Wes found his feet automatically moving forward to grasp the other man's hand. Warm, calloused hands against his, and Cameron's bright smile convinced Wes that coming here was the best decision he had made all week.

Cameron didn't drop his hand as he led Wes through the front of the bakery toward the back. "I'm taking my break," he called to the woman behind the counter. She nodded, but she was more engrossed with her phone and didn't look up.

Once the door to the kitchen closed, Cameron pushed Wes up against one of the high metal counters, still dusted with flour. His lips smashed against Wes's, heated and hungry. A whimper left his lips as Cameron fisted his hair, tilting his head back to deepen the kiss. Wes felt crowded with the cold rim of metal digging into his back while Cameron's body eclipsed his from the front.

It was exactly where Wes wanted to be.

He pushed his hips forward into Cameron's, eliciting a quiet groan from the other man. Cameron, however, took the opportunity to move his hands to Wes's backside, pulling him closer while he squeezed.

There would undoubtedly be flour handprints on his ass from that, but Wes couldn't care less. He would roll around in flour if it meant Cameron kept touching him. He was open to anything with Cameron.

Hot kisses trailed along Wes's jaw and down his neck as Cameron moved against him, and Wes closed his eyes to the feel of Cameron's lush lips on his skin. With shallow breaths and a heated body, Wes started to feel dizzy from all the sensations he was experiencing.

"You could bend me over this counter and I would be down with that," Wes managed to breathe out. He was so hard, so worked up, and he needed release.

But then Cameron pulled away quickly, his hands dropping from Wes's backside, and he abandoned his trail of kisses. Instead, he placed his hands on Wes's shoulders. "Wes, listen, I like you a lot, but I am not risking a health code violation for you. You're cute, but not that cute," Cameron said, trying to keep a straight face, but he failed miserably. His boyish grin cracked through, and he started to laugh.

And Wes couldn't help himself. He laughed too, his head slumping against Cameron's chest as he doubled over, his stomach cramping with the sensation of laughing so hard. "No, no, that's fair. I can keep it in my pants inside the kitchen," Wes finally said, straightening.

"Good, thank you for thinking of my business and the customers who eat here. Now, you came to see me?" Cameron gave him a small peck on his lips before pulling away to put space between them. The bigger man's eyes were still darkened, pupils blown wide, still as affected by their kiss as Wes was. Finding his breath took longer than Wes anticipated.

"I was done with classes, and I wanted to see you. Should I have texted first or was this like a bad idea and I shouldn't bother you at work?" Wes didn't know why he was suddenly freaking out about it. With a greeting like the one Cameron just gave him, clearly the other man wasn't upset about seeing Wes.

Cameron placed a finger under Wes's chin. "Hey, you should bother me at work whenever you feel like it. It's made my day seeing you." Cameron sounded so sincere and Wes knew he meant it. That was just one of the many reasons he liked Cameron so much. He was simply happy for Wes to be around. They didn't need to do anything more, they could enjoy each other's company without expectation.

"Any plans for tonight?" Cameron asked, cutting through Wes's thoughts.

He shook his head. "Not really. Well, I should say, not for the whole night. I was going to my sister's place for dinner." Then, before he could chicken out, he added, "Would you like to come?"

Cameron had hung out with Brie on many occasions, the same occasions that Wes had met him until recently. And he already knew Ezra, because everyone knew Ezra. But Wes inviting him to what amounted to a family dinner would definitely be a big step in a relationship. Were they at that stage? Sure, Wes had already met Camilla, but that was different. She was one person out of the whole family, they lived together, and she wanted to help Wes.

The smile Cameron gave him was glowing, and the adorable crinkle on the bridge of his nose appeared. "I would love that. Brie and Ezra are great, it's always nice to see them." And it would be nice for a change for his boyfriend to not hit on everyone at the table throughout the whole night. Brie had stopped letting him bring Apollo after two dinners because of that, and Wes felt, not for the first time, that he really should have listened to his little sister and friends. So much time had been wasted, and maybe that was time he could have spent with Cameron.

"They are pretty great, but I'm biased. I'll let Brie know you're coming, not that Ezra won't already prepare enough food for three times the amount of people. You might want to bring some Tupperware or something, because you'll go home with food. And there will be greens and healthy foods in there too. He's a tricky bastard like that." Wes laughed and Cameron's eyes sparkled with his own laughter.

They held onto each other for several long minutes, chatting about their day. Once again, Wes marveled at the ease of conversation between them. Before Apollo, he'd had many hookups and a few relationships but nothing was ever serious, none of them had the total ease around another person like he did around Cameron.

Apollo had been his longest relationship and even then, it was completely one-sided. The incubus never talked to him like that about mundane things. He never asked about Wes's day, or how he was feeling. When Wes was offered the associate professor position, rather than celebrate with him the way Wes wanted, with his friends, he took Wes back to his penthouse and fucked him all night. But the night wasn't about Wes, it was about Apollo. And after, when Wes got home late in the night, he felt hollow and the achievement didn't feel as great anymore.

Cameron wasn't like that. They had been dating for weeks now, and besides making out and wandering hands, they had kept things PG-13. Cameron was more interested in Wes as a person than in what his body could give him.

They stood in the back of the bakery, casually touching, as if to feel the warmth of each other without it being more. A niggling thought sat in the back of Wes's mind about whether he should tell Cameron about Apollo reaching out, but ultimately, he decided against it. What would be the point? It wasn't like Wes was going to do anything. He made his point to Apollo and now planned to ignore the incubus if he reached out again. *When* he reached out again. Wes had no doubts that he would. But that was his problem to deal with, not Cameron's.

"Do you need me to bring anything tonight?" Cameron's voice cut through Wes's thoughts. For a moment, he forgot what he was referring to before remembering the dinner.

"Nope, just yourself. Oh, and those little custard pastries! They are my favorite and my sister and I will definitely eat them all." Wes laughed and hoped that Cameron would agree to make them, as they were amazing.

Cameron laughed too, booming and full. "The quarkteilchen, yeah, those are a big hit here. I will bring what's left at the end of the day, unless you want me to bring a fresh batch."

Wes waved him off. "No, don't go through the extra work. Brie and I are food goblins. It doesn't matter to us if it's fresh. We're both foster kids, you know, and in some of our homes it was 'take what you can get.'" Wes smiled through his words, though the dull and aged pang of hurt and sadness still reverberated through him. Before Maddy, things were bad at some of the homes, and sometimes there was little to go around. With some of the larger group homes, you were lucky if things weren't stale most of the time.

But that didn't apply to his life now. Maddy had given him a good home with good food all the time. He had money to buy the groceries he wanted and needed and with everything else, he had a great brother-in-law who could cook like a professional chef.

"Well, I should get back to work. We're closing soon, and Abby has class after that," Cameron said, directing his thumb toward the front. He leaned in and planted a kiss on Wes's lips one last time.

"I'll see you tonight at seven," Wes said as he pulled away and started for the door.

Cameron winked in response, a grin on his face. Then he turned and started to clean up the counter. Wes walked out of the back and headed for the front door.

"You have flour on your butt, just so you know." Wes turned toward Abby, who stood behind the display case. She hadn't looked up from her phone.

Wes craned his neck to try to see, and just as he suspected, there were two large handprints in flour on his backside. He quickly tried to brush it off, smearing it more than actually removing it, while he flushed hot and embarrassed from head to toe. He was out the door and on his bike in seconds, trying to calm himself down on the ride home. But he rode with a huge grin on his face, looking forward to the evening ahead.

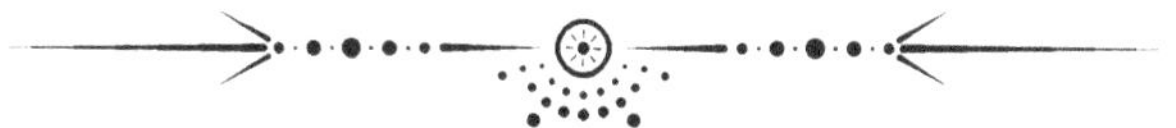

"You didn't respond, right?" Brie narrowed her eyes at her brother. Wes had just finished telling her about Apollo's messages. Because of course, Apollo would message on a day when Wes was perfectly happy. It was like the incubus knew Wes had plans and was trying his old tactics to ruin them. He had been just about ready to go to Brie and Ezra's place when the message popped up.

It was nearly the same as the first one, except it wasn't sent in the middle of the night. Apollo begged him to come over, adding more "I miss yous" and "we're so good together," like they were ever really together other than to have sex.

"No, not yet at least," Wes responded. He had instead slipped his phone back into his pocket, pressed the number two on the panel next to his door and walked through the portal Ezra had installed into the antique shop. Now, he and Brie leaned against the counter while a tourist roamed around the shelves. Normally, Brie wouldn't let them go this long. She tried to get humans out of the magical shop quickly, but her focus was so completely on her brother that she let them go.

Brie pointed an accusing finger at him. "Don't do it at all. You know how he is; he'll drag you back in and you'll be miserable again. Do not respond."

Wes sighed; she was right. And he wasn't going to respond, anyway. His days of dealing with Apollo's bullshit and love-bombing were over. Now he had Cameron, someone who treated him right and was actually interested in being his boyfriend. "I'm not. But fuck, it's not like I can avoid him forever. He's sort of already in our friend group and he comes here all the time. Eventually, I'll run into him."

"Wrong, he's not a part of *our* friend group, he's Ezra's friend. And that's more of a one-sided friendship, anyway, because Ezra gets just as annoyed at him as the rest of us. And if I could refuse him service, I would." Brie had never been a big fan of Apollo since their very first meeting. And had especially started hating him when Wes and he began dating. Or whatever they had been doing for three years.

"Believe it or not, he wasn't always so insufferable," came Ezra's voice from behind them. The man moved so stealthily that he was always creeping up on people. Only Wes jumped at the sound. Brie was used to it by now and had developed her own set of silent feet.

"Dude, don't do that!" Wes placed a hand over his racing heart, but received only a shrug from Ezra. "Was that before he became, you know, him?"

"Before his Fall, you mean? Yes, back then, he was actually nice to be around. Back then, he was a good friend, dependable, always more interested in the needs of others than his own. This place really corrupted him, he–" But Ezra was cut off from saying more by Brie.

"Oh my gods, do you mind?! Just go, you're not going to buy anything anyway," she snapped at the human customer, who had clearly been inching closer to the counter to listen in. The woman looked incredibly offended and opened her mouth to argue, but Brie cut her off as well. "Save it, lady. There is no manager. This is my place. No, I'm not losing a loyal customer. Don't care if you tell your friends. Get out."

The woman looked completely scandalized. Then she angrily clutched the strap of her purse and stomped out of the shop, the doorbell clanging loudly at her exit. "I fucking hate tourists. Nosy assholes," Brie muttered, more to herself than to the two men next to her.

"Just don't do that to our actual customers, sweetheart," Ezra said with a small affectionate smile aimed at her. He placed a gentle kiss on the top of his wife's head, and she looked up to smile back at him.

"Don't be gross, guys. I'm right here." Wes checked his phone to see the time. He half expected to get a message from Cameron canceling on him. That was something Apollo would have done; waited until the last minute to leave Wes hanging.

But, as if summoned, the shop door opened, the bell tinkling gently this time, and Cameron walked in carrying a large sealed plastic container. "Some woman told me not to come here because, and I quote, 'the owner is a real bitch who won't sell you anything.' Her words, not mine." He smiled as he walked to the trio at the counter.

Brie scoffed. "Bitch, that's the best she could come up with. I at least register as a fucking bitch, right? Should I be insulted?" She looked at her brother, and Wes nodded his head with a soft chuckle.

"So you want to be called something worse than a bitch?" Cameron asked, his brow wrinkled in confusion.

Brie rounded the counter and snatched the container of pastries from Cameron's hands. "Nobody wants to be called names, but if she's going to call me something, I expect some imagination. Bitch is so ordinary."

"And my sister is not ordinary," Wes said, beaming at Brie even as he grabbed the pastry container from her hands. She let out an indignant huff, but let him take it, anyway. There would be plenty to share between the two of them. Though their partners would be lucky to get even one.

Ezra held out his hand and pulled his wife close to his body once she had slipped her hand into his. "She is extraordinary," he whispered into her ear, though it was just loud enough for everyone to hear. Then he kissed her temple and led them all through the Storage Room door into their home.

"This is an awesome place." Cameron's eyes darted around the room, a similar reaction to the one Candy had had a few months prior. Everyone reacted the same way to Brie and Ezra's home. Even those in the magical community were awed by the casual magic of the space.

"Took me a few years to get it just right. Then this one moved in and suddenly I needed more space and furniture for all the guests I never had to deal with before," Ezra said with a small chuckle. He made his way back to the kitchen to work on dinner, while the other three took seats in the living room.

Pleasantries were exchanged between Brie and Cameron, and Wes was content to watch his sister and his boyfriend get to know each other better. All of their previous interactions had been good, and Brie had been pushing him toward Cameron for months. Well, she and Lily had. And they had been right all along. But then, Brie would have been happy for Wes to be with literally anyone other than Apollo.

"I'm really glad you two are together, finally. I love you, Wes, but seriously, I don't understand how you stayed with someone who constantly hit on everyone in your life, including me. Cameron, you seem like a decent person, and I expect you to treat my brother right. Or I will have to kick your ass." Brie lounged on the couch. Her threat held no weight, but Wes was completely sure she would find a way to make good on it if something bad happened between him and Cameron.

"Little Witch, literally everyone but you has magic. What are you going to do?" Wes laughed, patting her knee.

Brie crossed her arms and huffed. "I can still punch people. Ezra has been showing me how to fight for a while. You don't need magic if you have a fist."

"And not being able to die probably helps," Cameron added with a large smile.

"Again," mumbled Wes. Brie punched him in the arm and he had to restrain himself from rubbing the area. It actually did hurt; she had definitely gotten stronger. At least she was in a good headspace where they could joke about her dying. After everything that happened with Moloc years ago, she had been a mess. Therapy did wonders for her, but he knew from Ezra that she still occasionally had nightmares about it and woke up screaming. It had gotten better, though. She had gotten better.

Minutes later, Ezra called them all to the table for a spread of roast chicken, green beans with almonds, roasted potatoes, and the dreaded salad he insisted on for every meal. Cameron spent a considerable amount of time complimenting Ezra on each dish, making noises of appreciation as he tasted everything.

"Sweetheart, the dessert will still be there no matter how fast you eat your food," Ezra joked to his wife. Brie had been inhaling everything, while her eyes darted occasionally to the pastries on the kitchen counter. Brie loved food, especially if it was sweet. Food was something she and Wes had bonded over in their early years together.

"I really liked your family," Cameron said to Wes two hours later as they walked out of Brie and Ezra's apartment into the shop proper.

"Ezra is great. Brie is alright," Wes said with a laugh, leading the two of them to the front of the darkened shop. Cameron casually summoned a light in his hand so they could cross the room without hitting anything. Not that Wes needed the light to see. He knew the shop well enough to move around it without sight.

As Wes reached for the door, he had a sudden thought. An instant, all-consuming thought that he knew he had to act on. Whirling around to face Cameron, he gripped the ivory knit sweater Cameron wore and pulled him in for a kiss. Thick arms wrapped around Wes's body as Cameron pulled him close and Wes slid his arms up to rest around the larger man's shoulders.

There was a good chance that Brie and Ezra would be able to see what was happening in the shop with their magical security measures, but Wes couldn't find it within himself to care. All that mattered was the hot press of Cameron's body against his, muscled where he was lithe. His fingers brushed the edge of Cameron's silky brown hair, toying with the ends. Wes wasn't usually so bold, but he wanted more from Cameron, wanted to do more, and the only way he could think to get it was to initiate.

"Do you want to go to my place?" Wes asked between kisses, breathing heavy, his heart racing in his chest.

Cameron trailed hot kisses down his neck, and Wes almost forgot the question he'd just asked. "I thought we agreed to take it slow," he managed to force out between presses of his lips against Wes's skin.

"Glaciers move–aah–faster than us," Wes said, a moan breaking up his declaration.

"Get the fuck out of my shop and get a room before I get the hose," Brie's voice rang out across the room. She stood at the Storage Room door, her head peeking out around the door. Her face was covered in shadow, since Cameron had dropped the light and they were mostly in darkness. But Wes knew without a doubt there was a smile on her face, even if she didn't exactly want them to make out in the shop.

They jumped apart, hands falling away to their sides. Cold air seemed to wrap itself around Wes anywhere that was now bereft of Cameron's touch. Brie stared at them across the shop for a moment before she ducked back behind the door and it slammed closed behind her. The air was choked with tension. Wes didn't know what to do. Did he return to the question about Cameron going home with him, or did they just go their separate ways for the night after being caught by his sister as they made out like they were teenagers?

"So, your house?" Cameron asked as he grabbed Wes's hand and pulled him toward the front door.

Wes wasn't sure he had heard correctly at first before his brain caught up. He tugged on Cameron's hand to get him to stop. "My house. Come on." He pulled Cameron back toward the Storage Room door and ran his hand over the keypad until it reached the number for his house. The door clicked and Wes opened it, stepping through the portal into his living room with Cameron close on his heels.

CHAPTER 13

Wes had just enough time to thank the Goddess that he didn't have to explain the magic of the door before Cameron pulled him back and pushed him up against the front door. His lips smashed down on Wes's, taking and taking and taking from him. There was no room to breathe, no room to move. Wes was completely at the mercy of Cameron's sinful lips and wicked tongue.

Large hands gripped Wes's backside, holding him roughly, while the front of Cameron's body pinned him to the door. There was no space between them for Wes to plant his hands, so instead he wrapped his arms around Cameron's middle. He could feel every muscle in the other man's back, could feel the heat radiate from his skin even over the heavy sweater he wore.

The trail of hot kisses started down Wes's jaw, then moved lower and lower until Cameron sucked on the point where Wes's neck met his shoulder. Only the force of Cameron's hands on his ass held Wes up. His knees felt like Jell-O and were worthless at keeping him upright.

Still, he wanted more, wanted to feel more of Cameron against him. And for that, he needed several layers removed. "Get this off," Wes whined, tugging the bottom of Cameron's sweater, urging him to remove the garment.

Thrusting out his groin more to pin Wes to the door, Cameron removed his hands from Wes's body to reach behind his neck and pull the sweater over his head. He sent it flying with a quick toss over his shoulder. Cameron wasted no time getting back to his worshipping of Wes's body.

Finally, Wes had free roam of Cameron's bare chest, and it was glorious. Cameron radiated heat, like his body had adjusted itself to match the ovens he spent so much time around. Who needed sweaters or blankets when you can be wrapped up in Cameron's body for warmth?

When Cameron shivered, Wes tried to pull his hands away, worried his fingers were too cold. But Cameron tugged on his wrists and urged him to put them back on his body. "Don't stop. I like you touching me." His breath was ragged as he worked his way back up to Wes's mouth.

Wes put his hands back to work on exploring Cameron's body, allowing himself to appreciate every bit of exposed skin, his tapered waist and broad back, the toned arms, and finally his firm chest and abs which were covered in a dusting of dark brown hair all the way down to the waistband of his jeans.

His fingers grazed lightly over the front of Cameron's jeans, causing him to jerk forward, pressing farther against Wes. The moan that escaped his lips was rough and loud, and Wes wanted to hear it more. Slowly, he moved his hand across the bulge in Cameron's pants, feeling bolder as he cupped him through the fabric.

Cameron rolled his hips, jutting himself against Wes's hand. He wrapped a hand around Wes's wrist to still his motion. "You keep doing that and I'm going to cum right here." Cameron tipped his forehead against Wes's, his breathing barely under control. With one more kiss pressed against Wes's lips, Cameron put a little distance between them. "Go to your bedroom and strip," he said, his gaze unblinking on Wes.

Wes felt his spine straighten and his dick stiffen. Cameron's commanding voice made heat pool low in his stomach and he wanted more.

Wes didn't move, though. He was rooted to the spot. Lust pulsed through him, and his knees still felt weak. Cameron pulled him forward, away from the door. "Don't make me tell you again, Wesley." Cameron's voice became deeper, sultry, and commanding. He swatted at Wes's ass, which was enough to send Wes practically running to this room. Brain addled already, Wes nearly crashed through the door of his bathroom and had to retrace his steps back to his room. Clothing flew across the room as Wes removed his t-shirt, tripped over his jeans because he forgot to take his shoes off before removing his pants, and finally let everything else pile up across the room.

Standing naked in the middle of his room, Wes looked toward the bed, unsure if he should get on it or wait for Cameron. There wasn't time to think, though, as Cameron appeared in the doorway, his pupils blown wide, his face hungry. “Get on the bed,” his dark voice commanded, and Wes scrambled to obey.

Never in his life had Wes ever been so turned on. Cameron had all the control and Wes gladly relinquished it. Once he was on the bed, though, he didn’t know what to do. Did he lie down? Did he kneel?

The uncertainty didn’t last more than a second. “Sit against the headboard, Wesley.” Cameron waited as Wes positioned himself so his head rested against the wall, the headboard against his back, and waited, with his dick pointing straight up toward his stomach, rock hard. Wes felt as if he would literally die if Cameron didn’t touch him soon.

From the doorway, Cameron, still clad in his jeans, watched him. He had removed his shoes and socks. This was a side of Cameron that Wes never would have guessed. He expected sex with Cameron to be as sweet and gentle as Cameron was every day. But this, with the man’s eyes dark, a cocky grin on his face, and radiating so much BDE that Wes might cum just by looking at him, was nothing like Wes had expected.

Wes wanted more.

With lazy steps, Cameron made his way across the room, his eyes on Wes the whole time. He dipped a knee on the bed, letting his weight settle before he crawled up to Wes and sat back on his heels. Wes’s breathing picked up as Cameron ran his hands along the inside of Wes’s thighs, goosebumps rising in the wake of his warm, rough palms. “You’re so fucking hot,” Cameron said before claiming Wes’s mouth in a bruising kiss. Between them, Cameron moved his hand down Wes’s abdomen until he grasped his dick.

The loud moan that tore from Wes's throat was captured by Cameron's mouth.

Several lazy strokes had Wes racing toward an orgasm. He panted heavily, loving the way Cameron's callouses caught against the soft skin of his dick. With his head thrown back against the wall and his eyes closed, Wes gave in to the sensation of Cameron's glorious touch.

There was movement on the bed as Cameron adjusted his position. "Open your eyes, Wesley. You need to look at me." His command flowed through Wes's body like an electrical current and his eyes snapped open just in time to watch Cameron lower himself to take Wes's dick into his mouth, one hand still gripping him. The urge to close his eyes and surrender was strong, but Wes forced himself to keep looking. As Cameron began to bob his head along Wes's length, he kept his eyes trained on Wes. It was the most erotic sight Wes had ever witnessed, and he was entranced. Cameron pumped him as he sucked and the sounds that came from Wes were indecent at best. Loud and gravelly, he barely recognized his own voice as it filled the room.

With shaky hands, Wes reached forward and threaded his fingers through Cameron's soft hair, unsure if he wanted to push him away from the overwhelming pressure building, or pull him closer and let it all explode within him.

"I'm so fucking close." He managed to grunt out, his peak coming closer and closer. With a loud *pop*, Cameron's mouth was suddenly gone, his hand removed from Wes's dick altogether. The whine that tore out from Wes was needy and devastated. He wanted to cum so badly.

Cameron gave Wes's dick a teasing tap. "You'll cum when I say you can." He got off the bed and made quick work of his jeans. His eyes scanned the room, finally coming to rest on Wes's nightstand. "Lube?" he asked, pointing to the table drawer.

Wes nodded, panting too hard to use words. It felt as if his whole body was on fire from the denied orgasm. His skin itched with the need for release, and he wanted to cry from how turned on he was.

Cameron opened the drawer and pulled out a half-full bottle. "Water-based, good boy." Cameron's eyes turned toward Wes, and he couldn't help but preen under the praise even about something as mundane as buying the right lubricant.

"Get on your hands and knees, Wesley," came Cameron's next command and Wes scrambled to do as he was told. He looked over his shoulder and watched as Cameron pumped himself while he stared at Wes. The man had an impressive dick. Not massive like he would rip Wes apart, but with enough girth and length to be perfect. Wes's mouth watered at the sight. Maybe later he would let Wes return the favor with his mouth.

"That ass of yours is making me so hard." Cameron pressed his knee back on the bed and rubbed a hand over Wes's backside. Wes knew there wasn't much there, but he tried not to draw into himself, not let himself feel self-conscious about his body. His whole body shuddered at the feel of Cameron's skin on his.

The feel of the chilled lube sliding down the cleft of his backside caused him to shiver all over again. Cameron's fingers followed a second after, teasing his tight hole with two fingers before slowly pushing one into him. Wes groaned at the intrusion, squeezing around the digit. "I need you nice and ready for me, Wesley," Cameron said, his voice rough, like he could barely contain himself.

A little more lube and a second finger joined the first, pushing slowly into Wes's body, making room for more. Cameron plunged his fingers in slowly, working them back and forth in a hypnotic rhythm. Wes ground back against him, seeking more, more, more, craving release.

When finally Cameron removed his fingers, Wes felt like he could breathe again. But it was short-lived. Wes heard only the crinkle of a wrapper and a moment of suspense hung in the air before Cameron lined himself up and slowly pushed in. All the breath Wes managed to claim burst out of him in a loud moan that mingled in the air with Cameron's own. Inch by inch, Cameron settled himself against the back of Wes's thighs. Wes felt like his arms would give out any second from the overwhelming pleasure of Cameron's weight against him.

"Is this okay?" Cameron asked in a whisper, the commanding voice gone. Only his gentleness remained for the moment.

Wes nodded, not sure if he could actually say anything, as his mind was too focused on the feel of Cameron inside him.

Cameron stroked his hand from Wes's jaw to his ears. "I need you to use your words, love," he said, still in his gentle tone. This wasn't sexy dominant Cameron; this was sweet, sensitive Cameron checking in on him.

An overwhelming wave of warmth that had nothing to do with sex washed over Wes. This feeling was bright and comforting. It was too much and not enough at the same time. Nobody had ever asked him how he felt during sex. Nobody checked in on him or cared that much about his pleasure or limits. And it was something so simple, and yet, so important to Wes, even though he had never realized it. All he had ever wanted was to feel safe.

This was what real love felt like.

Not familial love.

Not friendship love.

Not the hope for love.

But real, unfettered love. That was what he felt for Cameron, and simply by asking how Wes felt during their most intimate moment, Wes suspected that Cameron might love him too.

"It's fucking amazing," Wes sighed, and it still wasn't enough to convey everything inside him, every large feeling he felt that he had never experienced before. But it was the closest thing he could come up with.

He could practically feel the smile on Cameron's lips. "Good. Now, grab the headboard." The commanding tone was back, Cameron's voice turning deeper, gravelly, and domineering. Wes nearly face-planted on the bed in his rush to grab his headboard and hold on, catching himself before he could hit the pillows.

Satisfied that Wes wasn't going to fall over mid-thrust, Cameron pulled out slowly, dragging out a low whine from Wes. But then he thrust in with such speed and force that the bed shook. He didn't stop, thrusting in and out with such vigor that the bed repeatedly slammed against the wall. Wes's head was wrenched back by his hair, awkwardly pulled to one side since the other side was shaved. From that angle, he could turn a little to see Cameron move behind him.

Cameron's other hand clutched tightly to Wes's hip, using it for leverage. He looked down to where he plunged into Wes, eyes transfixed on the spot where they joined, while Wes stared at him.

It didn't take long before Wes felt the pressure build again, and judging by the erratic rhythm Cameron barely kept contained, he was close too. The hand in Wes hair dropped and moved to reach around to grab his dick. It was too much, and the feral growl that erupted from Wes was like nothing he had ever done before, as he came in Cameron's hand.

A few more powerful thrusts and Cameron stilled, though he was silent as he spilled into Wes. Seconds ticked by before he carefully pulled out and collapsed on the bed next to Wes, whose arms finally gave out and he landed face down on the bed.

They lay there, side by side, panting heavily, heads fuzzy and dazed from their orgasms. As the fog of lust started to clear from Wes's mind, anxiety started to set in. What if Cameron left? He got what he wanted, and now he didn't have to stick around. It was something he was so used to after years with Apollo that he was ready for Cameron to leave and not say anything.

Cameron finally moved, rising from the bed to remove the condom and tie it off. Wes's heart raced in his chest, sadness already welling up at the thought of Cameron leaving. "Be right back," Cameron said, dashing out of the room completely naked. It was only a few seconds before he returned and crawled back into the bed, but all the while, Wes waited for him to say he was leaving, or to start picking up his clothes.

Cameron's strong arms wrapped around Wes and physically pulled him against his chest, his front to Wes's back. He lifted himself up slightly to pull the light blanket at the end of Wes's bed over them then curled himself around Wes's body.

"What are you doing?" Wes asked, unsure.

Cameron snuggled his face into the crook of Wes's neck. "Cuddling. If that's okay with you." It almost sounded like a question, like he didn't think Wes would want that.

Cuddling was definitely not something Wes was used to, not anymore. Nobody had cuddled him after sex in years. He was torn between being tense and wanting to melt into the feel of it. But in the end, his body made the decision for him. Cameron was simply too warm and felt too good against him for Wes to even contemplate moving.

"Yeah, it's alright with me," he whispered, reveling in the feel of Cameron's body wrapped around his. His eyelids felt heavy and slowly they lowered until Wes was lost in the safety and comfort of Cameron Griswold.

The buzzing of his phone woke Wes from one of the most restful nights of sleep he'd had in a long time. Cameron had slept beside him for several hours but left late into the night so he could open the bakery the next morning. By the time Wes saw him back through the portal and out through the door of Spirit Antiques so Cameron could get to his car, he was ready to crawl back into his bed for several hours more.

His phone buzzed again, drawing him further out of the dream state he had been in. He groaned loudly as he rolled over toward where his phone sat on the bedside table. The only person who would text him this early was Cameron, even though it was still too early for him to head to work. Another buzz of an incoming text came just as Wes grabbed the phone.

[Unknown: I'm so lonely without you.]

[Unknown: Darling, why don't you come over.]

[Unknown: I'll show you everything you've been missing. We can make up for lost time.]

Anxiety coursed through his body as he read over the texts. The number was new, but it was clearly Apollo. It had been months since their breakup without any contact, but now it was three times in one week.

Guess he's cycled through the rest of his regulars, Wes thought, bitterly. Not that he was jealous. Maybe at one point, he was, back in the early years when he and Apollo were together. But jealousy did nothing for him, and there was no appeal to Apollo anymore for him.

His phone buzzed in his hand again.

[Unknown: I'm so hard just thinking about you.]

Wes felt sick reading the text. Once upon a time, these messages would have been enough to send Wes scrambling out of bed to head across town to Apollo's place. He had been eager to please and to get attention from the man he thought he loved.

Now he was simply disgusted–with himself for letting Apollo do this to him for years and with Apollo for even thinking that late-night booty calls from unknown numbers were enough to have Wes crawling back. Wes had someone who cared about him. Who wouldn't text in the middle of the night just so he could get laid. Because Cameron respected Wes. And that, Wes realized, was the biggest problem with his relationship with Apollo; he didn't respect Wes. Not his time. Not his body. Not who he was as a person.

He knew he shouldn't respond. And he found that he didn't even want to, anyway. So he blocked the number, though he knew if Apollo was really determined, he would find another number to use. That was a problem for another day. Instead, Wes placed the phone back on the table and rolled over to sleep for a few more hours.

The last thought he had before he drifted off was that he should tell Cameron about what Apollo was doing. He wanted them to be transparent with each other, complete honesty. But he also didn't want Cameron to think Apollo was going to be a problem. And maybe he wouldn't be.

But he probably would.

The next morning, Wes felt lighter than ever. Class wasn't such a drudge because he knew without a doubt that he loved Cameron. Not that he was ready to tell him that. It was probably too soon, and he didn't want to freak him out or drive him away. But he knew, and that was enough for now. Though the thought equal parts excited him and scared the shit out of him.

Wes thought he had been in love with Apollo for years. But that feeling was nothing like what he had for Cameron. With Apollo, it always felt like work to love him, but with Cameron, it was effortless. It was as easy as breathing, something he did without conscious thought.

"Oh my god, stop smiling so much. It's making me sick," Candy groaned at him after the last student left the lecture hall.

"I'm not smiling. This is just how my face looks," Wes responded, knowing it was a lie. He had been smiling a lot that day, all through his classes, and even in his office while he was alone.

Candy rolled her eyes. "Let me guess. You totally got railed last night. Your big beefy boyfriend gave it to you hard. Whoopee for you, boss man." She picked up her bag and started to walk from the room.

Wes jogged to catch up. She had a much longer stride than he did, even managing to move much quicker in her sky-high shoes. "I'm sorry?" Wes said, though it sounded like a question. He wasn't sure how to respond.

Candy stopped and turned to him, and he was a little shocked to see she almost smiled. "Wes, I'm just fucking with you. Obviously, I'm happy for you. Like seriously, you deserve someone who makes you happy. And I like Cameron. He's a sweet guy and I think he's perfect for you."

"Stop being nice to me. It's weird, and it's making me uncomfortable," Wes joked, touched though he was by Candy's words. Her opinion meant a lot to him, and she was one of the best judges of character he knew. So if she approved of Cameron, he knew that things were good.

Candy gave him a shove, enough to push him back a half step, but not hard enough to knock him over. He laughed as she scowled back at him.

They continued walking down the hall and out of the building, silence between them. Finally, Wes spoke. "So we're having an Imbolc thing next week. Brie is insufferable about it since it's all about her namesake. We're doing a cleansing dunk in Crescent Lake and then a big dinner at Brie and Ezra's. Want to come?"

"Willingly submerging into a frozen ass lake for fun? That sounds horrible. Are you even allowed to do that? Plus, it's always muddy there." Candy raised an eyebrow at him.

"Are you saying you don't like the great outdoors? Because I find it strange that a *geologist*," he said the word with emphasis, "doesn't like getting dirty." Wes led them to his office, stopping to fill up coffee mugs from the ancient machine.

Candy waved him off with her free hand. “That’s family time, thank you. But fine, yes, I’ll do the crazy-stupid thing you and your crazy family have planned.” She acted like it was no big deal, but Wes didn’t miss the small smile on her lips as she turned away to head down to the basement where the rest of the TAs had their cramped offices.

CHAPTER 14

"For the record, I hated this last year and the year before that. I am here under duress," Ezra said in his deadpan voice.

"And I don't want to see any of you, except Lily, naked, yet here we are," Albert retorted, his tone haughty as usual.

"You both suck, and nobody cares what you think. Now strip." Brie clapped her hands and pointed to Ezra and Albert.

Lily pulled Candy close to her and Brie as they all shivered in the chilly night air. "You'll go in with us. The guys will do their thing and then we'll go next. Don't worry, it's like two seconds in and then there will be a warm blanket and alcohol by the fire." Lily put her arm around Candy's shoulder and Wes saw the telltale glow of magic on her fingertips, probably a warming spell.

There were six of them by the lake's edge. Wes was disappointed that Cameron couldn't join them for their Imbolc celebration, but his family had a tradition of cleaning out the whole house and their businesses, so he was spending time with them after a long day of cleaning. They had plans for the following day to hang out, so Wes had that to look forward to.

Since Ezra and Albert were in no way observant and were only there for their partners, Wes stood with his sister and friends to give blessing to the goddess Brigid. Once that was done, Wes rejoined the guys, and after quickly stripping down, the three waded into the water.

Immediately Wes's whole body began to shiver with the cold, like a thousand knives poked at the parts of his skin submerged. Ezra and Albert seemed completely unfazed by the temperature, which wasn't surprising since Ezra could use magic to keep himself warm and Albert was a vampire. It wasn't like he wasn't an ice block all the time, anyway.

Wes tried to think of the warming spell Camilla taught him at their last lesson. He had been working with her once a week since their explosive meeting, but he had yet to graduate beyond a few simple spells. Warming was one she taught him early on since the weather had turned bitterly cold. But Wes's mind short-circuited the minute he hit the freezing water and he couldn't grasp the spell. All he managed was a sharp shriek as the water closed in around him.

"Nope, I'm out. Thank you, Brigid for cleaning out the trash in my life, but I am not sacrificing my dick for this," Wes said as he made his way to the beach, slower than he would have liked, his feet sluggish in the water, his joints stiff from the cold.

Behind him, Ezra and Albert followed, though they were not in a big rush. Candy greeted him at the edge of the water with a towel held out wide, covering her face. "I don't want to see your junk, so put this on," she said from behind the towel. Wes ripped the towel from her hands, wrapped it around himself, and sprinted to the fire they'd made on the shore. The cloaking spell Ezra put up around their little campsite would keep anyone from noticing them.

Anyone human anyway.

Wes knew that surrounding the lake there were other magical beings doing something similar to what they were, but it was more of a feeling, rather than seeing anyone.

When he made it back to the fire, he dried himself off quickly and pulled his clothes on in a rush.

"Cold?" Brie asked with a laugh as she handed her brother a large flask that was full of Lily's homemade cherry mead. Lily's newest hobby was taking her fruits and turning them into alcohol, something her friends greatly enjoyed tasting.

Wes took a generous swallow before answering. "Shut up, you're next."

The three men stood on the beach while the women laughed and screamed in the water before they ran back to be wrapped in towels. The six of them huddled around the fire once they were all dressed again and passed several flasks of mead around the circle.

Wes took his phone out to text Cameron, at least to check in with him.

[Wes: I'm pretty sure my balls have ascended back into my body.]

[Cameron: That's the price you pay for jumping into a freezing lake like a crazy person.]

[Wes: At least there's alcohol here.]

[Cameron: Wes, babe, I'm at a Griswold family dinner. The only thing keeping us from killing each other is alcohol.]

[Cameron: And really bad karaoke. Dad has just started on Sweet Caroline.]

[Wes: Bah bah bah]

[Wes: Sounds like a fun time.]

[Cameron: You haven't heard my dad sing. We are not a particularly musical family.]

"Get the fuck off your phone, Wesley! This is family time!" Brie shouted as she snatched the phone away from her brother. Wes made to grab it back, but she held it in the hand opposite him and handed the phone over to Ezra.

The angel took it and promptly handed it back to Wes. "Traitor," Brie said, accusingly. But then she leaned into her husband's arm and placed her head on his shoulder.

"Let me just say goodbye to Cameron, and then no more phone," Wes said, typing out a quick bye to his boyfriend before shoving the phone back into his pocket.

He looked around the circle lit by firelight. His sister, the only family he had now, smiled brightly up at the love of her life. Ezra stared down at Brie with a soft expression that was meant only for her. Across from him, Albert stared into the flames, one hand wrapped around Lily's. Meanwhile, Lily sat next to Candy and talked animatedly with her free hand. And his friend, probably his best friend, rested her elbow on her curled-up knee while she listened intently, a small bemused smile on her face.

Everything seemed so simple in that moment, like life was easy for all of them. Nobody would know how much they all had gone through together over the last three-plus years. Brie had learned to cope with the horrors of dying at the hands of her husband's enemy. Lily and Albert were stronger than ever after the whole ordeal with Simon's vampire family trying to tear them apart. Even Candy seemed lighter now that she knew her mom was being cared for and she could finally live her life again.

Nothing could make the evening feel less than amazing. Wes was so grateful for his life, especially now that he was happy for the first time in years. The only thing that would have made it better was Cameron being there, sitting next to him by the fire, sharing smiles with the people who meant the most to Wes.

But, if Wes was lucky, and he hoped that he was, there would be plenty of holidays ahead to share with Cameron. And Wes couldn't wait for them.

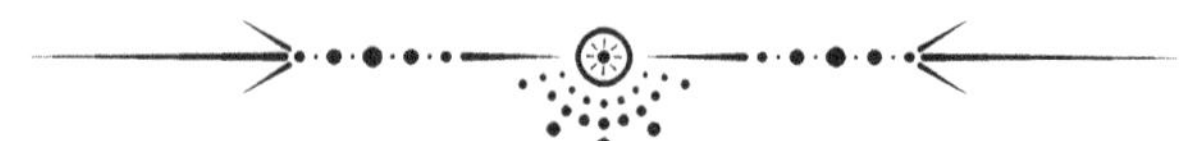

They chatted loudly as the group made their way into the Everett farmhouse. Lily's family insisted on hosting a late Imbolc dinner with everyone invited. The house was already crowded with Everett cousins, aunts, and uncles, as well as many family friends.

Her father, Damien, ruled over the kitchen, putting the finishing touches on the meal and smacking anyone who got close with a wooden spoon. Magic weaved around the kitchen as Damien directed the utensils to move to his whims.

The group split as they entered the living room; Lily, Ezra, and Brie went off to greet Granny, while Albert drifted off to the kitchen to help in any way Damien would allow him to. Wes grabbed Candy and led her to the family room where the older cousins stood around, passing drinks and chatting.

"Wesley St. James! It's been forever!" Lily's cousin Sequoia bellowed across the room. He was nearly a head taller than everyone else in the room and broad with rich brown skin, resembling the tree he was named after. His grin was wide as he pulled Wes in for a bone-crushing hug.

The air left his lungs as Sequoia squeezed him tightly, and all Wes could do was hold on to his arms. When he was finally released, Wes took a few deep breaths. "Literally saw you two weeks ago at family dinner." He was still a little breathless and his words were choked.

Sequoia laughed and slapped him on the back. The Everetts were an affectionately violent bunch. It just meant you were accepted. The other man's eyes darted to Candy, taking in her dark-clad appearance from head to toe. "And who is this beauty you've brought, Wes?" He extended his hand toward Candy, but when she took the offered palm, Sequoia brought her knuckles to his lips and kissed them.

Never in the time Wes had known her had Candy ever blushed, but there was an unmistakable pink tint to her cheeks. "Bet you say that to all the girls," she deadpanned, recovering quickly, though the pink remained.

"Only the exceptionally pretty ones," Sequoia said with a wink. "I'm Sequoia, the smartest Everett. I would say the prettiest too, but that's only until we're married." He placed another kiss on her hand and then slowly released it, which made Candy's cheeks burn brighter.

An elbow caught Sequoia in the chest, and he was pushed out of the way by his cousin, Oak. "Don't mind him. He's a total nerd. I'm Oak, the actual pretty one in the family." Oak was lighter-skinned and not nearly as tall as Sequoia. He shook Candy's hand without kissing it, and soon Candy was overwhelmed by the onslaught of Everett cousins introducing themselves.

"I thought you were ace?" Wes whispered to her once the introductions were done. Her eyes kept straying to Sequoia, who always smiled mischievously whenever he caught her looking.

It was Candy's turn to be violent as she punched his shoulder. "Idiot. I'm asexual, not aromantic. I'm open to enjoying the company of cute people who call me pretty. I just don't have interest in boning them."

Wes shrugged, slinging an arm around her shoulder. "Huh, learn something new every day."

"My sexuality is not your learning moment." Candy glared at him, even as she wrapped her arm around Wes's waist. "Now, I'm hungry. You said this would have food."

"Oh, there will be food. You think my boyfriend is a great kitchen witch, you haven't sat through a meal prepared by the master kitchen witch, Damien Everett. I wish he would adopt me so I could eat his cooking every day," Wes said, a dreamy look on his face. The smells from the kitchen were already filtering through the house, even with the overpowering smell of alcohol in the family room.

"Alright, assembled hooligans, time to eat!" Damien's voice rang through the house, amplified by magic to reach every part where people congregated. There was a mad scramble into the kitchen so people could load up plates. Wes and Candy held back, waiting for the first wave to clear before they made their way to the buffet set-up in the kitchen, which had definitely been expanded to accommodate the food and all the people passing through.

They laughed and ate with the rest of the Everett family and friends. Wes and Lily shared a knowing look as Sequoia sat down next to Candy and proceeded to stay there for the rest of the meal.

Dinner had just wrapped up, already late, when the door opened again and the last person Wes wanted to see walked in.

Apollo sauntered into the crowded house with two people Wes didn't know. One was an ethereal woman, who seemed to shimmer in the light, not just her glittering dress, but her skin as well, which was the brightest thing that shimmered. And there appeared to be gills on her neck. The other was a seemingly human woman, with dark curls and a rosy tint to her tan skin. She was dressed in a tight black dress, and her eyes scanned the crowd with disdain.

"I see the party has already started without me!" Apollo glanced around the room, his seductive smile in full force as he took in the assembled people.

His reception was lackluster at best, though. A large majority of the people in the house had, at one point or another, been on the receiving end of Apollo's advances or had actually slept with him. And with a few exceptions in that majority, most were ambivalent about his appearance.

"What the fuck is he doing here?" Brie was suddenly beside Wes, scowling as Apollo led his dates farther into the house.

"Party crashing, as usual." Ezra glowered at his friend, though Apollo had not caught sight of them yet. He was still too occupied with greeting every person on his way in to notice them. "Hyacinth had assured me he wasn't invited. Major holidays, yes, but the more intimate ones she's not telling him about," he continued, arms crossed tightly over his shirt.

Wes stood rooted to the spot. It was the first time since Yule that he had seen Apollo, and he didn't know what he should feel. There were so many emotions bubbling up within him that he wasn't sure if he should stand his ground and ignore Apollo, or sprint out of the party and go hide at home. He wished that Cameron were there, if only to hold his hand and comfort him during the moment.

But instead it was his sister who slipped her hand into his, while Candy wrapped her arm around his waist from the other side. The two women formed a protective and comforting barrier around him, and Wes lifted his chin high and turned his attention away from Apollo. Thinking of Cameron, Wes was able to contain the swooping in his stomach, but the prickle of awareness itched at the back of his neck.

For long minutes, he remained on edge, though he tried to remain engaged in conversation with his friends. They did their best to distract him, and it worked.

Until it didn't.

Because Wes could ignore Apollo when he was across the room surrounded by other people. He could not ignore the incubus when he walked right up to him and inserted himself into their huddled group.

"Hello, lamb. It's been a while and you haven't been returning my messages." His voice was velvety and seductive. He kept his eyes trained on Wes, ignoring the glowering looks from the others.

"Maybe there's a reason for that, Dickbag," Brie said, her voice almost a snarl. Out of all the people in their circle, she couldn't stand Apollo the most. She tolerated him for Ezra's sake, but even that was wearing thin.

Apollo turned his gaze to Brie, his smile curving higher. "Duckling, my invitation is always open to both St. James siblings. I'm sure your angel man keeps you very happy, but think of all the fun we could have." Ezra's arms shot out and wrapped around his wife before she could launch her fist into Apollo's face.

"You need to stop." Ezra's growl was surprising, considering the man was always neutral. But even Ezra had his limits, especially where Brie was concerned.

Apollo wasn't bothered by Ezra's reaction. His smirk was for both of them and Brie scoffed, murder in her eyes. "Let's get away from this creep." She tugged on Wes's arm and turned out of Ezra's restraining hold. Wes quickly turned to follow his sister, Candy gripping his hand, moved to follow.

Apollo's hand shot out and grabbed onto Wes's wrist. Not tightly, but enough to stall him. "Can we talk? For just a minute? I don't want to hold up the party." He sounded serious and his eyes were sober, not twinkling with the mischief that lingered below the surface mere seconds before. The look gave Wes pause. In all the years he had known him, Apollo was rarely, if ever, serious in any interaction. He lived his life carefree and frivolous. Avoid Apollo, refuse to hear him out, that was what Wes knew he should do. But that tone, that determined stoic look in his eyes, made Wes reconsider.

"Fine, but you have five minutes and then I'm out," Wes said, though he glanced at his sister, knowing she would disapprove. "Come get me if I'm not back in five, okay?" He said as a way to mollify her. Brie would be back by his side exactly at the end of the five minutes.

She huffed but pulled away, and Candy followed suit. There wasn't really a quiet place for them to go inside the house, so the two of them headed to the front porch. Apollo tried to slide his hand into Wes's, but Wes shook him off. The last thing he wanted was for Apollo to touch him.

"So, what do you want?" Wes said, his tone clipped, his eyes narrowed as he leaned against a porch post and crossed his arms tightly over his chest.

Apollo sent him one of his pouty looks. At one time, that look used to work on Wes. It would make him crumble under his own ire and he would comfort Apollo every time, even though he knew Apollo wasn't really put out. Now, he was hardened to the look, and it only served to make Wes more frustrated with the incubus.

"I miss you, and you're not returning my messages. I thought I would be direct and we could talk about us being together again." The seductive roll of his tone was back, and the twinkle was there in his eye again.

He really thinks if he gives me that come hither look, I'll just fall into his arms again.

It wasn't working, though. The constant pushing and pulling with Apollo wasn't his problem anymore. Wes had Cameron. He had a good and healthy relationship with a man who clearly was infatuated with him and liked him as a person, and not just for what he could offer in the bedroom.

"Not interested, and I would appreciate if you stopped messaging me all the time. I have a boyfriend I'm very happy with and who actually treats me like a person and not a dick with legs." The last part came out with more bite than Wes had intended. Maybe he hadn't noticed the simmering anger bubbling inside; the hurt and rage of spending years with someone who could not give more. Wes only had himself to blame for that. He always knew Apollo wouldn't give him more than that, but he couldn't stop being angry at Apollo too.

Apollo took half a step closer to Wes, crowding his space. "You can keep your boyfriend and we can still have fun together. We always had fun together. You don't have to tell him if it makes you feel better."

"If you think that would make me feel better, then you don't know me at all. I'm happy with Cameron. I wasn't happy with you. We're done, Apollo. I don't want anything from you other than for you to leave me alone." Wes moved away from the post, feeling crowded with the wood at his back and Apollo invading his space from the front.

The pout was back, but there was something more to the look, something that Wes had never seen before on Apollo's face.

Anger.

As far as Wes knew, Apollo never got angry. He rolled with whatever happened, even rejection, though that rarely happened.

Wes stared at him, unsure of what to say next or how to respond to this new emotion. Apollo's eyes began to glow. Their depths drew Wes in, holding his attention and causing him to lose all thought.

"We're meant to be together, lamb. Come home with me and let me show you pleasure like you've never known. Let me–" He was cut off by a hand covering his mouth. Wes was physically pulled away as Candy wrapped her arms around his middle.

"You're going to shut the fuck up right now. And if you ever use your power on my brother again, I will fucking gut you," Brie hissed from where she stood behind Apollo. She was the one covering his mouth, and she gave his jaw a tight squeeze, digging her nails into his flesh before letting go.

The front door opened, and Damien stepped out. His eyes narrowed as he took in the scene. "Apollo, it's time for you to leave. You know the rules in my house. We don't enchant people against their will. Now take your friends and go."

"How did he even know?" Apollo asked, not expecting an answer. He rubbed his jaw where little crescent indents from Brie's nails still marred his skin.

"The house has detection spells, moron," Brie spat. She grabbed her brother, and she and Candy ushered him inside. Nobody spared a backward glance at the incubus.

CHAPTER 15

Two weeks after Imbolc, Wes still hadn't told Cameron what had happened with Apollo. There had been no further contact from Apollo in that time, something Wes was grateful for, but it did little to ease his guilt.

I should tell him.

He had the same thought several times a week, but something held him back. Their relationship was still so new, and he didn't want to scare Cameron off and didn't want him to think there was any chance Wes still had any feelings for Apollo. He didn't. If it were possible, he would never see the incubus again. But that would require moving out of New Britain, and Wes would be damned if he would let his ex run him out of his home.

Maybe he wouldn't be a problem after what happened during Imbolc. It was too much to hope for, Wes knew, but he clung to that hope, anyway.

He needed to pull himself together. Cameron was coming over for pizza and a movie soon, and Wes wanted to be in the right headspace to enjoy a night with his boyfriend.

It was Valentine's Day, not that Wes was a big celebrant. Cameron had asked what he wanted to do for their first one together, but Wes hadn't wanted anything fancy. The thought of going out to dinner, let alone getting reservations anywhere, seemed like a ticket to a stiff night when they could just stay home and enjoy each other.

Clothing optional.

Yet, he couldn't stop the persistent nagging in his brain that Cameron should be aware of what was happening. But every time Wes thought about it, he spiraled into an anxiety-hole about how Cameron would react. Maybe he would dump him, not wanting to deal with the drama of an obsessive ex. Cameron didn't seem the type, but Wes couldn't know for sure. Their relationship was too new for that kind of drama.

It wasn't a problem until it was, and if that time came, Wes would handle it. Until then, he wouldn't burden his boyfriend with his problems. They were still in the honeymoon phase, and dumb exes were part of the relationship process.

The doorbell rang, pulling Wes out of his musings. A shot of excitement coursed through him, and his heart started to pound. Seeing Cameron was the best rush of dopamine he could get, and he craved it.

Without realizing it, Wes ran for the door, only coming to his senses at the last minute to slow his feet and answer the door like a sane person and not like an excited puppy overjoyed at their human's return. With his heart beating furiously in his chest, Wes opened the door to reveal a grinning Cameron on the other side, holding a bouquet of wildflowers.

He looked handsome and so delicious in a forest-green Henley and dark jeans that hugged his thick thighs. No flour in sight, though his hair was slightly mussed, like he had run his hand through it more than a few times.

"Hi," Cameron said shyly. They were both acting like it was their first date. It was absurd. They had already had sex a few times now, and yet, there they stood on Wes's doorstep, blushing and grinning like teenagers.

"Hi," Wes said, his voice more of a whisper. He cleared his throat. They were not awkward teenagers, and they didn't need to act like they were. "Why are we being weird? Let's not make this a whole thing. It's Valentine's Day, we are going to eat pizza, cuddle, and watch a movie. That's the plan. It's super romantic."

He tugged on Cameron's hand and pulled him inside the house. Cameron laughed, full and loud, as he entered the house. "Can we add chocolate somewhere in that plan? Because I brought chocolate pastries, which I made, obviously. And these delicious chocolate truffles, which my sister Catherine made. She's the family chocolatier."

They walked into the living room and Cameron set the tote bag of treats he had been carrying on the coffee table. "Yes, to chocolate. Always yes. And way to go, Catherine, for breaking the family mold." Wes laughed as he plopped down on the couch and picked up his phone to order the food.

Cameron shucked off his coat and placed it over the side of the couch before he sat down next to Wes. "She's the family rebel. Dad nearly disowned her when she told him. He said something about breaking over four hundred years of Griswold tradition. The man could handle a bisexual son and Camilla being a girl, but a chocolatier? Apparently, that was too much. He didn't speak to her for weeks."

"So, what made him come around?" Wes asked through a laugh.

Cameron grinned. "He finally tried one of her concoctions which had a low-dose love spell in them. It worked to get him to love the chocolate, gain twenty pounds, and then we all ran a marathon together. It was a weird family bonding thing, but afterward, Dad was okay with the family chocolatier."

"You're family sounds kind of crazy. Like the good kind of crazy, though, I'm not dissing them or anything." Wes put his hand on Cameron's leg to reassure him. Even if he didn't know from experience, Wes assumed Cameron's family wasn't all that different from any other.

Cameron placed his hand over Wes's and then threaded their fingers together. "They are, but I love them. And I think they would love you. If you wanted to meet them sometime." Wes watched as Cameron's cheeks turned pink. He kept his gaze focused on his leg, where their hands were entwined.

For a moment, Wes simply stared at Cameron, unsure of what to say. He had never been in a relationship that made it to the meet the family part. And Apollo had no family, so in all the years they were together, there wasn't anyone for Wes to meet since the only important person in Apollo's life seemed to be Ezra.

Wes bit his lip and squeezed Cameron's hand. "I would love to meet them. I mean, it's only fair. You've been around my sister and Ezra, and survived."

Cameron finally turned his head to look at Wes, his smile shy on his lips. "I can't guarantee your survival at a Griswold family dinner. There have been casualties in the past."

"How many people have you brought home and how many made it out alive?" Wes asked, staring at Cameron as he waited for the answer.

Cameron seemed to think for a moment. "Just one, my ex-wife. She made it through and still comes over for family dinners sometimes with her kid and wife. But every person Caroline has brought home never returns. She's the baby, though, so according to Dad, nobody is good enough for her."

"How do you deal with having all those siblings?" Wes had been in plenty of group homes growing up, or foster homes with multiple kids. But it wasn't the same as having multiple siblings, people you are stuck with for the rest of your life and who knew everything about you. Not even he and Brie had that since they were teenagers when they went to live with Maddy.

Cameron's sigh was deep and long-suffering as he ran a hand through his hair. "It hasn't always been easy. When we were growing up, my oldest sister, Charlee, used to fight with me and Camilla. She hated the idea of having siblings, and especially having two younger brothers following after her. Then Catherine came along and Cam and I got middle-child syndrome really bad. By the time Caroline came alone, Charlee lost interest in the rest of us, the two younger ones stuck together. And I've always had Camilla. She's my other half."

It was clear to Wes that Cameron and his twin shared a special bond by the way Cameron talked about her, and how they interacted with each other at Wes's disastrous magic lesson.

"That's kind of sweet. Am I going to have to worry about her trying to push me out if we get serious and, like, move in together? Will she stand creepily at the foot of the bed and glare at me in the middle of the night? Or try to off me because no one is good enough for her brother?" Wes was mostly joking. He also didn't want to focus on the idea that maybe he and Cameron might one day live together. Nope, things were still too new to think about that.

He was surprised when Cameron leaned over and placed a sweet kiss on his cheek. "Nah, Camilla likes you. Though the staring at you in the bed thing might happen. She has been known to sleepwalk, but she can't help that." Wes almost thought he was serious, but the wide grin Cameron fought to keep off his face gave him away.

Wes's phone vibrated on the couch next to him, and he picked it up, expecting it to be about their pizza delivery.

[Unknown: It's Valentine's, sweet one. Won't you be my valentine?]

The message came accompanied by a picture of Apollo wearing nothing but a red paper heart covering his dick. He made a kissy face in the picture with his eyes closed. It wasn't a picture Apollo had taken of himself. The giveaway was the visible face in the mirror behind Apollo's head. Which seemed to make it all that much worse; him wanting Wes while he had someone to fuck right there. Wes glared at the phone, trying to decide whether he was more angry or disgusted by the text.

"Pizza nearly here? Or did they cancel the order or something? You look pretty upset." Cameron didn't try to look over Wes's shoulder to see the phone, but he did place his larger hand on Wes's thigh. Wes jolted, realized he was still staring, and swiped out of his messages. He would block and delete Apollo's message later.

"Huh? No, just one of those spam texts. I hate them. I get excited thinking someone wants to talk to me and then it's like 'Hey, we've temporarily suspended your account, click this sketchy link.' Hate them." Wes didn't know why he was lying to Cameron about the message. He should just tell him what Apollo had been doing, show him the message, and let Cameron know he had no intention of responding and continue to block Apollo.

But he didn't want to worry Cameron; didn't want to burden him with his problem. And that's all Apollo was to him now, an annoying problem that would eventually go away. *Eventually* being the key word. Wes wasn't going to ruin a great night with his boyfriend over a dumb text from someone who couldn't understand the word no.

A few minutes later, the pizza arrived, and they set up dinner on the coffee table while Wes selected a movie for them. "So, what are we watching?" Cameron handed over a filled plate for Wes before sitting back with his own.

Wes tossed him a mischievous grin and winked. "It's a surprise."

Cameron gave him a dubious look but said nothing until Wes hit play. "*Phantom Menace*? We're watching *Episode One*? Really, Wesley?"

"It's tradition!" Wes shouted with a laugh as the opening notes of *Star Wars* blasted through the living room.

"How is watching *The Phantom Menace* tradition? I have to know." Cameron bit into his first slice and watched Wes intently.

Wes shoveled in half his pizza before he spoke again. "Okay, so I had a really bad breakup once. She was my first serious girlfriend, and I was very mopey, very miserable, and I was driving Brie insane with how many times I listened to the 'Black Parade' on repeat. So on Valentine's Day, which was like a week after the breakup, she and my mom stayed in with me. We ordered pizza and Brie put on this movie. It became our thing every Valentine's Day. Been going strong for well over a decade. See." He swiped through his phone to pull up his text exchange with Brie and pulled up the picture she sent earlier.

"Ezra isn't a *Star Wars* fan at all, but he watches every year with her." Cameron peered at the picture of Brie and Ezra's feet propped up with pizza on their laps, *The Phantom Menace* playing in the background. It was a very similar scene to their current situation.

Cameron twined his free hand with Wes's. "That's really sweet, actually. And who am I to break tradition? But just so you know, my favorite *Star Wars* is *Attack of the Clones*."

"Get out. This relationship was great and all, but there's a line. I have standards." Wes laughed, his finger extended toward the door.

"I lied! It's *Empire*, I swear!" Cameron laughed. He held his hands out in surrender and the two of them flopped back against the couch, laughing.

When their laughter had died down to soft chuckles, Wes turned his head to address Cameron again. "You're lucky you're cute and I really like you. Otherwise, your gorgeous ass would be out on the street."

They sat and watched the movie for a while, basking in okay pizza and each other's presence. Wes liked that he could just *be* with Cameron. There was no expectation of going out and doing something every time they were together. No expectation to fill every silence with sound. With Cameron, they could just exist in the same space, and it was comfortable.

No, not just comfortable.

It was perfect.

"I really like you too, Wes." Cameron's voice was soft, like he didn't want to break the peaceful quiet between them, but he had to say something. Their plates sat empty on the table, forgotten after the food ran out and they had turned their full attention to the movie. Which left Cameron's hands free to reach out and cradle Wes's jaw between his palms.

The kiss was gentle, soft, nothing heated. Wes found he craved that more than clawing at Cameron's clothes to get right to the act. Sometimes he just wanted to take his time kissing Cameron with no expectations of it turning into something more.

Kissing and cuddling was their only goal for the night, and Wes was contented with that. And Cameron didn't push him for more. They fell asleep snuggled under a blanket on the couch, the third movie of the night still playing in the background.

The vibrations of Wes's phone on the coffee table roused him late in the night. Half asleep still, he reached out, making sure not to nudge Cameron as he did, to check the screen. Wes was not fully aware enough to realize he should have left the phone alone, he should have turned it off entirely after the last text from Apollo.

[Unknown number: It's the first valentine's day without you and I feel so alone.]

[Unknown number: I remember this time last year when we were both covered in chocolate, licking it off each other. It was the best time of my long life.]

Wes huffed as he read the messages. He remembered last year a little differently. Apollo had grabbed a bottle of chocolate sauce, and without consulting Wes at all, had proceeded to pour it all over him, and then proceeded to rub his body against Wes until they were both covered in chocolate. The only thing Wes wanted to do at that moment was shower. He'd hated every second of it. And when they were done, Wes had to take a ride share home at two in the morning, still covered in chocolate.

[Wes: Leave me alone]

[Unknown number: Not until after you come over and you let me make you feel good.]

[Unknown number: But after that, I don't think you'll want me to leave you alone.]

[Wes: Fuck off, Apollo!]

Finally, Wes did what he should have done hours before; he turned off his phone and fell back to sleep, cuddled against the man who was quickly becoming the most important person in his life.

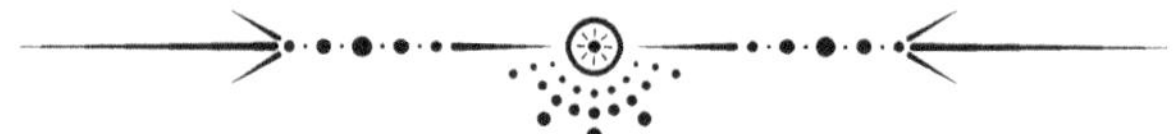

"It's too hard!" Wes moaned as the spell fizzled out. Camilla was trying to teach him how to deconstruct the compounds in a crystal. She said it would help him with his work, though Wes thought trying the spell was much harder than anything he did in grad school for his geology work.

"That's quitter talk, and I don't allow quitters. Now, try again. Really concentrate. The words don't matter as much as the intent. You want to see how the pieces of the crystal fit together, how the compound is formed.

You're asking it to show you its center." Camilla's tone was sharp, but not patronizing. She may be a brutal teacher, but she knew how to motivate.

"You're doing great, Wes. I'm so proud of you," Cameron said from where he stood against the wall, watching. The nice one to Camilla's hardass.

Wes flushed pink under the praise and smiled at his boyfriend. But Camilla's snapping fingers entered his line of sight, drawing his attention back to the task at hand. "Do I need to ask my brother to leave so you'll focus on the magic and not how handsome he is?"

The threat was enough to get Wes to focus back on the magic lesson and not on the hulking man giving him heart eyes off to the side. "I need him for good luck. I'm focused. Totally focused. He is in no way a distraction," Wes said as he stared ahead toward Camilla, unblinking.

"Oh my Goddess, Wesley, fucking blink already! It's creepy and definitely won't help your concentration when your eyes start to burn. You are worse than the kids I teach," Camilla said, her tone chastising.

Off to the side, Cameron snickered, but quieted quickly when his twin shot a glare across the room. Wes finally blinked and then closed his eyes, the better to focus his mind on the spell at hand.

Intent was the most important component of any spell. The problem was that Wes's mind tended to wander halfway through and it was hard to keep concentration when he was worried about messing up the words or the end result. Camilla had already had to spell away several shattered crystals, though Wes wasn't sure even magic could collect all the shards that exploded all over him, Camilla, the furniture, and the floor.

That was another of Camilla's magic lessons; all magic had its limitations. Cleaning spells included, Wes assumed, especially when it involved tiny shards of quartz.

"Picture how you want to see the crystal in your mind. Think about how you want it to blow itself apart slowly, so you can see the crystalline structure within, but without exploding it. It's part exploration, part containment," Camilla coached, her voice low and soothing, which did help Wes's concentration some.

"So it's like that show *Unearthed* where they 3D render things and blow it out in pieces to examine everything," Wes responded, keeping his eyes closed as he focused on the weight of the quartz in his hand.

A long-suffering sigh came from Camilla. "I don't know what that is, but sure, it's like that. Fucking nerd. Now, focus. Feel the weight in your hand."

And he did. He felt how warm the crystal was from being pressed against his body heat for so long. Felt the smooth planes of the sides and the jagged pointed pyramids that stuck out, the rough grainy texture at the base of the milky quartz. It was common, nothing special in color other than looking like someone poured milk during the fluid inclusion process when the crystal formed.

But Wes always found the beauty in the simple crystal. Common, ordinary, abundant, and yet still dependable. Wes called upon that dependability now, focusing on seeing the inside of the crystal that he knew by heart, anyway. With his eyes firmly shut, he concentrated on the intent and said to hell with the words; they were a distraction.

He felt it, that rush of magic flowing through him. It warmed his body all the way down to his fingertips and toes. The quartz heated unnaturally in his hand as the magic seeped into it, and Wes felt the weight of the crystal lift from his hand.

"Open your eyes, Wes." Camilla's voice was soft and low, probably not wanting to break his concentration.

Slowly, Wes let his eyelids drift open and inhaled sharply. Floating a few inches from his palm, the milky quartz had split, sheering itself along its crystalline structure. The pieces hovered there, contained within a sphere of magic that kept them from falling to the floor or floating away, perfectly poised for Wes to examine them.

Camilla appraised him with approving eyes, and for once Wes didn't feel like a total failure at magic. It was still a simple spell, something even children could accomplish, but Wes could feel his confidence building and that was a step in the right direction.

"Good. Now, put it back together. No cracks allowed," she said, prompting Wes to finish the spell.

If Wes had doubted it would be difficult to put the crystal to rights, he needn't have worried. The quartz wanted to be whole again, and it took only the barest brushes of magic for the pieces to snap back together and lower back into Wes's waiting palm. Not a single blemish remained, nothing to suggest that the crystal had once been in pieces.

Camilla opened her hand to take it from Wes and he dropped it into her waiting palm, feeling a little smug with himself. She examined it, turning the rock in her hand over and over, examining every angle. "You did well," she finally said as she handed the quartz back to Wes.

"Do I get a gold star sticker?" Wes smirked at Camilla, still riding on the high the magic gave him.

"Actually," Camilla said and grabbed her purse from the floor. After rummaging for a few seconds, she pulled out a clear rectangular box and opened it. "Here you go, a special star for a special boy." She placed a small shimmery gold star sticker on Wes's black Ramones t-shirt and patted his chest for emphasis.

"Hear that, honey, I'm a special boy." Wes smiled over his shoulder toward Cameron, who returned the smile with one of his own.

"I'm so proud of you," Cameron responded, finally leaving his post against the wall to join his sister and boyfriend. "Cammy, we'll see you Friday for family dinner?" he asked his sister.

Camilla chuckled. "Yeah, just prepare him, okay? It's not only that we're a loud bunch, we're also very intrusive and don't understand boundaries." With another laugh, she grabbed her stuff and was gone with a backward wave.

The joy of finally getting the spell right started to dissipate as Wes thought about the upcoming dinner. Meeting the family was a big deal, right? Camilla didn't count, that was only one family member and she and Cameron lived together, so she was around frequently.

But to be around the whole family, in their element, with Wes being the outsider, now that was daunting. It wasn't that Wes dreaded the idea of meeting them. He was worried they wouldn't like him. Especially because he was still rather useless at magic and Cameron came from a long line of powerful kitchen witches. They used magic as easily as they breathed, whereas he had just struggled for over an hour to do a simple spell.

There wasn't much to relate to with them, either. Besides being bad at magic, Wes wasn't a particularly good cook. He had his go-to recipes from Maddy, but he was still limited. He didn't have much experience with a large family and would probably sit off to the side, quiet and forgotten.

And what if they thought what he did for a living was stupid? Sure, maybe to other people, geology wasn't the sexist science out there, but Wes lived and breathed it. Since he had gone to live with Maddy, he had been obsessed with minerals, crystals, and just plain rocks. They made sense to him and were just as complex as dealing with people, without the anxiety that came attached with interactions.

"I know that look, and even though I know it won't do much good, I'm still going to tell you to stop worrying." Cameron's voice broke through his anxiety spiral. It was true that Cameron telling him not to worry wasn't going to do much, but it pulled Wes out of his own head long enough to push it off to the back of his mind.

"I'll try to not overthink and play out every awful scenario in my head," Wes said with a small smile, weak though it was.

Cameron leaned over and kissed him sweetly on the lips. "That's all I can ask from my special boy," he said with a wink.

“Ew, gross. Nope, not into that. Just stop,” Wes said as he playfully shoved Cameron away. The two of them laughed and more tension eased out of Wes. Sure, Friday may be overwhelming. But he would still have Cameron by his side, and an ally in Camilla. He would be fine. He would get through it, and who knows, maybe Cameron’s family would accept him.

Maybe.

CHAPTER 16

Friday classes had started to drag. Now that it was officially March, as of twelve hours ago, it meant spring was just around the corner and students would start skipping classes en mass to enjoy the turning weather.

Not that the weather had turned yet. It was still cold as hell and dreary all the time, but Wes could feel it coming soon. Two more months left in the year and somehow that was going to seem like the longest two months of all their lives.

He had one more class after lunch, so he took the time to relax in his office. The door remained shut but unlocked, and with no office hours today and Candy in another class, he didn't have to worry about anybody bothering him.

Since Cameron had come into his life, things had been less quiet. Just a few months ago, Wes had dreaded how much quiet was in his life, but now he was grateful for the few moments he got to himself. It turned out that being in a real couple made it more exciting to be around other couples. Who knew?

Even with the dinner at Cameron's family home that night, he was excited about the weekend. Meeting Cameron's family was exciting, even with the anxiety. Then Sunday he was meeting with his D&D group after a few weeks off. They had ended their previous campaign and took a much-needed break. Barring any scheduling conflicts, they wouldn't take another break until late April, when Samson would take off for Passover. And they were all invited to the Seder this year, though Wes wasn't sure if he was curious enough about what a vampire Seder looked like to find out and attend.

Which left all of Saturday afternoon to spend with Cameron, at least, after he was done at the bakery. Then they could sleep in on Sunday and be lazy together. Wes didn't care if they stayed at his or Cameron's house. At least when they stayed at Cameron's, Camilla usually made waffles on Sunday mornings, and the four of them, including Camilla's boyfriend Tim, would sit around and eat too much, and talk all morning.

Maybe he would hang out with his sister on Saturday morning. It had been a while since just the two of them had done anything together. With both of them having partners, and friends with partners, they didn't do much alone anymore. Not like they used it.

Wes decided to push all thoughts of weekend plans aside and let his head be empty for a moment.

Easier said than done, of course. Because then his mind moved toward chores he needed to finish, like laundry; errands he needed to run, like picking up his

Lamictal from the pharmacy soon; and that he needed to make his shopping list.

"Be Zen, brain," he whispered to himself. His voice sounded louder in the small room than he had meant. He placed his head on the desk, cradled against papers he should grade soon, but would probably hand off to Candy. She didn't mind taking the work, since that was part of her job, but Wes still felt guilty making her do it all.

The paper was scratchy against his forehead, cheap printer paper was not known for its soothing texture, but Wes kept his head where it was. He could honestly fall asleep like that. A little nap at his desk might be what he needed to relax a little. But at the angle he sat now, he would no doubt wake up with a sore neck and back. One of those fun things they tell you happens when you get old, but that old apparently means as soon as you turn thirty.

Still, Wes would have been content to while away the time before his next class, sitting unmoving at his desk.

But then the door to his office burst open, the door catching on the chair across from Wes's desk, causing it to move a few inches. And there in the doorway, in a forest green knit sweater and designer jeans, stood Apollo.

Despite there having been no sun for over a week, he still looked like he stepped in from a day in the summer rays. What skin was visible was golden and radiated heat. His golden hair was swept up off his ears, and had the right mixture of looking put together with a bit of sex hair. It probably was sex hair. It was after ten in the morning, Apollo would be well on his way through a healthy day of sexing everyone up.

"Wes, darling! There you are!" He swept into the room and shut the door behind him. Wes wished he hadn't, but he was too stunned by Apollo's appearance to say anything at first.

"What are you doing here?" Wes finally managed, and there was a steeliness to his words. He didn't want Apollo here, didn't want him in his little sanctuary. And he especially didn't want Apollo here today of all days when Wes was already an anxiety-riddled mess as he waited for the evening dinner with Cameron's family.

Apollo gave Wes his favorite fake pout and plopped down into the chair he had hit with the door. "Poor manners, Wes. I thought you would be happy to see me. It's been a month, and we barely talked last time I saw you." He clapped his hands together as if that would dispel the negativity that surrounded their last encounter. "But now, we've all had some time to cool our heads and we can get past all this animosity."

Wes sighed and sat back in his chair. Any hope of relaxing before his next class was gone. "I don't have any animosity toward you, Apollo. I just want you to leave me alone and accept that we're over. For good. So, get out of my office before I call campus security."

The incubus made no move to leave. Instead, he lounged farther back in his chair, settling in for a long conversation. "Oh, you mean David Connor? Head of campus security? He's an old friend. I'm sure he'd be more than happy to see me." Wes had never wanted to punch a smirk off someone's face as badly as he did now. Because, of course Apollo knew the head of security, and his tone said he knew the man intimately.

Is there anybody in this town he hasn't fucked? Wes knew the answer was a close no, with likely his inner circle being the only exception.

"Of course you know him, and probably the whole force. Can you please just go? I'm really not in the mood for this." Wes hoped that would be enough, though he knew very well it was wishful thinking. Apollo would leave when he felt like it, and that likely wouldn't be until Wes caved to his wants.

"Why so touchy today? Where is my happy Wes? I miss him. Though I know a good way to help you relax. I can even crawl under the desk and we can be really discreet about it." The lascivious look he shot Wes was enough to make his skin crawl. He couldn't stand for anyone other than Cameron to look at him like that. Cameron was special, and those looks were for the bedroom only, which Wes liked. Sure, he liked being desired by Cameron sexually, but he also knew Cameron desired him for all of himself, not just what his dick could do.

"I'll pass. I have a boyfriend, and he takes care of my needs. My stress has nothing to do with not getting laid." Wes crossed his arms tightly across his chest. It was his best attempt at keeping closed off and distant from Apollo. There was a time when Wes would have told Apollo everything, because, despite the unrequited love, Apollo did care about Wes in his own way. He still listened, and they did talk and share, rare as that was.

Leaning forward in his chair, Apollo's expression changed. It was softer, concerned almost. "Wesley," he said quietly, and Wes sat straighter in his chair. Apollo never called him by his full name. It was always nicknames or just Wes. "I know I come off strong and we are no longer lovers, much as I hate that. But we were close. You know you can still tell me anything, even if we're not sleeping together."

The tone, the demeanor, it all threw Wes off his guard. He didn't think when he answered, because it was all so caring, so unlike Apollo. "I'm meeting Cameron's family tonight. I'm worried they won't like me," he found himself whispering. Regret was instant. Apollo didn't need to know this. Shouldn't know this. Because without a doubt he would try something, sabotage something.

For now, though, Apollo's smile dropped, and he stared at Wes with soft eyes. "There has never been, nor will there ever be, a person who doesn't like you, Wesley. You are one of the most wonderful people I know, and I know a lot of people. They'll love you." It was the kindest thing Apollo had ever said to him. It was probably the kindest thing Apollo had ever said to anyone, if Wes had to guess. But rather than being a comfort, it threw him off balance. He wasn't used to this side of Apollo, and if anything, it stressed him out more.

"Thanks," he mumbled, turning his gaze away from the man in front of him. He couldn't deal with that at all. Apollo being his horny self and turning up to proposition him again and again? Sure he could handle that. But Apollo being kind, offering up words of reassurance and gentleness? Nope, he couldn't wrap his head around that and everything within Wes rejected it. There was more to it than that. Apollo was working a new angle to try to flatten Wes's defenses. Wes would accept the sentiment for what it was: nice, but with a motive.

"I need to go. I have another class soon," Wes said, breaking the weird tension in the room. He stood up and Apollo followed suit.

The grin returned to Apollo's face, all seriousness gone. "Well then, I guess I'll see you around. Maybe respond to one of my texts soon." He winked and then was gone. Wes sighed heavily and closed his eyes. He didn't want to deal with Apollo anymore, and the whole encounter had thrown him off even more.

But he would get through the next class, get through the rest of the day. And then when it came time for dinner with Cameron's family, he would get through that too. Because he could handle anything and Cameron's family would love him.

"Brie, I am so not going to get through this. I feel like I'm going to throw up!" Wes came barreling into Spirit Antiques through the Storage Room door, already yelling for his sister.

She sat on the stool behind the counter, consulting the large and dusty ledger book that had long ago become a permanent fixture. Her head shot around, a smile on her lips. "It's going to be fine. You're not going to throw up, because if you do, I'm making you clean it up yourself. I won't let the shop do it for you."

"You're evil, you know that?" Wes retorted as he made his way to the counter.

Brie flashed him a mischievous look. "I learned it from my big brother. Or do you not remember that one time in high school I came home super drunk?"

"You puked on my bedroom floor, Bridget. You walked into my room in the middle of the night, emptied your stomach, and then tried to just walk off to your bed. Of course, I was going to make you clean it up." He tried not to laugh and to maintain his serious-brother face, but it didn't work and his face cracked into a grin. At the time, it was horrible. The smell took forever to finally dissipate, even after Brie cleaned and then Wes cleaned again several times. For weeks he teased her about it, much to Brie's annoyance. Now, over a decade later, it was something to laugh about. Yet, Wes had no doubt in his mind that Brie would absolutely make him clean up his mess if he did vomit, despite the access to a magical building that could do it easily.

"Okay, vomiting aside, I'm nervous. Cameron is going to be here in like thirty minutes and then it's into the Griswold fire. I'm a human disaster and they are going to take one look at me and know that." Wes wanted to grab at his hair, but he had actually spent time and effort to style it on the long side and gave the other side a fresh shave. So instead, he shoved his fists into his pockets to keep from fidgeting.

After his last class of the day, Wes had returned home to get ready. He had exactly two nice outfits, one of which he wore to his sister's wedding. The other was a dark green button-down with dark jeans that were neither faded nor ripped. He wasn't going to show up for a family dinner in formal wear or his usual geology-themed shirt or a band shirt and ripped jeans. As he stood in front of his bathroom mirror fixing his hair, he thought about the need to update his wardrobe. Now that he was a professor, an actual professional, he should have more than one nice thing to wear. Eventually, he would have to attend conferences and speak in front of his peers. Plus, over half the stuff he wore on a daily basis had been part of his collection since high school.

Wes by no means felt like a grown adult, but maybe it was time to start looking and acting like one occasionally.

"Wes, you look great. The Griswolds are going to love you because you are, like, the least offensive person and are super easy to get along with. You won me over in, like, five minutes after we met. It took all of a day for you to feel like my brother. Cameron's family is going to adopt you into their fold so fast. Just don't forget about your actual sister when they do." She crossed her arms and jutted out her hip. Wes couldn't stop himself from opening his arms and wrapping her in a tight hug.

"I love you, Little Witch. You'll always be my family first. Everyone else is second." He placed a small kiss on her temple, and the siblings continued to hug each other for a while. Wes slowly felt the anxiety leave his body, and he took several steadying breaths against Brie's hair.

After several long moments, Brie pushed him away. "Okay, enough lovey-dovey shit. Your boyfriend will be here soon, and I have regulars coming in. We can do some quick shots in the break room if it'll make you feel better."

It was a tempting offer, though Wes didn't know how much it would actually help. Instead, he shook his head. "Nah, that probably won't help the sick feeling in my stomach." She nodded in return and the two of them lapsed into silence for a minute.

Wes pulled his phone from his back pocket to check the time. Cameron would arrive soon. The moment was coming up quicker than he wanted and Wes was absolutely not ready for it. "You don't think this is too fast, do you? I mean, meeting the family is like a big deal and we haven't even dropped the L-word yet."

That was moving too fast, wasn't it? Wes wasn't sure. With Apollo, he didn't say "I love you" until a year into their relationship and he never heard it back. There had been no family of Apollo's to meet, and Apollo knew his sister before he met Wes, so there really wasn't a framework there to go off of.

None of Wes's relationships before Apollo had ever been serious enough. Saying I love you to his high school girlfriend wasn't really love, especially since they broke up the minute they both got to college and immediately wanted to hook up with other people. There was never a meeting of the families then because they weren't really interested in forever.

"Wes, you're an adult. You don't have to call it the L-word. And you two have been dating, what, three months now and haven't made any confession of feelings?" Brie asked, incredulously.

"Sorry, not all of us say 'I love you' five seconds after getting together with our partner," Wes deadpanned with a roll of his eyes.

His sister didn't bother with a retort. It wasn't a fair statement. Her relationship with Ezra had been odd in the beginning. They did things in a weird order because of all the shit that went down between them and the Morrigan, and that asshole Moloc. And even still, when she had told Ezra she loved him, it was very unintentional, or so Brie said.

Wes sighed, and once again fought the urge to put his hands in his hair. He turned and leaned back against the counter next to Brie, his gaze fixed on the Storage Room door. "I do love him, you know. I didn't think I would let myself love someone after all that with Apollo, but it was easy. Cameron is so easy to love, it's like breathing."

There was a twinkle in Brie's eye, usually a sign of mischief on her part. "You should tell him that. Right now." The doorbell tinkled behind Wes and he whirled around to see Cameron walk through the door.

"Hey, it's the St. James duo! What are you telling me?" His grin was wide, all those white teeth on display. Dazzling was the word for it; Cameron's smile was dazzling. His beautiful chocolate brown hair curled around his face, and his green eyes sparkled with mirth. It took a moment for Wes to draw his gaze from Cameron's face to take in his outfit.

"What are you wearing?" Wes asked, incredulous. Cameron walked farther into the shop, twirling with his arms outstretched as he went, like he was walking the runway. The jeans were simple dark denim, sculpted so perfectly to show off every line of Cameron's lower half. But the sweater he wore was quite the sight. It was obviously hand knit, though by a practiced hand, and it was butter yellow. Like fresh butter yellow. And in the middle of the chest was a large, black, knit "C."

"You like it? My mom made a ton of these one year when she was laid up after breaking her leg. She just knitted for days. Now we all have these sweaters. There's easily several dozen shades, and we pass them around and take turns wearing the different colors to family dinners when it's cold. I got the yellow tonight because, according to Charlee, I don't have to impress you with my plumage."

Beside Wes, Brie snorted. "Are you from a family of peacocks, then?"

Cameron turned his wide grin toward Brie. "The Griswolds are known for their peacocking. Baking is only the second-best thing we're good at." The three of them burst into laughter, chuckling for a few solid seconds.

"So, what were you supposed to tell me when I walked in?" Cameron's tone wasn't accusing or anything, indeed, it was light and joyful. But that didn't stop the lead weight in Wes's stomach from dropping further.

Wes tried to turn toward his sister for an out, but as he did, he realized she was no longer there. The click of the Storage Room door half a second later was the only indication she had been there at all.

She's picked up too much from her husband, Wes thought, still wigged out by his sister's ability to move quickly and silently like Ezra.

Wes took a fortifying breath. There was nothing scary about telling the person you were head over heels with that you were in love with them. Could Cameron reject him? Sure, there was always that possibility. But Wes had been through that before. He could handle it. Yet, Wes knew that Cameron was not the type of person to do something like that. If their time together was any indication of feelings, he knew Cameron felt the same, or at least close to the same, as Wes did.

With that knowledge in mind, Wes spoke. "I love you. And I just wanted you to know before we go see your family so you know I wasn't pressured or anything to say it, or so, like, things don't get weird there. Because I do love you, and yeah, that's it." Wes ended his little speech and felt incredibly awkward as he waited for Cameron to say something.

The large man didn't make him wait or suffer for more than a second. Instead, he crossed the room in three great strides until he stood next to Wes, who turned to face him. Cameron cupped Wes's face and pulled him in for a fierce, claiming kiss.

It was fire and passion and yet, there was a tenderness behind the press of his lips against Wes's. In that kiss, Wes could feel the acknowledgment of his words and what they meant, and this was Cameron saying them back. His heart felt so light, he was afraid it would float right out of his body and keep going until it was out of sight and in the clouds.

When Cameron pulled away, his eyes were shining. He rested his forehead against Wes's and they stood wrapped around each other for a long minute. "I love you too. I wanted to tell you sooner, but I didn't want to scare you off. Thank you for telling me first, so this was at your speed. Whatever makes you comfortable, Wes, that's what I want. And I love you so much."

With one more press of his lips against Cameron's, Wes pulled away but kept his hands on Cameron's arms. "This was not how I planned to start the night, but I'm lucky my little sister got on my case. Totally worth her nagging me."

Cameron laughed, and Wes could feel it reverberate under his fingertips. "Remind me to send her a whole basket of every dessert I make. But we should get going first. Mom will lose it if we're late. The whole world will fall apart, apparently. And then maybe we can go to your place after and explore this whole love thing a little more?"

Wes nodded enthusiastically. "Yes, I would like that very much."

They exited the shop arm in arm with matching grins on their faces, and Wes had never felt so incandescently happy in his life.

Until Cameron's car pulled up to a large white colonial house with dark red shutters. The place was massive, easily the biggest house Wes had ever seen up close. A single candle burned in every window, even in the ones with electric lights beyond them. The sight was both inviting and overwhelming.

"I think your childhood home is bigger than every place I've lived in combined," Wes said, arresting his movement on the sidewalk. He couldn't help but gawk at the place. If anything, he felt even more intimidated by the night ahead in the colossal house.

Cameron gazed up at his childhood home and shrugged. "It's been the Griswold homestead forever. My some-odd great-grandfather built it and generations of Griswolds just kept adding to it." This was said nonchalantly, like it was normal to grow up in a multi-generational home, passed from descendent to descendent. The thought alone was more than Wes could imagine, though that probably said more about his life experience than what other families were like.

Cameron threaded his fingers through Wes's and squeezed gently. "Come on, let's get inside and you can meet everyone. I promise it won't be bad, but it might be a bit overwhelming. My family is... well, they are a lot."

With a fortifying breath, Wes nodded and let Cameron lead him up the small steps and to the door. As soon as they entered the house, they were blasted by noise. Wes didn't see anybody at first, since there was only a staircase in front of him and open doorways that lead to other parts of the house, but Cameron quickly pulled him off to the left into what was clearly a family room filled with people.

The room held an array of furniture, with nothing matching, and plenty not even from the same century. A fire crackled merrily in the large hearth, and lining the wallpapered walls were dozens of framed photographs of the family, from school pictures to formal portraits to candid shots from vacations past. And filling the room with bubbling talk were at least ten people mingling on couches or standing, chatting excitedly with each other.

Wes's eyes immediately landed on Camilla, a familiar face that he needed to fortify himself. She smiled brightly and stood from the couch she was perched on, ending the conversation she was having with a dark-skinned Indian man with a small smile on his lips.

"You made it!" She hugged Wes close, crushing him against her chest until there was no more air left in his lungs.

"Please don't kill my boyfriend, Cammy. We can't afford to lose another rug to wrap him in," Cameron said, throwing a wink Wes's way. Camilla pulled her brother into a similar bone-crushing hug after giving him a playful shove.

Camilla moved to Wes's side and put her hands on his shoulders, turning him toward the assembled group. "Everyone, this is Cameron's boyfriend, Wes. He's a guardian. Now be nice to him. He's sweet and shy, but he can and will produce his light sword if needed."

"That's what she said," one of the women with blonde ends on her chocolate brown hair fake coughed.

Camilla sighed dramatically. "For fuck's sake, Charlee, your daughter is in the room."

Wes finally noticed a small child sitting on the floor next to the couch where her mother sat. She couldn't have been older than three or four, and she sat with a tablet resting on her knees.

"Sadhika's watching *Bluey*, it's fine," Charlee said in response, patting her daughter's head affectionately.

A woman with light brown hair streaked with gray crossed the room to stand in front of Wes and Cameron. She was only a few inches shorter than her son and daughter and stood at the same height as Wes. "I'm Emily, the mom of this group of rapscallions. It's so wonderful to finally meet you, Wes. Cameron has told us so much about you." She cupped his face and pulled him in to kiss his cheek with a loud smack. A rush of joy and sadness swept through him. Maddy used to do the same thing when he would come home from college. The minute he walked through the door, there she was, making him bend over so she could reach his face and plant loud kisses on his cheeks before pulling him into a tight hug.

"Em, give the boy some space. You're making him sad," the Indian man on the couch said with only a hint of an accent, rising to his feet to join the group greeting Wes.

"Oh, no, you're not making me sad. Sorry, no. It's just ... my mom, my adoptive mom, used to do that. It just made me think of her." Wes felt his whole body warm. He didn't expect to have to explain himself.

The man who spoke put out his hand toward Wes. "Sorry, I didn't mean to put you on the spot. I'm Dharamdev, but please, call me Dhara. I'm Charlee's husband."

"And he's an empath who yet can't seem to read the room." Another woman walked up, her hair more blonde than brown, though her features were like that of her older siblings. She elbowed Dhara in the biceps playfully, though he flinched away. "Hi, I'm Cat. It's so nice to meet you, Wes. My big brother has pretty much talked about you non-stop and we probably already know more about you than you'll be comfortable with."

Now there was a daunting thought. Wes tried not to panic at the idea, but then he started to panic about not panicking because then Dhara might pick up on that and announce it to the room. The slide of Cameron's fingers through his was enough to pull him out of his spiraling and ground him into the here and now. It didn't matter how the night would go, because he had the man he loved by his side. There was nothing Wes couldn't handle now. Hopefully.

Emily pulled the two of them farther into the room and offered them a drink. She was a gracious host, making sure Wes was comfortable, and that his glass never got below half full. The rest of the family in the room were great conversation and made Wes feel welcome. He had yet to meet Caroline and Cameron's dad since they were on dinner duty tonight, but he was assured he would meet them soon enough.

The front door opened and shut suddenly, and a willowy man with pale skin and a face covered in freckles swept into the room. He was already in the process of removing his outer layers and when he removed his dark-colored cap, a pair of bright red fox ears were revealed, nestled in his bright red hair. "Sorry, I'm late. I had to switch up my office hours this week and apparently ending times are a suggestion for the overzealous. Oh, hey! Wes!" The man finally took a breath and noticed Wes sitting on the couch next to Cameron.

"Owen!" Wes sprang to his feet and embraced the newcomer. "I didn't expect to see you here. Or the, you know..." Wes made a gesture to suggest the ears.

Owen's laugh was loud and from his chest. "Yeah, well, being a fox spirit isn't something you usually advertise, even to colleagues. Or I guess, now you're one of the bosses."

"You two know each other?" Charlee asked from her spot on another couch.

Owen walked up to Cat and bent to kiss her sweetly before plopping down onto a patchwork chair. "Yeah, Wes is an associate professor in my department, actually. I don't TA for him though, since he's all about mineralogy and I'm over in paleontology. He was my TA for some classes the last few years, though." He turned his attention toward Wes again. "When Cat told me Cameron was bringing his boyfriend to meet everyone, I had no idea it was you. Small world!"

Wes laughed, and he instantly felt more at ease. Not that the Griswolds had made him feel uncomfortable, but it was nice to have another face he knew surrounding him, like there was someone else to vouch for him.

"Dinner's ready if you all want to get your asses in here," a gruff feminine voice called from where Wes assumed the kitchen was.

"Caroline! Watch the language, we have guests," Emily yelled back as they all stood to start dinner. Wes followed Cameron out of the room and down a hallway covered in framed photos and artwork from school days gone by. The décor of the Griswold home was obviously centered around the family that grew up there.

A pair of pocket doors were thrown open to welcome them into the massive dining room. It was clearly meant to hold a large number of guests and had high ceilings, a sturdy wooden table that would look right at home at some medieval banquet hall, and a whole back wall of windows, though nothing could be seen in the darkness beyond.

A petite blonde woman, Caroline no doubt, her hair tossed over her shoulder in a long braid, placed a covered dish on the table next to several others. The table was set for thirteen, and Wes wondered if there was another person expected.

"We always add an extra place setting just in case. You never know when someone might drop in," Emily said, reading the confusion he didn't realize was on his face.

"After years of us all bringing home strays, it just made sense to always be prepared. We still have friends from when we were growing up who'll stop by just to see Mom and Dad. They practically raised everyone else's kids while they raised us." Cameron laughed and his siblings joined in. It was easy for Wes to imagine the house full of people constantly. Every room seemed to radiate a coziness, a feeling of home, even though it was nothing like what he had growing up. And the Griswolds seemed exactly the kind of people who took in everyone and claimed them as their own.

A man with a thick head of pure white hair walked into the room, juggling three bottles of wine in his arms. He held up one at a time and let them float out of his hand to set themselves on the table at dedicated intervals. His attention turned to the assembled group and when his eyes landed on Wes, a wide smile crossed his face.

With just a few long strides, he stood in front of Wes and wrapped him up in a bear hug. So that was where Camilla got it from. "You must be Wes! I'm Christopher, the dad to all these gremlins. It is so great to finally meet you. I hope you are hungry, because me and Sweet Caroline cooked up something special tonight."

As a collective, four of the Griswold siblings belted out a "bah bah baaah" as their dad referred to their youngest sibling by her nickname. Only Caroline herself refrained and groaned loudly.

"I hate this family," she grumbled with an eye-roll. But there was a small smile on her lips that hinted she didn't mind so much.

"Hush, you love us. Otherwise, you wouldn't still live at home where we can all find you easily," Charlee said as she threw her arm around her much shorter sister and pulled her close for a hug.

Caroline extracted herself from Charlee's embrace and settled into one of the chairs at the table. "I live at home because it's saving me money while I get my shop open. Mom and Dad don't care."

"That's right, we don't. And none of you can judge, Charlee. You lived here well into your twenties before you met Dhara. And we thank him every day for taking you off our hands." Emily patted her son-in-law's arm affectionately.

There was so much laughter and banter going on around him that Wes let himself ease into the feeling. This was how a family acted with one another, and it really wasn't all that different from the dynamic he shared with Brie. Maybe they weren't so far off on the whole typical family thing after all.

"Don't mind them. They are always like this," Cameron whispered as they took their seats.

"And by this, he means absolutely charming and inviting, and clearly we all love each other very much," Cat said, taking the spot across from Wes. Camilla plopped down on his other side, with Tim next to her. The table filled quickly, and all talking stopped for several minutes while everyone filled their plates and started to eat.

A large stock pot sat in the middle of the table and turned out to be a thick etouffee. Chunks of celery, onion, and green peppers swam around perfectly cooked shrimp. When Caroline removed the lid, the smell of home assaulted Wes's senses.

Despite all of Maddy's cooking lessons, the only recipe Wes could ever perfect was his adoptive mom's etouffee recipe. More than pizza, the dish was his comfort food. Smelling it now, while not exactly like Maddy's, she always put spoonfuls of hot sauce in hers, it still filled him with emotion and memories.

A large dish of white rice was uncovered next to the stockpot, ready to be placed in bowls and smothered with the gravy-like dish. Beyond that, a large bowl of mixed greens sat next to an assortment of salad dressings. "Cameron told us your mom was Cajun, so I thought this might put you at ease with us. We're a lot, so I figured this might help a little." Caroline fidgeted in her seat and tried to keep eye contact with Wes as she spoke. But her eyes darted away, like she was nervous about the food.

For a moment, Wes was at a loss for words. A person he had never met before put time and thought into doing something nice for him simply because it would make him feel more comfortable. The fact that Cameron had told his family about Maddy served as further proof of why he was an amazing person. Now that he sat at the dinner table, one of his most favorite and precious dishes presented to him, Wes realized that tonight wasn't just Cameron presenting his new boyfriend, it was a welcome into the Griswold family. It was acceptance that Wes would be around and they would count him as one of their own.

Wes swallowed the lump of emotion choking him to finally answer. "It's perfect. Thank you. Maddy used to make this when my sister or I were sick. This means a lot to me." Cameron's hand on his knee, gently squeezing, was enough to keep Wes from completely breaking down.

The moment passed and everyone dug into the meal. Bottles of wine were passed around the table, glasses filled and drained quickly. Chatter flowed up and down and across the table while bowls were emptied and second and third helpings were ladled out. Wes doubted there would be any leftovers after the meal.

Once everyone had their fill, Christopher brought out a large plate of fluffy beignets liberally dusted with powdered sugar. "I've never made these before, and honestly, I don't know how anyone makes them without magic. I would have burned my whole body if I had to put them in the oil by hand." Christopher handed the plate around, beaming with pride as everyone settled at least two on their plates.

"Dad doesn't do any frying. Not since 'The Incident,'" Cameron explained to Wes.

"The Incident?" Wes asked, confused, but curious to know the story.

"The Great Falafel Fire of 1997," Charlee said in a loud conspiratorial whisper.

Wes side-eyed Cameron, waiting for him to get on with the story. Cameron laughed with his whole chest. "It's not as epic as it sounds. Dad tried to make falafel once and ended up starting a grease fire. The falafel ended up being hard as rocks and we had to get a new oven. He's never done anything with deep frying in hot oil since."

"I wasn't even born yet when it happened, and yet I still have to explain to people why dad doesn't fry anything," Caroline half yelled, half laughed across the table.

The laughter rang out around the table. The story was clearly a family favorite and told often, and yet they all still laughed like it was the first time. "But you can use magic. Why not just do that so you didn't burn the place down?" Wes asked between laughs.

"Because he forgot! He was so into the idea of making falafel that he didn't think to use any magic. Like, how do you suddenly forget you're a witch and then almost burn down your family home?" This time it was Camilla who spoke, cackling next to Wes, the wine sloshing in her glass as she bent over laughing at the table.

Christopher pointed a finger at his daughter from around his wineglass. "Now listen here, missy, I didn't forget. I was simply caught up in the culinary moment. If things had gone to plan, you would have loved the falafel."

"Oh, we all know that's not true!" Cameron jumped into the fray. "Cammy and I lived exclusively off pizza rolls and bagel bites at that time. There's no way we would have eaten anything even remotely green, fried or not."

"Well, that confirms I have the eating habits of a five-year-old," Wes joked, and Cameron smiled at him and placed a kiss on his temple.

"Enough out of all of you. Eat your beignets," Christopher chortled.

Wes didn't have to be told twice. He bit into the hot dough and immediately his senses were overwhelmed. The taste was warm, cinnamon, and sweet. But then there were fireworks behind his eyes, like real fireworks. The most unexpected thought was the sound of jazz music in his ears. If he closed his eyes, he could easily imagine he was in the heart of New Orleans for a moment. Or better yet, his memory went back to Mabon celebrations from years past, with Maddy playing jazz in the house during the day, and booming fireworks during the celebrations at night. It was a feeling he wanted to hold on to for a while.

"Good stuff, right? It's a spell I've been working on for my newest line of truffles, and Dad was gracious enough to let me use it on his beignets," Caroline said, beaming with pride. Everyone around the table complimented her spell and Christopher's fine attempt at frying.

The mood was light, and the room rang with laughter for the rest of dinner. More wine was brought out as they adjourned back to the living room. At some point, Dhara took Sadhika up to one of the guest rooms to sleep, the little girl, long black hair covering her small face, snuggled into her father's side as he carried her up the stairs. When Dhara joined them again, the group was well into another bottle of wine and talking loudly at each other across the room.

Wes couldn't remember the last time he had smiled so much. Cameron's family was easy to talk to, not only was conversation natural, but more likely than not, Wes was dragged into a family story that had been told hundreds of times before and would be told a hundred times still. All the tension and anxiety he had carried all day was long gone. The wine helped him relax into the couch and the warmth from Cameron's body next to his made Wes feel content and drowsy.

It took a moment for Wes to register the vibration in his back pocket. But the second time it happened, seconds after the first, Wes remembered where his phone was. He lifted his hips enough to pull it out and checked the screen.

[Unknown: I can have you out of that house in two minutes and show you a better night if you give me the chance.]

"Everything okay?" Cameron's voice broke through as Wes stared down at the screen. Wes caught himself from jumping at the intrusion. He quickly darkened the screen so that Cameron wouldn't see and shoved the phone back into his pocket and then leaned up against Cameron's side.

"Yup, just my sister asking if she needed to come save me," he said nonchalantly. He didn't like lying to Cameron, but it wasn't the place to tell his boyfriend that an ex was starting to borderline stalk him. It was Wes's problem to deal with. And maybe once Apollo had taken the many hints and backed off, then Wes would let Cameron know. Apollo was bound to get bored, eventually.

Cameron grinned at him. "Sounds like something my sisters would ask. She really loves you."

Wes's insides twisted and his skin felt itchy. "Yeah... yeah, she does."

CHAPTER 17

Cameron left Wes's house early the next morning after Wes claimed he had papers to grade since he gave Candy some time off, which was true. But the guilt that had laid like a stone in his stomach for the remainder of the previous night, and even through their lovemaking into the early hours, was still there in the morning. He couldn't shake the text Apollo sent and how he had immediately lied to Cameron about it.

For the remainder of the morning, Wes contemplated responding to the message. Not that he knew what to say. Telling Apollo to stop so far hadn't worked. Rather than continue to let Apollo contact him from other numbers, Wes finally made the executive decision to unblock Apollo's number and text him directly.

[Wes: Please stop texting me. You knew last night was a big deal for me. You didn't have to say anything.]

It took less than a minute for Apollo to text back.

[Apollo: Hey you unblocked my number, I'll take it. And don't be mad, I was just outside and would have happily created a diversion for you.]

[Wes: That's really fucking creepy. Why were you following me?]

[Apollo: I wasn't. I happened to know where you would be since you told me, and I made myself available in the neighborhood.]

[Wes: Yeah, still not any less creepy.]

[Wes: Please just leave me alone. Don't make me get something to banish you with from Ezra.]

Not that he thought Ezra would give him something like that. He and Apollo were friends, of a sort, and Wes wasn't sure what could actually banish an incubus. There was probably something. Like an enchanted chastity belt or something weird like that.

[Apollo: Ezra wouldn't. He loves me in his own way. I've been around too long to be banished.]

[Wes: Just stop, Apollo. Please.]

[Apollo: See you later, lamb.]

Wes didn't know what to make of that. Would Apollo show up in his office again, or would he lay off for a while? There really wasn't a way to be sure with

Apollo. He was a wild card and played by his own rules. Which were really no rules and let anarchy reign so long as it brought pleasure.

Feeling like shit, Wes wasted the rest of his Saturday curled up on his couch watching endless streams of the Great British Bake Off. Cameron texted in the early afternoon to say "I love you" and how much the previous night had meant to him. Wes put all the energy he had left into responding like normal. He should be with Cameron right now, enjoying a beautiful yet cold Saturday with the man he loved. Instead, he wasted his day wallowing in the guilt he created for himself and didn't move from his couch.

Maybe he should invite Cameron over to discuss what was happening with Apollo. But then he would have to explain that Apollo had been texting him for weeks and had started to show up at his office, and was now following him around town. What if Cameron thought he was still keeping in active contact with Apollo this whole time? Then he might think they had jumped into a relationship too soon after Wes and Apollo broke up and he would break up with Wes and then everything would suck.

Wes was spiraling again. He had let himself get so much into his own head that he was creating more problems than actually existed. So he focused and went over the facts in his head.

One, he would handle Apollo, because that was his problem and not Cameron's. The boundary needed to be made clear and finite and he shouldn't need to have his boyfriend make that boundary for him.

Two, he loved Cameron. They were going to be fine, despite all of Apollo's attempts to make waves. For three years, Wes had languished in an unrequited relationship. There hadn't been a need to check out of it when one of the people supposedly in the relationship wasn't actually in it. Sure, there had been that sense of loss when Wes finally broke up with Apollo, but they had never really been together, not in all the years they had been involved.

Wes's phone vibrated on the table, and he thought about leaving it if there was a chance it was Apollo again. But he picked it up anyway and saw Brie's name.

[Brie: Come to the shop, we have sandwiches.]

[Wes: I'm there.]

He pushed himself off the couch, shoved his phone into his back pocket, and made for his front door. The portal into Spirit Antiques issued a warm glow from the shop side, and Wes was grateful for the cozy feeling as he entered.

"Wow, you look like shit," came Candy's voice as he closed the door behind him.

Wes ran a hand through the long side of his hair, fingers catching on the tangles. Did he remember to brush his hair? Probably not by the feel of it. "Thanks, I put a lot of effort into looking this bad," he deadpanned.

"She's right. You do look like shit. I thought Cameron stayed over? I didn't expect you to show up for at least twenty minutes. The sandwiches aren't even here yet and we ordered one for him. Did you guys fight or something?" Brie asked, grabbing Wes's hand and pulling him close so she could examine him.

Wes let himself be manhandled by his sister. It wasn't like she would find what was wrong with him by poking and prodding him on the outside. Across from them, Candy leaned over with her elbows on the wooden counter. She looked warm in an oversized black sweater dress with her hair styled into two messy buns on the top of her head. Her makeup was just as dramatic on a Saturday afternoon as it was any other day. It was definitely a cozy goth day for her.

His sister was also wearing a sweater in black, though judging by how big it was, it was most certainly Ezra's, and he was most certainly never getting it back. "You can stop now. I'm not sick or anything. And no, we didn't fight. I'm having an off day, my brain is dumb sometimes. It's no big deal."

Brie narrowed her eyes at him, but stepped away to give him space. "You took your meds, right?" Wes nodded. He had been extra vigilant the last few months. Even with them, he still had some off days, and with everything on his mind, well, there wasn't much he could do about it.

"Well, food will be here soon and that will make things a little better," Brie said, fixing her face into a smile, probably for Wes's sake.

The three of them chatted for several minutes before the door opened, the bell tinkling Lily's arrival. "Sorry, I'm late. I had some trouble ... getting out of bed." Her cheeks held a little pink. Her olive green overalls were completely clean, which meant she probably hadn't even made it to her garden either.

"Ew, please don't. Albert and I just got to a good place. Don't ruin it," Brie groaned loudly. She put on the act like she and Lily didn't share the intimate details of their relationships regularly.

It was nice to relax with the women in his life, the three who meant the most to him. Wes was sure that Camilla was slowly joining that circle, but he wasn't sure if that would be weird to ask his boyfriend's twin to hang out. Not yet anyway. Things had been going so well with Cameron that Wes tended to forget that they had only been dating for a few short months, though it felt like years. Which made the fact he was hiding Apollo's persistent contact that much more troublesome. But Wes had to believe that Apollo would go away eventually, that Wes could only hold his attention for so long before the incubus flitted off to his next object of desire.

As if summoned by his thoughts, the door opened, the bell tinkling the arrival of Apollo himself into the antique shop. In one hand he carried two plastic bags filled with food containers. With the other hand, he gestured grandly. "Hello, all you lovely beauties! I come bearing food for you all." His smile was bright, blindingly so, reminding Wes of why he had fallen in love with him. But the thought left a sour taste in his mouth and he wished Apollo would stop looking at them all like they were meant to be devoured.

"We ordered sandwiches, so no need. Now, get out, Jerkwad," Brie spit out as she glared daggers as Apollo approached them.

He pouted, jutting out his lip like he was hurt by her words, though the glint in his eye said he was ready to play. "Ah, but I anticipated this and just so happened to run into the delivery guy on my way, so I took the food off his hands. Don't worry, I tipped him very well. And I got his number." The pout was gone, replaced by his customary smirk as he held his phone up as evidence of his conquest.

"Let me guess, you also just so happened to order your own lunch and decided to join us?" Candy's deadpan voice accompanied her narrowed eyes.

Apollo turned his sparkling eyes on Candy. "As a matter of fact I did, my dark flower."

Candy responded with an eye roll that went on far too long, showing clearly her opinion of Apollo. Luckily, she had never spent significant time with him and hadn't been subjected to his constant flirtations.

"And to think I used to be a welcomed guest at this fine establishment." Apollo laughed like he wasn't the subject of glares and bubbling disdain.

"You were never a welcomed guest. You were tolerated at best, but that was before you broke my brother's heart and have literally hit on all of us a million times, to the point where your very presence makes us uncomfortable." Brie looked ready to leap over the counter and maul the incubus. "Now, leave the food and get out, or do I have to call Ezra to make you?"

The smile on Apollo's face didn't falter even as he set the bags of food on the counter, and walked back out, throwing a wink and a salacious grin over his shoulder without any complaint.

Wes had said nothing during the entire encounter, but he observed from behind his sister. He didn't miss the way Apollo kept eye contact with him when he wasn't looking at Candy. Even when he was addressing Brie, Apollo's eyes remained several inches above her head, staring at Wes instead.

"I swear he's following me now," Wes said, after the door was shut and Apollo was gone from view. "He came to my office yesterday, and he's been texting me basically every night. But whatever, he'll go away, eventually."

"You haven't told Cameron about it yet, though," Lily said. It wasn't a question, likely because her gift of sight already told her as much.

"You see something about that? Does he find out and it all blows up in my face or something?" Wes couldn't quite keep the sharpness from his tone, though he didn't mean it.

His sister glared at him. "Dude, chill. You don't have to snap at Lils. She didn't need to see anything for us all to know you haven't told Cameron shit about what's going on with Apollo. Which makes you an idiot, but I don't think any of us are going to bother telling you what to do about it since you'll just blow us off like you've done for years, anyway."

Wes couldn't help but feel chastised. She was right, snapping at Lily was wrong. And it wasn't like what she had said wasn't true. Brie's words cut him the most because they were also true. He just didn't want to hear them. The three women would certainly tell him that Cameron had a right to know and Wes knew he would ignore their advice and do what he thought best, because that's how he was.

Suddenly, Wes no longer felt like being around people.

"I'm just going to head home. I'm not hungry anymore." He turned away from them and quickly punched the number for his apartment before disappearing beyond the Storage Room door before anyone could stop him. Once the door closed behind him, Wes leaned against it and sighed deeply. Maybe if he had listened to his sister and friends years ago, he wouldn't be in this mess now. But choices had been made, and Wes knew he was going to continue to make the wrong ones.

His phone vibrated in his pocket and Wes almost didn't reach for it, afraid it would be Apollo. With his state of mind, he didn't know if he was strong enough not to reply, even just to fight. But he took it out, anyway. A flicker of happiness sparked in him at seeing Cameron's name above a text.

[Cameron: Hope you're having a good day. Can I bring lunch to you on Monday?]

[Wes: I would like that so much. I'm out of class at 11 and don't have another until 1. We can go out or have lunch in my office.]

[Cameron: Let me bring you something to your office at around 11:30.]

[Cameron: I'll leave you to the rest of your Saturday. Don't work too hard. Love you.]

[Wes: Love you too.]

He let a small smile cross his features, for once looking forward to a Monday. None of his problems mattered when he had Cameron. Apollo would get bored in his own time and move on. Brie would forgive him for being an ass, eventually. Everything would be okay soon enough.

At least, he hoped.

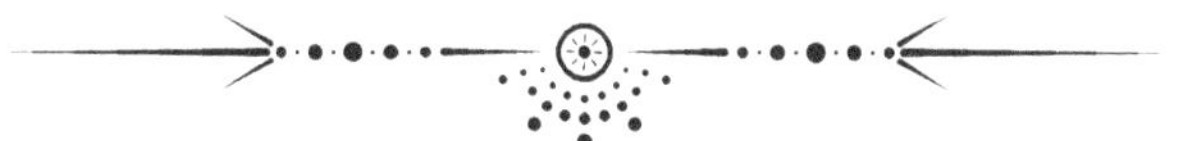

Wes had to stop himself from running back to his office. All he wanted was to see Cameron and enjoy a bit of quiet with his boyfriend. A student stopped him on the way out of class to ask a few questions about an upcoming paper and he was delayed longer than he liked. Cameron would be at his office soon, and Wes didn't want to keep him waiting.

When he finally got to his office door, there was already someone standing beside it in the hallway, but it wasn't Cameron. Apollo leaned against the wall, chatting with one of the undergrads who worked in the office. She wasn't even twenty-one, for fuck's sake, and Apollo was very clearly doing what he did best.

"Ah, there you are, sweetness. I was just telling Danielle here about a great party I'm hosting this weekend and how she should absolutely come." Apollo had that glint in his eye that belied the double entendre. "Wes will be there too. I think the three of us will have a fab time."

Danielle giggled and smiled at Apollo like knew exactly the kind of time they could have. Wes watched as the two exchanged numbers and then Danielle walked off with a sway in her hips that was definitely more for Apollo's enjoyment than any way she would normally walk.

Wes rolled his eyes and unlocked his office door, trying in vain to shut it behind him before Apollo followed him in. But Apollo pushed the door open and settled himself in a seat before Wes could do much else.

"What are you doing here again?" Wes asked, annoyed as he walked around the desk and set his bag down. He hoped that Apollo would leave quickly, afraid that Cameron would arrive while the incubus was still there.

Apollo was unphased by Wes's tone and sprawled out on the chair. "I actually did come to invite you to the party. Everyone will be there and I think you should come. You need fun, Wes, not to stay home all the time on the couch with your simple-minded baker, thick though he may be.

"Maybe I like just staying on my couch and hanging out with my boyfriend. Did you ever consider in all that time we were together that I really didn't like parties or constantly going out?" Wes shot back. Apollo never cared to know what Wes liked outside of sex. It didn't matter that Wes was too introverted to really enjoy parties, that he preferred to stay home and enjoy the company of a small group. Apollo's world was loud and full of people all the time, and Wes hated every minute of it.

Apollo's arrogant air was in full force. "Lamb, there's no way you can enjoy just sitting there all night, not having any fun, any pleasure. Letting him cook for you when you could have some of the best food in town every night. It all seems so domesticated."

"How do you even know that's what we do? Watching my house or something?" Wes was only half joking. He didn't want to think about Apollo actually watching his house, peering through his windows to see him and Cameron on his couch having a quiet night in, or worse, seeing their intimate time together.

"I don't call it watching so much as checking in. How can you trust that witch in your home when you don't really know him? You don't know him like you know me. I don't think he's right for you, sweetling. You need me, and I need you. We're perfect together and maybe I can work on being more affectionate. I know you like that." Apollo carried on as if he didn't actually admit to stalking Wes's house. And then to ramble on like all of that was a good excuse as to why they should get back together. Wes couldn't believe what he was hearing.

"What the fuck are you even talking about? We've been broken up for months now. I'm happy with someone else. We were terrible for each other. I wasn't willing to wait around and be just your bang buddy anymore, and you will never commit to anyone. You never have. That's not the life I wanted, that's not the relationship I wanted." Wes didn't know how he could be clearer, and was amazed at himself that he was able to keep his tone even and his emotions in check. It was a herculean effort not to scream and want to throttle Apollo.

But then something passed over Apollo's face, something Wes had never seen. He looked ... tired.

And not like he had a long day of fucking everything in sight kind of tired, but instead it was a bone-weary exhaustion. Apollo's smirk slipped from his face, and for once, Wes saw that he actually grimaced. There was no glow of magic to his countenance, no sparkle in his eyes. Instead, his shoulders slumped a little, and he seemed to turn in on himself; the golden god diminished.

But it was gone like a passing shadow and Apollo straightened up in his chair and plastered on his trademark arrogant smile. "We'll see about that, dearest. We'll see." He rose from the chair, shot Wes a wink, and left the room without saying anything further.

A sense of foreboding filled the room and the unease in Wes's stomach heightened. Was that a threat? Or, knowing Apollo, it was a challenge. Either way, Wes was now on edge.

Less than two minutes later, Cameron's large frame filled Wes's doorway, a bright smile on his lips and a bag of food dangling from his hand. "I brought waffles! And there's a side salad which Brie told me I had to get because Ezra said that you both needed more greens. Which I think means I have to bring St. Paddy's Day-themed treats over to their place soon because at least it'll be green." Cameron was bubbly and bright and exactly what Wes needed after the tense encounter with Apollo.

"Hey, you okay?" Cameron asked as he dropped the takeout bag on the desk. He walked around to stand next to Wes and placed a hand on his shoulder, and leaned down to kiss the top of his head.

"Yeah, I'm okay. Long day already. And I'm starving. Please feed me." Wes gave a weak smile and tried to shake off the meeting with Apollo. All he wanted was to enjoy a drama- and stress-free lunch with the man he loved.

For the whole of their lunch, he let Cameron dominate the conversation, responding at appropriate times and engaging when needed. But his head wasn't completely there, and he knew Cameron could tell. "I don't want to keep you. If you need anything, just let me know, okay? I mean it, Wes, anything. I want to take care of you." The love that shone in Cameron's eyes made Wes's heart ache. How had he ended up with such a caring and wonderful man as Cameron? Hell, how did he even deserve someone like the hulking witch before him?

With quick movements, Wes rose from his chair and stood between Cameron's spread legs, leaned forward, and pressed a soft kiss to his lips. With a small moan, Cameron leaned into the kiss, taking more of what Wes offered as he cupped the back of Wes's neck to hold him there. Once they pulled apart, panting for breath, Wes rested his forehead against Cameron's. "I'm sorry. My head is jumbled today. I'll get it together, I promise."

With a chaste kiss to Wes's lips, Cameron pulled away, though his hand remained on the back of Wes's neck. "Hey, it's okay to be jumbled. You don't have to promise me anything. Take your time and just, you know, be." There Cameron went again, being perfect and understanding, and once again Wes found himself unable to figure out what that man saw in him.

A few more kisses were exchanged before Cameron left, taking their empty containers with him. Wes sat back in his chair, his mind filtering through the events of the last hour. Between the creepy vibes Apollo had thrown and Cameron's unconditional caring and love, it all left Wes in a swirl of emotions. Still, he had a class to teach soon and needed to get himself pulled together and focused. Easier said than done.

CHAPTER 18

For the next month, Wes became increasingly paranoid. At night, especially when Cameron was coming over, he would look out every window and scan the darkness for any sign of Apollo. The late-night messages didn't stop either. If anything, on days when Wes stayed at his own home alone, they increased, coming through at all hours of the night. No amount of blocking numbers ever seemed to stop it. It was like Apollo had decided their last meeting was indeed a challenge, and he was prepared to wear Wes down.

Sleep was a distant memory for Wes. Between the texts, which had made him start turning off his phone at night, and constantly feeling on edge that he was being watched, Wes could barely sleep anymore. Candy spent more time in his office than her own lately, since he was afraid that without her there, Apollo might try to stop by again. At least Candy was a buffer, probably the best one out there. And for once, she didn't pester him about his change in behavior. Likely it was because, after the last disastrous lunch at his sister's, the women in his life had collectively decided that giving Wes any sort of advice was useless and they were going to let him fail on his own.

"Can't you do anything to make him stop?" If his tone sounded pleading, it was because it was meant to be. Wes was desperate, which is how he found himself whining to his brother-in-law in the Storage Room of his antique shop.

Ezra, who until then had kept his attention on the tablet he was using to record inventory, finally looked directly at Wes, his gaze dark and penetrating. "Wesley, I have known Apollo for time infinite, and I still haven't figured out how to make him stop. But if it makes you feel any better, he wasn't an obsessive and annoying fuckhead before he became an incubus." Ezra's attention turned back to the tablet, where he marked something with the stylus he was holding.

"Yeah, that actually doesn't make me feel better, surprisingly," he said with an eye roll. Not that Ezra noticed, or likely cared. He got enough of those from his wife.

There Wes sat in the middle of a magical room filled with countless enchantments and items of immense power and yet he felt powerless in every part of his life. "What about you, Room? You got anything that can tame an incubus?" Wes cast his question out into the room itself. Not that it could answer, not conventionally anyway.

"It'll probably give you a sex doll that has electrified orifices," Ezra mumbled, though he kept his attention on his inventory task.

Wes whipped his head around. "Did it actually do that?"

Ezra's responding sigh was deep. "You would think that would have stopped him." Ezra looked up, then, and gave Wes an unblinking stare. "It didn't." Then he turned back to his tablet and continued to let Wes stew in his own misery.

After a few seconds of nothing further from Ezra and the Storage Room not magically producing the answer to all his problems, Wes decided to head out. He only took one step before something hard and small bounced off the top of his head and he barely caught it in his hands as it fell. "What the fuck?!" he gasped in pain. With one hand, he rubbed the spot where the object hit him, while he held what appeared to be a small wooden box in the other.

The box wasn't very large, vaguely the shape of a ring box in black walnut with brass hinges. Holding it up to eye level, Wes examined it from the outside. There was nothing on the box, no markings or identifiers to indicate what was inside the box. Just the polished wood and darkened hinges.

"Hey, Ezra! What's this? The Room just dropped it on me." He held up the box for Ezra to see. His brother-in-law reluctantly set aside his tablet, walked over to Wes, and took the offered box from his hand.

The hinges creaked softly when Ezra opened the box, not fazed by opening a mysterious container randomly dropped by a magical room. "I forgot I had this," he said, picking up whatever was in the box.

"Not surprising, considering how much stuff is in here. But what is it?" Wes asked again, unable to see what was in the box.

The angel finally held up the object, which looked like a crystal, purple in color and white at the base. "An impressive piece of amethyst. Is the Storage Room giving me pretty gifts now? Because I will absolutely take it," Wes said, directing that last bit toward the greater room.

With a curious look, Ezra inspected the crystal from all angles. "It's not simply a pretty piece of amethyst. This belonged to Giacomo Casanova when he was living in France the second time. He made a name for himself then as an alchemist and was known to keep these and similar gems around his home. This one in particular, he claimed, was used to soothe and purify his sexual urges, though I think that did little for him."

Reaching over, he handed the crystal to Wes for him to inspect. The moment his fingers touched the cool surface, he felt the magic pulse within. Perhaps at one point, it was a simple crystal, meant to sit on a shelf to impress visitors, but over the years, the personality of the person imprinted itself, and a new kind of magic formed within the crystalline structure.

Seems like Camilla's magic lessons are paying off, Wes thought. Not only had they covered spells, but the practicals of magic as well. Grateful for the knowledge, Wes inspected the crystal, feeling the smooth lines and the pyramids on top.

"Wait. *The* Casanova? Like the guy who fucked his way through Europe?" Wes asked, incredulous.

Ezra made a noise that sounded like a harrumph. "Mino was more than a professional lover. He was quite brilliant, though he was also a prolific grifter."

"Friend of yours, I take it?" Wes snorted. In his long years, his brother-in-law had met and befriended many of what most would consider historical figures. It never ceased to amaze him the things Ezra had seen, and out of all of that, he chose his sister to share his life with. And Brie would experience that too. She would live forever with Ezra, while Wes would grow old, die, and turn to dust long before Brie tired of immortality.

Ezra handed the box over next. "Not exactly. He frequented my shop when it was located in Paris for a brief time. I hated that city and it's good I left when I did." A visible shudder took over Ezra's body for a second, and Wes decided not to ask.

The amethyst didn't grow warmer in his hand. Instead, it felt even cooler the longer he held it. But the magic still pulsed there, ready and waiting. "So why did the Storage Room give this to me?" Wes placed the crystal back into the box and closed the lid, careful to shut it gently rather than snap it shut.

The tablet was back in Ezra's hand by the time Wes looked up at him, his attention already turning back to his work. It was several moments before Ezra finally answered and even then, he didn't look up. "As I said, it was used for purifying sexual desires by one of the most notorious libertines known to man. Figure it out, Wesley."

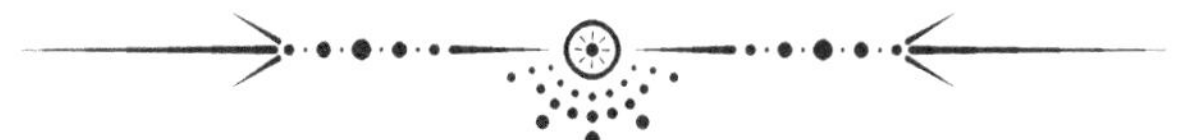

Figure it out, Wesley. Yeah, figured part of it out, Dickhead!

While he lounged on his couch, Wes stared at where the open box with the amethyst piece nestled inside sat on the coffee table in front of him. Obviously, it was meant to help him with his Apollo problem. The question was, how did it work and what did it do exactly? Ezra hadn't been any more forthcoming with answers by the time Wes left. Actually, he seemed more annoyed Wes had stayed as long as he did.

One thing Wes had learned over the years was that Ezra liked to be left alone to do his work, unless it was Brie bothering him. And even then, he gave her a hard time about it. That annoyance only encouraged Wes to bother him more, and Ezra had to remind him on several occasions that Wes did not, in fact, work at Spirit Antiques, and if he didn't stop bothering him, he would be banned from the Storage Room.

[Wes: Can you ask your charming husband how to work the crystal and what it's supposed to do?]

[Brie: Crystal?]

[Wes: Just ask him, he'll know what I'm talking about.]

Several minutes went by before Brie texted him back, and Wes had spent the whole time staring at the crystal. It was a remarkable piece, small though it was. The purples were magnificently deep, maintaining the color all the way down, when often the gem would become more transparent.

[Brie: He said, and I quote, it purifies sexual energies and that he's not spelling it out for you anymore.]

[Brie: And that the thing needing purified needs to hold it and the spell is *je suis lib*éré.]

[Brie: Are you going to tell me what's this about or do I have to make Ezra tell me?]

[Wes: Ask your husband. He was sooo helpful today.]

[Wes: That was sarcasm, btw.]

After he received the middle finger emoji from his sister, Wes dropped the phone on the couch beside him and studied the crystal again. Ezra wouldn't have let him take the thing if he didn't want him to use it. Hell, the Storage Room dropped it on his head. Clearly, it too had an opinion on things.

If that small thing could purify sexual desires, then maybe it really was the key to calming things with Apollo. At the very least, it would take away Apollo's desire for him. But what if it did more? What if he couldn't get it up ever again and Wes just killed Apollo's sex drive? What would happen to an incubus that couldn't have sex? Wes didn't want to hurt Apollo. He just wanted to be left alone to enjoy his life with Cameron.

Maybe he simply shouldn't use it, at least not yet. There was always a chance, small though it was, that Apollo would grow bored with the chase and move on. It seemed unlikely, though, especially after their encounter in Wes's office.

With a body-shaking groan, Wes threw his head back against the couch and pulled at the long-stranded side of his hair. Ex-boyfriends should not cause this big of a problem. Especially not to the point of wanting to use magic to get them to go away. Yet he was seriously contemplating using a magic crystal with only a vague idea of what it actually did. Not a real comforting thought.

Using a sock-covered foot, Wes closed the box on the coffee table without looking, instead letting his head remain firmly pressed against the back of the couch. If he didn't look at it, he wouldn't think about it. The logic was flawed, but it made Wes feel a little better.

His phone was back in his hand a moment later. What he really needed now was Cameron. They hadn't seen each other much since their awkward lunch, and Wes was determined to make it up to him.

With a few quick texts, they made plans for the evening, with Cameron set to arrive at Wes's place around six, and then they would order something for dinner. Determined that he would have a good night with the man he loved, Wes put the box containing Casanova's crystal on his bookshelf, deciding it would stay there until he figured out what he wanted to do.

He settled in to wait for Cameron. The prospect of a night in with some of their favorite takeout sounded like the best way to spend an evening. Wes didn't want parties and events, or late-night booty calls that ended with him in the back of a ride share at three in the morning because he wasn't allowed to sleep over. Instead, he loved their relaxed dinners at home, make-out sessions on his couch, and sex that was gentle or rough depending on how they were feeling, and after falling asleep wrapped in the arms of the man who loved him. Being with Cameron, dating Cameron, was easy, and not in a complacent way, because Wes wanted easy. He wanted uncomplicated and to be comfortable in a relationship. Cameron gave him all of that and more.

Once Wes heard the knock on his front door, he quickly forgot about the amethyst. When he was ready, he would deal with it. For now, Cameron's smile greeted him like a blast of sunshine on the darkest day, and all of Wes's other worries melted away.

"Hey! Is everything okay?" Cameron's smile slipped a little as he took in Wes's face. He stepped closer and cupped Wes's jaw in his large hands, worry clouding his green eyes. Gently, Wes placed his hands over Cameron's and pulled them away, but kept his hands on Cameron's.

"Yeah, everything's fine. Come in," he said and was quick to turn away so Cameron couldn't read any more on his face. Dropping one hand, Wes tugged Cameron into the house and closed the door behind them.

"You've seemed a little off lately. Seriously, Wes, if there's something going on, talk to me. I know I can't solve your problems, but I'm one hundred percent here if you need me." There was a hint of pleading in Cameron's tone, mixed with worry and sincerity. It gutted Wes to hear his boyfriend sound like that. He didn't want to worry Cameron. But still, he didn't feel comfortable putting any of his problems on him. That wasn't fair to Cameron, and Wes had to learn to handle his issues on his own.

Without looking at Cameron's face, Wes squeezed his hand. "I know. I'll try to be honest with you." The lie tasted like ash on his tongue, but he couldn't force the truth out. Not yet.

Beltane was approaching faster than Wes anticipated. How it was nearly May, he couldn't even guess. The Everetts were planning a small celebration at the farm, small by Everett standards anyway. Plans had already been set to add extra excitement for Brie's birthday.

Wes was excited about the holiday, though. Growing up, Maddy loved Beltane, and they always spent the early part of the day celebrating Brie, and the second half of the day celebrating with their community. Since Ezra and Lily and all the rest had come into their lives, they made a point of making the day extra special for Brie. After everything she had been through, Wes loved to see her smile on her birthday the most.

The excitement, though, was heightened by the fact that Cameron would attend with him. Normally, the Griswolds did their own thing with their coven, which was basically all the other Griswolds and distant relations. Witch covens were not particularly varied in their traditions from what Wes had gathered. Though he only had experience with two old Connecticut covens.

In exchange for Cameron spending Beltane with Wes and his family, Wes in turn had to bring Brie and Ezra to a Griswold family dinner some time in the near future. Something he more told Brie than actually asked her about, and according to her, Ezra had no say in the matter, anyway.

Sometimes it felt like things were moving too fast with Cameron. They hadn't even been together six months and already they were throwing themselves into family mingling. The idea of it should have scared Wes. Should have, but didn't.

"Are you even listening to me?" Candy's voice cut through his thoughts. She was annoyed. That was obvious, more so than usual, anyway. With some effort, Wes focused back on her, hit with the sudden guilt of being caught ignoring her. He hadn't meant to. His mind just kept wandering off lately.

He shook his head. "No, sorry. My brain has checked out today. What were you saying?"

Candy rolled her eyes and crossed her arms tightly across her black-clad chest. "I was asking if there was anything I needed to bring to the Beltane party. I've never been to one before. Also, present for Brie?"

"You don't have to bring anything, just yourself. Unless you want to bring some flowers from your home garden, if you have one. That's always fun to weave together with flowers from other gardens, kind of a binding of energies. I would say any of your desserts, but then you will have to pass the judgment of not only Albert, but Damien Everett, and honestly, I would be more worried about Damien than Albert. And for a present..."

Wes trailed off, unsure of what to recommend for a gift. Everybody, Wes included, always gave Brie a new plant. She had so many that Ezra was talking about conjuring a greenhouse for their place. What else did his sister like?

"Pick your favorite book and get her that. She likes to read new things, and she loves it when people give her their favorites." That seemed like a great idea and Wes kicked himself for not thinking of it sooner. Now he would have to look for a book to get her along with the sassafras he made Ezra order for him.

Candy nodded as she leaned over to pick up her bag from the ground. "Okay, Boss. Well, you are clearly preoccupied and as much fun as staring at your absent-brained face is, I'm going to do something actually productive."

Another wave of guilt hit Wes as Candy closed the door behind her. He hadn't meant to ignore her. He just couldn't seem to focus lately. Even with turning off his phone each night, the anxiety of what he would find the next morning was enough to keep him up. Or the thought of Apollo watching him, never knowing when or where, put him on edge every day. On top of having a pseudo-stalker, he still had to work to be present in all his relationships: with Cameron, his family, his friends, his students. Only a handful of people knew Apollo wasn't leaving him alone, but Wes hadn't even told his sister how bad it was getting.

As if summoned by mere thought, a knock came on Wes's office door, and without waiting, Apollo burst through the door with a flourish. It had become a weekly thing, and always on days when Cameron planned to stop over for a bit. It was like a game to Apollo, to get to Wes first and dart away just before Cameron arrived, leaving Wes frustrated and annoyed. He could never fully enjoy his lunches with Cameron because of Apollo's bullshit.

"Go away," Wes said by way of greeting. There was no bandwidth left for him to deal with Apollo's taunting and cajoling.

Apollo slapped on his playful pout as if this really was a game they were playing together and not a one-sided manipulation. "That's hardly a way to say hi. Why don't you try again, and this time do it with a kiss?" He turned the pout into an exaggerated lip pucker with a wink to go with it.

"Haven't you tormented me enough?!" Wes felt like yelling, but he doubted very much that his colleagues in the adjacent offices would appreciate that. Instead, he filled his tone with steel and hoped that would convey anger effectively. "You never leave me alone, no matter what I say. That's some serious stalker shit and you need to stop. Like seriously, you can fuck literally anyone in this town. Why are you bothering me? My dick isn't made of fucking gold."

Wes's glare would quell any other man, but Apollo let the look slide off him like he was made of Teflon. All of Wes's anger, frustration, and accusations meant nothing to Apollo because he didn't care about consequences. He felt like a fool for ever thinking that telling

Apollo to back off would work. There was no handling him on his own. The incubus would do what he liked, Wes's wishes be damned.

Apollo advanced toward Wes, moving around the desk so he could stand close. Wes wanted to step back, step away, to put as much space between them as he possibly could in his small office. But that would mean backing down, that Apollo could cow him and that would only embolden the incubus more, and he would continue to force himself into Wes's life more aggressively.

A warm touch on his jaw, a finger caressed down his face. It was all meant to be gentle and coaxing, but Wes cringed at Apollo's touch and couldn't help stepping back. "My sweet lost lamb, you know you can't escape me forever. You were meant to be mine. You just need time to realize that."

It took everything in Wes not to scream and hurl everything on his desk at Apollo. "You only want me because you can't have me. Say I go back to you, I know how this goes. Everything will be good for a time, but you can't commit to anything or anyone. You'll want me for sex, but you'll have a new date for every outing. You'll kick me out of your place in the middle of the night because I can't sleep over. You'll treat me like a body that you can possess and you won't care that I'm actually a person. Nothing will change from how it was before." He took another step back and put the office chair between them. "So get the fuck out of my office and leave me alone, Apollo!"

His voice rang in the small room, louder than he intended, but he didn't care. While Apollo's grin was wide and mischievous, he did move away from Wes and back toward the closed door. "I'll be seeing you around soon, sweetling. And I can't wait." Then he flung the door open wide, and there in the doorway, mouth agape and hurt in his beautiful green eyes, stood Cameron, holding two cups of coffee.

"Ooooo, I can feel the drama building. As much as I'd love to see how this all plays out, I'm afraid I have my own lunch party to get to. I'll see you around, darling," Apollo said with a wave over his shoulder and a wink toward Cameron.

Wes was horrified. He stared at Cameron, eyes wide, and he felt ice rush through his veins. He had no way of knowing what Cameron was thinking by looking at him. Many times, Wes had told Cameron that he wanted nothing to do with Apollo, and he meant it. But it wouldn't look like that to him, not with Apollo just leaving his office. And what if he heard them arguing? He probably had, judging by the face he was making when Apollo opened the door.

"Cameron, please. I can explain." Wes felt panic rising within him. If he didn't tell Cameron everything right away, he might not get another chance.

"Explain? Yeah, I would say you have a lot to explain. How long has this been going on?" Cameron's tone was accusatory, but there was nothing but pain in his eyes.

"There's nothing going on between us. Come in so we can talk. I don't want to do this in the hall." Wes moved away from the door so Cameron could enter. Once the door was shut and locked behind them, Cameron moved to the far wall of Wes's office, putting as much distance between them as he could. He leveled his gaze at Wes, and for the first time since they had started dating, Cameron wasn't smiling. His lips were set in a hard line, and he stood and waited for Wes to start.

Wes ran a hand through his hair and took a deep breath. "Cameron, I swear to you there is nothing going on between me and Apollo. He's been basically stalking me for a while. That's why I've been so on edge lately. He sends me messages all night from different numbers. At least once a week he stops by my office, and I know for a fact that he's had my house watched and he follows where I go. Today, he knew you were coming by and wanted to escalate things more. He seems to think this is all just a hurdle to getting me back and, eventually, I'll crack. I don't want that, Cameron. I want you, and I want Apollo to leave me alone. But the more I tell him to fuck off, the more he sees it as a challenge. I don't know what to do." By the end, Wes gripped his hair so tightly he worried he would pull out clumps.

Cameron set the coffees he had been gripping on the top of a black filing cabinet next to him. The sigh that escaped his lips was deep, and he closed his eyes for several seconds. "How long?"

"How long what?" Wes asked, not entirely sure how to answer.

"How long has he been doing this?" Cameron sounded exasperated.

Wes shrugged, trying to play it off as not that big of a deal. "A few months. It's been getting worse the last few weeks."

Cameron stared at him like he had just said something crazy. "Months?! Months, Wes! He's been doing this for months and you didn't think to tell me that your ex-boyfriend was stalking you? What the hell, Wesley?"

Shame was the only thing Wes felt now. All other emotions were pushed down under the crushing weight of that one. For months, he had made excuses about why he shouldn't tell Cameron and now that he looked back, they were all flimsy excuses. It all boiled down to Wes was scared. He didn't want to be a burden to anyone and wanted to handle his problems himself. But more than that, he was scared of losing Cameron and didn't want anything to jeopardize what they had. And this is where his fear had gotten him.

"I thought... I thought I could handle it. That he would eventually get bored when I didn't come crawling back and he would leave me alone." Wes couldn't look Cameron in the eye, couldn't face the disappointment there.

His eyes remained on the floor even as Cameron sighed deeply again. "If you had been further in your magical training, you would know more about incubi than that. They don't get bored like that. Once they have something in their sights, they are persistent. They covet, it's part of their nature. And you would have known that and gotten help months ago if you had talked to me."

"I know, I should have–"

"But you didn't. You didn't trust me, Wes. Relationships are built on trust, and you didn't trust me enough to help keep you safe. And now I don't know if I can trust you to be honest with me." Cameron grabbed one of the coffees from the filing cabinet and started for the door.

Wes panicked. He didn't want Cameron to leave, didn't want things to end like this. "Are we breaking up?" He couldn't hide the quiver in his voice. His heart was breaking, and he only had himself to blame.

Cameron's hand rested on the door handle and he shook his head. "I think you just need some time to sort yourself out. I don't want to break up, but I think some time apart might be good for both of us. I love you, Wes. But you are a mess, and you need to fix this. You need to earn my trust back."

He didn't wait for Wes's response. Cameron stepped out into the hall and closed the door softly behind him.

"I love you too," Wes whispered to the door before he crumbled in on himself and sat on his office floor to cry.

CHAPTER 19

Wes was going through the motions of getting ready for the Beltane festivities. For two weeks he had felt detached from everything, like he was watching his life being lived for him while he was a third-party observer.

For two weeks, he hadn't spoken to Cameron, not in person, anyway. He sent texts telling Cameron that he loved him and he missed him. All he got in response were curt responses to respect his wish for time apart and simple reassurances that he loved Wes. Not that it was much comfort. Wes still felt like his heart had been ripped in two and then stomped on and all that was left was a gaping, oozing hole where his heart used to be.

Several times a day, he had to remind himself that Cameron had not broken up with him. They were simply taking some time apart because Wes was a fucking moron. He just didn't know how to make things right. Yes, he should have told Cameron the minute Apollo started messaging him from random numbers. And he definitely should have told him when Apollo started to escalate. But he didn't, and now Wes didn't know what to do. Telling Apollo to fuck off didn't work. The incubus played by his own rules and didn't give a damn what anybody else said.

Was there any way to get an incubus to stop pursuing something they wanted? That sounded like a question for Camilla, but Wes didn't feel like he could ask her. If Cameron wasn't speaking to him right now, Wes didn't think his twin would either. And he would certainly ask about Cameron if he was actually brave enough to call Camilla.

There was always Ezra, but he didn't seem particularly interested in helping Wes when he thought a problem was of his own creating.

The thought of his brother-in-law sparked an idea. He had forgotten entirely about the amethyst the Storage Room had thrown at him. It was still at his house on the bookshelf, forgotten, and more or less, a decoration.

Not that he knew entirely what would happen if he used the crystal against Apollo, but he was beyond the point of caring. He had let Apollo ruin too much already. His sister was still mad at him from the other week. Cameron wasn't speaking to him. His students could even tell something was off with him, shooting worried glances his way throughout the lecture, or staring at each other, unsure.

There was no alternative. He needed to use the amethyst. Why else would the Storage Room give it to him if it didn't want him to use it? And it wasn't like Wes hadn't noticed for a while how tired Apollo looked. That was a man who did everything to keep up appearances, and it was weighing on him.

Or maybe Wes was trying to reason with himself that it would be a kindness, rather than face the guilt of what could happen if he used the magic against Apollo. Just as likely, nothing would happen if he used the crystal. It might not even be powerful enough to stymie even one flare of lust.

It doesn't matter. I have to try something.

Wes was resolute. He couldn't keep living with the shadow of Apollo everywhere. Now there was a good chance he would lose Cameron over this, and he couldn't handle even thinking about that. For the last three years, he had given away his love and received nothing in return, and now, finally, someone loved him completely, and he couldn't let that go. Wouldn't let that go just to be dragged back into the hell he had been living in.

Papers were thrown haphazardly into his bag, and Wes barely spared a moment to lock his office door before he started to race for home. The amethyst was on his bookshelf, exactly where he had set it that night before Cameron came over. He needed to get home, grab it, and finish things with Apollo. With grim determination, he pedaled hard through the streets of New Britain, thankful that his house wasn't too far from campus.

When he reached his front door, he didn't bother trying to dig for the keys he had tossed into his bag. With a practiced gesture and a command to open, the door unlocked itself and swung open. At least Camilla's magic lessons had proved useful.

But as Wes stepped through the door, he stopped in his tracks. Sitting around his living room were Brie,

Lily, Candy, and surprisingly, Camilla. They looked at him expectantly, their faces solemn.

"What are you all doing here?" he asked, his gaze going straight to his sister first. Whatever was happening, she was behind it.

"You know why we're here, Wes," his sister said quickly.

Because, of course, they all knew what was going to happen and what he was going to do before he even thought about it. There was only one person who would know what Wes had decided in his office and had had enough time to assemble a group. His gaze flicked to Lily, and he tried to conjure up anger at her psychic intrusion again, but he couldn't. There was no fire within him. The determination from moments ago was gone.

"I take it you saw me making the decision? Maybe even the outcome?" Wes plopped down heavily on his couch next to his sister, though his question was directed at Lily.

Lily fidgeted with her hands in her lap and didn't look at him. "You know I can't always control these things. I don't know everything that happened before, or why you suddenly made a decision. But I gleaned enough to know you needed us today, and we're here."

"And not just us, Ezra is closing the shop and picking up food. Albert can meet us when the sun is down. They want to help you too." It was Candy who spoke this time. Wonderful, sarcastic, Candy, who had only just been introduced to their crazy fucked up magical world a few months ago. She took it all in stride and Wes admired the way she could adapt so easily.

Brie snorted. "Ezra wants to help because he cares about Wes. Albert just can't stand Apollo and wants to see him suffer."

A surprised laugh was pulled from Wes's throat. The vampire and he weren't friends exactly, but the guy was fun to be around sometimes, and he was fiercely loyal to those in his circle. But the fact that his brother-in-law wanted to help him deal with a person, a friend, whom he had known for millennia, well, that was actually something meaningful.

"And don't worry, my brother will come around. Just give him some space. If it's any consolation, he's been miserable the last two weeks. He's baking like shit." This time it was Camilla who spoke, and she gave him a sympathetic look. If anyone would know how Cameron was feeling, it would be his identical twin.

"I didn't mean to hurt him. I thought I could take care of this on my own and it wouldn't have to be his problem. I'm used to doing things alone, handling my own problems." It wasn't a comfort to tell her that. Nor was it a good excuse, but it was all Wes had.

Brie patted his arm. "You're full of shit, Wesley St. James. That may have been the case when you were younger, but you've been my big brother since we were teenagers. We've handled everything together."

"You mean how you handled not telling me you were working in a magic antique shop and how I didn't tell you for years that I knew you were the host to the spirit of an ancient goddess that my family served? Because, yeah, we handled that one so well." The eye roll was truly reflexive. At that point, Wes wasn't sure which one of them had introduced the high level of sarcasm into their demeanor, Brie or him. He only knew that both St. James siblings were highly sarcastic people, and both used it as a defense for everything.

Brie sighed deeply. "Point taken. Okay, well, we don't do things on our own anymore. Better?"

He shrugged. "Sure, I guess. So what's the plan then? The Storage Room gave me this amethyst to use, but I'm not sure if it'll actually work. And if it does work, how?" His eyes darted up to where the purple crystal sat in its box on the shelf. Right out in the open and he could have taken it with him any time. Maybe all of this would have been over already if he had the guts to carry it with him. Maybe then Cameron wouldn't have had to know and they would have continued to live blissfully happy together without having to worry about Apollo.

But that wasn't reality. And now Wes had to face the desperate measures needed to fix a problem that had gone on for far too long.

"No, no, no, there's no plan. The Storage Room gave you a thing, you have to use it. That's your plan. We're here for moral support only," Candy said, pointing a finger at Wes.

"And to eat. Ezra is on his way with the food, it'll be like–" Brie's words were cut off by Wes's front door opening and Ezra entering through the portal from the Storage Room. "Now," Brie finished unnecessarily. She got up from the couch and walked to her husband, kissed him on the cheek, then grabbed some of the bags he was carrying over to Wes's kitchen table.

Wes stood to join his sister at the table, realizing how hungry he was and not even bothering to wait for his uninvited guests to join them. "So, you've all taken over my house, plan to make a mess, and meanwhile, I have to deal with my problems by myself? What kind of shit deal is this? I was there for you and Lily when you had your problems." He stared accusingly at his sister and then Lily, who seemed completely unbothered by his words as she helped herself to the takeout containers.

"I would say in Brie's case, you mostly got yourself hurt rather than helped. And if I recall, you were there for moral support only when Simon came to town. If anything, I would say our little band functions on moral support rather than practical support." Ezra's contribution to the conversation was absolutely right, but it wasn't what Wes wanted to hear. No, what he wanted to hear was that someone else would take care of the problem for him and he could go find Cameron and grovel for a while. That was unlikely to happen, though.

"Think of this more as an intervention than like a war council. You need to get your shit straightened out, and we're here to make sure you do it. Today." Candy started to fill the paper plate Brie handed her with a little something from every container, though she still had a free hand to point at him with a pair of chopsticks.

The glare Wes sent her way was half-hearted. In truth, he was glad she was there with the rest of them. "You've changed since you've learned about magic. You used to be sweet and innocent, and now look at you." His tone was teasing, even as he started to feel anxiety rush through him.

Candy snorted. "I have never been sweet nor innocent and if you ever tell anyone that I am, I will have to kill you." The rest of them laughed, except Wes. He knew better than to laugh.

They sat around his living room eating the food that Ezra brought. Every bite was difficult to swallow for Wes. That day, he was going to do it and there was no getting out of it. Food was what he needed, he knew that, but none of it had any taste.

"Do you know where he'll be?" Brie's voice cut through his thoughts. It took Wes a moment to realize the words were directed at him.

Truly, Wes had no idea. Apollo never kept a set schedule except for his day to visit Spirit Antiques. There were parties and socials, orgies and raves constantly happening and Apollo liked to make the rounds. If he felt in the mood, he would even hit up the frat parties on campus, which only creeped Wes out. "Honestly, he could be literally anywhere, with anyone. I have no idea."

"You could always invite him over here. Home turf advantage and we'll be here if you need us," Camilla said, setting down her empty plate on the coffee table.

Inviting Apollo over would be the easiest way, but that would require messaging him, which would only serve to heighten Wes's anxieties. He wanted to avoid any further text contact. That, and there was no guarantee he would come over. When they were dating, Apollo never came to Wes's place, not once, even when Wes asked him to.

"I'm not sure he'll actually come if I invite him. He's never been here," Wes responded. The group stared at him in disbelief.

"Wait, you were together for years and he never even came to your place? Did you like super glue those rose-tinted glasses to your face, or were you just that oblivious to the red flags that guy was throwing up like confetti?" Candy put her face in her hand, like she was embarrassed on his behalf.

Now that he had to say it out loud, yeah, it sounded horrible and he should have known pretty early on that things with Apollo were never going to work. Superglued, rose-tinted glasses indeed.

Embarrassment flushed through him. Each person in the room had told him over and over again that Apollo wasn't good for him, and like a stubborn ass, he had ignored them all and let himself suffer, hoping that things would change one day. He had let so much slide, or simply refused to see how messed up the way Apollo treated him really was. And for what? Some mind-blowing sex and the fear of being alone?

Did he deserve Cameron? Wes wasn't entirely convinced, but he did know he deserved better than Apollo. And he would spend forever trying to be the kind of man who was worthy of Cameron's love. Not just Cameron's love though. Wes wanted to be a man worthy of his own self-love.

First things first though, he needed to take care of Apollo once and for all. No was not a complete sentence when it came to Apollo. The chase mattered more to him, not Wes himself. Because if he ever got Wes back, well then, the thrill of chasing him would be gone and the incubus would have to find something else to go after, leaving Wes trailing after him with a broken heart.

Wes wasn't sure what he was most angry at himself for; wasting years of his life on someone who was a walking red flag, or not asking for help sooner on getting Apollo out of his life. He was an idiot on both counts. He should have just listened when he could have, or asked for help right away when he knew Apollo wouldn't leave him alone.

"I'm such a moron," Wes mumbled, though everyone could hear him clearly.

Brie moved closer to throw her arm around his shoulders. "Yeah, you're a real dingus, but you're still my big brother and I love you."

"Love you too." Wes leaned his head against his sister's shoulder and for a moment let himself relax into her side.

"Apollo is at a house party. I texted you the address." Lily's voice broke through the sibling moment.

Wes's head whipped up, and he looked at the witch still holding her phone. With a slight smirk on his lips, he spoke to her. "House party? It's like six in the afternoon. On a Tuesday!" Wes sighed, less surprised than how he sounded. "Well, thanks to the Sight, I get out of having to text him myself."

Lily laughed and shook her head. "Or, you know, I just texted Esmerelda and asked where he was."

"You texted Esmerelda, of all people?" Wes asked, incredulous. He had never liked Esmerelda because he always saw her as competition for Apollo's affection, something Apollo had definitely instigated on more than a few occasions, but there was no reason to harbor the dislike. Easier said than done though, and he still felt a tinge of annoyance.

"I had her number. We're friends," Lily defended.

"What are you talking about? We're your only friends," Wes shot back, though he had a hard time keeping the laugh from his voice, the annoyance fading quickly.

Lily opened her mouth and held up a finger as if to make a point, but then dropped her hand. "Okay, that's true. But I am friendly with other people. Esmerelda is one of those people. Now, you have things to do, so get your butt over there and take care of things."

Eyes scanning the room, Wes looked into the faces of his family and saw only encouragement and hope. "Are you okay with this?" His attention landed on Ezra. Everyone else in the room was no fan of Apollo. They hadn't known him as long and he made most of them extremely uncomfortable with his constant sexual comments toward them. But Ezra was Apollo's friend, whether he liked it or not, there was simply too much history between them.

"I can't speak for him, but I've known Apollo a long time. Even I can see he's tired. He wants what all the Fallen want. He wants to go home. So, yes, I'm okay with this. I wouldn't have let you take the crystal if I wasn't sure it was the right thing to do." Ezra's tone was measured, but he answered without pause. Any compunctions he may have had on the matter had clearly already been thought through.

A feeling of unease settled in Wes's stomach. Sure, he could go to the party, which likely had humans, confront Apollo and use magic, and risk a bunch of random humans seeing. It wasn't the best plan, but it was the easiest for Wes.

But maybe this time the easiest wasn't the best solution. Because truthfully, Wes had no idea how Apollo would react. Wes had never seen him have any inclinations toward violence. Hell, he had never seen Apollo even get a little angry. When the incubus had joined their group to rescue Brie, he hadn't even bothered to fight when he was needed. Still, he was never put in direct harm, and Wes had no idea if Apollo would lash out. He didn't want to take the chance of getting hurt or being the reason others got hurt in the process.

"Do you think..." He paused, unsure if he wanted to voice his concern. "Do you think it would be better to have him come to the shop? Like for safety reasons? I don't think he'll get violent or anything, but I want the assurance he and I will be safe. Is that cool?" Again he looked at Ezra as he posed his question.

Ezra nodded, not surprising Wes. Ezra opened his shop to all who needed it, and he had the protective magics around the place in case anything went sideways. With a head nod back toward his brother-in-law, Wes was resolute as he pulled out his phone and texted the last number Apollo had used for one of his late-night texts.

[Wes: Meet me at Spirit in ten.]

It was a vague message, promising nothing, yet Wes knew it would be like a siren song to Apollo and he would be there in half the time. Just the idea that

Wes might give in to his whims would be enough to draw Apollo from his debauched partying to go to an antique shop in the late afternoon. Besides, his incubus logic would see an opportunity to get what he wanted and then he could go right back to partying.

The night was young.

A moment later, Wes's phone pinged with Apollo's response. A thumbs-up emoji and a kissy face emoji. Mere seconds later, he sent an eggplant emoji. Wes rolled his eyes as he shoved the phone back into his pocket.

"He's on his way, and, of course, he thinks he's about to get dicked down. Okay, I need the crystal and a reminder of the magic words, please." Candy grabbed the crystal from where it sat on the shelf again, and it was passed around the room until it reached Wes's waiting hand.

"*Je suis libéré.* I know French isn't your strong suit, but please try to remember." Ezra leveled him with an unblinking stare that Wes couldn't help but flinch away from.

Wes stood and stretched, mentally preparing himself. "Sadly, my French is better than my Spanish. My parents were from Mexico and I don't even speak their language. How sad is that?"

"You know plenty of swear words in Spanish and French," Brie said. "Maddy had a ... colorful Creole vocabulary sometimes." The last she said to the rest of the group, making a face as she tried to describe the way Maddy vented her frustrations without her kids knowing what she said. They had learned pretty quickly, though.

Joking aside, and with the thought of Maddy to give him strength, Wes walked to his front door and punched the number for the shop. "Oh shit, is the place locked up since you both are here?" He turned back to Ezra, who was already standing and making his way toward the door.

"I'll open it up and stay nearby. Just in case. Everyone else can stay here until it's done. Brie, sweetheart, I'm not leaving the door cracked for you to spy. Please, for once, listen." Ezra gave one last lingering look at his wife before walking through the portal.

Wes took a fortifying breath and stepped through after Ezra, shutting the door firmly behind him.

CHAPTER 20

On the other side of the portal, the shop was dark, though daylight still filtered in from the front windows and a few items on the shelves glowed of their own volition. Ezra was already standing at the door, flipping the lock but leaving the sign on closed. The last thing they needed was a tourist to wander in while in the middle of a magical working.

"Do you want me out here, or would you prefer I stay in the Storage Room?" Ezra came to stand next to Wes beside the counter. He snapped his fingers once, and the lights came on in the shop before he crossed his arms over his chest and waited for Wes's response. Sometimes Wes forgot that under all the broody exterior, his brother-in-law was an extremely caring and considerate person. He loved Brie unconditionally, and treated Wes like his own brother, since he realized early on the St. James siblings were a package deal. And Wes was grateful for that consideration, more than he could say aloud.

"Please stay. You're like an insurance policy and I'll feel better having you around. If that's cool with you." When it came down to it, Wes knew the words rang true. Even if asking for help was hard for him, the prospect of facing Apollo alone did not sound thrilling. None of it sounded thrilling, but the strength of presence from Ezra was enough to hold his resolve.

The two men stood together behind the antique shop's counter, waiting for the arrival of the incubus. Ezra stood perfectly straight, arms crossed tightly, face neutral, basically his usual look. But Wes strove for an air of indifference, with one hip resting against the counter, one hand planted palm down on the wood so he could lean. He kept the door in sight from the corner of his eye and waited. No words passed between the two of them, and the silence was thick, pressing against Wes's chest, trying to stop his lungs. Or maybe that was all in his head, the fear of the unknown.

When the bell above the door tinkled, Wes nearly jumped out of his skin. He kept upright, but his breath quickened and his heartbeat ran so wild that it felt like his chest was cracking.

"Oh, excellent! It's two for one tonight. And I have been such a good boy." Apollo's voice sounded like a car crash to Wes's ears; grating metal and broken glass, promises of carnage and destruction. He wanted this over now.

With a fortifying breath, Wes turned his body to face Apollo across the counter. If the polished wood stood between them, Wes could use it like a barrier, keep himself safe even if he didn't know what from.

"Apollo. We need to talk." He congratulated himself on how even his tone was, how unbothered he sounded. He certainly didn't feel that way inside.

Apollo was already nodding his head, and the lust in his eyes could clearly be seen. He thought he'd won, that the chase for Wes was over and he would get back what he thought of as his. It made Wes's heart hurt to see. To know that if Wes gave in to Apollo tonight, he would be right back to the sad mess of a person he was before he'd met Cameron. Apollo would find something new to chase and the thrill of Wes would be over. Not that Wes had any intention of giving Apollo any more of his time. It was time to end the menace that was Apollo the incubus.

"Oh, there will be plenty of time for talking later, lamb. I have a few better ideas for what we can do with our mouths. I certainly wouldn't mind if Ezra decided to join us, either. Maybe you should bring your wife, make it that much more fun." Apollo winked at Ezra, and the man scowled deeply in return.

If Wes thought Ezra had any doubts about what he was about to do, Wes was sure those doubts were long gone now too. The angel looked very near to jumping over the counter to throttle Apollo before Wes even came close to performing the magic.

"That's not what we're doing. This has gone on long enough, Apollo. We're all tired of how you treat us. How you treat everyone around you. I'm tired of feeling like just a body around you. I'm tired of saying no and you not listening. And I suspect that you're tired too." His eyes remained trained on Apollo's. Another reason to have Ezra beside him, just in case Apollo tried to use his hypnotic power again.

And then he saw, clear as day. The thing that for years he thought he saw when he sometimes looked at Apollo but never caught it clearly.

Sadness.

Exhaustion.

Emptiness.

It was all there in his deep blue eyes. Unlike all those other times, the look in Apollo's eyes didn't alter right away. It was like seeing the weight of the world resting on the incubus. Even his shoulders seemed to shrink as if pushed low by a heavy burden.

For once, Apollo looked completely diminished. The golden hue that seemed to resonate from his skin dimmed, and for just a second, he looked utterly exhausted and beaten down.

Then, in the space of a heartbeat, the broken man before him vanished, and Apollo was once again the exuberant golden god he always was.

"Tired? Me? Darling, it's in my nature to go on forever. I never tire." He laughed, his customary smirk back on his face. And yet it all seemed so forced, so fragile. His face showed more vulnerability in seconds than it ever had in the years they were together, and Wes was sure he was making the right decision.

Wes shot Ezra a side-eyed glance before he turned his attention back to Apollo. "Come here. I need to give you something." With the words of the spell running through his mind, Wes waited as Apollo drew closer to him. Thankfully, the incubus stopped across the counter, rather than coming around the side to stand next to Wes.

Apollo leaned far over the wooden surface. "Is it a kiss? I've missed those."

"Hold out your hand," Wes instructed, taking a page from Ezra's book and keeping his voice flat. Either Apollo trusted Wes more than he realized or he had little regard for safety in general, because he held out his hand, palm up, without question.

Running his fingers across the flat smooth surface of the amethyst one last time, Wes stretched out his hand and placed the crystal into Apollo's outstretched palm. Rather than removing his hand right away, Wes curled Apollo's fingers around the crystal and held on.

"Is this some kind of geologist mating thing? It's new to me, but I am very open to anything." Apollo's smirk was startlingly at ease, considering what Wes was about to do. His heart clenched like in a vice, but then he knew it was time.

"*Je suis libéré.*" Wes's voice came out as barely more than a whisper, strained and lacking the conviction he had hoped for. Instead, it was a sad sound, almost pained. Because that was how Wes felt, sad and pained at what he knew was the right thing to do.

Apollo had just enough time to look puzzled before his blue eyes rolled back into his head and his fingers clutched the amethyst in a tight grip, knuckles quickly turning white. A purple glow seemed to emanate from his skin, the edges swirling unrestrained around him before finally channeling into a flowing river of purple light down Apollo's arm and into the hand wrapped around the amethyst. It looked as if the crystal was sucking up all the magical energy coming from within Apollo.

There was no sound, which disturbed Wes more. He thought there might have been screaming or begging from Apollo, literally any noise at all. But it was as if the sound had been turned off. A complete absence of sound remained unbroken, even by his own breathing.

Wes didn't know what he had expected would happen once he activated the spell. Movement and sound, certainly, but that was all vague. Without sound, he felt disjointed and wrong, and Apollo didn't move an inch. The purple glow flowing its way into the crystal was the only movement in the entire room. The whole tableau, Apollo standing stock still with only the whites of his eyes showing and no noise, was disquieting.

If Wes could tear his eyes away from the scene before him, he would have looked at Ezra. But his brother-in-law stood behind him, out of his line of sight, and he too, was caught up in the unsettling event he was a part of.

After days, or maybe minutes, it could even have been seconds, Wes wasn't sure, the glow finally dissipated. Apollo's eyes closed entirely, his chin fell forward, and he stumbled half a step before catching himself against the counter. The amethyst tumbled from his hand onto the wood below, still faintly glowing. Apollo's hands came down on the counter to steady himself and he stood hunched over, breathing heavily.

Sound returned suddenly, loud and jarring. It was like Wes could hear all three of their heartbeats, like a trio of large drums. It was overwhelming after the silence of the past few moments. Wes didn't know what to do now. Whether he should say something or turn tail and run back through the Storage Room door and hide in his room.

Before him, Apollo's whole body heaved and a silver light began to emanate from his body. In a whoosh of feathers, a pair of wings sprang from his back, stretching out wide and magnificent. They looked very similar to Ezra's, though Wes had only seen those a handful of times.

Apollo reached up a hand over his shoulder, his movements tentative, his head still tilted down with his eyes closed. As his fingertips touched the first feather, he let out a long, heavy sigh, followed immediately by a choked sob. Tears started to flow in streams down his cheeks, and Wes wasn't sure if the sounds were of joy or anguish. Maybe both.

Neither Wes nor Ezra said anything, letting Apollo have his moment to experience all of his emotions. It was several minutes before his tears began to slow and his breathing started to even out. Finally, Apollo lifted his head and opened his eyes.

They were no longer blue.

Instead, Apollo stared at Wes with eyes like quicksilver, and they were alight with happiness. Wes studied him for a second, noting that his golden skin had lightened and shone as if there were glittering silver stars below the skin. Every part of him now seemed to show the same subdued color, and to Wes, he looked all the more radiant for it. Though Apollo still wore the designer jeans and short-sleeved button-down he came in wearing, he didn't look anything like he had before. Even his aura had calmed. Apollo had always carried an aura of frenetic exuberance, but that was gone as he stared deeply into Wes's face.

A large smile spread across his features, but it was nothing like his usual grins and smirks. No, this smile was wide, wholesome, and caused crinkles to form by his eyes. "Wes..." He seemed at a loss for words for a moment. In just saying Wes's name though, his voice was different. Wes couldn't quite pin down how, but it wasn't the sensual tone that he had come to associate with Apollo.

It took a moment more for Apollo to organize his thoughts. "Wes ... I ... thank you. This is something I've wanted for so long, but was too afraid to ask for myself." He made no move toward Wes, which Wes was grateful for, but instead Apollo stared at him before his eyes moved to Ezra.

"My friend, I think I have you to thank as well, though I admit, I thought you would be the one to do it." Apollo's smile was small for Ezra, but his eyes, those oddly silver eyes, held nothing but affection in them.

Ezra shrugged, not letting any emotion slip through his stony exterior. "It was as much for Wes as for you. You both needed the closure if everyone was going to be happy." At Wes's questioning look, Ezra continued, "Apollo has been wanting this for many years. He was cursed thousands of years ago. A few months ago, he approached me, asking if I had anything to help him. I didn't think I did until the Storage Room gave you the amethyst."

A bubble of annoyance floated up in Wes's stomach. "Wait, you made me agonize over this for weeks, when you could have just said I was helping him? You're a real dick sometimes, Ezra!" Ezra's shrug did nothing to quell his annoyance, but Wes knew better than to push it. Ezra was the kind of person who didn't put too much thought into how things got done so long as they got done, eventually.

"Why didn't you just ask your mom to do it? She's, like, a god, or whatever," Wes said after a beat.

Again, Ezra shrugged, but at least he had the courtesy to follow up with an explanation. "My mother is the one who cursed him during his Fall. And you've only met the nice side of my mother," he said with a pointed stare.

A noise from Apollo made them both turn toward him. "Oh!" he exclaimed loudly, then he pulled the waistband of his jeans away from his body and looked down. "Finally!"

Confusion colored Wes's face. "Did you just check out your dick right in the middle of the store? Are we sure this thing worked right?" He pointed at the amethyst still sitting on the counter as he turned his face toward Ezra.

But it was Apollo who answered his question. "Not checking out my dick, because it's gone. I didn't have anything there before my Fall, and now it's all gone. I'm like a Ken doll again!"

"Uh ... congrats?" Wes said slowly, unsure of how to react.

But Ezra was there again with an explanation. "Believe it or not, Apollo was touch-adverse before his Fall. He asked my mother to remove parts he didn't want."

"And when I got too curious about the human world and Fell, she cursed me to be an incubus where I would have to rely upon the touch of others to live," Apollo finished.

"Well, that's just ..." Wes paused to think of a more delicate way to phrase it. He came up with nothing. "Nah, that's just really fucked up. Ezra, your mom is kind of horrible."

A crack of thunder shook the store, despite the sunshine still streaming through the windows. Wes stumbled, crashing his hip into the corner of the counter painfully. "Yes, it is very much kind of a god thing. At least you didn't call her something worse. I've seen her smite a man. Right in the middle of the road."

"Do you think she'll let me go home?" Apollo's voice was so soft, so uncertain. Wes had never heard him sound like that before.

But Ezra nodded, and he even let a small closed-lip smile slip through for his friend. And as if summoned by his nod, a golden light descended around Apollo, like it was ready to beam him up.

Apollo's eyes locked with Wes's. "I'm sorry for everything. You deserve to be loved, Wes. Not just by your sister and friends, but by Cameron too. I'm so sorry I got in the way of that." There was no sadness in his eyes. Instead, his features were soft and serene. It was all Wes could have wanted for Apollo.

Wes knew he had limited time left to say something, so he didn't hold back. "I loved you. Despite what you were, I loved you. I hope you find happiness again. I really do. Because you also deserve that."

And that was all that needed to be said. Apollo nodded once, and then the golden light brightened and Wes had to avert his eyes. When he turned back, the light and Apollo were gone. Wes and Ezra stood alone in the antique shop, with the afternoon sun streaming through the windows as if nothing had happened.

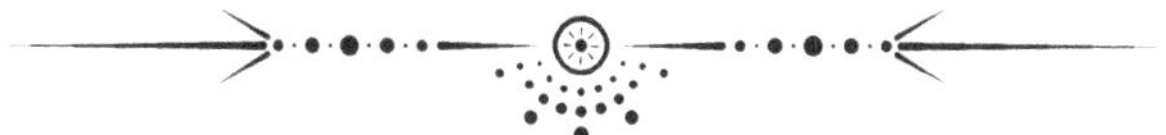

The sun had set an hour earlier, and Wes sat on his couch alone. Brie had shoved everyone out of his house after he and Ezra returned from the shop and explained what happened. His sister offered to stay, but Wes found that he really didn't want the company at the moment. It was better if he had time to think and come to terms with what had happened.

Ezra had also asked if he wanted to talk, but Wes wasn't in the mood to talk to his brother-in-law. He would forgive him eventually for misleading him and letting him sit on his guilt for weeks. It wouldn't have been so bad if Ezra had just informed him that Apollo wanted this because Wes had loved Apollo once and would have done anything to help him. So he was going to stay mad at Ezra for a few days, and then they would talk and he would probably get over it. And Wes would absolutely demand a favor from Ezra to be used whenever.

All that mattered now was that Apollo was free, no longer under the incubus curse. Though Wes's problems weren't over. He needed to talk to Cameron, to face up to his mistakes about how he had handled the problems he had with Apollo, and now that things were resolved, what their future together looked like.

If they even were still together.

Wes wasn't sure where their relationship was. Cameron said they weren't breaking up, but he also hadn't heard from him in forever. Camilla had updated him on how Cameron was doing, though it didn't make him feel any better knowing Cameron was hurting too.

Maybe I should text him. At least let him know things are done with Apollo.

Wes took out his phone to do just that when a knock came at his door. It wasn't from the shop, because Brie or Ezra would simply burst right in. He wasn't in the mood for visitors, and everyone he associated with had already been at his house earlier. Maybe Candy or Camilla left something behind and had come back to get it.

Slowly, Wes dragged himself to the door and swung it open. But it wasn't Candy or Camilla on his doorstep.

It was Cameron.

He looked disheveled. Not in the sexy, just-showed-up-after-a-long-day-of-making-magic-with-baked-goods kind of way he usually did. There were deep purple bags under his eyes. Beautiful green eyes that had dulled and lost their sparkle. There was no easy smile on his face, only a sad frown that Wes hated immediately. His chocolatey brown hair looked like it hadn't been brushed in days and stood on end. And there wasn't even a smudge of flour anywhere on him.

Wes was sure he didn't look much better, but seeing Cameron like that made the guilt return two-fold since he knew he was the cause.

"Hi." Cameron's voice was barely above a whisper, and he seemed to be breathing rapidly. Wes could understand. His own heart had started to beat rapidly and his breathing had sped up.

"Hi," Wes responded quietly. They stared at each other for several long seconds. Neither moved. Wes's hand was still on the door handle.

Cameron rubbed the back of his head nervously. "Uh, can I come in? I think we should talk."

Wes nodded and stepped aside, not sure how he should respond, so he figured silence was best for now since Cameron had made the first move by coming over.

They settled on opposite ends of Wes's couch, not quite looking at each other. Silence fell thickly between them once again for nearly a minute before Cameron spoke. "Camilla told me what happened with Apollo. I'm so sorry you had to go through that, Wes. And I'm angry at Ezra for making you feel that guilt for so long when he knew it was what Apollo wanted. That was uncool and unkind of him and I've made sure to have words with him first. With your sister's help. I'm not mad at you anymore for not telling me what was going on. Yes, I was hurt and pissed off at the time, but I guess I realize now that unburdening your problems on others doesn't come easily to you. I need to be more understanding. But you also need to be able to trust me, to be able to come to me with your problems if this is going to work. We're partners, and if you can't treat me like your partner, then I don't think we can make it. I'm all in with you, Wes."

Finished with his speech, Cameron looked at Wes. There was no expectation in his look, just a calm blankness that Wes wanted gone. He wanted that glint of joy back in Cameron's eyes. He wanted the brilliant smile that lit up his whole face. He wanted that damn beautiful crinkle to appear on the bridge of his nose. It was his fault that Cameron was diminished, and so it was his job to bring that light back.

"I fucked up big. I know that now. And you're right, it's hard for me to rely on other people. Even my sister can tell you that and we've stuck together through everything. I need to do better, to try. I want to be your partner, I want to be your everything. Because I love you. I really, really love you. I'm also an idiot, and I hope you'll forgive me and maybe let us try again."

He couldn't look at Cameron. He didn't want to see what look might be there. Not that he thought Cameron would reject him. He wouldn't be here if that was the case. But he didn't feel like he deserved understanding, either. Nor sympathy, or any emotions other than tentative acceptance.

He felt the couch move as Cameron scooted closer. "Look at me, Wesley," Cameron said, his tone commanding. Wes didn't want to, but he couldn't deny Cameron when he used that voice. Slowly, he moved his face up to look Cameron in the eye, and there he saw the light come back to Cameron's face. He saw love and understanding and everything he didn't dare to hope for in that face.

Cameron cupped Wes's jaw. "You listen to me, Wesley St. James. I love you. Fiercely. I want to be with you. But you will give me all of yourself, or nothing. No more secrets. No more shouldering all the burden. That goes both ways. You hold me accountable too. We can do this together." With all the words out, Cameron leaned forward and pressed a gentle kiss to Wes's lips.

How he had missed those lips! Gentle kisses were not going to be enough. Two weeks without Cameron had made Wes desperate for his touch, and their kiss quickly turned heated. They couldn't get enough of each other's mouths and hands started to roam over skin. Wes pawed at Cameron's shirt, trying to remove it before Cameron finally pulled away long enough to pull it over his head. Wes's shirt followed soon after, thrown somewhere around the living room.

Easing Wes down on the couch, Cameron maneuvered his body to hover over Wes, deepening the kiss further. Kisses moved from Wes's mouth, Cameron dragging his lips across Wes's jaw, down his neck to his chest, and farther still. When Cameron moved down the couch and to the waistband of Wes's jeans, he looked up at Wes, asking permission with his eyes before he unbuttoned anything.

Wes nodded so hard that he worried he might pull something in his neck, but none of that mattered the minute Cameron popped the button on his jeans and slid the zipper down. All thoughts fled then and all he could focus on was every minute movement Cameron made. Slower than Wes liked, Cameron peeled down Wes's jeans and boxers, finally allowing his growing erection to spring free. Cameron gave it a few slow pumps before lowering his mouth and gently licked the tip of Wes's dick.

The moment was arousing and maddening all at once. Wes didn't want sweet and tender. He needed Cameron like he needed air. Their separation had nearly driven him crazy, and his head clouded with lust.

"Cameron, please!" His words were pleading. He didn't care how he sounded, Wes wanted and wanted and wanted, and the tentative licks and slow pumps of his dick weren't going to cut it.

Cameron smiled against the head of him, mischievous. The man knew he had power over Wes. He always did. A power that Wes gave freely, but still. "You need more, Wesley?" Cameron's grin was wide as he pulled his mouth away, but he still kept up the slow rhythm with his hand.

Wes could only nod, the movement driving him to the brink of insanity. He only had a second to brace himself as Cameron's grin grew wide and then he descended on Wes, taking him deep into his mouth and sucking hard.

It was a wonder Wes didn't explode that instant, but he managed to hold himself back, not willing to let things end too quickly. A herculean effort, really, as Cameron was very good with his mouth. Still, despite Wes's best efforts, it only took minutes of work for Cameron's skilled mouth and clever hand to bring him to orgasm and he spilled down Cameron's throat with a shout pouring from his lips.

With a loud pop, Cameron pulled away, sitting back on his heels at the far end of the couch, a smug smile on his lips. "I missed that so much. You taste amazing." He was exceedingly pleased with himself and Wes couldn't fault him for that since his brain had ceased to function and he was still waiting for his vision to fully clear again. It had felt like ages since Wes had cum that hard.

"Now, once you can move again, you are going to bend yourself over this couch and get ready for me," Cameron said in his most domineering voice. The sound sent shivers up Wes's spine, and even though his whole body felt boneless, he scrambled to comply, eager to have Cameron inside him. His knees rested on the couch cushion, and he planted his elbows on the back of the couch and waited. Craning his head over his shoulder, Wes watched as Cameron flicked his wrist, a pale light surrounded his hand before a second later, a bottle of lube to appeared there. The same bottle Wes kept in his room for Cameron's visits.

Wes could never not marvel at the casual way Cameron performed magic. Even with his lessons from Camilla, Wes's own displays were not nearly so effortless. But all thoughts of spells and magic went out the window as Cameron began to prepare his body. And then Wes was lost completely as Cameron slowly pushed into him, gliding in inch by inch with expert control.

Once fully seated, Cameron stilled his movements, giving Wes time to adjust. "Okay?" Cameron's voice was soft, letting his dominant side drop for a moment to check in with Wes.

Wes nodded, wiggling his ass against the intrusion to encourage Cameron to move. "I need words,

Wesley." While Cameron's tone was commanding, it was still gentle.

"Please move, Cameron. I need you." Wes really was a mess around Cameron, but it felt too good and he needed more.

And Cameron didn't hold back when he finally began. He set a punishing pace, pushing into Wes hard and fast, hands gripping his hips so hard that Wes knew there would be fingerprint bruises on his skin for days.

Thrusts becoming erratic, Cameron bent over Wes's back, one arm moving to wrap around Wes's chest. Cameron held Wes close as he spilled inside him, his shout loud in Wes's ear, filling the room. For several seconds, Cameron rested his weight against Wes's back and they remained curled together like that, Cameron still buried deep within Wes.

Then slowly, Cameron pulled out and flopped down on the couch, taking Wes with him, situating him on top. Their bodies were slick with sweat and their skin stuck together in every place they touched. Cameron's arms banded around Wes, and Wes could feel his eyes dropping, his mind getting fuzzy.

"I love you," Cameron whispered into Wes's hair. Wes smiled against Cameron's chest and then let his eyes close and fell into the first restful sleep he'd had in weeks.

EPILOGUE

Three months later

"You'll have to share the secret of how your mom can make boozy lemonade that gets you this fucked up from one glass and yet doesn't taste like alcohol at all. That's the real magic," Wes said, his head light from the drink despite only having one relatively small glass.

Cameron's cheeks and nose were pink from the alcohol, a sure sign that he was well on his way to being drunk. "Griswold family secret. You don't get the recipe until you marry me." He grinned widely, the smile that Wes loved more than anything.

"Dude, it hasn't even been a year. But I want a Halloween proposal. Not a Samhain one. I'm talking cheesy Halloween with, like, jack-o'-lanterns spelling out 'Will you marry me?' That's a requirement." Wes laughed, only half joking. He could absolutely see himself marrying Cameron one day.

Cameron snorted into his own lemonade. "And then we bob for apples and the ring is stuck in the apple when you bring it up."

"Perfect. I'm allergic to nickel, so don't cheap out on me." The two of them descended into fits of laughter, enjoying the way the boozy lemonade made them giddy and enjoying the sunshine at the Fourth of July party at the Everett farm.

Though the covens didn't associate much, the Everetts had invited the Griswolds. The farm was nearly as packed as it was during the annual Samhain celebration now that the Everetts had expanded their family with a bunch of strays and their partners and their families.

With so many witches in attendance, the fireworks display for the evening was going to be, for lack of a better word, explosive. Wes just hoped he was sober enough to enjoy it, though he doubted very much that he would be if he kept drinking Emily Griswold's lemonade.

"You know you have to mingle with everybody and not only hang out with each other. It's not like you don't spend every waking moment together, anyway." Brie sidled up to Wes's side, her own cup of lemonade in hand.

Wes threw his free arm around his sister's shoulders. "You're one to talk. This is the first time I've seen you without your husband all day."

Brie wrapped an arm around her brother's middle and looked over to where Ezra was talking with Damien Everett. "That's because Ezra is socially awkward and has known most of these people since they were babies. Now, Cameron, I love you, but shoo. I haven't seen my brother in days."

Cameron smiled, kissed Wes softly, placed a kiss on Brie's cheek, and walked over to where Candy stood conversing with several of the Everett cousins, including Sequoia, as well as two of his sisters.

"So what's up, Little Witch? It's been like two days." Wes squeezed his sister's shoulder and looked down at her.

"Well, Catherine Fry is coming into town and wants to stop by and see us."

"You're old mentor? Wasn't she just here last year for something?" Wes could remember Brie telling him about that but didn't actually see the woman.

Brie shrugged. "She was supposed to be, but never showed. She said she got detained in Thailand, and I don't know if there's a story there or like she was just held up at the airport or something."

Wes laughed, his thoughts playing out pretty much every scenario, not that he knew the woman well. "Maybe she's become a criminal mastermind after she left academia and got caught up in a smuggling ring."

Brie laughed along with him. "Always a possibility. Who's to say she wasn't one before? She's lived a hella long life, after all. I wonder how mortality is treating her?"

"You'll find out soon enough if she shows up this time," Wes responded.

"Right. It'll be nice to see her, though. I'm sure she'll have some stories from her adventures. It's been four years and now that she doesn't have to be near Ezra, she's probably done a lot," Brie said thoughtfully.

Wes nodded, not nearly as excited, but that was due only to the fact he didn't have a personal relationship with the woman. "For sure. But now let's talk about our adventures coming up. Japan at the end of the month! It's going to be so fucking hot."

Despite now being in their thirties, the siblings hadn't done much traveling. There was always school, and not having the extra money to do much. Brie and Ezra did take an extended honeymoon, but Wes hadn't had the luxury of traveling outside of the continental United States. He had barely left Connecticut.

He watched as Brie's face lit up with excitement. "I honestly can't wait. Sure, it'll be hot as balls, but it's still going to be fun. And you'll have Cameron with you, so it'll be like an extended double date. I'm really looking forward to visiting Nara."

"Why Nara? I thought you were stoked for Kyoto?" Wes asked. He was just happy to travel. Every place would be exciting for him. Doubly so, because he would have Cameron with him.

"Yeah, I mean, I'm excited for Kyoto. But you can feed the deer in Nara. They just walk right up to you!" Brie's excitement was infectious and Wes couldn't help the smile on his face at his sister's glee.

"It's going to be great," he said, pulling her in for a proper one-armed hug.

"Definitely. But first, I have to get through the visit with Dr. Fry. I really am excited to see her. Maybe she's been to Japan recently and can give some tips for traveling." Brie raised her glass to her husband, who had started walking toward the siblings.

Wes nodded. "Yeah, that would be cool. Anyway, your other half is ready to be saved, so I'm going to go find my boyfriend and stuff my face with Damien's cooking before I get drunk off my ass on this." He held up his now empty glass before releasing Brie.

She waved at him and then turned to her husband. Wes made his way over to his boyfriend and his best friend. There were so many good people in his life and Wes felt incredibly lucky.

Things had been rough for the last several years, and Wes hadn't realized how bad things were until he finally had something good in his life. And he wasn't about to waste a single moment of it. Cameron came into his life when he needed him most, and Wes planned to spend the rest of his life thanking Cameron for saving him. Not just from his relationship with Apollo, but also from himself.

As he joined the group that included Cameron and Candy, Wes felt an overwhelming sense of joy at all the magic in his life.

Book Club Questions

1. This book is intended to not only be a romance about two people, but it's also about someone learning to love themselves. How is Wes's character relatable in that regard?

2. Should Wes have handled his problems better, rather than waiting around for years?

3. Toxic relationships don't always appear obvious to the people in the relationships. Discuss why you think Wes stayed with Apollo for so long if he thought things weren't going to change.

4. Food is obviously a big part of the series. What kind of magic would you want added to your favorite dish?

5. Was Cameron right to want space from Wes? In your opinion, should they have just broken up and had a reconciliation, or was it best to take a break?

6. Ezra doesn't inform Wes that Apollo wants to be rid of the curse. Do you feel like he should have been more open with Wes from the beginning, or do you feel he had his reasons?

7. While it's easy to hate Apollo for how he behaves with everyone, he is acting on the nature of his curse. Do you find Apollo's actions excusable or unforgivable?

8. Cameron is a very forgiving character. Do you think he should have forgiven Wes more quickly, or do you think he was too harsh?

Author Bio

Kait Disney-Leugers is an author of fantasy stories with lots of romance. Originally from Ohio, she has a degree in history from Ohio University. She now lives in Maryland with her husband and two kids, and uses her history degree to be insufferable while watching historical movies and shows.

When not writing in the dead of night once everyone else is asleep, she enjoys playing D&D, trying in vain to get through her giant pile of books, and baking bread to 90s hip hop.

More books from 4 Horsemen Publications

Fantasy, SciFi, & Paranormal Romance

Amanda Fasciano
Waking Up Dead
Dead Vessel
The Dead Show
Dead Revelations

Beau Lake
The Beast Beside Me
The Beast Within Me
Taming the Beast: Novella
The Beast After Me
Charming the Beast
The Beast Like Me
An Eye for Emeralds
Swimming in Sapphires
Pining for Pearls

Chelsea Burton Dunn
By Moonlight
Moonbound
Bloodthirsty

D. Lambert
Rydan
Celebrant
Northlander
Esparan
King
Traitor
His Last Name

Danielle Orsino
Locked Out of Heaven
Thine Eyes of Mercy
From the Ashes
Kingdom Come
Fire, Ice, Acid, & Heart
A Fae is Done

J.M. Paquette
Klauden's Ring
Solyn's Body
The Inbetween
Hannah's Heart
Call Me Forth
Invite Me In
Keep Me Close
Heart of Stone

Jessica Salina
Not My Time
To Be Normal

Kait Disney-Leugers
Antique Magic
Blood Magic

Kyle Sorrell
Munderworld
Potarium

Lyra R. Saenz
Prelude
Falsetto in the Woods: Novella
Ragtime Swing
Sonata
Song of the Sea
The Devil's Trill
Bercuese
To Heal a Songbird
Ghost March
Nocturne

Paige Lavoie
I'm in Love with Mothman
Dear Galaxy

Robert J. Lewis
Shadow Guardian and the Three Bears
Shadow Guardian and the Big Bad Wolf

T.S. Simons
Project Hemisphere
The Space Between
Infinity
Circle of Protections
Sessrúmnir
The 45th Parallel

Valerie Willis
Cedric: The Demonic Knight
Romasanta: Father of Werewolves
The Oracle: Keeper of the Gaea's Gate
Artemis: Eye of Gaea
King Incubus: A New Reign
Queen Succubus: Holder of the Crown
Val's House of Musings: A Mixed Genre Short Story Collection

V.C. Willis
The Prince's Priest
The Priest's Assassin
The Assassin's Saint
The Champion's Lord

Paranormal & Urban Fantasy

Amanda Fasciano
Waking Up Dead
Dead Vessel

Beau Lake
The Beast Beside Me
The Beast Within Me
Taming the Beast: Novella
The Beast After Me
Charming the Beast

The Beast Like Me
An Eye for Emeralds
Swimming in Sapphires
Pining for Pearls

The Devil's Trill
Bercuese
To Heal a Songbird
Ghost March
Nocturne

Chelsea Burton Dunn

By Moonlight

J.M. Paquette

Call Me Forth
Invite Me In
Keep Me Close

Jessica Salina

Not My Time

Kait Disney-Leugers

Antique Magic

Lyra R. Saenz

Prelude
Falsetto in the Woods: Novella
Ragtime Swing
Sonata
Song of the Sea

Megan Mackie

The Saint of Liars
The Devil's Day
The Finder of the Lucky Devil

Paige Lavoie

I'm in Love with Mothman

Robert J. Lewis

Shadow Guardian and the Three Bears

Valerie Willis

Cedric: The Demonic Knight
Romasanta: Father of Werewolves
The Oracle: Keeper of the Gaea's Gate
Artemis: Eye of Gaea
King Incubus: A New Reign

Printed in the USA
CPSIA information can be obtained
at www.ICGtesting.com
CBHW030154230124
3688CB00003B/39